T0166590

Chef's Special

Susan X Meagher

Chef's Special

THIS TRADE PAPERBACK ORIGINAL IS PUBLISHED BY BRISK PRESS, BRIELLE, NJ 08730.

COVER DESIGN AND LAYOUT BY: CAROLYN NORMAN

FIRST PRINTING: DECEMBER 2016

ISBN-13: 978-0-9966774-7-9

By Susan X Meagher

Novels

Arbor Vitae
All That Matters
Cherry Grove
Girl Meets Girl
The Lies That Bind
The Legacy
Doublecrossed
Smooth Sailing
How To Wrangle a Woman
Almost Heaven
The Crush
The Reunion
Inside Out
Out of Whack
Homecoming
The Right Time
Summer of Love
Chef's Special

Serial Novel

I Found My Heart In San Francisco

Awakenings: Book One
Beginnings: Book Two
Coalescence: Book Three
Disclosures: Book Four
Entwined: Book Five
Fidelity: Book Six
Getaway: Book Seven
Honesty: Book Eight
Intentions: Book Nine
Journeys: Book Ten
Karma: Book Eleven
Lifeline: Book Twelve
Monogamy: Book Thirteen
Nurture: Book Fourteen
Osmosis: Book Fifteen
Paradigm: Book Sixteen
Quandary: Book Seventeen
Renewal: Book Eighteen
Synchronicity: Book Nineteen
Trust: Book Twenty

Anthologies

Undercover Tales
Outsiders

acknowledgements

As always, to my beloved wife, Carrie, who supports me unfailingly in every part of my life.

Gemma provided significant guidance and feedback, particularly concerning Cayman, but her observations were spot-on no matter where the characters roamed.

Mary J picked up the ball to give me great advice about Detroit. It always helps to have the perspective of a native.

Catherine Lane paused her own writerly efforts to provide a final read-through, and I'm very grateful that she did.

Dedication

To all of the hardworking women and men who labor for our culinary pleasure. If you enjoy dining out, thank them for giving up their evening so you can enjoy yours.

One cannot think well, love well, sleep well if one has not dined well.

Virginia Wolff

Chapter One

AN OPPRESSIVELY HUMID AUGUST morning enveloped Emily like a shroud the moment she stepped out of her apartment building. Summer in New York was often brutal, but this year had to clinch the title for stickiness.

The flagstone path to the sidewalk was littered with a styrofoam container filled with some nasty-looking Chinese food, and she edged it off the stone with the toe of her running shoe. To be a good neighbor, she normally picked up whatever had made its way onto their little patch of real estate, but she drew the line at rancid food. She had a strong stomach, but having a hand covered in God-knew-what wasn't the way to start the day.

Her mostly quiet block was still sleepy, with her fellow working-class residents snoozing within their mid-sized apartment buildings. Just one enterprising neighbor, the drug dealer who controlled the opposite side of the street, was open for business. Today, two beefy kids and a pair of ferocious dogs were keeping watch. For some reason, she found their presence reassuring. The drug sales prevented other mischief, like burglaries and car theft. Not that she'd ever be able to afford a car, but it was nice to know it would be unmolested if she chanced upon one.

Just before she reached Roosevelt, she paused for a moment, trying to get herself in the right mindset for her trip. But it was hard to stay cool when it was barely eight in the morning and a petroleum-laden combination of oil and gas already wafted off the blacktop. A food delivery guy, ripe as a dumpster, swept by on his bike, probably taking breakfast to some lazy bum who couldn't make himself a bowl of cereal. Yeah, it was going to be hard to chill today.

When she turned onto the heavily commercial street she met the full impact of her dense, urban neighborhood, with the acrid exhaust of creeping cars nearly suffocating her. When a Prius cab matched her stride for a block it was like a mini-vacation from the pollution, and she breathed in deeply, savoring a few moments of cleanish air.

In those few seconds, scents from the neighborhood restaurants started to register, with each spot beginning to fire up their ovens to send heady plumes of smoke into the skies. The Columbian and Ecuadorian places, redolent of masa, onions, chorizo, and eggs, made her stomach perk up. When she passed a street cart displaying appetizing photos of arepas con queso, she almost pulled out her wallet. But she'd had breakfast, and being on time was more important than satisfying her grumbling tummy.

Sweat trickled down her back by the time she reached the train. For once the "E" was pulling into the station as she clambered up the innumerable stairs, and she grabbed the handrail to take them two at a time. Maybe catching a train quickly was a harbinger of good things to come? She wasn't usually a believer in omens, but she'd gladly take one.

On a good day, the ride only took a half hour, not long at all. But being jammed into a sardine can with a hundred and fifty people, each not caring who they stepped on to wedge in, sucked no matter how long it lasted. Thank god morning rush hour was something she hardly ever had to suffer through.

A mass of people exited at forty-second street, then another exodus at thirty-fourth gave her not only room to breathe, but a coveted seat. She stretched out a little, amused at how she always savored the chance to sit, even for just a few stops.

"Hey."

She didn't look up after registering the presence of a guy standing right in front of her. It had taken a few years in the city to learn the tricks, but she'd perfected the art of selective deafness. If you didn't wall yourself off a little, you'd be constantly harassed. Then a gruff voice said, "Emily, right?"

Her head snapped up and she recognized a guy she'd worked with years earlier. Mentally, she rolled through the names of the dozens of people she'd labored alongside. "Randy?"

"Andy," he said, sticking his hand out to shake. "You still at Defarge?"

"No, not for a few years. I'm at Henri now. You?"

"Saziato." Andy was a big guy, seeming even bigger as he loomed over Emily, holding onto the rails above his head to steady himself. "Looking to move though. Heard about anything good?"

Trying to make her expression blank as slate, she shook her head. She didn't recall much about Andy, but the last thing she wanted was extra competition. She'd been trying to get on at Blake, a modern, French-inspired place for months now, and wasn't going to spoil her chances by sharing the lead.

"Why you going in this early? Do they serve breakfast at Henri?"

"Nah," she said, chuckling at the thought. "Chef can't manage to roll in before five."

As the doors opened, he said, "Isn't this your stop?"

She wasn't great at coming up with instant responses, especially lies. "Yeah. I've got to…" Her mind went blank, then she almost spit out that she was going for one of the most important interviews she'd ever been on, the very last thing she wanted to admit!

A leer he probably thought was sexy crooked his mouth. "Got a girl downtown?"

Oh, right! Andy was the grill cook who was obsessed with her being gay.

Trying to appear nonchalant, Emily shrugged. "You know how it is."

"I wish I did," he said, grinning at her like he was about to drool.

The train slowed, then the conductor called out a garbled, "Canal Street."

"Gotta go," she said, giving him a pat on the arm as she slipped past. "Good luck on finding a new spot."

"Have fun!" He called out, clearly imagining her having the day she wished she was going to have. But instead of a morning roll in the hay, she was going to be selling her skills to a person everyone agreed was tough to impress.

Once she'd popped her head out of the bowels of the subway, Emily looked at her phone to check the directions. Ten minutes to spare. Now the sweat slid down her sides in rivulets, as much from anxiety as heat.

At a noisy, dusty demolition site, she scurried under a protective roof that stopped bricks from conking people on the head, bracing herself for the inevitable catcalls. Luckily, most of the guys were actually working, but a few had time to make clicking or kissing sounds at her. Not for the first time, she reminded herself that the guys weren't performing to attract her. Only a moron would think overtures more suited to lure a hungry cat would compel a woman to respond. No, guys did this for each other, which had always seemed pretty gay to her, but whatever. She ignored them, as always, kept her head down and walked a little faster.

Then she was standing in front of the building, looking up at a black awning that spread across an entire storefront. The name of the place stood out clearly in neat, slim, blood-red letters above the entryway.

Blake.

She took in the sign for a minute. Was working eighty hours a week simply to have your name splashed across an awning worth it? Of course it was. There wasn't a question in her mind.

For just a second, she pictured her own name up there. It would take years, and a ton of good breaks, but she had a fighting chance, especially if she could nail this job.

The entry door was locked, but that was to be expected. If you unlocked your front door at nine, you'd have a restaurant full of miscreants by 9:10. On instinct, she walked down the block and slid between buildings, hoping to find a loading dock, sighing with relief when she spotted it. A civilian wouldn't realize what a difference a dock made, but it was a thousand times easier than having to muscle provisions down narrow stairs into a dark, dank basement. Been there, had the backache to show for it.

This dock was taller than many, and it took a real stretch to get up that first step. Pushing her way into the building through heavy steel doors, she stood in the silent, gleaming kitchen for a moment.

Why did kitchens seems so benign early in the morning? This one was quieter and cleaner than most, more like an operating room than a place to cook. No heat, no mess, only the smell of a mild disinfectant. Gleaming stainless steel surrounded her, waiting for a bunch of soldiers of fortune to turn it into a hellish mess.

A tall, slim, dark-haired woman emerged from an office. It was *her*. Emily was rooted in place. She'd seen pictures of her, of course. Had seen her interviewed on TV once or twice. But neither photos nor television had done her justice.

It wasn't that she was pretty—though she was. It wasn't that she had rock-star hair—though she did. It was her style, an elegant grace that gave her an aura. She'd moved just fifteen feet or so, coming toward Emily, but in that time the woman's calm presence made the unspoken promise that she was in charge.

A charming, friendly smile split her lips to reveal straight, white teeth. "Blake Chadwick," she said, extending her hand. It was strong, sure, and callused, the hand of a woman who worked hard. Before Emily could get a word out, she added, "You're Emily Desjardins." The name rolled off her tongue as if she were a native French speaker. Impressive.

"I am," Emily agreed, nodding decisively.

Blake took a look toward her office, but didn't move that way, instead leading Emily to a high table nearby. Two metal stools flanked it and they each took one. The table, stainless, utilitarian, held a printer and computer, the keyboard overlaid with a multicolor silicone cover. Food wasn't going to make those keys sticky. It wouldn't dare.

Emily waited while Blake angled the computer, typed in a few keystrokes and read for a minute, chin resting in her hand. "I have your resume here," she murmured, concentrating. "Got it." Her head nodded decisively. "You're Marcel's sous chef." Then she leaned back, crossed her arms over her chest, and smiled. "He raves about you."

"He's a good man. A good chef."

"He is. He's been showing people how it's done longer than most of us have been alive. How long have you been sous?"

"Two years."

Blake nodded. "Two years is long enough. If you're good, you have to push yourself. You could get fat and lazy at Henri, even though it's a great little place. You rarely change the menu, right?"

"We have specials…"

"But nearly everyone orders the same five or six entrées, and those never change. If you tinker with them, your guests complain."

"That's true. But we try to keep things fresh with our—"

"Of course you *try*, but it's difficult when your guests have been visiting for thirty years." She leaned close to the computer, with her eyes scanning across the text for a minute. Then she slid the computer back to its former place, precisely on the edge of the table, right in the middle. "Marcel's doing you a favor by getting you placed before he packs it in. His farmhouse in the Garonne Valley is waiting for him." A wistful look came over her features. "Have you been?"

"To the Garonne Valley? No, I haven't."

"It's lovely. I worked not too far from there for a while." She grasped a notebook and a pen, then started to jot something down. When she looked up again, a pensive smile covered her face for a few seconds. "A large part of me longs to return." Her eyes went unfocused, with her voice remaining soft and slow. "The mindset of a French cook is so different. Better," she added, not allowing for a varying opinion. "In New York, innovation is too highly regarded. In France, technique is paramount. Perfect technique. Every single night."

"That's should be something we all aspire to."

Her gaze landed on Emily, eyes so dark as to appear black, simmering with a flash of anger. "But we don't." With a heavy sigh, she dropped her chin back into her hand. "I respect the chef who can replicate a good dish time and again much more than one who can create something unique, even something fantastic—then not be in the mood to push himself the next day. Children," she grumbled. "Spoiled children who think they walk on water."

Emily had to respond. Had to think of some way to let this woman know who she was. "I agree, of course," she got out, despite having those dark eyes settle onto her again. "But we have to innovate, don't we? Otherwise, we'd all be mimicking Escoffier every night."

"Of course. Of course. That's obvious." A tiny frown pulled her dark eyebrows together. "We agree, yes?"

"We do." She wasn't a hundred percent sure what she was agreeing to, but she thought they were somewhere near the same wavelength.

"Tell me about Henri. You have…what? Forty seats?"

"Forty-six if you include the bar."

"We have ninety." She looked up and smiled, the fire leaving her eyes, replaced by a warm confidence. It wasn't a haughty expression, but you couldn't miss her certainty that ninety was the proper number to have. "Ninety-eight if I include the bar, which I don't, since we only serve charcuterie and cheese there." Her gaze narrowed. "Going from forty to ninety will be a challenge."

"True, but I think I'm ready."

"Don't think," she said, a touch of irritation showing. "Know."

"Yes, Chef."

"We have two sous chefs, one for meat and one for fish. You work alone now, right?"

"Right."

"Here, the sous divide the work. I don't care how, but I like one to be in by ten, and the other by noon. Ideally, the early one can leave by ten, but that doesn't happen very often." She leaned over the small table and spoke very earnestly. "The early shift is harder in every way, but that's the one I want you for."

Emily's heart started to slam in her chest. It sounded like she already had the job!

"Grant Boyd is the other sous. He's a good cook, and he's not afraid of kicking butts when they need it, but I need someone who will focus on *my* restaurant. Grant always has one eye on getting his own place. I think he keeps his best ideas for himself, so I'm unable to trust him. Marcel says you love to create. True?"

"Yes, Chef. That's why I cook."

"Are you willing to give me your ideas? Your *best* ideas?"

"Yes, Chef. Absolutely."

"Are you able to get up early?"

"Yes, Chef. I'm in by nine most days."

Her brow knit as her words dropped from her mouth like cubes of ice. "I have no tolerance for being late. *None.*"

"No, Chef."

"Let me repeat. I will not tolerate a chef, a prep cook, a dishwasher, or a server who can't be on time. Every day."

"I understand, Chef."

"I run a tight ship, Emily, and I rarely give people a second chance." She was quiet for a few seconds, giving her words the opportunity to sink in. "Do you understand?"

"Yes, Chef."

Blake stood up, extended her hand, and they shook again. "Cook for me," she said, her expression brightening when a lovely smile peeked out.

"What would you like me to cook?"

"Surprise me." She glided by, slapped Emily on the back and disappeared into her office.

Standing on wobbly legs, Emily was sure someone had snuck in and set her feet into wet cement. This was like being dropped into a stranger's apartment, blindfolded, and told to have dinner on the table in an hour.

While she'd assumed she'd have to cook, she'd expected *some* guidance. Or at least a quick tour. Even though professional kitchens were vaguely similar, they all had hidden secrets. Secrets she'd have to suss out on her own.

Standing there like a stooge wasn't going to get the job done, so she looked for a place to change. Her gaze settled on the hallway just behind Blake's office. If she was designing a kitchen she'd put the locker room right there. *Ah-ha!* They thought alike—on at least one small detail. After tightening the drawstring waist on her pinstripe pants and buttoning up her chef's whites, she slid into her trusty clogs. Just having the right shoes on started to let her feel more in control. But when she reached into her tote bag and withdrew her knife roll, everything snapped into place. When you had your trusty tools, you could work anywhere.

Now back in the kitchen, she sharpened her senses to figure out where to set up. The cooks would be coming in soon and they wouldn't want her in their spots. Then the first scent of the day wafted by. Someone was roasting bones for stock. Heading for the scent, she spied an opening in the far wall. A prep kitchen, nearly as big as the main kitchen in her current shop, was tucked behind that wall, allowing the cooks a place to do the heavy, dirty work while staying out of the flow of traffic. A brawny Latin man stood with his back to her, chopping onions so fast white bits flew into the air.

"Hi," she said, startling him.

He turned his head and nodded, with his flashing knife never slowing. "Buenos dias."

Oh, shit. Not knowing Spanish well was going to be the death of her. "Buenos dias. Mi llama is…é…Emily."

The man grinned, his gruff exterior fading to make him appear approachable and friendly. "I forget I use Spanish." He stuck out a beefy hand to shake. "Carlos. Morning prep."

"Good to meet you, Carlos. I'm interviewing for the sous job, and I need to cook. Should I do it in here?"

"Sí. Yes. It will be not good in the kitchen. There's room here. Do you need for me to show you around?"

She looked at the huge pile of onions he had to get through. "I can snoop around and figure it out. All kitchens are basically the same, right?"

"This one is cleaner," he said soberly. "Chef will not stand for mess."

"I can tell. I'll be back." She wandered around, finding the walk-ins, the big, chilled rooms where everything perishable was kept. Fish filled the first one she tried. When she closed her eyes and breathed in, the clean, sweet, tang of the sea was all she detected. Absolutely perfect. Everything was covered in crushed ice, and laid out just the way she liked it. Same for the meat walk-in. Even dairy was stunningly well-organized. This woman ran a *very* tight ship.

After checking out all of the dry goods in the pantry, Emily went back to the prep kitchen, where she spied two under-counter refrigerators. All sorts of goodies were hiding in there, stuff that had been opened and only partially used, the portions too small for a first course. A few ideas started to bloom in her imagination. She knew Blake had trained in France, and had worked there for a while, so she decided to make her bones with some classic French dishes she'd learned in cooking school. Without thinking, she took her main knives from the roll and ran them over her steel a few times. They were already razor sharp, but doing something mechanical let her get into the zone. It was time to cook.

Emily knew better than to assume she'd have free reign, but she hadn't considered all of the competition she'd face in getting her hands on the combi oven.

The damned oven was a miracle of modern technology, able to do everything from dehydrate to steam, at temperatures from one to six hundred degrees. She'd missed having one every single day in Henri's antiquated setup. Today, when she'd spotted the oven, she'd blithely assumed she'd use it for her custard, as well as roasting potatoes. But Blake only had one of them, and it was being used to proof dough for dinner rolls. Shut-out, she went back to basics, using a bain-marie to start on her custard, while cursing her naive assumptions.

It had only been an hour, but when Blake walked into the prep kitchen she already seemed less laid-back than she'd been at nine. Gone were the pressed blouse and jeans, replaced with a perfectly-fitted, blindingly white jacket, blood red piping slashing down and across her body. Atop her breast, "Blake" was emblazoned in the same color and font as the awning, with "Blake Chadwick" in small block type below. Nice. No additional titles, like "Chef de Cuisine," or "Executive Chef" wasting space. Her name was enough.

She went to Carlos and slapped him on the back. When he didn't respond, she wrapped her arms around him and shook him back and forth until he giggled like a child. Amazingly, she planted a kiss on his cheek. "Do you know what I want, Carlos?"

"Yes, but I tell you again you cannot have me."

She chuckled. "I'd love some vichyssoise. Don't you like a good, cold soup on a hot day?"

"I don't like cold soup. I don't know how to make it, anyway." He winked at Emily. "I don't know where you will get such a soup."

"I don't know either," she said, sighing. "But I sure would like some." She sauntered out of the kitchen, not giving Emily a single glance.

Fuck!

She was really cranking on the first courses, and if she took time to peel potatoes she might screw up her custard. But if Chef wanted vichyssoise, she was damned well going to get it.

An hour later, Blake breezed through again. The whole kitchen was alive now, even though Emily could only hear, and not see the commotion in the main room. She was surrounded by four young commis, the poorly-paid newbies no good kitchen could do without. The big kitchen had to be cooler, so their presence indicated the other space was jammed. Each of them was bent over, with their faces hovering just above their work. One used a pair of spoons to form a pâtè into tiny football-shaped orbs, his concentration easily as intense as if he were on the NYPD bomb squad. Another arranged violets around a cold seafood terrine, using long tweezers to place each like a mistake of a millimeter would be catastrophic. The woman to her left was dicing masses of carrots and celery, her knife a blur of motion, while the guy to her right turned a mound of basil into a chiffonade. None of them had spoken a word since they'd arrived.

Blake jumped up to sit on the work surface, catching Emily's eye, then speaking to her like it was just the two of them, perhaps sitting on a park bench in the Tuileries.

"When I was a kid, I worked for a guy in Nice. He told me you could judge the quality of a cook by her béarnaise. I'm not sure why he thought that, given it's not a difficult sauce." She seemed pensive. "I've never been able to prove him wrong, though. A good béarnaise says something about a cook."

Fuck!

She hadn't been planning a beef dish, but now she had to produce one. And with another entrée, she'd need another side dish. Blake had to have seen she wasn't doing beef. She was just fucking with her!

When Blake began to speak to a commis, Emily paused to give her a good, long look. Her hair, jet black, curly and shortish, was now messy, like she'd been running her hands through it. And her jacket wasn't pristine any longer, with a splash of something brown along a hip and some golden spatters at her chest. Oddly, she was chewing gum, a habit Emily had rarely seen in a good kitchen. The gum chewing and her perch on the counter made her seem very young, but anyone would have known she was in charge. Oddly, though she seemed more tense, more focused, there was a lightness to her affect that hadn't been there earlier. This was clearly a woman who loved the chaos of a kitchen. Blake jumped down by putting her hands near her seat and lifting her body weight with just her arms. Then her feet hit the floor without a sound and she glided away.

By three thirty, heat flowed into the prep kitchen in waves, the noise in the main kitchen having grown until it was a dull roar. The hoods over the ovens rumbled, pans clanked against cast iron grates, muted voices, bursts of laughter, and a few shouted profanities punctuated the air repeatedly. Every possible scent lingered in the languid breeze, most of them pretty appealing. She turned to the guy who'd been next to her for five hours, a word not having passed between them. His body odor was the one sour note she'd been catching all afternoon, but he probably couldn't help it. A steaming hot kitchen on a steaming hot day was a bad marriage. "Hey, will you go tell Chef I'll be plating at four?"

He'd obviously been there long enough to know to obey anyone who spoke with authority. "Yes, Chef." She smiled as she started to make the fucking béarnaise. It was nice to outrank someone.

A few minutes later, a woman Emily hadn't seen before stuck her head in and caught the kid's attention. "Whipped cream," she said, entering fully to drop a five quart stainless tub on the counter. "Fill that, okay?"

"Yes, Chef."

His trembling voice made Emily look up from her own work to see him staring at the tub like it was going to bite him. *Damn.* She was too busy to get involved, but she couldn't let the poor guy wet himself.

"Need help?" she asked quietly.

"Service isn't for hours. If I make it now, it'll be a soupy mess."

Relieved at how easy his problem was to solve, she said, "Get some gelatin and heat it until it melts. Whip that in and it'll stand all day."

He gave her a suspicious look, then his gaze landed back onto the empty tub. "Are you sure?"

"Am I sure?" Rolling her eyes, she said, "Stabilizing whipped cream isn't brain surgery. I learned it in cooking school, just like you should have. But even if I hadn't been paying attention back then, I majored in chemistry in college."

He blinked at her, like he couldn't figure out why she'd told him that.

"I understand the science." She took her eyes off her sauce for a second, fixing him with a glare. "When you're a commis, you don't have time to question people senior to you. If someone offers help, accept it and get going. Now!" He ran to the pantry, where she hoped he'd stay until she finished. His body odor was so bad it was screwing with her ability to taste. Nothing in her béarnaise should have made it smell vaguely of armpits.

At four o'clock on the dot, Blake strode in, one hundred percent business. No hugs for Carlos. No sitting on the counter like a kid watching her mom cook. Not even a glance at Emily. Her focus was one hundred percent on the food, lying in the bright light like edible jewels.

The plates were laid out in three groupings, each a first course and entrée. The vichyssoise, the only soup she'd prepared, sat slightly above the other dishes. To the far left was a starter of sea urchin custard with baby squid. That paired with tenderloin of beef, the fucking béarnaise sauce and Dauphinoise potatoes. In the center was another first course of roasted eel, dotted with foie gras and sitting atop Swiss chard. Its entrée was glazed sweetbreads with roasted fennel and slices of caramelized pear. Lastly, quenelles of pike "Lyonnaise" were the first course, paired with an entrée of smoked Arctic char over Beluga lentils, with a stripe of carrot puree making the fish pop visually.

Blake took the fork and knife that lay atop a pressed napkin, bent over so close her nose almost touched the food, and moved along the line, inspecting each dish like she was searching for an improperly placed molecule. As she moved, she made some quiet but appreciative noises, especially when she passed the eel and the sweetbreads. Then she boldly dug in, carving and eating exactly one substantial bite from every dish. Except for the soup. She must have really wanted that, for she saved it until the end and ate every bit, quickly.

When she finished, she put her spoon down and finally made eye contact. "How much time will you need?"

"For…?"

A small smile broke through. "To do this all again."

Fuck!

Emily's blood pressure rose so quickly, she felt faint.

"Before you can start," Blake said slowly, her impish grin widening.

"Oh! Two weeks. I can start in two weeks."

"Two weeks it is." She stuck her hand out again and they shook one more time. As she turned to leave, Blake said, "Find someone who'll appreciate that. We're about to have the family meal, but that's better." Almost to herself, she added, "Much better."

Emily greedily grabbed the sea urchin custard and the quenelles for herself. She was starving, and there was no way she was giving those up to strangers who might not appreciate how hard she'd worked to prepare them. Then she addressed the kids in the kitchen, none of whom had stopped their work while Blake sampled. "Help yourselves, guys. God knows it's a rare day you get a decent meal in a professional kitchen."

Emily shuffled into her apartment just after eleven that night, fairly early for her. Chef Henri had been remarkably generous in not only giving her an excellent recommendation, but allowing her to burst into his kitchen just before service that afternoon. She'd never been more relieved to have a slow night. Just seventy covers, well spaced. If they'd had a tough crowd she might have sunk to the floor and bawled.

She was on her third episode of a show that detailed how complex machinery was made when a key jiggled in the lock. Hoping it was Chase, she called out, "Congratulate me!"

He stomped down the hall, turned and stood in the doorway, a broad smile lighting his face. "I knew you'd get it! You're ready for the big time, baby!"

Chase knew as much about cooking as she did about playwriting, but that didn't stop them from being the other's biggest fan. "I'd better be. Chef made it clear she doesn't screw around."

He dropped his beat-up nylon briefcase and walked over to pull her to her feet and give her a good, long hug. They'd recently celebrated their fourteenth year of friendship, really just an excuse to go to a favorite Sichuan place and reminisce about meeting at Michigan during freshman orientation. "How are we going to celebrate? There's not much open…"

"Chef Henri gave me a great bottle of wine for Christmas. Want to split it?"

"Red?"

"Of course." She got up to get the bottle. "Like you'd turn down white." She'd hidden it in her room, under her jeans in the chest of drawers. Their regular roommates, Olivia and Ray, a pair of flight attendants who lived in Florida and Texas, respectively, shared the third bedroom. Ray was gay, and Olivia was married to a man, but that didn't stop them from bunking together. Neither of them was there more than once a week, making them nearly ideal roommates. They were upstanding people, but they sometimes brought stragglers or other FAs who'd gotten stuck at LaGuardia to crash. Emily had learned the hard way to hide any liquor she didn't want guzzled.

She pulled the cork to let the wine breathe for a moment. They didn't have proper glasses, so a pair of plastic cups from a convenience store would have to do.

Chase was sitting on the sofa, eagerly holding both hands out when she returned. "Hold your horses, bucko," she chided. "Want me to pour your half right now? Or do you want to act like you're only going to have a little?"

"Load me up. I've been driving all day and my nerves are shot."

Given that he made his living teaching playwriting at an arts college in Manhattan, that made no sense. As she poured liberally, she asked, "Driving what? You don't have a car."

"My buddy Ethan's been driving for Uber. He was sick today so I borrowed his car and took over for him. People are *ass*holes," he moaned. "But I cleared two hundred bucks, so it was worth being shat on." He tilted his cup and clicked it against Emily's. "To my best friend, who's also the best chef, and the best roommate. I'll never be able to afford to eat at the restaurant she'll one day own, but she's the kind of woman who'll bring me primo scraps."

"If I ever own a restaurant, I'll keep a table just for you. Don't start licking your chops yet, though. I've got to impress a lot of people to get to a point where I can lure in some investors."

"You'll get there," he said, his confidence in her never dimming. "Tell me about this woman you'll be working for. Should I have heard of her?"

"Mmm…if you followed food closely you would have, but she doesn't have her own show or anything. She's just a hard-working chef at a well-rated place in TriBeCa. Like everyone at her level, she busts her butt trying to hold onto her four stars from *The Times*."

"Cute?"

She summoned up a memory of Blake. "Cute's not the word," she said thoughtfully. "Pretty. Sexy. Edgy. I doubt she was ever cute. Even as a baby I bet those big, dark, penetrating eyes made people call her striking or beautiful."

"Pictures, please." He grabbed her laptop, placed it in her lap, then sat back with an expectant look on his face.

Emily called up the images tab on her browser and did a quick search. Hundreds of shots popped up, many of them duplicates. She opened the one that made Blake look most intimidating; standing, unsmiling, with her arms crossed over her chest and a cleaver held like she was about to hurl it.

"Yow! If she had a whip in her hand rather than a knife, I'd be sure she was a first class domme."

"She could definitely pull it off. But I think that's a front. She was…" She thought for a few seconds, trying to decide how to categorize her. "She was nice. Much nicer than I thought she'd be. She even has a sense of humor. Hold on." She found another photo, one of Blake at an awards ceremony, giving a fellow chef an utterly charming smile. "She was more like this in person."

"Wow," he said, gazing at the picture for a long time. "She's something, Em."

"Yeah, I know. If I saw her on the street, I'd follow her like a bloodhound just to get a good look. But her commis acted like they were walking on eggshells."

"Commis are…?"

"Interns, basically. Recent cooking school grads for the most part. They seemed terrified of her."

"But you still think you'll like it?" he asked, squinting.

"I think I'll work my butt off. But she studied in France and she's widely regarded as one of the best classically trained young chefs in New York."

"That sounds…good." He was so sweet, so eager to be supportive, but not sure of how best to do that.

"I've got a lot to learn, and I know she can teach me."

"Learn?" His eyes saucered. "You've been cooking for eight years!"

Emily smiled at how little he truly understood her world. He wanted to know more, but she acknowledged it was hard to comprehend the details without having immersed yourself in the scene. "I know how to cook. But I don't know how to run a big kitchen. Or how to split my time between publicizing myself and keeping the kitchen running perfectly. Or how to reliably turn a profit. It's the business side I need to learn. I love Chef Henri, but he's very old school. If he didn't own his building, he'd have lost the place years ago."

"Maybe this woman will teach you how to work fewer hours for a lot more money."

She pinched his cheek—hard. "Blake Chadwick is not a magician. Chefs work hard for little pay. Kinda like playwrights."

"But at least I can do my job sitting on my butt in coffeehouses."

Her cell phone chirped and Emily glanced at the unfamiliar number. "If this is another call for Wah Lung Lo Chinese…"

"Yeah," she growled, sick to death of the almost nightly wrong numbers.

"Emily? Blake Chadwick."

Her heart started to race. If she was calling to fire her already…

"Yes, Chef?"

"I was too busy to talk about details this afternoon. Do you know the salary I'm offering?"

"Yes, Chef." She didn't add that it was two thousand less than she was currently making. What she'd learn had better make up for working harder for less.

"Did we discuss your whites?"

"No, Chef."

"Right. Well, if you want the restaurant name on them, I'll give you a contact at the place where we have them embroidered. Or you can wear them bare." She paused, and Emily heard her chewing something. Probably eating dinner. She took a look at the clock. 1:30. "Or with your name. Whatever you want. I'm not picky."

"Yes, Chef."

"But don't wear whites with another kitchen's name on them," she warned. "I hate that."

"No, Chef."

"For pants…" She trailed off, letting several seconds pass. "Don't wear checks. At my place those are for prep cooks. Black or grey are fine. Stripes…" She sighed. "If you have to."

"Yes, Chef."

"Oh. I'd rather you didn't wear those clownishly big pants that some people seem to like, but if you really need the room…"

"No, Chef, I don't."

She took a bite of something crunchy, making Emily hold the phone away from her ear. "We supply the usual white half-aprons. But I don't mind if you wear a full one. Any color." She paused for a few seconds. "Not too loud, though. I like my kitchen on the sedate side."

"Yes, Chef."

"So...black or grey or green. *Dark* green, though." Another noisy bite. "Mmm...let's say black or grey."

"Yes, Chef."

"No toques. And no scarves on your head. We're chefs, not pirates."

"No, Chef."

"We have baker's caps in grey, with a stripe." She paused. "That's best."

"Yes, Chef."

"Anything else? Do you have any questions?"

"No, Chef."

"Great. See you."

Emily hit the "end" button and met Chase's gaze. "I'm not going to say more than 'Yes, Chef' and 'No, Chef' for the next two or three years." She took a slug of her wine, enjoying the warm tingle as it went down. "I'm not picky. Ha!

Chapter Two

ON THE FIRST DAY AT her new job, Emily arrived at nine, determined to get the lay of the land before things got busy. After scampering up the loading dock like a rat, she went in and let the quiet peace soothe her for a few moments. Then she went into the locker room to change. She'd brought four coats and three pairs of pants, and now hung them in a locker marked "SOUS". Every once in a while she saw her title written somewhere, invariably laughing a little when she did. Technically, "sous" meant she was subordinate only to the head chef. But the term literally meant "under chef," which was kinda odd. Maybe it sounded better in France.

Once she was dressed and had put her street clothes away, she went out into the main kitchen, where muted sounds came from behind the half-wall. That was probably Carlos. Even without taking a peek, she knew he was making fish stock from the scent of mirepoix combining with all of the bones and fish heads from the previous day. While tempted to chat with him while he worked and maybe get some info on the inner workings of the kitchen, she decided he was probably too busy for that.

Going back to the tall table outside Blake's office, she saw a clipboard labeled "SOUS" lying there. A handwritten note said, "Emily—Check in the deliveries. I'll be in by 11. Grant." The other sous. The one Blake didn't completely trust.

Using the invoices on the clipboard to tick off every single item stacked up on the loading dock, Emily found only a case of Demerara sugar that wasn't on the order sheets, so she set that aside.

She'd just gone back to the desk when a tall, fairly handsome guy strutted in. Dark glasses, slicked back dirty blond hair, a snug T-shirt and skinny jeans made him look more like a musician than a chef, but a tattoo of the tip of a knife blade peeked out from above his collarbone to extend along his neck. Definitely a chef.

"Grant," he said, sticking out a hand. "Emily?"

"Yeah. Good to meet you."

He held onto her hand a beat longer than necessary. "I'm not shaking your hand just because we're meeting. Chef makes us shake in and shake out every day."

"Shake in?"

"Yeah." He went into the locker room, continuing to talk. "She thinks it shows respect for the work and each other. But it also makes everyone announce they're here. No one can sneak by if you have to shake in." He emerged with an apron over his street clothes. "Where have you worked?"

Most people got out a few niceties before they interrogated you, but Grant must have thought her resume was all that mattered. "I was sous at Henri for two years, a line cook at Defarge for two before that, and an assistant for fish at Farmstand for a year and a half. I did an externship at a place in the Hudson Valley before that."

"You went to the CIA?"

"I did."

A small smile broke through his studied disinterest. "Me too. But we weren't in the same class." He lifted his sunglasses, his having left them on this long beginning to make him look like a douche. "I remember all of the good-looking women. Especially the blondes."

"I graduated nine years ago," she said, ignoring his attempted compliment.

"Eight for me. I'm twenty-five. You?"

What a prick! "I was twenty-five once. You can swipe my driver's license out of the locker when I'm not looking if you want my birthdate."

"Touchy," he grinned, clearly sure he'd scored a point. "Why'd you start so late?"

"I went to college. And a year of grad school, too." She gave him a sickly sweet smile. "I guess I'm an underachiever."

"Why waste your time learning stuff you'll never use? I took the GED after my junior year of high school and headed up to Hyde Park."

"No reason," she agreed, having zero interest in trying to convince this guy that college had allowed her to mature. That was something it seemed he was still working on.

"Okay. Let's get cracking before the boss comes in. You did the deliveries?"

"I did."

"Keep an eye on the dry goods guy—"

"He slipped an extra case of sugar in," she said, cutting him off.

"Send it back. He's always trying shit like that."

"I checked everything in at my last job. I'm used to the game."

"Right. Here's the deal—anything special, like caviar, foie gras, vintage balsamic, unique cheese… All of that goes into Chef's office fridge. She'll kill you if she finds anything really expensive lying out where people can lift it."

"Got it. Does stuff wander off much?"

"Not much." He shrugged. "Beer…mostly beer."

"I'd expect that. Beer always walks."

"Make sure everyone clocks in. I'll check them out at the end of the day, but you sign the time cards. You approve overtime and do the schedule too. And all the ordering."

"And you do what? Specifically."

He blinked, like he hadn't expected her to call him on his BS. "I cook the family meal, I do the Z report at the end of the day, and I make the list for you to do the ordering. It's fair," he stressed, frowning.

"Okay. Chef said we should work it out. We'll try it your way and see if it really is fair."

He rolled his eyes, and headed for the fish walk-in. "Do you want to make tagliatelle or butcher fish?"

"I'll take fish."

"Good. My pasta will amaze you."

She followed along, thinking that Blake might be the easier of the two to work with.

At noon, Blake sauntered in via the loading dock doors, pausing to move around the kitchen, shaking hands, while adding a few words to those she seemed to know well. Emily had finished butchering her fish, and was just marking time until she knew what the specials would be for the day. Surreptitiously, she watched Blake work the room. She had such an elegant way of moving, her posture ramrod straight, with a crisp, sea green summery blouse making her look like she'd just come from a nice walk in the park. Her hair shone black as Beluga caviar, with gentle waves framing her lovely face. Then Blake turned abruptly and clapped Emily on the shoulder, startling her. "Glad to have you on board, Emily." After shaking her hand, she continued on to Grant, leaving Emily with what she knew was a silly grin on her face. It was like having the queen pick you out of the crowd for a special greeting, and she didn't have the self-control to act like it hadn't given her a boost.

Now finished shaking in, Blake walked over to the doors that led to the dining room, fiddled with a sound system hidden behind a stainless cover, then propped the doors open, allowing a blast of music to penetrate the room. The Smiths? Funny choice. But Emily could see her liking the British alt-rock scene. It somehow fit. On the way to her office, she sang along quietly, the lyrics just brushing Emily's ear. "A jumped-up pantry boy. He didn't know his place…" A second after Blake detoured into the staff bathroom she stormed right back out, good mood obliterated.

Standing in the middle of the kitchen, she called out in full voice, "Meeting!"

Everyone stopped. Not a sound for two or three seconds, then five people scurried out of the prep kitchen, and two dishwashers flew from their separate nook, their hands dripping water onto the floor.

"I must not have made myself clear," she said, her tone now relatively quiet, modulated. "Toilet seats are to be returned to the *horizontal* position." She held her hand out in front of herself, showing what she meant by horizontal. "Urine must be directed *inside* the bowl. Not on the rim. I understand everyone doesn't have the skill or the ability to hit the bowl every time, but every one of you can take a paper towel and clean up after yourself." Her heated gaze scanned the crowd. "I'm locking the bathroom," she declared. A startled gasp sounded from behind Emily. "If you want to use it, ask me for the key. After you've finished, it had better be as clean as it was at the beginning of the day. I'll be checking. As will Emily, our new sous, and Grant." She glared at each face in turn. "Got that?"

"Oui, Chef," came the nearly unanimous reply. Only Emily's "Yes," stuck out, making it clear she wasn't a member of the team yet.

Her expression softened, then Blake met Emily's eyes and said, "I'm sorry to give her such an unpleasant welcome, but you all know how I feel about the bathroom." She cleared her throat and a smile finally returned to her face. "Emily Desjardins comes to us from Henri, in Gramercy, where she was sous. You might also have run into her at Defarge or Farmstand. Introduce yourselves to her when you get a chance."

Then Blake strode toward her office, calling out, "Sous!" Emily and Grant scampered after her, like ducklings after their mother. When they entered, she closed the door. "I know they think I'm an asshole, but leaving the bathroom dirty means they aren't fastidious. Dirty people can't be trusted to make clean food. Both of you keep an eye on it. I'll put a closed-circuit camera in there if I have to."

"Oui, Chef," they said, with Emily adopting the nomenclature. She just hoped she wasn't the one charged with reviewing the pee-cam footage. There was only so much you wanted to know about your fellow cooks, and their bathroom habits wasn't on the list.

"Okay." Blake sat down at her desk, then popped a piece of gum into her mouth as she turned to Emily. "Are you ready to discuss today's specials?"

"Oui, Chef," she said, taking the chair next to the door. Grant excused himself, leaving them alone. Blake must have already told him his input wasn't necessary.

"I was in such a damn good mood," Blake said, leaning back in her chair. "Having you here is going to make things *so* much better. I was floating on air when I walked in, looking forward to being able to relax. I've been covering for three weeks now, and I'm wrecked."

"You have?" Emily knew she looked stunned, but that's because she was. Chef Henri would have called an agency and had someone—anyone—in there the day after his sous left.

"Who else can do it? If I thought Brady was ready to move up, I would have moved him." She tossed another piece of gum into her mouth, her jaw muscles popping from the rigor of her chewing. "Have you met Brady?"

"No, Chef. Just Grant and Carlos so far."

"Brady's your poissonnier. You'll like him. He's got the knack for cooking fish, and he never causes trouble. With a little seasoning, he'll be ready to move up, hopefully by the time Grant runs off to pick up his first Michelin star." Her smirk showed she thought he had a while to go before that happened. "Grant and I have an end of service meeting every night, and we decide on a special entrée or two, but we never get to first courses. Too tired. You and I will do that in the morning. Ça va?"

"Oui, Chef." Her distant memories of high school French were going to have to sharpen.

"Any ideas?"

"A few. I looked in the prep fridge this morning and pulled out things we can burn through. If we're careful, we have enough black truffles for a risotto…"

"Good," Blake said, making a note. "What else?"

"Wild striped bass tartare?"

"Good. Now something without protein."

"Some great sweet corn came in. How about a velouté?"

"I like it," she said, with a satisfied grin forming. "Chilled, right?"

"Right."

She made another note. "Which one do you want?"

"To make?"

After placing her chin on her hand, she batted those gorgeous brown eyes. "Yes, Emily. We have to *make* the food."

"I know!" she said, her cheeks blazing. "I meant…I don't know how you do things here."

"I'm sorry for teasing you," she said, and she honestly did look sorry. "I can be a smartass."

"I don't mind. Really. So, Grant and I split up the specials?"

"All three of us do. I like to make at least one dish every day. Keeps me sharp."

Emily wasn't sure exactly what Chef meant by saying she liked to "make" a dish. Did they each prep enough for service? Or make a single serving to test it out? She could have asked Grant, but thought it smarter to get her directions from the horse's mouth. "How far do we go? With the specials, that is."

She shrugged. "It depends. If you can make the whole thing, go ahead. But if it's something that has to be fired, the line cooks obviously handle that. So..." She looked at her note. "We'll make enough sea bass and velouté for..." She leaned in and looked at her computer, which she'd booted up the second she'd sat down. "We're full tonight, so make enough for a hundred portions. But just one order of risotto. We make that to order."

"To *order*?" Emily got out, stunned. "You don't precook the rice?"

Blake gave her a half-smile. "We do, but just before service. I don't like the texture when you cool it completely." She made a face. "It can be chalky."

"Got it," she said, the realization hitting her once again that Chef wasn't fucking around with quality. In eight years, Emily had never worked at a place where the risotto wasn't half cooked in the morning, then spread out on cookie sheets to rest in a cooler for hours before service.

"If you don't have a preference, I'd like the velouté." Blake tapped her lip with her pencil. "Tarragon?"

"Perfect."

"And something to add a little crunch, I think. I'll play around and see what works. If I can't think of anything else, I'll make some croûtons."

"Got it. I'll take the tartare."

"That leaves Grant with the risotto." She stood. "Have your dish ready by three thirty. We present the specials to the FOH at four, and I like to have time to tinker."

Present the specials to the front of the house staff? The servers got a vote? Chef Henri would have laughed. Then a tendril of anxiety shot through her. What if the servers didn't like a dish? Would they have to start over? *Jesus!* Shakily, she got up to move to the door, remembering to add, "Oui, Chef."

Blake stood as well, and got close. When she spoke, her voice was soft, almost like they were peers, maybe even friends. "It's very nice having someone to kick things around with." She clapped Emily on the shoulder, with her smile growing. "I can't tell you how nice it was not to have to think of today's specials. You just saved me ten minutes, which I truly appreciate."

As Emily started for the door, Blake said, "After my temper tantrum over the bathroom, I assume I don't have to give you the lecture about cleanliness?"

"No, Chef," she said, shaking her head soberly.

Blake started to move back to her desk to sit down, then made a silly face and stayed right where she was. "I can't help myself. That big 'A' in the window means the health inspector whipped through here in minutes, happy as a clam. Keeping that grade is paramount." As she leaning over slightly, Emily was struck by the intensity that shone in her gaze. "I know it's easy to forget this, but we're not just selling food. People trust us, Emily. They pay good money for the certainty that they're not going to get a stomach virus from something we've let sit in the cooler too long. Don't *ever* forget that."

"I won't, Chef."

"Great. Now get out there and kick some butt."

Emily was beaming as she walked out of the office. She'd been an employee for less than half a day and was already thinking of ways to get more of those shoulder squeezes.

In nine years she'd only worked for guys. People she'd respected, but hadn't lusted after. *That* had officially changed. Blake was not only ridiculously attractive, she was fiery, a characteristic Emily had always been drawn to. But she'd been working long enough to understand how little you truly got to know your head chef. She'd have to resign herself to an occasional fantasy about her new boss—when she wasn't too tired to even bother with a fantasy to lull herself to sleep.

In the few minutes Emily had been gone, new faces had populated the kitchen. She could have had Grant introduce her, but he was conspicuously absent. She'd smelled smoke on him when he'd come in that morning, so she moved to the back door and looked outside. As she'd suspected, he was out on the loading dock with an older guy, short, wiry and gaunt. Typical seasoned line cook. "Grant," she said as she approached, "you're on for a black truffle risotto. Go light on the truffles. We're stretching them."

"What else?" he asked, taking a long drag on his cigarette.

"Just that."

"No, what are the other specials."

"Oh. I'm making a striped bass tartare and Chef's handling a corn velouté."

"That's it?"

"Uh-huh. She just wanted three."

"Good. Sometimes she goes nuts and wants four or five. That really busts our balls." He shrugged. "I think I'd rather make the tartare."

"Sorry," she said, turning to go back inside. "I called it." She normally would have been much more collegial. But Grant was clearly the kind of guy who pushed you as far as he could. He was going to find out she was tougher to move than she looked.

The busiest times of the day were the first hours and the last hours. Things were often a little chill early in the afternoon, and that was the case today. Deciding not to force the staff to come to her, Emily walked around the kitchen and introduced herself.

In a way, she was everyone's boss. Or co-boss with Grant. But her specific responsibilities would be for the fish dishes and all of their accompanying sides. That meant two cooks reported directly to her: Brady, the clean-cut poissonnier, and Alicia, her entremetier. Emily thought it funny that they used more French terms than her old place —given Chef Henri was French and Blake clearly American. But every chef had her quirks. Usually many of them.

While it was easier to say that Brady was the fish cook, while Alicia prepared the accompanying sides and sauces, Emily was going to have to recall, and stick to Chef's classic French terminology.

Watching Alicia move around Brady to get things in order so she could start on a sauce, Emily had to face the fact that she was now wedged between a gorgeous boss and an equally beautiful employee. But she wasn't worried about having Alicia get under her skin. By the time they really got going, every worker was simply another pair of skilled hands. By end of service, she was sure she wouldn't even recall that Alicia was a woman, much less a pretty one.

She was still chuckling to herself at how each of them had pointed out a full box of disposable gloves prominently displayed upon a stainless shelf above each station. Both Brady and Alicia demonstrated that it took less than a second for them to grab a pair and get them on —something they only had to do when someone gave the signal the health inspector was about to enter the kitchen. At least Blake gave them a little wiggle-room there. No one liked to cook with their hands encased in gloves.

Grant eventually sauntered back in with Jameson, his rôtisseur, or grill chef as she would have called him before today. She followed him into the prep kitchen, and watched him break down a side of beef with quick, sure strokes, while they chatted. The meat entremetier was Cleveland, a pleasant seeming guy with a nice smile who lived with his wife and two kids just a few blocks away from Emily.

While talking to the cooks, Emily learned that even though the terms were different, the process was just what she was used to. The menu was built from a backbone of standards, which changed with the seasons, along with a few special first courses and entrées. Given that Henri's menu had been in a bit of a rut, she hoped to use her time to figure out how to keep the menu fresh, a requirement in today's market, while not overwhelming the staff. That was a delicate balance, one Chef Henri had never bothered with.

Now that the four line cooks on the hot side were all in, they'd start on their mise en place, the individual elements of the dishes they'd be making that night. Nothing was more important than having your ingredients properly and amply prepared. A hand-written copy of the menu was tacked up above each station, and Emily watched Alicia neatly arrange piles of herbs before she knocked them down to their proper sizes for the dishes in question. *Good knife-work.* The kid had skills.

Emily didn't have to cook during service, so handling her first course would be the only time she'd get her hands dirty. At Henri, even though she was sous, in many ways she'd been a glorified line cook. Rare was the night she wasn't cooking while trying to keep the whole line moving along. Being at Blake was a promotion in every way.

Setting up alongside Brady, Emily got to work on her striped bass. It was a beautiful fish, with a sweet smell and a perfect feel. "Do we weigh out the portions or go by feel?" she asked absently.

He let out a soft bark of a laugh. "That's a joke, right? 175 grams for entrées, a hundred for a first course. If she wants something different, trust me, she'll tell you."

Blake emerged from the prep kitchen, staring intently at her phone. "We're looking at over two hundred covers tonight, people. Don't be stingy with your mise."

"Oui, Chef," they all replied, keeping their heads down.

Emily had underestimated how long it would take to prepare enough tartare for a hundred first courses. Ten thousand grams of sea bass, chopped down to pieces the size of a kernel of corn, was a lot of fish. But she made it on time by kicking into a higher gear for the last hour, ignoring the sweat rolling down her body, puddling in her clogs. Alongside the tartare, sat a spicy green papaya salad to which she was adding a final grinding of pepper when Blake appeared and placed her corn velouté on the counter. She tapped her foot as she chewed the hell out of her gum, waiting for Grant. He arrived a minute later, sweat dripping from his ears onto the shoulders of his jacket. On a hot day, that prep kitchen was like hades.

Blake looked at all three dishes, then turned them a hundred and eighty degrees, obviously checking to make sure they were perfect from all angles. She tasted each, then frowned over her own dish, mumbling something under her breath. Emily let out a relieved breath when her own creation garnered a slight smile. "Excellent," Blake said. "Now make a fresh order for four p.m." Her gaze landed on Grant. "Sharp." When he started to walk back to the prep kitchen Blake regarded Emily for a second. "Taste my velouté?"

After grabbing a fresh spoon, Emily took a sip, letting her taste buds focus on the savory dish. "Perfect," she said, nodding thoughtfully. "I don't taste any thyme, which is good. It might have competed with the tarragon."

Blake nodded, then leaned against the counter to speak collegially. "I usually make a sachet of thyme, bay leaf and black peppercorns, but I eliminated the thyme today."

"Good call. The whole corn kernels you put in liven it up. I like the crunch."

"Not too crisp? I left them raw so they'd pop, but I want to keep the velvety texture."

"You did." Emily looked up at her, catching a hint of a smile.

"Thanks. The papaya salad makes your tartare. Good addition. I appreciate that you knew it would work, and didn't come to me for approval." Her eyes narrowed, and she spoke with more intensity, although less volume. "So long as you stick with what we generally do, you can fly solo, Emily. We use great product to make delicious food. Unique is great. Showy isn't. This is a restaurant, not an art gallery."

Then she was gone, headed back to her office. The moment Blake stepped away, people gravitated to the food, like sharks after chum. There really wasn't much to share, and it disappeared in seconds, empty plates showing only tiny remnants of the creations that had rested there moments before. Emily always told her friends that she'd never been around hungrier, less picky eaters than cooks. She swore they'd eat sautéed tires if you'd left a plate of them sitting around.

At four on the button, Emily, Grant, and Blake stood in the dining room, displaying their creations to the front of the house staff, a motley collection of servers slumped against walls and straddling chairs. Most were wearing shorts or yoga pants, with T-shirts and tank tops revealing a lot of skin. During service, Emily was sure they'd be well dressed, upright, attentive, and engaged, but now they looked like people who'd stayed out way too late the night before. Almost to a person they seemed more interested in crawling under a table for a nap than hearing about specials.

Surprisingly, Blake didn't speak. Grant took over, selling the dishes like he was trying to unload used cars on a lot. Blake leaned against a wall, appearing bored and antsy at the same time.

Emily hadn't yet seen the dining room, and she was surprised by its simplicity. There was an undercurrent of richness in the fabric on the chairs and the wall coverings, but clean, elegant lines were at the forefront. The tables were spaced far enough from each other for guests to be able to converse in private, and Grant's voice didn't echo—a nice change from most places in TriBeCa, where cacophony was the rule of the day. The music had been turned off a little earlier, replaced by the tinkle of silverware as busboys quickly set it out.

Two bartenders were getting their mise ready, busily slicing limes and oranges, while a guy in a nice suit, probably the front of the house manager, bustled about, speaking softly to everyone he passed.

Grant was selling the hell out of Blake's corn velouté, making it sound so good Emily was disappointed she hadn't gotten a bowl. Now the servers perked up and dug in, demolishing the food with slightly more restraint than the cooks had shown. "What's in the papaya salad?" a bearded, stocky guy asked.

"Emily?" Grant said, turning to her.

"Pardon me," Blake interrupted, pushing away from the wall to come to life. "I didn't introduce our new sous chef. This is Emily Desjardins. Emily? Your papaya?"

Hearing Blake speak her name caught Emily by surprise. She not only used the proper French pronunciation of her surname, her given name now had a Gallic flair as well. More like Emi-leé. Blake hadn't done that before, but maybe making the velouté had transported her back to France without realizing she'd gone. Emily forcefully brushed aside her musings to focus on the food. "Thank you, Chef. This dish is close to a classic som tam, with papaya, peanuts, chilies, basil, coriander, shrimp paste, fish sauce, honey and lime juice." She thought for a second. "It's about a five out of ten on the heat scale. Not for wimps." A thought occurred to her. "We can't take the peanuts out, and we can't make it less spicy. I apologize in advance to your guests who won't be able to enjoy it."

Blake put a hand on her shoulder as they returned to the kitchen. "Nice job. I like having the servers know something's spicy up front. Saves us from having it returned." She paused and turned to survey her domain. "Do you like the dining room?"

"It's very nice. Both elegant and calming."

"I suppose it is," she said, looking around thoughtfully. "One of the owner's wives decorated it."

"You're not…?"

"The owner?" She laughed, not looking particularly amused. "I don't own a square inch of this place. I'm a hired hand, just like you."

Everything that could be done to prepare for service had been done. Now they had almost forty-five minutes to burn before the first guests would arrive. That wasn't enough time to fully relax, but it was better than nothing.

While the dishwashers sprawled out on the floor of their nook, resting their heads on rolled-up towels, the smokers went outside to stand on the scorching hot loading dock in the full sun and fill their lungs with a thousand chemicals, nicotine the most precious. Emily sat at the sous' desk and checked her phone. Sometimes sitting for a few minutes rejuvenated her, but just as often it made standing again an awfully big effort.

Blake was in her office, talking to the suited guy from the front of the house. Her voice kept rising above his, with names repeatedly carrying over the general noise. Emily could just see inside, catching sight of Blake standing over a large plastic rectangle that covered her desk. That was probably a schematic of the restaurant. Did she really work with the maitre d'hotel to make sure their guests were seated in the right spots? Emily gawped at the scene, completely stunned. When did she have time to do all of the paperwork involved in running a restaurant? Grant said he did the Z report, the tally of every dollar that came in that day, but that was the tip of the iceberg. *Damn.* Compared to Blake, Chef Henri had been on a permanent vacation.

Grant sauntered in from the loading dock, looked around, then walked over to Emily. "I'll check all of the stations before service. Will you make sure we've got enough plates? Raul, our chef de plonge, sometimes forgets to bring them out."

"Chef what?" she asked, too distracted by her phone to have listened carefully.

"Our head dishwasher."

"Chef de plonge?" she said, pronouncing it with more of a French accent than Grant had used. "I've worked in places that call them plongeurs, but never a chef."

"He's the boss, so he's a chef. One of her many, many quirks," he said, leaning over to whisper. "She's talented, everyone knows that. But she's got some weird-ass ideas. If she gets a vibe about a person's work ethic she ignores his training or even experience. Like the new pastry assistant." He pointed to a goth-looking young woman named Raven. Emily had noticed tattoos of cookies, cakes and pies decorating her hands, but it was her blue-black hair that caught your attention. Magic-Marker hair as Chase called it.

"What's wrong with Raven?"

"She's like seventeen!" he fumed, albeit quietly. "No formal training —at all. Zero experience. But she came in here about six times, begging for a chance. She made some shit Chef liked and bang! She's the pastry assistant."

"Maybe she can sense talent, Grant. Or drive."

"Nah. She'd rather have someone reliable, like Jameson, than someone with drive. She likes plodders."

"A kitchen full of people with tons of drive would make us all nuts. Trust me. A good kitchen needs a mix." She slapped him on the shoulder, hoping he took it as a light-hearted gesture. "We can't have too many of you." Taking a look at the office, she saw that Blake was still talking. "What's the FOH guy's name?"

He started to walk away, with his hand fluttering dismissively in the air. "Thierry something. The FOH is another world. One we don't have to care about."

At five p.m., Blake came out with her apron on. It was a unique one, unsurprisingly. Grey, of course, since she liked things to be sedate, but it didn't loop around her neck. Instead, the straps went over her shoulders to cross at the middle of her back, a style Emily was going to find and copy. She couldn't count the number of times she'd gotten a heat rash from a sweaty apron strap.

Every other cook wore a baker's cap, a brimless cotton hat that kept sweat from falling into the food. But Blake was bareheaded, with the bright lights making her black waves gleam.

She stood at the pass, the elevated stainless counter at the center of the hot cooking area. Grant, his rôtisseur, and his entremetier stood to her left, ready to cook any kind of meat along with the required vegetables, sauces and garnishes. Emily, her poissonnier and her entremetier were at her right, doing the same for fish, pasta and vegetarian dishes.

Those four line cooks, Jameson, Cleveland, Brady, and Alicia, were the center of the action for most entrées. But a kitchen didn't live on hot food alone. Off the heat was a whole section devoted to food that was chilled or served at room temp. Besides Lorelei, the rail-thin thirty-something pastry chef, and Raven, her assistant, a wild child named April was the garde manger—responsible for all salads, cold hors d'oeuvres, terrines, pâtés, and charcuterie. Taking a quick look, you would have been sure she'd just stepped in from a hurricane. Her hair, a unique shade of lilac, pointed in at least twenty different directions. She easily won the most tattoos contest as well, with one arm covered in black and white cartoons, with the other filled with vividly decorated, very brightly colored skulls, the ones used in Mexico for the Day of the

Dead. Strangely, there was something light-hearted about them, despite their grim nature.

Emily could tell April had skills. She'd whipped through her mise in no time, and now had Emily's papaya salad ready to plate. She'd just have to add the precise portions of tartare Emily had weighed and stored in the refrigerator near April's station. But that was just one of a dozen other dishes she'd be responsible for. Garde manger was a damn tough job, but the salad chef rarely got credit for juggling far more dishes than anyone else on the line.

Emily took a look at Blake, poised for action. Her feet were spread shoulder-width apart, exactly the way they trained you in cooking school. The heat lamps at the pass bathed her skin in a golden hue that made her look robust and healthy. The printer that would soon start spitting out chits was silent, but she kept glancing at it, as though wondering where the first of their two hundred covers were. Just then the first one started to print. 5:05. People weren't wasting any time tonight.

Blake whipped it from the printer and called out in a clear, strong voice, "Ordering. Table six. One bass, one velouté, one duck, one skate wing."

"Oui, Chef," all of the cooks responded as one. Then April got to work, sending the bass, the papaya salad and the velouté down the line. The velouté was in a bowl, with everything else on a thin metal tray. Since it went past her, Emily touched the back of a fresh spoon to the velouté and tasted it, finding it perfectly seasoned. Since she'd made the other dishes herself, she didn't need to taste them again. Then Blake took the tartare and the salad and plated it, arranging the fish atop the papaya beautifully. Emily had plated at her last job, so this was a tiny demotion, but she didn't mind. It would be a good learning experience to watch Blake not only plate the food but expedite it as well.

"Pick up, table six," she called and a strikingly suave man from Ghana named JoJo dashed in and placed the dishes on his tray before hustling back out.

Emily had always called the guys who delivered food and picked up the spent plates back waiters or back servers. But the new sheriff in town wanted French titles, so French titles they would have. She'd chuckled earlier in the day upon meeting the four "commis de rang." They were all Ghanaian, resembled each other vaguely, and were somehow related, as were Carlos and Norma, the morning and afternoon prep cooks. Whoever the first of their clan had been, he or she must have been dead solid certain their relatives would measure up. If there was a screw-up, Blake would have fired not only the relative you recommended, but you.

The orders started to come in fitfully, with a minute or two between them. That was a nice pace, but Emily knew it wouldn't last. Brady fired a monkfish, and when it arrived Emily whipped a metal rod from her breast pocket and stuck it deep into the flesh. When she removed the cake tester, she put it to her bottom lip. Just warm, the perfect temp for fish. She let the plate slide along to Blake, who arranged it so artistically, settling it among three tiny side dishes, that Emily was a little in awe. The woman had mad skills.

Some escalloped potatoes slid by and Emily tasted them. Grasping the hot casserole dish with a towel, she scooted back down the line and spoke quietly to Alicia. "You've got too light a hand with your seasonings. Go bolder with the salt on the potatoes and add garlic to the turnip puree."

"Oui, chef," she said, nodding as she rushed to prepare the next dish.

Emily added a little salt to the potatoes, then moved back down the line and handed the dish over. Blake gave her a look, but didn't add a question. That was much appreciated. Emily's staff would only respect her if they knew Blake trusted her judgment.

The chits started coming every thirty seconds, then every fifteen. All at once, they were spitting out continually. Blake's strong voice kept calling, "Ordering," as she read off each ticket.

"Shit!" As the word left April's lips, Emily was beside her.

"What's wrong?"

"I'm almost out of mushrooms, watercress and endive. People are ordering a fuckload of salads tonight."

Emily was tempted to lecture her, but that could wait. She breezed by Blake, quietly said, "Cover me," then ran for the prep kitchen where she grabbed two young commis and instructed one to chop the watercress and the other to clean and dry the endive. Then she took a tub of hen of the woods mushrooms, wiped them clean and sliced them according to the plan. It took almost ten minutes, but April was resupplied with no need to cross items off the menu, always an embarrassment for both the server and the restaurant.

When Emily returned to her post, Blake was so busy expediting she no longer had time to plate. Grant had been doing it all, but now Emily stepped in and plated the fish dishes. She thought she was good at this, having done it for two years, but Blake's presentation was a large step better. More artistic in every way. Luckily, Grant's was as weak as her own, but Blake didn't seem to notice. She was so busy barking out orders and making sure everything was ready for an entire table at once that she couldn't have spared a second to look.

The last chit spit out at 11:55. Five minutes to fucking midnight, when they were supposed to close at eleven. Luckily, it was only for a salad and dessert. They all stood on their shaking legs and stared at the printer for another minute. Silence.

"We're out," Blake called, finally sounding tired. "Good job, people. Very good job. Two hundred and thirteen covers, and not one legitimate complaint about the food." She moved to the far side of the kitchen, shaking each person's hand as she worked her way around. When she got to Emily, she gave her a quick, wan smile. "Excellent job. We gave very good value for money tonight." She leaned in and added, "Next time, have the commis replenish if someone runs out of mise. You're too valuable to step away." Her voice grew louder and she took a look at Grant. "But at least you *did* something rather than just stand there with your dick in your hand."

Wow. She busted Grant's chops all day long! But he didn't seem to care a bit, letting a smirk settle onto his face. Blake went to a corner of the cold area, where busboys had stored every wine bottle with more than an ounce remaining. Grabbing the bottle with the most in it, she called, "Grant? End of service meeting," and strode to her office, with a burst of energy making her look like she could go for another few hours.

Emily watched them disappear, then she used all of her remaining strength to head for the lockers to change. Thank god Grant was responsible for breaking the kitchen down. If she'd had to do that, she might have fallen on her knife.

"Emily?"

Stopping mid-stride, Emily poked her head into Blake's office. "Yes, Chef?"

"It's bluefish season. We'll have a good supply tomorrow. Think of a nice way to prepare them."

"Yes, Chef."

Blake was doodling on a pad, not looking up. "Do you have any other thoughts? With it so hot, I want something light."

Emily snuck a look at Grant, his expression blank. This was *his* job. A big part of it. Offering her ideas would relieve him of thinking of his own. But she couldn't blow Blake off just to make a point. She slid into the office and said, "Why don't we make an entrée salad? The papaya sold well. We could do a Thai beef thing."

"Too ethnic," Grant grumbled. "I've already had three ideas shot down. We don't want anything too unique."

"Too *weird*," Blake said, not looking up. "I'm not opposed to your salad, Emily, but we'd need to make it ours. People don't want to pay thirty-five bucks for an entrée they can buy for ten at their local Thai joint."

Emily picked up a pencil and started to write down ingredients, thinking of what she could add to create depth and a little extravagance to the dish. She was so tired her brain wasn't working at full capacity, but they had to come up with a good menu, and the faster they finished, the sooner they could leave.

It only took another five minutes to come to an agreement, thanks to Blake's addition of a light variation on a croque-madame, along with a skirt steak with a spicy chimichurri sauce.

While she changed, Emily's mouth began to water while thinking about how good some perfectly poached eggs would be right then. All she had to do was hear about a favorite food to want it, and the loving way Blake had described her croque-madame made her want to wander the streets, looking for a French bistro that was still open. But when she arrived at the back door, her two cooks and the pastry team were standing there, clearly waiting for her. "We're taking you out," Brady said, giving her a big smile. "Where do you want to go?"

Home? Please let me go home! But she couldn't refuse, tired as she was. You had to bond with your fellow cooks, and the time-honored way to do that was via alcohol. "You guys choose. I've been over in Gramercy for two years, so I'm out of touch."

"They'll let me in at Knicks," Raven said. "Is that cool?"

Emily recalled Grant saying Raven was only seventeen. He might have pulled that number out of thin air, but maybe he was right. Now the question was whether Emily should contribute to the delinquency of a minor. A minor who kinda worked for her. "Why don't we go somewhere and eat? Then we don't have to worry about it."

"Nah," Raven said. "It's cool. Jimmy lets me in 'cause I don't drink. We go there all the time."

"Okay. Sounds good." Maybe the youth of America were more prudent than her own generation had been.

The bar was just a few blocks away, and blessedly close to a subway line Emily could use to transfer to one that would eventually take her home. Raven lingered outside the door, saying, "Anybody wanna get high before we go in?" Ahh…the youth of America leapt into the depths of depravity just as the previous generation had.

Lorelei, Raven's boss, joined her, with Emily wondering if they'd brought a secret stash of baked goods for when they got the munchies. She and Brady and April went inside, and she let her eyes adjust to the strange blue lights that dotted the room. It was a dive—pure and simple. A big jukebox was playing a punk rock classic, and a dozen people, mostly very young, lounged around the pool table. Everyone was barely dressed, given the heat, and the place smelled like stale beer and sweat. But there was something oddly homey about it, and Jimmy, the bartender, was friendly and attentive.

"New boss," Brady told the barman as they found and gathered stools for all of them to sit close. "Treat her right."

A shot of something and a cold beer were placed in front of her. "Welcome to the neighborhood," Jimmy said.

Emily stared at the drinks, feeling two sets of eyes watching her. *What the hell.* She downed the shot, a fairly decent whiskey, then pounded the beer, encouraged by her new co-workers. It was like being back in college. But her body wasn't twenty any more, and she knew she was long past being able to convince it to ignore the ravages of time.

By one thirty Grant had moved his stool very close as they watched Raven and Lorelei attempt to play pool while remarkably high. Neither woman could hit a straight shot, and Emily thoughtfully pondered the intelligence of getting absolutely ripped with an underage employee. A few hits were one thing, but these women were boneless.

"I haven't been out with co-workers for years," Emily mused. "I kind of missed it."

He let out a laugh. "I have never met anyone who doesn't go out. Only a..." His mouth shut quickly, then he tentatively said, "Are you in AA or something?"

"I suck at it if I am." She raised her beer so the glass touched his nose. "I've been out a million times. Just never as sous. There were only six cooks at Henri, and all of them had families they wanted to get home to."

Grant had already bought her a round, so it was her turn. He drank much faster than she did, and she was well aware it was a fool's errand to try to match a guy drink-for-drink. While her bottle was half full, Grant's was empty. Signaling to Jimmy, she pulled out a ten and said, "Set Grant up again, will you?"

Jimmy put down two shots and one beer, took her ten and added a wink. Great. More booze. Just what she needed. But Grant raised his shot and waited for her to do the same. They touched their glasses together and she downed hers, shivering as it hit her gut. The rest of her beer went down pretty smoothly after that, and she leaned back against the bar, with the stress and strain of standing for fifteen hours easing as the analgesic effect of the alcohol worked its way through her system.

Grant dropped an arm around her shoulders and tugged on her. "Don't act like the boss when we're out. Once we leave the kitchen, we're all the same."

"But we're *not.* I'd prefer that my staff like me, but if I had to choose, I'd rather have their respect."

"We're equals. And *I* like you," he said, his lips close to her ear. "I like you a lot. You're the best looking cook Blake's ever hired."

She patted him on the leg. "Nice to know, but you'd better find someone who likes guys if you want to get laid."

His arm fell as he jerked up straight. "You're a dyke?"

"All the way through," she confirmed, enjoying the stunned look he gave her. She never tried to act or look straight, but had to admit it was nice to be able to pass, letting her cuddle with a woman in the straightest bar and not get a single sour look. While it sucked that her affect gave her straight privilege, there wasn't much she could do about it. Even when she was dressed in her dykiest clothes, guys hit on her. Okay. Maybe it wasn't truly a privilege to look straight. Sometimes it was a huge pain in the ass.

Grant grabbed Brady and yanked on him until he stood right in front of them. "Did you know Emily was gay?" he demanded.

Brady chuckled, his normally sharp eyes now muddled and fuzzy. "Nope. And I was all ready to sleep with her to get promoted."

"How would that work?" Emily asked. "I'd have to fire myself to promote you."

"Oh, yeah." His lazy smile made him look as dumb as an ox. "I didn't think that through. I'll still sleep with you, though. You're a sizzler."

"Much appreciated," she said. "But I'm good."

Raven came over to the group, her eyes mere slits. "We're gonna go smoke. Anybody?"

"Emily's a dyke," Brady informed her.

"Me too," Raven said, leaning close and speaking abnormally loud. "Most of the time."

"I'm full-time," Emily said.

Then she found another shot in her hand, with Brady toasting, "To dykes! They rule the world!"

She could hardly disagree with that. Besides, the whiskey was tasting better and better.

At three, Emily stumbled out of the bar with her new friends. They were a great group. Generous, fun, and…something else she couldn't think of. Brady lived in the Bronx, so they went down to the 6 train together, a line which would one day get her to Queens if she was lucky. "I've got to change at fifty-something," she said. "Remind me."

"Got it." He tried to tap his temple, missing by an inch or two to poke himself in the eye.

They leaned against each other on the platform, then nearly fell into an empty car when the train pulled in. She'd lived in New York long enough to know that an empty subway car was always a bad deal, but she was too slow to process information. Yep. Someone had just used this one as a urinal. They could move to the next car as soon as they stopped. But Brady was big and soft enough to make a nice pillow. They'd move in a second or two…

Emily jerked awake when a guy with two huge suitcases let one roll over her foot. "Hey!" she called out grumpily, her arm jutting out in reflex. As her hand fell, she patted the big, lumpy mattress, then slowly realized it was a human being. Her eyes opened, then slowly focused on the tall apartment buildings they were flying by.

Fuck!

"Brady," she said, grabbing him by the shoulder and shaking him. "Where are we?"

He opened an eye, then closed it quickly. "The Bronx, I guess. Lemme know when we get to a hundred and twenty fifth. I've gotta change to the 5."

"Third Avenue, a hundred and thirty eighth street," the conductor's voice squawked.

Emily slapped at him again. "We're on a hundred and thirty eighth."

"Can't be. Haven't got to a hundred and twenty fifth yet."

"A hundred and thirty eighth is bigger than…what you said. We passed it."

His eyes blinked slowly. "There's no stop at a hundred and thirty eighth."

"The conductor just said we're stopping there. Come on, wake up."

He managed to keep his eyes open, then gazed around like he'd been transported to another land. "I don't know where we are…"

The doors opened, and she grabbed his arm to pull him from the car. "This is the Bronx. You live here. How in the hell do I get to Queens?"

"No idea," he said, tipping face-first into a post, where his open mouth rested against grimy steel bearing a hundred years of flaking paint and hard use.

Grasping him by the hand, she tugged hard, making him stumble behind her until they were in front of a large subway map, now looking like a plate of colorful spaghetti; blue, red, orange, and green strands trailing off dizzily. Carefully, she traced the 6 line back down to a hundred and twenty fifth, where Brady should have changed.

"What street do you live on?"

"A hundred and fifty third," he said, looking proud of himself. If her sense of direction wasn't as trashed as the rest of her brain, they weren't all that far away from his street. But her stop, a little dot of blue that none of the nearby spaghetti strands reached, was going to require dragging her ass all the way back down a billion blocks, then a change to the E, then the walk home. Fuck it.

Once she got him moving, Brady was pretty well able to walk a straightish line. They descended the steep stairs, both holding onto the railings like they were lifelines. There was a rowdy club a half block away, with people loitering in front, smoking. A battered black car cruised by, looking for pickups. Emily hailed it, then poured Brady in. "What's your address?" she asked.

He managed to recite it, with Emily and the driver taking him at his word. The trip didn't take long, and she forced herself to stay awake just in case the driver tried to take them on a two-hour payday. They pulled up in front of a big, old building and Emily gave the driver every dollar she had. That only left him with a dollar tip, which he grumbled about in a language she couldn't understand, but she was tapped out.

She and Brady stood in front of the building and his head slowly turned to give her a boozy smile. "Are we gonna sleep together?"

"If you don't have a spare couch we are." *How in the hell had a simple drink turned into this?*

Chapter Three

THE PHONE ALARM BLEATED and brayed at nine. Emily fought her roiling stomach and spinning head to get her bearings. Work… drinks…drunk…Brady. *That's* whose heavy arm was draped across her gut. She reached down, patting around frantically until she was able to reassure herself they were both fully clothed. It probably wouldn't have been a good idea to have her first sexual encounter with a man be with her new employee—while she was blasted.

After rolling out of the full size bed, she grabbed onto the wall to steady herself. She had, at most, fifteen minutes to get to the train. Stumbling and bumping into walls, she made it to the bathroom, but made the mistake of taking a look at the shower. She would never know how she hadn't barfed at the sight. No one had *ever* cleaned the damned thing. From the day the enamel had been sprayed on until today, not one cleaning implement had ever touched it. She hated to go to work dirty, but since she didn't have clean clothes, it hardly mattered.

She spent a good five minutes washing her face, repeatedly splashing cold water on her bloodshot eyes, trying to take some of the puffiness from them. Then she found a comb that she held under hot water for a minute to kill anything that lived on it. If your face was clean and your hair was combed you didn't look too bad, right? A woman must have lived there or visited frequently, because three ponytail bands lay near the comb. Hoping the woman didn't have lice, she pulled her hair back and wrapped a band around it. Not too bad. Now she simply looked like a hung-over ghost. But at least her face was clean!

Rifling through Brady's wallet like a thief, she took two of his nine dollars, leaving a note that she'd repay him at work. She wanted to check to make sure he'd set an alarm, but there was no clock and his phone was hidden somewhere. She would have woken him, but as long as he arrived before Blake she could cover for him. There was no one to do the same for her.

After exiting his building and listening to the ambient noise for a minute to see if she could hear an elevated train anywhere near, she spotted a Dominican restaurant a few doors down. Emily stumbled in, so jonesing for coffee that she was ready to beg. It was a small place, and a motherly woman used a little stovetop pot to make the nectar of the gods just for her. Dark, sweet, and frothy. It was only a dollar, and Emily gave her both of her purloined bills. She would have paid twenty for something so good.

She couldn't see or hear a train, but her phone found one and guided her there quickly. Some of her friends questioned paying so much for a smart phone, but it had saved her countless hours of wandering around lost. After getting on the train, Emily stayed on it all the way downtown, even though she would have been closer to work if she'd changed. But she trusted her feet more than the MTA to get her somewhere without delay. When she and a few hundred other harried laborers were dumped out at Canal, she had ten minutes to cover eight blocks. It was hot, hotter than the day before, which had been awful, and much more humid. She'd made the mistake of wearing a dark blue cotton blouse and khakis the previous day, trying to look crisp for her first day at her new job. But neither cotton nor khakis took well to sleeping in them—especially with a man's heavy arm draped across you in a sweltering apartment. Catching sight of herself in a store window, she had to admit she looked like she'd slept in her clothes. But her hair was combed!

When she got to the construction site near the restaurant not one guy was tempted to catcall her. Damn, she must have looked awful! She ran the last two blocks, huffing and puffing like she was carrying a heavy weight on her back, but she succeeded in climbing onto the loading dock at ten—on the button. As Emily wheeled around the corner, she stopped dead in her tracks when Blake stared at her from her office door. The look she gave wasn't unkind, but her words were pointed.

"You're probably trying to fit in, but being a professional they can rely on is going to work much better than being someone they can drink under the table." She turned to go back to her desk. "If you hurl, don't do it in front of your staff. That's an amateur move."

After changing into her chef clothes, Emily went into Blake's office, expecting a longer lecture. But she jumped right into the day's business. "PPX tonight," she said, looking at a long list of names she'd written onto a pad.

"PPX?"

"Personne particulièrement extraordinaire." She cocked her head. "Marcel doesn't use the PX terms to show how important a guest is?"

"We used metals. Brass, silver, gold, platinum."

"Ahh. Well, these are the terms I learned when I was just starting out, so I feel comfortable with them." After yanking a paper copy of the dining room floor plan from the wall, she pointed at a table near the kitchen. "Two of the owners are coming in tonight, and this is where they like to sit. They always want something off the menu, but nothing's coming to me. Can you help?"

"Sure. Anything in particular they like to eat?"

"They'll eat anything. Especially Vincenzo. He had to get fat for his last movie, and he seems to want to stay there."

Her extremities tingled and her voice came out in a squeak. "Vincenzo Amato is an owner?"

"Uh-huh," she said, doodling on the pad. "One of four. I'm not sure what his share is, but he eats enough to put us out of business."

Holy fuck! Vincenzo was around Emily's age, but had been in the business since he was a child. Now he was one of the biggest stars on the planet and she was going to have to feed him.

Blake looked up at her. "Star struck?"

"A little. I want to make sure he's happy."

A tired-sounding sigh passed Blake's lips. "He's just a guy, Emily. A guy who's always got a supermodel on his arm and a billion paparazzi following him, but he's still just a guy. Make something good and he'll love it."

"Yes, Chef. I will."

Blake acted like she wasn't anxious about the owners coming in, but that was BS. Emily could feel the tension radiating off her every time she passed by, nitpicking at every station. They'd worked like dogs getting five first courses ready for the afternoon presentation, and after Grant had done his sales job to the front of the house they went back into the kitchen. Blake stuck her hand in her pants pocket, extracted a five dollar bill and slapped it on the counter next to Raven. Then the kid pulled out a pack of cigarettes, handed one to Blake and pocketed the five. After Blake stepped out onto the loading dock, Emily stared after her. What in the hell was that?

She had a few minutes, so she went to the desk and checked her phone, catching a text that had just arrived from Chase.

"In the nabe. Free?"

"I've got twenty."

"Alley?"

He was well used to the back alley ways of restaurant people.

"Loading dock. Same difference."

A minute later, Emily went out to the dock. She jumped off and gave Chase a hug when he slid between the buildings to appear in the hot sunlight. They chatted for a while, with her telling him about Vincenzo coming for dinner, and him relating a funny story about a clueless kid in a class he was teaching. Chase looked up sharply and Emily turned to see Blake approach.

"Hi," she said, extending her hand. "Blake Chadwick."

"This is Chase Larkin," Emily said.

Chase put his arm around her shoulders. He was just like a proud parent, boasting about her whenever he got the chance. "You made a wise move hiring Emily. She's going to be huge."

Blake smiled so broadly her teeth showed. "I can't disagree with you. If she can keep bringing it like she did last night, there's no reason why she won't zoom to the top."

He looked like he was going to squeal with delight, but he controlled himself. "Emily's been raving about *you* for weeks now. She's so thankful to get this opportunity."

Emily elbowed him in the gut. "Don't tell my secrets!" She caught Blake's gaze. "We live together, so he has to listen to me yap all night."

"Ahh. Where do you two live?"

"Jackson Heights. Queens," Emily added.

Her brows knit together, as though she was giving this a great deal of thought. "I've been to Queens, but I don't think I've been to your neighborhood."

"We're ten minutes from LaGuardia."

"Ahh, then I've definitely been there." She shook Chase's hand again and excused herself. "Got to run. Big night."

"Nice to meet you," Chase called after her, staring at the door she pushed through to enter the restaurant. "She's a lot prettier than her photos," he said, with a dreamy look on his face. "How do you avoid just staring at her all day?"

"I don't have time to stare at her or anything else. And if I don't get back in there in the next minute, she'll kick my butt." She kissed his cheek. "Give me two bucks, will you? I slept with my fish chef last night and robbed him while he was passed out drunk."

He shook his head as he extracted his wallet. "After fourteen years, you still manage to surprise me."

She went back in, marveling at the fact that it was cooler inside than out. Blake was right next to the door, and she leaned over and spoke quietly. "I haven't seen you hurl today. How's the head?"

Emily was stuck. Tell the truth? To say she'd had to gag down bile when she went into the fish walk-in that morning? That every scent rising from a pan made her stomach turn? That the smell of smoke that blasted from Chef's mouth was about to make her retch? She *wished* she was the type to only get a headache from a hangover. "It's fine. No problem."

Very seriously, Blake spoke even more quietly. "If that's true, you'd better consider cutting back. I will *not* have another binge drinker in here."

"No, Chef," she said, while mentally kicking herself. There was no right answer! She couldn't admit she was off her game, but if she could drink all night with no ill effects she was nothing but trouble. Great! Now all Blake had to do was find out she'd slept with Brady. *Near* Brady. That would totally cement her reputation as a screw-up!

The first half of service went surprisingly well, mainly because their reservations were heavily tilted toward the second half. Knowing it might be her only chance, Emily ran for the bathroom. Blake's order about the door being locked had devolved by noon. Now the key was stuck in the knob, where it dangled. Emily understood the need to keep the place clean, but you couldn't lock a bathroom that twenty people shared. It was madness.

Two of the dishwashers…check that…plongeurs were waiting outside when she finished. She eased past them and got right back into the game, focusing on the dishes that passed by her. Then Blake leaned over and said, "Cover me." Emily blinked in surprise. She hadn't considered that Blake used a bathroom, or had any normal human needs like the rest of them. Two minutes later the kitchen froze when Blake stood in the center of the room and demanded, "Who used the bathroom last?" She strode over to Emily. "Was it you? If so—you're fired."

"No!" She was stunned into silence. She hated rats. Hated the mere thought of throwing another employee to the wolves. Especially for something so minor…so picky…so stupid…

"Then who was it? Someone peed on the seat and didn't have the decency to clean it off."

Emily stared back at her for a full minute, heat passing between them as the kitchen grew strangely still. The printer chugged out orders, all of them falling onto the pass, unread. "It wasn't me," she finally said, unblinking.

From around the corner, Raul, the chef de plonge, appeared. "Maybe I forget to pick up the seat. I was in a hurry," he said, his voice quiet but easily heard in the otherwise still room.

"Pack up," Blake said, looking like she'd been punched in the gut. She moved to him and shook his hand, then impulsively wrapped her arms around him for a hug. Emily'd heard he'd been with her since she'd been a sous, and had followed her when she'd opened her own place.

Just like that—Raul, with his fantastic attitude and voracious appetite for hard work—was gone. Over a few drops of piss. Emily's stomach turned as she watched the man go to the locker to get his things. Not being allowed to finish your shift was humiliating, but when she caught a look at Blake, she felt almost as bad for her. She looked like she was going to cry, but she popped two pieces of gum into her mouth and took out her frustration on it. She'd better have a good dentist or jaw surgeon. She was going to need it.

Twice during the long night Blake was called on to go into the dining room to kiss ass. She clearly hated it, but when you had to use other people to fund your dream, they owned a piece of it, and you. At 10:30, a couple entered the kitchen with Thierry, the maitre d', trying to stop them without seeming to.

"I'm sure Blake will come out and talk with you in a moment," he said, his eyes wide when he met Blake's dark glower.

The guy, early forties, dark hair and bronzed skin, sidled up to Blake and tossed an arm around her shoulders. "It's fine, Thierry. Blake doesn't mind."

Emily could see her resist the urge to throw the arm off, or maybe take a bite out of it. But she compelled herself to be not just tolerant, but pleasant. "I'd much rather sit out there and open another bottle of Barolo with all of you, but duty calls."

"You've got all of these people in here running the place just fine." He moved to stand right next to Emily. "I don't think I know you," he said, giving her a long, puzzled look.

Her voice was a little tight, but Blake introduced her. "This is our new sous chef, Emily Desjardins."

Emily smiled briefly and met his gaze, hoping Blake was able to divert his attention. Pans were stacking up next to her, each needing her focus.

"Where are you from, Emily?" He didn't seem like a horrible creep, but he had that 'I've got enough money to own you and everything in the room' vibe that she'd never cared for. "Detroit," she said, sticking a fresh fork into a pan of roasted beets and digging into the smallest one for a taste. "Perfect," she called down to Alicia.

"Detroit? You don't look like you're from Detroit."

Oh, Jesus!

"Well, I am." She moved around him with the beets and set them on the pass. Then she tested a whole branzino, finding it just a few degrees undercooked. It would come up to temp after resting for a moment, but was too close for comfort. "Right on the edge with that one," she said, addressing Brady. "Careful."

"Yes, Chef."

"You meant you're from Grosse Pointe or Birmingham, right?"

Emily hadn't caught the guy's name, but she didn't care who he was or what he did for a living. He was in the way. Not pausing in her duties, she said tersely. "I meant Detroit. University District." Turning her head to address Brady after poking her probe into another branzino, she said, "Perfect temp on that one. Good job."

She could feel the guy's interest evaporate, then he moved over to stand right beside Blake, nearly touching her. "You've got quite an assembly line here. No socializing allowed, huh?" Addressing the group, he said, "You guys can spare her for an hour, can't you?"

"No!" most of them shouted, with Emily's voice the loudest.

"See?" Blake said, smiling. "We work as a team. You can't win a ballgame without a catcher."

The guy's wife or girlfriend wandered in and went to the pastry area, standing next to Lorelei, who was trying to assemble a multi-layered, airy concoction of flaky goodness. Layers of pâte brisée had to line up just right or fall like a stone, requiring both mastery and focus.

"Can you make me some unsweetened whipped cream?" the woman asked as Lorelei was doing her most delicate work.

"Let's go grab a bottle of that wine," Blake said loudly. "Send out some cream when you get a chance, okay, Lorelei?"

"Oui, Chef," Lorelei said, obviously relieved to have her stalker ejected.

"I wish my kids were that responsive," the woman said. "How do you get them to snap to it like that?"

"Mutual respect and working toward a common goal," Blake said as she placed a hand on both of their backs and guided them through the door.

Just after eleven, Blake walked back into the kitchen and paused, regarding the whole group with a black look.

Grant caught it, removed something from the breast pocket of his coat and extended it in her direction. "Need some of this?" he asked. The light hit it and Emily could see it was an electronic cigarette.

The glare grew more heated. "I don't need more temptation, Grant. Those things are the work of the devil." She turned and made for her office. "Take over for Emily, please."

Emily sent the entrée she was working on to Grant and took off for the office. Blake had removed her apron and opened her jacket, revealing a skin-tight, white nylon tank top.

Jesus!

Where had she been hiding those breasts? Emily tried not to stare, but who could blame her? If Blake paraded around the dining room with her jacket off business would be up by fifty percent!

"I bet you had a worse day than I did," Blake said, letting her head drop to the back of her chair, "given that you've had to deal with a hangover." She picked her head up and made eye contact. "But I bet I'm close."

"I think you win. I know you didn't want to fire Raul. And I know you *really* didn't want to spend the evening with those people."

"That's the god damned truth." She ran her hands through her hair, tousling it to make it look even better. "Sitting there drinking up the profits so they can whine about how low our margins are."

"That's why they were here? To complain?" It was cool to speak so freely, so much like peers. Must've been the wine.

"No, they really like the food, and they know I don't alert the tabloids that they're here. But even after three and a half years they still don't believe how small our margins are. They seem to think we should be throwing off thousands of dollars of profit a day, which isn't humanly possible."

"Not when you hog a table for four hours, eat nine first courses and six mains."

"Don't forget the wine. Five bottles." She chuckled, her face relaxing into a warm smile. "I think I had most of one to myself." She reached across the narrow room and gripped Emily's shoulder. "I'm truly sorry about the bathroom incident. I would've felt like shit if I'd had to fire you after two days."

"But you would have," Emily said, looking directly at her, unblinking.

"Of course I would have. But I would have felt like shit." She picked up her phone. "Not as bad as I feel about firing Raul, one of the best damn employees I've ever had, but pretty bad." Grumbling, she dialed a number. "Now I've got to find him a new job. One where they don't mind that he can't hit the toilet." Her eyes met Emily's with the tinny sound of a ring in the background. "I can understand not wanting to take the time to raise the seat. I can understand having your aim off. I can't understand not noticing."

"Chase and I have lived together on and off for ten years, and he's very compliant now. But that required years of vigilance on my part. Personally, I don't know why they don't sit down, but Chase looks at me like I'm crazy to suggest it."

"Nunzio? Blake Chadwick. I'm not sure which of your restaurants needs a fantastic head dishwasher, but you're going to want to create a job for my guy if you don't have one already." She rolled her eyes at Emily, grinning at herself for laying it on so thick.

She nodded as the other person spoke, then said, "I fired a guy I've been with for eight years because he dribbled a little pee on the toilet seat." Leaning back in her chair, she started to laugh. "I wish people were exaggerating when they say I'm a nitpicking jerk, but they're not."

Emily got up to let Blake continue to sell Raul's skills and work ethic to a guy she hoped was a little more laid back—at least about the bathroom.

Emily was already dragging when she entered the kitchen on Wednesday. This was always the toughest day for her. Two days away from her last day off, and four until the next one. This morning, four days seemed very, very far in the future.

She'd just changed into her whites when Carlos caught her eye. "Problema," he said, holding up his cell phone. "Rodrigo calls. He must go to Mexico for his mother's funeral."

"I'm sorry to hear that," Emily said, then it hit her that she had to replace him—stat. Since Blake had fired the chief dishwasher, losing a second guy was unimaginable. She already had a call in to a staffing agency to replace Raul, but she hadn't even gotten a list of candidates yet, much less interviewed anyone.

"He has a cousin…" Carlos said.

"Bring him in," Emily said, not caring if the cousin had ever seen a plate or a glass.

"He has experience. Mucho."

"Excellent. Can you make the call, Carlos? The faster he can get here, the better."

"Sì. I will call now. Rodrigo says his cousin does not speak the good English…"

"I don't care if he speaks a word, so long as he can keep that dishwasher loaded."

Hector seemed like a good fit. Bright eyed, energetic, and well versed in his trade. Emily would have relaxed at that point, but Alicia, her entremetier, wasn't in yet. She was due by eleven, and it was dangerously close to noon. At five 'til, Blake came through the door, a limp smile on her face. She'd just started to shake everyone in when Alicia burst past her, cheeks flushed.

Emily grasped Alicia by the arm and herded her into the locker room. "An hour? You're an hour late? When you know Chef's always here by noon?"

"I'm *so* sorry. I've been having problems at home…"

Emily looked at her carefully. Alicia had clearly been crying, with her big brown eyes swollen and puffy, and splotches of pink tinted her cheeks. "I'm sorry you're having a tough time, but you know how little patience Chef has with lateness."

"I know. I know," she said, closing her eyes tightly. "I tried so hard to get here on time, but…" She shivered roughly. "I couldn't do it."

Emily patted her on the back, touched by how shaken up the young woman seemed. She thought about some of her own misadventures when she was in her early twenties. Everyone screwed up once in a while. An hour wasn't going to ruin the place. "Hurry up and change, but I want you here by ten tomorrow to make up for today. Got it?"

"Yes, yes, I'll be here early. Thanks, Emily. Thanks for understanding."

She left her to change and almost walked right into Blake, who was standing in her doorway. She crooked a finger and sat down behind her desk when Emily entered. "Close the door, please."

"Alicia's having some problems at home. I'm having her come in an hour early tomorrow to make up for today—"

"You can't fix today's problem tomorrow."

"But this is the first time she's been late—"

"Since you've been here," Blake said, cutting her off. "She was late twice before you started. That's twice in just over a year." She sat there, still as a rock for a few moments. "I warned her very clearly last time. Bring her in here. I'm firing her."

"No!"

Blake's head snapped up and she stared, open mouthed.

"I already told her she could make it up." Emily knew she should back down, but it was important for her staff to trust her to make decisions and stick by them. "I'd appreciate it if you'd let me handle this, since I already told Alicia she could make up the time."

Blake, clearly surprised, looked down and took in a deep breath. Finally, she nodded. "We'll compromise. Bring the best commis out to trail her. I want her to know there's someone with drive and talent—lurking."

"Is that really necessary?"

"Go," she decreed, waving a hand.

Glumly, Emily went to ask Carlos which of the young interns was the best. It would be humiliating for Alicia to have a trainee right beside her all day. Everyone would know she was being punished. But Blake had delivered a direct order, and nothing Emily had learned so far indicated she was just talking out of her toque when she did that.

Despite the rocky start, they all got into a groove and managed to have the day's specials explained to the FOH staff right on time. Once service started, Blake actually seemed in a good mood, humming along to the music that periodically seeped into the kitchen when a commis de rang flung a door to the dining room open. Blake seemed to be running on a different track from the rest of them, seeing more, focusing harder, as she plated and organized orders.

This was the part of running a restaurant that Emily needed to work on. She knew what a good expediter should do, but the actual job seemed just out of her reach. The task was pretty straightforward, if not a little imposing. Keep track of every dish for every diner. An outsider would probably think they could do it if they had a little experience. They'd be wrong.

You had chits coming at you fast, and you had to make sure the cooks knew when to start each dish to insure it was finished simultaneously with the rest of the items for the table. It was hard to do for a party of two. But for eight or ten? Good luck.

Once the expediter got the first courses out, you had to pay attention to the back-waiters returning with the spent plates. Emily was having a hell of a time remembering to call the guys commis de rang, but everyone else did, so she had to get on board. Once the commis de rang announced that the first course was clear, Blake ordered the entrées fired. But throw in an overcooked steak or a guest who forgot about her shellfish allergy until her sea bass, dotted with cockles, appeared in front of her—and you had a mess.

Every restaurant needed a top notch expediter. Both for the guests and the cooks. It was demoralizing for a cook to see her perfectly cooked fish languishing under the heat lamp if the expediter didn't leave enough time for a duck breast to be cooked well done.

Here, with ninety seats, Blake was keeping track of anywhere from twenty-five to thirty-five tables, depending on how they set the dining room up that night. It was all fun and games until the expediter didn't see a note on the Point of Sale system that a guest needed gluten-free pasta. At the very least, that guest would write a scathing review on all forms of social media, accusing the restaurant of attempted murder. At most, there would be a loud, tearful confrontation in the dining room, with the entire meal comped to try to calm the guest down. *Then* you'd get a scathing review. The anonymity of the internet let people bash the hell out of you for trying your best.

Emily had only seen her work for a few days, but Blake was the best expediter she'd seen. Even though Emily loved Chef Henri, his best days were behind him. He knew exactly what to do, of course, but he wasn't energetic enough to keep up. That didn't look like it would ever be a problem for Blake. Air-traffic controllers didn't pay as close attention as she did to the details. She was an all-star in the part of her craft that got no recognition, but made or broke a restaurant.

Hector came bustling out to the pass with a fresh supply of plates and Blake gave him a quick look. "Who in the hell is that?" she said as he headed back to the dishwashing area.

Damn!

The woman didn't miss a trick! Hector looked so much like Rodrigo their own mothers might mistake them. "Rodrigo's mother died and he went to Mexico for the funeral. Hector's his cousin."

Blake leaned over and quietly said, "I assume you checked Hector's immigration status."

Fuck!

Three pans slid down the line, and Emily tasted everything before sending them on to Blake. Her attention now split, she went over the incident in her head. Blake hadn't really asked a question, right? You didn't have to volunteer information without a direct question, did you? Luckily, Blake didn't follow up, but that didn't stop Emily from obsessing about it for the next four hours. There was no way they could get through service without Hector, but she'd put the restaurant in jeopardy by not checking to make sure he was a legal resident. She had no idea if they'd be closed down or simply fined if the INS did a spot check, and she really, really didn't want to find out.

The moment their last ticket was closed she ran to the dishwashing area. Hector was doggedly scraping food from a batch of plates, his face flushed, his white jacket splashed with water and suds. Knowing Hector didn't have a good grasp of the language, she found Alberto breaking down his work station. "Alberto, could you do me a favor and ask Hector to bring proof of his immigration status tomorrow?"

"Si," he said, ambling over to the frantically working young guy. They spoke for just a second, then Alberto walked back, shaking his head. "He has nothing," he said, shrugging.

Her heart sank as she walked over to Hector, who was looking at her from the corner of his eye. "Sorry," she said, clapping him on the back. "Adios, amigo." She held up a finger, went to her locker and took out every dollar she'd taken from the ATM that morning. She'd agreed to pay him ten bucks an hour, and he'd been there for twelve. Yanking six twenties from the bunch of ten, she went back and handed it to him. "Gracias," she said as he gave her a questioning look, but stuffed the money into his pocket and went back to the locker room to change. She looked at the eighty bucks she had to last a full week. Screwing up was not the key to financial stability. But she couldn't afford to put an undocumented worker on the payroll, and she wasn't about to ask Blake to cash him out.

Fuck it all.

She was so paranoid, Emily stayed and finished the dishes after Hector departed. She felt like she'd run a marathon when she dragged herself by Blake's office, hoping she'd left. Just her luck, she was sitting there, typing on her computer.

"May I?" Emily asked after poking her head in.

"Sure. Come in." Her head cocked. "Why are you still here? You're supposed to have the early shift."

"I was washing dishes."

One of Blake's perfectly curved eyebrows rose. "Rodrigo sent us an undocumented worker?"

"Yes, but I don't blame him. He knew we were in a tough spot with Raul gone. But I have no excuse. I know full well I have to check people's status. I screwed up."

"Yes, you did." Blake rested her chin atop her hand. "But I'm impressed you took responsibility. I'd already forgotten about it."

"I might screw up, but I never cover up."

A small smile slowly bloomed. "I prefer screw-ups to cover-ups any day. But your screw-up was a bad one, Emily. You've got to use your head."

"Yes, Chef. It won't happen again."

"It'd better not, because any fines we get because of your mistakes will come out of your paycheck."

"Yes, Chef."

As she got up, Blake said, "Hector can't be on the payroll. I'll give you some petty cash to pay him for the day."

"I already did."

Both eyebrows shot up. "Where'd you get a key for a cash register?"

"I paid him out of my pocket. My screwup—my money."

Blake didn't reply, but Emily saw something in those dark eyes worth a whole lot more than a hundred and twenty bucks. Blake's respect.

With a burst of energy, she went to the desk outside the office. It was late in normal people's time, but the shaft of the evening for restaurant workers. So she got on the phone and started calling everyone she knew in the biz. Someone had to know a dishwasher who was just itching to get to work. If she didn't find anyone, she was going to have to get up early and call the staffing agency to light a fire under them. A temp and a permanent dishwasher had to be on the job by five at the latest.

While making her calls, she watched the cooks industriously break down their stations. Alicia was taking up the padded runners that kept people from sliding on grease and spills, clearly trying to do some extra work to ingratiate herself with Emily. Not a bad move.

Chapter Four

THE NEXT MORNING, EMILY was working alongside Alicia, who'd dutifully come in at ten o'clock. Together, they went through the day's deliveries, a job she was sure the young woman had never done. But when you were late you had to do some scut work to make the lesson sink in.

Grant came in at eleven, his usual time, then Emily lost track of him. She was starving, and thought she might run to a food truck usually parked a block away that sold good burritos, but Grant wasn't in the kitchen.

She found him in the prep kitchen, showing two commis how to dehydrate thin slices of beef and then break them like glass, creating shards of meat for some dish he could obviously see in his head. But what he saw wasn't on their menu, and they didn't have time to play around.

"Can I talk to you?"

He made a face, but followed her out to the loading dock, which was still mostly in shade. "What's up?"

"It's great that you want to show the interns some tricks, but we don't have time to do that in the morning."

"You've got the kitchen under control." He took out his electronic cigarette and took a puff. "There's nothing wrong with giving these guys more than just a couple of bucks per hour."

"I agree. So do it after the presentation. Some days you have a full hour to kill."

"Nah. That won't work. Everyone needs a break by then."

She stared at him until he met her eyes. "Well, I need a break now. Right now." She took off her apron, tossed it toward him, and jumped from the loading dock. "I'll be back in fifteen minutes," she said, waving as she strode down the alley, hoping he covered for her.

The first time Emily walked by the office after she returned, Blake's soft voice said, "Can you come in here?"

Irrationally, she was sure she was going to be axed. Sure that Blake had realized she'd left the kitchen unsupervised for fifteen minutes. But Blake merely gave her a curious smile and said, "Got any ideas for the specials?"

Relieved beyond measure, Emily took a chair and started to rattle off the ideas she'd kicked around the night before while trying to fall asleep.

They tinkered with her suggestions, and Blake added a couple of her own, then she started doodling, often a bad sign. "What's the busiest time of our day?" she asked, almost conversationally.

"Right now, Chef."

"I agree." She looked up, her dark eyes fixing Emily like she was an animal trying to flee a predator. "Do you think someone needs to be actively supervising during the busiest part of the day?"

"I do," she said, nodding.

"I do, too. So why did you take off when Grant was busy in the prep kitchen?"

There was no way she was going to tell the whole truth. It wasn't necessary and might make her look like she couldn't handle things. "I'm…trying to work some things out with Grant. It's taking a little time for us to get in sync."

Blake leaned back in her chair and popped a piece of her nicotine gum. Poor thing. She was hooked on that crap. "You know, I was a little reticent to hire my first woman sous." She narrowed her gaze and looked at Emily carefully, plainly assessing her. "Especially one who looks like you. I knew you could cook, but you don't look very tough and I was worried Grant would try to exploit you."

"I'm not going to let him—or anyone else do that," she said, trying to look as no-nonsense as she felt.

"Good." She let a smile show. "But don't leave the kitchen unsupervised again. It looks bad to the staff."

"Yes, Chef." She stood up to leave, feeling like she'd scaled a small barrier. It was clear Grant wasn't going to play by her rules, but just as clear Blake wasn't truly angry with her for skipping out. Not bad. Not bad at all.

Thierry was in Blake's office for at least an hour every afternoon, going over reservations, making notes and adjustments to the seating chart. This was the part of running a restaurant that Emily had little interest in. But given how much time and effort Blake spent on it, it was obviously something that couldn't be overlooked.

The dining room could be arranged in almost any configuration, but it required creativity to do it right. Important guests wanted to be seen, but they didn't want anyone close enough to hear their conversation. And a few regulars wanted the same table every time they came, something that could be tough to do if you had a few big groups you were trying to cram in.

But Blake put in the time to maximize their space and keep the guests happy. It was constant pressure, with her cell phone buzzing through the day with updates on reservations and last minute requests. This was something Chef Henri didn't ever bother with. Their regulars came in and were treated like family. Everyone else filled in the bare spots. But you couldn't do that when you were striving to pay a big mortgage and make a profit for four partners. Each seat had to bring in the maximum.

After Grant raved about that night's specials to the FOH, Emily followed Blake back into her office. "I came up with ideas for six first courses and six entrées," she said, dropping the sheet onto Blake's desk.

Blake looked up at her quizzically.

"These are unique things. Expensive. We'll probably lose money on each one. But they'll be ideal for our PPX. I assigned a number to each dish, so we can make a note on the Point of Sale system for that PPX when we whip one of these out. That'll let us have our ducks in a row for six visits. No repeats on either the first course or the entrée."

A very pleased smile curled Blake's lips. "Our ducks like to be in rows, huh?" She picked up the list and looked it over carefully.

"Excellent stuff here, Emily. Unique and modern. Not the same old crap these guys get at every high-end place."

"Thank you," she said, knowing she was blushing. "I tried to make the dishes decadent, but not too rich or calorie laden. Most of our PPX barely eat. Except Vincenzo," she added, chuckling.

"This is very good," Blake said again. She looked as pleased as Emily had seen her.

Score!

"We always have these ingredients on hand." She ran her finger down the list. "Tonight, let's make number six for a first course, and number three for an entrée for our very special guests. I'll explain this to Thierry, so he can make a note in the system." She stood up and snapped her coat down to straighten it. "Did you know Jonathan Tweed was joining us?"

"I had no idea! I read his cookbook when I was a kid. I'm a big fan."

"He doesn't need fans," she said, not unkindly. "He needs something unique to eat."

"Yes, Chef. He'll have that." She started for the kitchen, but stopped when Blake spoke again.

"What kind of music do you listen to?"

"Indie, I guess."

"Indie…what? Who do you listen to?"

"I was listening to Lissie on the way in." At Blake's blank look, she added, "I like Adele, Brandi Carlile, Neko Case, Sarah McLachlan…"

Blake nodded, looking like she was going to laugh. "Will you have Grant put some music on? Tell him to crank it."

Emily started to leave, then stopped and stared at Blake. "Did you just insult my musical tastes?"

Blake was unable to take the smirk off her face. "I'll listen to Sarah McLachlan when I want to daydream about angels and kittens. To cook, I need to rock."

/

At ten o'clock that night, deep in the weeds, Emily was forced to peel herself away from her station, leaving Grant all alone. Blake had been called to the dining room fifteen minutes earlier, and it was clear they'd go down in flames without her back in her spot. But Grant didn't have the nerve to fetch her, leaving Emily to decide what was worse—having service ruined, or drawing Blake's wrath for interrupting her. It was actually a close call, but she knew it shouldn't be. Service came first.

Grabbing a fresh apron, she tied it around her hips and walked briskly into the dining room, trying to catch Blake's eye without drawing too much attention to herself. Blake was talking to Emily's first chef crush—Jonathan Tweed. There was no way she could march over there and interrupt. Yet she knew she had to.

A pair of twenty-something women were seated at the table closest to the kitchen passthrough, and they caught her attention for precious seconds. One of the women looked vaguely embarrassed, but the other was giving her server, a patient-looking guy who often asked perceptive questions during presentation, a thorough tongue-lashing. "I don't care what you're serving," she said, each word loud and filled with contempt. "I want the lime cheesecake with vanilla ice cream."

"I'm so sorry," the guy said, actually looking like he was. "But we're serving the cheesecake with pineapple sorbet. I'm afraid we don't have vanilla ice cream on the menu."

"What kind of place doesn't have vanilla ice cream lying around? You're lying right to my face!"

"I'm not, ma'am," he said, still calm. "We make all of our ice cream in house, and we didn't make vanilla today."

She blew out a breath, then spoke like she was addressing a dimwit, each word carefully enunciated. "Go to the store and get it." She met her friend's eyes. "Can you believe this? Every bodega in town has ten kinds of vanilla ice cream. I'm not about to pay eleven dollars for dry cheesecake just because they're too stupid to have a carton in the freezer." One of the Ghanaian commis du rang walked by, catching the guest's eye. "Send one of them if you don't want to go," she said, rudely pointing. "He's not doing anything important."

From the corner of her eye, Emily saw Blake move over to the entrance and speak to Thierry. Then she sailed back toward the kitchen, giving Emily a look that nearly burned her skin. As she slapped herself back into action, two of the commis du rang descended upon the table, blocking her exit. In a matter of seconds every single dish and piece of cutlery had been cleared from the ice-cream complainer's table. Thierry was next to her, leaning over to speak quietly to the furious woman.

"Are you fucking kidding me?" she shouted. "You can't tell me to leave! We're not finished."

He spoke again, very quietly. Emily didn't know him at all, but even she could see that whatever he'd said, he was sticking to.

Outraged, the women gathered up their gargantuan purses and stormed out, grumbling about the horrible way they'd been treated. As they crossed the entryway, several other diners applauded, quietly, like they didn't want to add to the fray, but wanted Thierry to know they appreciated his actions. His head nod was barely perceptible, then he glided back to his podium, order restored.

No one had paid much attention to Emily, and she slid back into the kitchen, ready to explain to Blake why she'd come after her. But Blake not only didn't chide her, she didn't acknowledge she'd been gone. She was standing in Emily's spot, tasting a side dish, then she carried the dish to the pass and started to plate the order.

Emily reclaimed her place and they started to make a dent in the backlog, slowly hacking their way out of the weeds.

At midnight, Emily lurked outside of Blake's office, under the cover of checking the schedule for the week, but in reality waiting to get her butt chewed. She wouldn't be able to sleep knowing she'd be walking into a lecture in the morning, so she'd decided to get it over with. Grant was in the office, rocking back on a metal chair, looking like he might fall on his head. When the chair hit the floor, he got up and went back into the kitchen to supervise clean up, and Emily went to the opening and stood there, waiting to be acknowledged. Blake looked up, seemingly surprised to see her. "Yeah?"

Emily entered, not taking a seat. "I wanted to apologize for going into the dining room—"

"No need," she said, sticking a hand up to cut her off. "Grant told me you guys were going under for the third time. Production is always more important than my being out front, kissing butt." She leaned back in her seat and let a weak smile cover her face. "Hell of a night, right?"

That seemed like an invitation to chat, so Emily took a chair. "Sure was. What was the deal with the women you tossed? I've never seen sober customers get the bum's rush."

"Bum's rush?" A short bark of a laugh made her eyes twinkle. "I like that expression. I guess it's accurate, too." She stuck her hands in the air and stretched, yawning while she did. "I can't have people treating my people like that. If you don't stand up for your staff, you ruin morale."

"Yeah but…" She wanted to say more, but thought she'd better not.

"Go on," Blake said, "I can see you've got an opinion."

"Yeah, I do." She took a breath. "You supported the staff, but you also made an enemy. If that incident isn't all over social media, with you sounding like an ogre…"

"Yeah, that's gonna happen. You've got to pick your battles. Tonight, I decided I wanted her out of my restaurant, no matter what." Her smile grew a little. "Tomorrow, I might put up with someone twice as foolish."

"She was gone in seconds," Emily said. "Do the commis practice?"

Now Blake's laugh sounded easy and relaxed. "Probably. The FOH runs like a well-oiled machine thanks to Thierry." She sat up straight and started to organize the papers on her desk, a sure sign she was ready to pack up. "Not a bad night. I made an enemy, got stiffed for two meals and a bottle of wine, and almost went down in flames. And tomorrow we get to do it all again."

"You got stiffed?" Emily stood and started to ease herself out the door.

"I comped their meal. Had to," she added as she reached for a tote bag she sometimes carried things home in. "That spoiled brat nailed me for three hundred bucks."

Emily nodded, then continued on to the lockers. She wasn't at all sure she would have handled things the way Blake had. Making an enemy, particularly one who would no doubt bash them from one end of the internet to the other, was a loser's bet. But Blake didn't seem to have a moment's doubt about it. Not surprisingly.

When Emily returned to the kitchen, Blake was exiting through the back doors. Giving her just a few seconds to get a head start, Emily snuck out and stealthily followed her down the alley. She wasn't usually the type of person to lurk around an alley, following a woman home. But Chef was such an enigma. So tough and curt and no-nonsense, but with such a sweet smile and easy laugh, even though both emerged infrequently. It was the rarity of that smile that made the craving Emily had to know more about her more acute. Blake was on her phone, chatting away as she walked, posture still erect, crisp blue and white checked shirt fluttering in the warm breeze.

Where did she live? Was there someone waiting for her? Man? Woman? Cat? Python? Any of them were equally likely, and as Emily peeled off to go to her subway she gave her a final glance, watching her stride grow longer as she started to walk more quickly. Emily truly hoped that over time they got to know each other better. A couple of hours rolling around in bed would be a fantastic way to start, but that was as likely as Blake laughing about finding drips of pee on the toilet seat. Not gonna happen.

Emily had only been on the job for two weeks, but when Blake came in that Monday morning the darkness of her mood chilled the kitchen as abruptly as the cold fall wind that blew through the bedroom window the night before.

Everyone traded surreptitious glances, with their shared anxiety spiking. They were like kids in an unsettled, unpredictable home. You never knew if dad was going to come after you with a belt, so you'd learned to stay clear long before the leather landed on your butt.

After dropping off a crate of something in her office, Blake walked around and shook everyone in. But her affect made it seem like she was getting ready to fire the whole bunch of them.

"Emily?" she called when she'd finished her rounds. "My office."

Surprisingly, their morning chat was roughly the same as always, the only difference in how unreceptive Blake was to suggestions. After allowing Emily to explain two specials she'd conjured, Blake knocked both down like annoying flies. Then Emily pulled an idea out of nowhere. "How about watermelon three ways?"

Blake looked up, clearly engaged. "Name 'em."

"Mmm... A salad with watermelon chunks, tart feta and a few drops of our best Balsamic. Pickled rind. Watermelon sorbet."

"Do you have good product?"

"Uh-huh. We got three big watermelons in this morning. Carlos said they were primo."

"Great. But a granita would be better than the sorbet. Crisper." Nodding she said, "I'm going to make a tomato tarte Tatin. I'll take it from start to finish."

"Sounds good. Do you want me to write up the description for the menu?"

"I'll do that. I'm not sure where I'll end up. I might add caramelized onions if the tomatoes aren't as good as they should be." She dragged the crate she'd carried in earlier onto her desk, revealing pear-shaped cherry tomatoes. They might have been from her garden for all Emily knew. She could just see her standing out among her plants, ordering the tomatoes to ripen properly. One of the tiny orbs went into her mouth. "No need for onions. They're very good. Maybe basil..." She looked like she was a million miles away as she took her crate and headed for the prep kitchen. A minute later she was back, grabbing her apron and knife roll. What in the hell? Blake, distracted?

A while later, Emily spotted her in the prep kitchen, along with two commis, peeling the tiny tomatoes. Emily continued along her own list of specials, losing track of time. She'd finished her two dishes, and was going to help Grant out with one of his, a real bear of a prep job. Blake and the two commis were still in the same spot, now nearly finished with the crate. Say what you would about the woman, she wasn't a slacker.

At three o'clock, Blake walked up to Emily, still seeming off her game, either distracted or anxious. "Have you seen Grant?"

"Not for a while, but—"

Storming over to the loading dock, Blake stayed right at the door and yelled, "Grant!" He strolled in a minute later, unbowed. The guy was almost impossible to rattle. Stunningly, she grabbed him by the shoulder of his jacket and dragged him behind her, slamming her office door when he cleared it. Everyone stopped, all of them listening as she reamed him a new one. Emily was torn between telling everyone to stop eavesdropping and get back to work, or just acting like nothing was happening. She chose the latter. It wouldn't hurt them to get a preview of what could happen to them if they weren't careful today.

"The choice is yours," Blake shouted. "Are your cigarettes worth more than your job?"

"No, Chef."

"Good answer. If I catch you smoking again before the presentation, you…are…gone!"

He emerged, red-faced, with Blake right behind him. Loudly, she declared, "If you must smoke, do it *after* the presentation. Period. I'm not paying you people to stink up my kitchen all day." She went back into her office and slammed the door, making it rattle. Everyone got back to work, knives whipping through produce, meat slipping from bones. Only the sounds of food changing from one form to another filled the kitchen. Words abandoned them all.

Emily surreptitiously watched to see when Blake would emerge. She clearly had a bad temper, everyone knew that. But it usually ran hot and fast. She'd yell for a moment and then it would be over. But not today. Her door remained closed for over an hour.

Grant made the family meal, whipping up tacos from bits of meat he'd found in the cooler. Some chicken, a little pork, and beef he'd cubed into tiny pieces. He added rice and beans, but it was still a sad-looking mess. They didn't keep salsa, and he hadn't made any, so the already bland dish was even more uninspired. No one would complain, though. They knew they got the leftovers, and had resigned themselves to that fact.

Everyone grabbed a plate and ate standing at their stations, with what little conversation there was hushed and brief. People were clearly worried that the belt might come out at any minute, and they wanted to protect their backsides. Grant had made plenty, so Emily assembled a plate and knocked at Blake's door.

"Yes?"

She opened the door and stuck just the plate in. "Hungry?"

The plate was taken from her hand, then a grumbled, "Thank you," came out. Even when she was mad, she still had manners.

A few minutes later, Blake emerged, once again furious. She stood in front of Emily and demanded, "Who made the family meal?"

Emily was surprised and pleased when Grant looked up, cleared his throat, and said. "I did."

"Each of us pay two dollars a day to be fed a decent meal. You just screwed us out of a dollar fifty. Try to *act* like you care."

Then she strode into the prep kitchen and threw herself into finishing her tarte. Her dismissal of the meal had ruined everyone's appetite, and each member of the team took their plate to the trash and dumped it. Then they all got back to work, not a joke or even a burst of profanity breaking the silence for the rest of the afternoon.

The presentation to the servers was looming, with Blake leaning against a counter, waiting for Emily to finish. Absently, Blake took a fork and pierced a Brussels Sprout Cleveland was roasting. That was an odd thing for her to do. She usually let Emily and Grant have sole domain over the sides, but today she was nothing if not unpredictable. A sour look came over her as she chewed, and once again every member of the team watched her while trying not to look like they were. The rumbling of the hoods over the stoves sounded painfully loud in the otherwise silent kitchen. Then Blake grabbed two towels, took the steaming hot pan and dumped the contents into the trash, before tossing it into the air to catch it with the toe of her clog. It zipped across the kitchen, a blur of stainless as it slammed into a walk-in, leaving a noticeable dent. If anyone had been walking by, a heavy pan flying through the air would have killed them!

"If you can't tell when Brussels Sprouts have turned bitter, you're not competent to work here." Her heated gaze fell to Emily. "How old were those?"

"They came in yesterday, Chef."

"They...were...old," she snarled. "Did you taste them?"

"No, Chef." That was crazy! No one tasted a raw Brussels Sprout!

"I thought as much. Come up with a new side for the duck. A *fresh* one. Then call the purveyor and read him the riot act about those Brussels Sprouts. I won't pay for spoiled produce."

After grabbing some cleaning supplies, she strode over to the walk-in. Carefully, the way she did everything, she cleaned the mess, then took the pan to the dishwashers while everyone tried not to make eye contact, with her or each other.

When she returned to the prep kitchen, the whole staff let out a relieved breath. With any luck, she'd stay there until service. Emily snuck over to the trash, picked out a sprout and bit into it. Closing her eyes, she breathed in, forcing every hint of flavor through her nose. It was fine. Perfectly fine. Then Grant came over and did the same thing. He shrugged, made eye contact with Emily and shook his head. Then Brady and Alicia followed suit, every one of them completely perplexed.

Cleveland reached for a sprout, freezing when a loud voice rang out from the prep kitchen, making them all shudder. "Chemicals begin to release the moment a vegetable is picked, altering the taste. If you can't sense those changes as acutely as I can, that's not my problem."

How could she tell, from behind a solid wall, that they were challenging her? Uncanny!

The tension in the overheated room grew worse as the night went on. Blake didn't blow up again, but everyone feared she would. Emily actually hoped for a small explosion, just to clear the air. At 8:15, Blake went to her office, put on a fresh coat and emerged with her hair neatly arranged. A white apron was settled onto her hips, not her usual working apron, and Emily caught her checking her reflection on some shiny stainless steel.

She fussed at the pass, decorating plates with extra élan. Then when the order for table four came in, she barked at Grant to cover for her, then strode toward the dining room.

JoJo, the debonair, slightly excitable commis de rang, raced in as she exited. "Her mother and father are here," he said, his wide eyes mixing excitement with terror. "Pray to god you don't make a mistake!"

Emily met Grant's eyes and they each dove for the order. "PRS table four," Emily called out, having snagged it.

Silence. Not a "Oui, Chef" in the bunch.

"What's a PRS?" Cleveland asked, his voice so quiet it was barely audible.

"P...X... Oh, fuck. VIPS! VIPS at table four. What can you send out immediately?" she demanded of April, the salads and cold appetizers chef.

"Oysters," she called back. "Ready now!"

They were already arranged on a tray mounded with crushed ice, and Emily tasted the mignonette carefully before putting the platter into JoJo's waiting hands. Then she studied the chit. They'd each ordered the tarte, along with one order of Emily's watermelon salad. They must have been massive tomato fans to inspire Chef to spend her whole day making the damned tarte.

Perfectly plated first courses were on their way out the door one minute after JoJo returned with the oyster shells. Every member of the staff waited on pins and needles while they fought through the incoming orders. After fifteen gut-churning minutes, JoJo ran back in with the empty tarte plates. "Table four is clear!" he declared, clearly elated. "Fire the entrées."

"Monk in four!" Brady called, alerting Jameson to have the duck breast ready at precisely the same time.

"Duck in four!" Jameson confirmed.

"Since when does JoJo expedite?" Grant grumbled.

Everyone was off their game, with each of them stumbling over the other to do the job perfectly. Emily watched Jameson set a timer, then heat a knob of butter and begin to ladle it over the duck breast, fat and protein sizzling under the heat. Both entrées arrived simultaneously, along with their sides, which Grant and Emily tasted with every bit of their concentration. Then they plated and called out, in unison, "Pick up, table four."

The orders continued to pour in, but Emily knew every member of the staff was stuck on only one table, where duck & monkfish were hopefully being savored to death.

Blake returned, the tense set of her shoulders now relaxed, her arms moving easily at her sides. "Emily, the gentleman at table four would like to speak with you. Your watermelon salad was a big hit. Ordering," she called out in her smooth, rich voice. "One tarte, one foie, two sea bass."

"Oui, Chef!"

Emily almost hyperventilated as she pushed through the door into the dining room. But the oasis of calm felt like a tender hug compared to the chaotic kitchen. Here, people spoke in low tones, glassware tinkled softly, and lilting laughs made it seem like everyone was having a hell of a good time.

A couple, who looked significantly younger than her own parents, looked up when she approached table four. Mr. Chadwick was handsome enough, but nothing unique; just another middle-aged guy whose hair showed hints of grey in the sandy strands near his temples, with an expensive suit and a rep tie covering his trim frame. But Emily blinked in surprise when her eyes settled on his date. There was no way this was Blake's mom. Though she was a true beauty, the woman couldn't have been over forty. Dark, wavy hair, delicate, fine features, and impressive cleavage peeked out of a thin, filmy, print dress expressly made to show it off, but in a tasteful, discrete fashion.

Emily tried not to stare, but now that she really took her in, the woman looked too much like Blake not to be her mother. *Wow.* Had she given birth when she was ten? Emily's own parents might have been around the same age, but her parents looked like people in their mid-fifties. A few extra pounds had crept up on them, and their clothes were made for comfort over style. Her mom had briefly debated coloring her hair, but decided the reward wasn't worth the time or expense, and Emily was certain her father didn't have an opinion on her decision.

Mrs. Chadwick, on the other hand, looked like maintaining a youthful visage was a full-time job, and Emily had to admit she kicked ass at it. Blake's dad, however, looked older than his wife, like he was weighted down, maybe at having to pay for the fountain of youth his wife drank from.

He half stood and shook Emily's hand. "I enjoyed the watermelon salad a great deal. Blake said that was your creation."

"Oh, it wasn't anything unique." She almost bit her tongue. Don't diminish the specials! "But I'm pleased you enjoyed it."

Mrs. Chadwick poked the tines of her fork at the glistening fish. "Is this cooked through?" She looked up at Emily, dark eyes clearly concerned. "The first bite seemed fine, but now…"

"Yes, ma'am. If you cook it any longer, it dries out." That didn't convince her, and the fork continued to poke. "But I'm happy to make you something else. *Anything*." She knew she seemed like a dog trying to please her mistress, but that's because she was in exactly that position.

"No, thank you," she said, placing her fork down and folding her hands. "I don't eat meat, and I don't care for trout."

"Then I'll cook you a new piece, and leave it on the fire a minute longer. Just because I think something's done, doesn't mean I'm right. I'll be back in five minutes with—"

"No. Really. Don't bother." She picked up a roll and started to add a sliver of butter, sliced so thin it barely existed. "I love the rolls Blake makes, but I never let myself indulge." She offered up a dazzling smile, with Emily realizing she was being dismissed.

"I'll leave you alone so you can enjoy your meal."

"Good to meet you," Mrs. Chadwick said, even though Emily hadn't had the brains to introduce herself. What a dope she was!

She nearly ran back to her post, where Blake was testing a piece of sea bass. "Thanks for handling that," she said, meeting Emily's eyes.

Handling that? That's how you referred to your parents' visit? But Emily didn't have time to worry about the comment. She was too busy obsessing about the damned monkfish. Obviously, she had to mention it to Blake, but she didn't want to make a big deal out of it in front of the rest of the staff, who were giving her questioning glances, silently asking for information from the front lines.

Ten minutes later, JoJo returned with the plates. "Table four, clear," he said, his voice quiet, eyes downcast. Blake looked up sharply. A good hundred and forty grams of the monkfish was still on the plate.

"Emily," she said, a threat in her voice, "are you certain the monk was cooked properly?"

"One hundred percent, Chef." She was more sure of that fish than she was her own name. "Your…guest was unsure of it, so I offered to refire it or make anything else she wanted."

"And?"

"She didn't want anything else."

Blake stared at her for a few seconds, then pinched off a big bite with her thumb and forefinger, her eyes closing as she tasted it. "Perfect," she agreed. "Good job. If people want dry fish, they have to order it that way."

Whew! That was a close one! Emily's life had flashed before her eyes—all because of the internal temperature of the ugliest fish in the sea. And some kind of mother issues she didn't want to dwell on.

Even though they'd been stunningly busy during the shaft of the evening, things settled down around ten. Oddly, Emily preferred being swamped. When you had time to reflect, your body's signals could actually reach your mind, letting you feel the ache in your legs, and your back, and the tension that built up between your shoulders as the day wore on.

For a change, Blake also seemed distracted, and she shocked Emily when she said, "Can you take over, Grant? Emily and I are going to get a head start on tomorrow's specials, then she's going home." Turning toward Emily with a tired smile, she said, "I haven't forgotten that I promised you could leave at ten when it wasn't crazy."

"No problem," he said, eagerly stepping up to the pass, looking like he'd gotten a second wind from his temporary promotion.

Blake made a detour to grab two bottles of wine, each with a few ounces left, then headed for her office. Emily patted Brady and Alicia as she left, trailing along to enter the office behind Blake.

"Shut the door, please," Blake said, making Emily's heart start to race. Then she added, "I can't stop myself from second-guessing Grant if I can hear him."

Emily closed the door, then sat down, her clammy hands drying now that the danger had passed. When Blake started to unbutton her jacket, Emily did the same, smiling when a small fan appeared on the desk and started to cool them both down. "I wonder if the heat has broken?" Blake asked, like someone was preventing her from sticking her head outside to see for herself. "When I was a kid, all I wanted was summer. But now…" She leaned back in her chair and stretched like a cat. "I can't wait for fall."

"Me too. But I'm not crazy about winter, so I'd like to get to October and stay there."

"Nice thought." She stood, stretched dramatically, then took her jacket off, once again revealing a tank top so tight it clearly would have revealed if her nipples were hard—but a quick glance showed they were not.

Emily watched her go through a stretching routine more suited to the Olympics than a small office, while trying hard to not stare—or leer. Blake stood tall and stuck her arms straight up in the air, then clasped her hands together and bent at the waist, hitting every point on the compass. It was like walking by an open window, with a gorgeous woman inside doing some sexy calisthenic routine. But even though Blake was thrusting those fantastic breasts right at her, Emily forced herself not to look. It was just pervy to try to catch an eyeful when the woman in question wasn't performing for you.

Finally, Emily resorted to putting her hand over her forehead, blocking her view. Then she was able to think of food. "Tomatoes are still great," she said. "Wanna make that tarte Tatin again?"

Blake stopped mid-stretch, then barked out a laugh. "Fuck you very much," she said, smiling. "I'll have you know that was one awesome dish. But would it have killed me to leave the damn skins on? If I'd called it a rustic tart, I could have saved myself, and the two commis I dragged into it, a load of work."

"That never seems to be a consideration for you."

Blake bent at the waist and let her arms dangle, making her voice a little muffled when she said, "Maybe it should be. There's a tipping point where you're doing more than your guests can appreciate. I think I passed it today." When she stood, her curls pointed in new directions, and her cheeks were bright pink. "Next time I do something stupid like that, remind me of what I said tonight."

"Uhm…" Emily waited until she was looking at her to say, "Do you really think I'm going to tell you when you're doing more than I'd do? There's a reason your name's on the awning."

"Yeah, I guess there is," she agreed, now sitting down and sticking her feet out as far as she could get them. "But I can be blindly unreasonable, and that's not good for the staff."

"I think you're going to have to have a staff therapist if you want someone to tell you you're being unreasonable. You do know we're scared of you, don't you?"

The most adorable smile Emily had ever seen settled upon her face. "I want you to be."

"Then you've got your wish."

That smile stayed right where it was, and all of a sudden Emily could see Blake in twenty years. Still gorgeous, still achingly sexy, but with a more mature, more seasoned attitude.

It was crazy to even consider, but she had an irrational desire to stick with her as they both matured in the job. It would be fantastic to be able to remain with someone you respected and knew well. Over time, she'd be able to tell her to knock it off when she started to peel an entire crate of cherry tomatoes. But that wasn't how the business worked. You learned, you progressed, and you moved up. If you got burnt out or developed a drinking problem, you moved down. But she'd never heard of an enterprising sous sticking with a head chef for decades. Even having the instinct to do that showed you weren't very enterprising. She watched Blake as she began to doodle, rendering a very nice representation of her tarte. Even though they couldn't work together for decades, she hoped they'd still be in touch—or, even better, touching. Now *that* was a nice fantasy for a cool September night, and, for a change, she was going to get home early enough to actually do something with her frisky libido.

Chapter Five

A WEEK LATER, ON A warm, humid Saturday night, Emily stood at her station at nine o'clock, silently pleading with the clock to move faster. Not only was the dining room stuffed with three tables of PPX, they also had two tables holding their most loyal guests, couples who were extraordinary simply because they visited at least once a month.

Emily kicked herself for creating a special side dish that had turned into a huge pain to assemble properly. It had seemed pretty simple when she'd pitched the idea, a savory mille-feuille. Instead of pastry cream, she used purees of carrot, parsnip, and rutabaga, all nestled on the thin sheets of puff pastry. Then a stylish "B" was piped on top using whipped potatoes in a pastry bag. She'd made it herself for the presentation, and it had been perfect. But the kitchen had been ten degrees cooler then, they weren't under choking time constraints, and the puff pastry hadn't started to droop.

Brady and Jameson, the meat and fish chefs, were sailing along. But Alicia and Cleveland, their assistants, were both in the weeds—all because of Emily's idea. They'd each made a tray of the dish just before service, but the pastry wilted by the time the first ten covers had gone out. So they had to toss the rest of the tray, put fresh sheets of puff pastry in the cooler, then run to grab some and make each mille-feuille fresh. As usual when something was going badly, the duck and sea bream associated with it were the best sellers of the night, forcing them to dash for the cooler constantly.

The kitchen had been hot all day, but it grew oppressive as the night wore on. By nine, Emily began to feel like she was running in deep sand just to keep up. She must have spaced for a moment, for she jerked to attention when Blake grabbed her by the jacket and said, "Alicia's going down. Bail her out."

Immediately, she nestled in beside Alicia and started to make the mille-feuille herself. Cleveland, from across the gap that separated the two main stations, gave her a pleading look. "I'll handle all of the mille-feuille," she said, gulping. That was the right thing to do, but it sucked. For the next two hours, she piped purée onto delicate squares of pastry, assembling each one like a sculpture—which meant her own job fell onto Blake's shoulders, who now had to taste all of the other sides when they got to her. As Emily pulled another sheet of pastry from the cooler she silently pledged, to herself and her coworkers, to never, ever come up with another dish so time-consuming and easy to ruin. She knew she'd break the vow, yet was dead certain she'd make a valiant effort.

At eleven fifteen, a single chit spit out and Blake grabbed it. "Two quiche Provençal, two asparagus salads, and one country pâté. All at once." She made eye contact with Emily and gave her a wan smile. "No mille-feuille. My kind of guests." Then she slapped her hand on the pass. "We are out, people. Thank you for busting your butts tonight. I know it was a tough one, but you all did a wonderful job."

She started for her office, calling, "Grant, let's go." He followed along behind her, with the rest of the staff starting to break down their stations. Lorelei headed for the dishwashing area, gathered the partially drunk bottles of wine, then grabbed a funnel and combined all of the reds into a couple of bottles, all of the whites into another pair. Then she moved around the kitchen with some plastic glasses, offering the wine to anyone interested. This was a common practice that Emily rarely took advantage of. Having everything from a Beaujolais to a Barolo mixed together was too sacrilegious, akin to putting all of their main courses in a blender and seeing what kind of glop came out. But she wasn't going to miss out on a nightcap, already having decided to open a decent bottle when she got home. When you were as wound up as they all were after that shit storm, you had to do something to calm down, and alcohol was all she had. No wonder half the cooks she knew had a drinking problem.

Grant must have had some great ideas for the next day's entrée, for he was back out in the kitchen in moments, supervising the clean-up while Emily was still getting changed. On her way past Blake's office, she caught sight of her, leaning back in her chair, feet up on the desk. Emily wasn't sure she was speaking to her, but when she heard Blake clearly say, "Know what I'm glad of?" she poked her head in.

"Were you talking to me?"

"Uh-huh." Her hands were laced behind her head, elbows forward as she did a few crunches, grunting softly with each rep.

Emily entered the office, then sat down when Blake didn't rush to speak.

After she finished her mini-workout, she said, "I'm glad New York hasn't legalized marijuana."

Emily let out a short laugh. "Okay, I'll bite. Why are you glad New York hasn't legalized marijuana?"

She released her grip, let her hands fall to her sides, then sat up straight. "Because I'd be sitting here, getting bone-numbingly high at the end of a night like this. Then I'd start going through the walk-ins, chowing down on everything that looked good. I'd get caught, and then I'd get fired. All because of a legal drug."

Emily didn't mention that their pastry chef and her assistant were always carrying, since she realized Blake was talking out of her hat. She actually appeared to want to converse, and Emily seized every opportunity for a real chat. "What do you do to relax after a rough night? I was going to go home and drink what I hope is a good bottle of wine I've been saving."

She nodded. "That's not rare for me either. I hate to spend my Sunday with a hangover, though." A sly little smile broke through as she picked up a pencil and started drawing wine bottles. "You can obviously hold your liquor, given that you powered through your second day. When I took a look at you that morning, I was sure you were going to hurl."

"Lesson learned," Emily said, playfully grabbing her head and holding it. "I'm not able to keep up, so I haven't tried again."

Blake cocked her head, then let her eyes shift to meet Emily's for a few seconds. "No other ways to calm down?"

Did she really want to know this? Emily was about to tell her nothing relaxed her as well as a good roll in the hay, but she wasn't sure Blake wanted the conversation to be *that* casual.

"You don't do yoga or anything like that?" Blake continued, saving Emily the embarrassment of talking about the rejuvenating powers of a few orgasms.

"No, I've never gotten into yoga or meditation or any of those other things my sister's always politely suggesting."

"How about a steam bath?"

She shrugged. "My tub's really short, and there's a window in the bath that doesn't seal properly. The steam would be gone in two seconds."

The slight smile grew. "I meant a real steam bath. A schvitz."

"Oh! I've never been to one. Do they help?"

She started to neaten her desk, stacking piles of papers on all four corners of her desk pad. Then she stood, looked at Emily and said, "I think it's time you decided for yourself."

"Where...?"

"East Village. Go hail a cab while I lock up."

Emily got up, made a bee-line for the rear exit, and quickly moved between their building and the restaurant next door. By the time a cabbie saw her raised hand, Blake was next to her. "Good job," she said as she grasped the rear door handle and urged Emily inside.

It was strange, very strange to be in a cab with Blake. While they got along well, their interactions were exclusively work-based, even if their rare conversations veered off food once in a while. But this promised to be something entirely different and Emily was on pins and needles trying to figure out exactly what it was.

Blake took over and gave the cabbie the address, then scooted up so her head was even with the plexiglass safety divider most drivers left open. Then she directed him, in detail, like he was a student driver and she was the instructor. Leave it to her to have to be in control.

It didn't take long to get across town, given Blake's innate GPS, and they got out in front of an old, vaguely seedy building with a faded blue neon sign that hung vertically, clearly stating, "Steam." A smile lit her face when Blake looked up at it. "I bet this place is over a hundred years old. They don't make them like this anymore."

When Blake opened the front door, Emily stepped inside, hit with a surfeit of scents she wasn't sure she could identify. Definitely eucalyptus, but that was all she was certain of. Steam had a weird scent, probably from the individual chemical properties of not only water but the pipes it traveled through.

An elderly woman who might have spent her youth palling around with Stalin greeted them. Or, more accurately, ignored them. But Blake didn't let that stop her. She planted an arm on the podium the woman stood behind and said, "Platza. Two." She held up her fingers in a "V".

Emily's hand twitched, poised to tap Blake on the shoulder to ask what the charge would be. She had no idea what platza was, but if it cost more than twenty-five bucks, it wasn't in the budget. Then Blake confidently whipped out a charge card and handed it over, making Emily's money worries disappear in an instant.

At the sight of plastic, the woman came briefly to life, taking the card and running it through a modern card reader.

After Blake signed, the woman crooked her finger, directing them to tiny enclosures. Blake was in the adjoining one, and Emily could hear her amused voice through the thin walls.

"Fancy, huh?"

"Very. Do I just leave my stuff in here?"

"No. Our friendly hostess will give you a key to a locker. She must have forgotten. Just put on the robe and get ready for a novel experience."

"A novel, relaxing experience, right?" she asked, all of a sudden not so sure what she was in for.

"Eventually," Blake said, chuckling.

They emerged from their little booths, both covered in tissue-thin white terry robes, disposable rubber flip-flops on their feet. Blake filled her robe to capacity, with her broad shoulders straining the fabric. She gave Emily a toothy grin. "Ready to relax?"

Their hostess reappeared to shove keys on plastic wristbands at them. "Come," she said, pushing through a door to indicate some tiny lockers. Then she pointed to a set of stairs lit with fairly dim bulbs.

Two burly women appeared in the murky light, silently guarding a wooden door, both wearing a variation of white surgical scrubs that ended at their knees. "Platza?" one of them asked.

Blake nodded, then boldly entered the room, which nearly knocked Emily to her knees as she followed. "We'll die in here!" she whispered, stunned by the heat.

"It's only two hundred degrees. Kinda like the kitchen in August."

Long benches lined the walls, with a huge wooden bucket in the center of the room. The women entered, each bearing fistfuls of tree branches dotted with leaves.

"What in the hell..." Emily muttered.

"You're gonna love it," Blake said confidently. Then she unfastened her robe and lay face down on a bench. Her attendant picked up a couple of towels, then started to peel the robe from her shoulders. Some strange instinct made Emily turn away, not allowing her even the briefest glimpse of Blake's body. Maybe she just didn't want to see something she could never have. She lay down, then allowed her attendant to remove the robe. She was naked for just seconds before towels were draped across her.

Her attendant pulled a smaller bucket from the large one, then water just this side of freezing was poured down her body. "Ahhhh!" she screamed, sounding like a child in a haunted house.

Blake laughed, then gasped as the icy water was poured onto her. "It would have been nice of me to warn you about the water," she said, laughing a little, "but it's kind of like hazing. You don't want to spoil the fun for the pledges."

"Oh, yeah, that was fun. What's next? Ripping the hair from my head?"

"Even better," Blake said, her voice rising as the attendants began to wail on them with the soapy branches. Emily stuffed her fist in her mouth so she didn't cry out again as they were beaten mercilessly. After a few seconds the shock wore off and she realized it didn't exactly hurt, but she couldn't quite quantify the sensation. It was like being drummed on, firmly, repeatedly, ceaselessly. She hadn't gotten a good look at her attendant's arms, but they must have been like stone. You couldn't wield sopping wet, soapy tree branches all day and have flabby guns.

"Do you come here to recruit?" Emily asked, raising her voice to be heard over the constant slapping.

Blake laughed at that. "I guess I could. If Jameson leaves, I'm coming here to look for my next butcher."

Another bucket of water hit her, but Emily had been prepared, now keeping an eye on her attendant. It didn't help to know it was coming, but she had time to clap a hand over her mouth, reducing her scream to a whimper.

Then her masseuse climbed onto her body, kneeling on her butt, with her hands on her shoulders. She couldn't see what Blake was up to, but she started to hear grunts that matched her own as the woman crawled around like a toddler, working her hands and her knees into every sore, stress-filled spot. It was one of those "good for you" things, the kind of sensation that was pleasant only after it was over. When a knee was actually grinding into your butt, you had trouble believing that, but when the branch-drumming began again, you forgot about individual parts of your body and let yourself grow limp. Until another bucket of water hit you. "Damn it," Emily yelped.

"Part of the process—" Blake said, her words cut off by another gasp.

The masseuse climbed down, then helped Emily sit up. She was a little woozy, and the room was now murky from steam, but she followed along when her hand was tugged on firmly. They exited, then went to an open shower, where she was doused with tepid water rinsing off the billions of bubbles the soap left on her skin. Then she was guided to a small pool. Her attendant pointed at the water and she got in, assuming it was a hot tub. "Holy shit!" she cried as the ice-cold water hit her thighs.

The room was so dim, and the needles that seemed to pierce every inch of her shin distracted her from seeing Blake walk by. But an evil laugh bubbled up. "It would have been even nicer of me to tell you about the cold pool. But you never would have gotten in if I had."

"And how would that have hurt me?" she said, speaking over the water splashing over Blake's head.

"Part of the experience," she called out. "Are you relaxed yet?"

"Intermittently."

"Well, I'm about to take a dip in the cold pool, and knowing it's in my future doesn't make it more inviting."

"Enjoy," Emily said as her attendant extended a hand and lifted her from the tub like she were a twig.

Now that her skin was a frozen shell over a toasty center, she was helped back into her robe and led down a hallway. Seeing a sign indicating a bathroom, she signaled to her handler and went inside to pee, although how she had any fluid left in her body was a puzzlement. Her trusty minder was waiting to lead her to a frosted glass door. The attendant wanted her robe, so she gave it to her, accepting a very small, thin bath towel in exchange. Pushing open the door, obviously the New York entrance to hell, she cried out again, continually embarrassed by her outbursts. Going into a stunningly hot space when you couldn't see the hand in front of your face wasn't fun when you were mildly claustrophobic, but then the door opened and a calm, low voice broke through the heavy steam. "Emily?"

"Pounded like a piece of veal, but still standing," she said, trying to orient herself. The room was tiled and every sound echoed.

"Make a solemn vow that you won't let me fall asleep, okay? I did that once and it took me a day to get rehydrated."

"I can't guarantee anything." Through the fog she saw a vague shape. "Are you by the door?"

"Yeah. We're the only ones in here."

Emily bumped into something solid, reached down and felt a bench running along the wall. Then she heard Blake's skin slap onto what must have been a higher bench. Not wanting to get all up in her face, she stayed on the bottom and covered herself with the towel. "I've decided this is relaxing, even though it was like being whipped around in a stand mixer, then shoved into the cooler, and now the Combi when it's set to its maximum."

"It kind of is," she agreed, her voice sounding lower when it bounced off the walls. "But we'd never fit in the Combi."

"I wouldn't have said this a half hour ago, but this was just what I needed. Thanks."

"I thought you'd like it. You don't look very tough, but I know you are."

That was a nice compliment, and Emily savored it for a second. Then, all of a sudden, Blake was sitting next to her. A towel covered her, mostly, but she wasn't obsessive about making sure every inch was hidden. Emily consciously kept her eyes front and center. Seeing Blake naked, or even better, partially naked, was only something that could hurt her. She needed every bit of her concentration at work, and thinking of her boss's probably luscious body would only make her job harder.

"Got a question for you," Blake said.

"Yeah?"

"Would you be upset if I relieved Grant of his menu-devising duties?"

"Completely?"

There was a pause, then she said, "Not if you think that's unfair."

"Well," she said, trying to think through a brain that was as fog-enveloped as the room. "I'm not crazy about doing an important part of his job."

"Right." Blake slapped her hands together, the sound sharp and ringing in the tiled room. After a few seconds, she said, "I could give him time cards."

"Have I been screwing up…?"

"No," she said, her voice firm and decisive. "You're doing a fine job, Emily." She paused for another second. "Make that excellent. Everything Marcel said about you is true."

"Thanks," she said, glad the fog obscured her face. It would be embarrassing to let Blake see her beaming with pride.

"I told you before that I don't think Grant gives me his best ideas, but I've finally figured out that his palate just doesn't mesh with mine. Your suggestions make my mouth water, and that's important to me. I hate to put something on the menu that I'm not excited about, but I truly don't have the time or the energy to come up with fresh first courses and mains every day." She let out a sigh. "But I acknowledge it's more work, and it will probably guarantee you won't get to leave early."

Emily didn't remind her that leaving early was a fairy tale often repeated but never realized.

"So, if you're willing to switch things around, think about what you'd like to give up to even out the workload."

"Scheduling," she said, not even taking a second to ponder it. "It's a pain in the butt, and almost impossible to make everyone happy."

"Done. I'll call him tomorrow to give him a day to get used to the idea." She slapped Emily's bare shoulder, then moved back up to the higher level. "It wouldn't kill us to sleep a little, would it?"

"I'm not sure I'd mind if it did. If we survive, promise you won't leave without me. I'm lost on the Lower East Side."

"Don't worry about a thing," Blake said, her voice so full of confidence Emily let herself relax, fully relax. It was hotter than hades, but her muscles were loose and pliable for the first time in what felt like forever. Getting this treat for free—well, for having to take over part of Grant's job—was still a bargain.

Chase had been craving Brazilian food all summer, but it took until two o'clock on Sunday afternoon for he and Emily to finally head to his favorite place in Astoria to get it. While neither of them minded a long subway ride, they both hated to take buses, so the commitment to hop on the Q102 for coxinhas and some moqueca de camarão was a serious one.

Emily tried to stay in the shade of a bodega's awning while they waited for the bus to arrive. After taking out her phone, she looked up a note she'd previously made and said, "If I made a batch of gazpacho today, would you eat it during the week?"

He laughed, shaking his head. "When have I ever turned my nose up at anything you've made?"

"Could be a first. I've just got to buy limes and tomatillos, and we're good."

As she slipped her phone back into her pocket, he said, "I'm not complaining, but you've got a lot of spark today. Most Sundays you either want to eat *or* cook. Not both."

"I've been rejuvenated," she said, sticking her arms straight out at her sides and flapping her hands. "Some Russian weightlifter pummeled me into a limp mass of flesh at around one in the morning, but I feel great today. I'm not even dehydrated, despite falling asleep in the schvitz."

He stepped back and gave her a long look, making both moves as dramatic as possible. "Russian weightlifters and a schvitz? Were you trapped in an avant-garde play?"

"Sometimes it feels like I am, but this was just your usual 'I'll have your back beaten with birch leaves if you'll scratch mine' kind of thing."

"Again," he said, narrowing his eyes into a faux glower, "you're speaking more like Ionesco than yourself."

She could have lobbed another puzzling statement at him, but it was hot and the bus was barreling toward them, so she cut it short. "Blake wanted me to take over some of Grant's duties, so she took me to the Russian baths and paid for me to be pummeled. Literally. Just to soften me up. Literally." She stuck her hand out to signal to the driver they wanted to board. A minute later they'd threaded their way through the standees to settle near the rear of the bus.

Chase still had a puzzled look on his face, and as they lurched away from the stop he said, "It's kind of strange to have your boss send you to a massage parlor, but not the strangest thing that's ever happened to you in the odd world of kitchens."

"She didn't send me. We went together."

"Together? You and the inscrutable Blake Chadwick socialized?" His eyebrows moved up and down a few times. "That must mean she likes you."

Shrugging, Emily said, "She likes me plenty. I'm working my butt off, I don't have a drinking problem, and I don't complain."

"That's true of everyone to hear you talk." He laughed a little. "Except for the drinking problem. But I bet she doesn't go out for a steam bath with everyone."

"Probably not. Mainly because she wouldn't be in the steam with any of the guys. She had to make me goofy from the heat to get me to do her bidding."

"Naked?" he asked, with not a nanosecond between her statement and his question.

"Yes, Chase, we were both bare-assed naked in a steam room." She laughed as his eyes got bigger and he blinked them rapidly. "Stop using me in your homemade porn!"

"I'm blurring your face out," he insisted, still with a silly grin on his face. "I'm seeing all of her with just a few parts of you peripherally involved." With a jerk, he stared at her. "Why did she want to be naked with you? Is she into you?"

"No!" She slapped at him, making the nearby bus riders give them a quick look to ascertain there wasn't going to be any real violence. "She was manipulating me, but not in the fun way."

"Are you sure?" his gaze was penetrating, unblinking.

"Of course I'm sure. To her, I'm a good pair of hands and a palate that roughly matches hers."

He nodded soberly. "What is she to you?"

"Uhm..." Her cheeks were starting to flush, but she didn't want to bare her soul about Blake. It was too cliche to admit she ran around the kitchen like a golden retriever puppy, just begging for a scratch under the chin from her mistress—who coincidentally was as hot as a ghost pepper.

Chase put his arm around her shoulders, then banged into her as the bus took a wide turn. "There's nothing wrong with having a crush on your boss, Em. Maybe it'll make the day go faster if you fantasize about her."

Giving him another slap, she said, “You shouldn’t be encouraging me! It’s hard enough to keep my head down and focus like a laser all day. If I’m dreaming about humping my boss in the walk-in…”

With a dreamy look in his eyes, he said, “I’m about to unspool another reel of my homemade porn. Women grinding against each other in a cold room, their nipples so hard—”

Emily slapped her hand over his mouth, then let out a devilish laugh. “I’m stealing that one for *my* porn reel. Wake me when we get to Astoria.”

CHAPTER SIX

THEIR WINDOWS WERE CLOSED more than they were open, the trees had lost many of their leaves, and Emily's moisture lotion was getting a workout. Fall had descended upon them after their strangely warm September, coming on fast and furious.

Late one night, Emily and Chase demolished a big container of hot and sour soup while an old movie played on Chase's laptop. They sat shoulder to shoulder on the lumpy sofa, only giving a portion of their attention to Henry Fonda. "Are you going home for Thanksgiving?" Chase asked.

"Home?" She thought for a moment. "Can't. We're serving. Wish I could though. I miss the hell out of my family. How about you?"

"Yeah, I'm going. Want me to stop by your parents' house on the way from the airport?"

He was such a sweetheart. He'd have to go an hour out of his way to do that. "You know, I'd really like that. So would they."

Chuckling, he said, "Anything to spend less time with my family. I'd love to skip, but my mom takes Thanksgiving very seriously."

"Mmm." Emily thought for a minute. "I think my dad likes it better than my mom. Maybe because all he has to do is eat." She thought of her father's eyes lighting up when her mom put the turkey on the table.

"You didn't work Thanksgiving at Henri, did you?"

"Nope. But we worked Christmas. I'd make that trade any time."

"Oh, right. You get two whole weeks off. Doesn't it cost an awful lot to shutter the place for that long?"

"If you've got to close, Christmas is the time to do it. It can be busy, but you don't get many of your regulars. It's a touristy crowd."

"Tourists don't spend real money?"

She gave him a playful pinch. "Yes, Chase, they do. But I don't think Blake's as invested in turning out covers as she is in keeping the regulars happy. Plus, she'll drop dead if she doesn't get a vacation, and God knows she doesn't trust me or Grant to run the place."

"She's there every night?"

"Every night. Cooking much of the day, expediting all night. She's the hardest working chef I've ever worked for, as well as the most focused. I'm sure she could get a show on TV and make some easy money, but she likes to cook."

He grasped her cheek and gave it a pinch. "And that's the real reason you've got a crush on her. You always like people who respect food as much as you do."

"She's got me beat, buddy. Or at least we tie. Blake's easily as big a food nerd as I am."

On a blustery November morning, Blake burst through the back doors, the heavy scarf she'd looped around her neck fluttering in the breeze. "Who's ready to go with me to the South of France?"

Only Emily, Grant and Alicia were in the kitchen, and each lifted a hand.

"Good. We'll go as soon as service is over. Emily?" She walked by, with a scent of something a little different, a little more floral floating in the air as she passed. Emily followed her into her office, and when the scarf was tossed to the other chair, she realized it bore some perfume, probably left over from the previous winter. Wherever it came from, it was nice. Sexy.

"I'd like a hearty soup for one of the specials," Blake said as she picked up her pencil and started to draw a bowl, then put some tendrils of vapor above it.

Emily snapped back into work mode, dismissing the thought of bare skin and spicy perfume that threatened to wake her libido. "We've got some hot chilis… How about an African peanut-based soup?"

Blake looked up from her drawing. "In four years, I don't think we've ever served an African soup."

"It's a big continent. One little soup could slip right in, almost unnoticed."

"How do you make it ours?"

"Maybe we don't," she said, trying to think of a new angle.

An eyebrow lifted.

"We have a lot of regulars, right?"

"We'd better, if we want to stay in business."

"I bet their palates get fatigued with all of our decadent first courses. Why don't we introduce a fairly simple soup? Something hearty and different."

A dubious frown covered her face, but she kept drawing. "How do I charge fifteen dollars for a simple soup?"

"Well, that's my other thought. I can use chicken legs and wings, yams, cilantro… Nothing expensive. We could charge like eight bucks for it. It won't cost more than two to make, so we'd still have a hefty margin. Besides being something different, our regulars might like being able to pare a little off the bill."

"Do we want people to pare the bill down?" She was now trying to draw a yam, making a pretty good attempt.

"Sure. What do we care if they spend less, if we spend less by omitting all of the high-priced ingredients? Isn't the margin what's important?"

Blake nodded decisively. "I take your point. Make your soup. We'll have the cooks taste it, and if they like it, it's on." She met Emily's gaze. "I like that you're thinking of our bottom-line. It's easy to get caught up in bigger, richer, more expensive and forget that our job is to make people happy."

A thrill chased through her. Damn, she loved having the boss pat her on the head. "I like rich food more than your average guy, but I couldn't eat it every night. I'm just trying to think like a guest."

"That's an excellent instinct, Emily. One you should always hold on to." She looked down at her notes. "One more first course and we can get this menu cracking. I had an idea when I was walking over here this morning. Did we get any mahi-mahi in?"

/

That night, the main courses for a table of PXs, important people who hadn't risen to the particulièrement level of extraordinary, were ready to hit the flame. "Fire four skate wings for table six," Blake called out.

"Four skate in four," Brady replied.

Getting four portions of the same dish finished at exactly the same time, particularly something as thin and easy to overcook as skate, was a pain. Brady had four pans going simultaneously, his hands moving from handle to handle, giving each pan a rough shake. After she'd tested each portion for temperature, Emily tasted the side dishes and slid them all down to the pass. As she watched Blake smear a ribbon of pea puree across a gleaming white plate, she instinctively grabbed a plate from the stack and mirrored her. She was half a second behind, but as Blake finished her second entrée Emily dotted the edge of her second plate with sauce and slammed the squeeze bottle down.

At that moment, she realized she'd sliced a part of Blake's job away from her without comment—or permission. But in the half second they had to breathe while the next order was spitting out, Blake gave her a wry smile. "I'd better stay on my toes. My sous is gaining on me."

If Emily hadn't been so tired, she would have wiggled her tail like a pup. Blake moved past her on the way to the dining room to fawn over the PXs. As she went, she squeezed Emily's shoulder and murmured a quiet, "You continue to impress me."

The next morning, Emily walked down Roosevelt Avenue, heading for the subway. It was a blustery day, with the leaden gray skies so low she felt like she could jump up and touch the clouds. But she was too tired to even consider jumping. The wet cold made her joints ache, and she longed to return to bed to give her creaky body a break. But if every cook stayed home when she didn't feel great, every professional kitchen would be empty.

Normally, she made a bee-line for the train in order to get to work as swiftly as possible. But today she stopped at a favorite Pakistani place and had a second breakfast to try to boost her mood. A bowl of creamy porridge with dried fruit laced throughout didn't make the skies any less gray or foreboding, but it warmed her up inside, and that was a small victory.

Entering the kitchen a minute before ten, Emily was surprised to spot Blake in her office, still in her civilian clothes. She didn't look up when Emily passed by on her way to change, but on the way back Emily came to a halt when those stormy, dark eyes landed on her. "Do you ever wonder why we bother?" Blake said, her head tilting slightly.

That had to be a trick question. Edging away from the door, itching to get to work, Emily tossed off a noncommittal, "Not really."

After taking another step, she thought she'd gotten past the danger, but Blake sounded so sad when she said, "Then you must not read reviews," that Emily put on the brakes and backpedaled.

"We got a bad review?" she asked, sticking her head into the office.

Blake used a single finger to shove her phone across the desk, touching it like it was toxic.

Now all the way inside the office, Emily picked up the phone and took a look, expecting to read something horrible from one of the few legitimate publications that bothered to review restaurants. Instead, she found a long screed from some jerk named "Gour May" on a popular crowd-sourced review site. As she read, she kept sneaking glances at Blake, who truly seemed disconsolate.

"Do you know this guy?" Emily finally asked.

Dark eyebrows shot up. "Know him? Of course not." She sat up straighter in her chair, then started organizing her desk, something she often did when she was agitated. "Do you think I'd hang out with an imbecile who'd slam me in public?"

"No, I suppose not…" She took in a breath and tried to figure out what was going on. Taking another look at the post, Emily took a wild guess. "It must hurt to have someone go after you personally. And be so utterly wrong," she added.

Blake's head shook dismissively. "I can take it. Some jerks are intimidated by women." When their eyes met, Emily took in the fire burning in Blake's gaze. "What I can't stand is having our food criticized by an idiot who knows *nothing*. If he'd had a poorly prepared meal, he would have every right to bitch about it. But he didn't, Emily. That dish was perfect." She picked up a pencil and rolled it between her fingers for a few moments, stewing. With a loud snap the pencil lay in two pieces, then both halves were flung against the far wall. "You came up with that one," she said, her voice bubbling with anger. "Years of training and experimentation let you pair those scallops with that tart green apple." A reluctant smile curled her lips. "I still remember how it tasted. It gave the scallops a distinct character. It was *unique*," she said, a massive compliment from Blake.

"Thank you, Chef." That compliment warmed her far more than the porridge had. "It was a good dish."

"It was excellent," Blake insisted. "Yet this ignoramus, who doesn't understand food at *all*, has the nerve to bitch about it. This is our livelihood," she said, her eyes opening wide. "He's screwing with our profession!"

"Yeah, I guess..." What was there to say? Some people were jerks. Was that a surprise?

"I like poetry," Blake said. She shrugged. "*Some* poetry. But I don't have a deep understanding of it. I would have to be an asshole to read a poem and then go to some poetry review site and slam the poet. I'm not knowledgable enough to understand the quality of the work." Another pencil found its way into her hands and Emily kept her eyes on it, preparing to twitch when this one cracked. "I can have an opinion, but I shouldn't be so full of myself to try to influence other people based on that *unschooled* opinion." She blinked a few times, hurt still visible in her eyes. "Does that make sense?"

"Perfect," Emily said, finally getting Blake's point. "This guy," she said, tapping her finger onto the phone, "implied we were lazy and cheap to use an apple to enhance the flavor of the scallop. Questioning our motives like that isn't just mean-spirited, it's ignorant. Part of dining in a restaurant like this is to get a fresh take on things. To have someone help you discover unique elements in familiar foods."

"Exactly," she said, slamming her hand onto the desk so hard some papers levitated. "We're not a tradition-bound New York steakhouse, where you want the same thing done the same way every time."

"That's not us," Emily agreed. "And most of our customers love us. You can't let a few get you down."

"It's hard not to," Blake grumbled. She lifted her head again and met Emily's gaze. "Not when I put so much of my heart and soul into it."

Emily almost teared up. Of all of the people she'd worked with, she and Blake were most simpatico. They weren't doing this for the money or the acclaim. They did it because they *had* to. It was a calling. She stood and lingered in the doorway for a moment, wishing she could help vanquish the hurt feelings the guy's review had left. She was about to say something, but realized platitudes never helped. Instead, she said, "I'm gonna go check in the fish. Then we're gonna come up with a few first courses that will please our toughest, most discerning critics—us." As she slipped from the door, she could see a half smile tug at the corner of Blake's mouth.

Success!

Later that morning, when she should have been working on time cards, Emily found herself on the review site, checking out the slam. She'd never looked at internet reviews for any place she'd worked, and was amazed that they'd amassed almost a thousand of them. Of that number, over six hundred of them were four stars. Another two hundred and fifty were three. That left a hundred and fifty people who were vaguely to very unhappy with their meals. That seemed like a lot, so she dove deep, scanning every one star review. Some were valid, like the couple whose food wasn't piping hot. Things like that happened in a frantic kitchen on a Saturday night. Ideally, the customer complained to the server and they got a re-fire, but most people didn't want to do that. It was easier to anonymously blast a restaurant online. But, as Emily waded through the other reviews, she decided most were truly ridiculous. How was it Blake's fault that a guy spent three hundred bucks on dinner and didn't score with his date? As she continued to read, she got more and more downhearted. Then a flash of clarity filled her and she closed the tab. All she could do was cook to the best of her abilities. If people wanted to bitch, there wasn't a thing she could do about it. But she resolved to never again look at another review site. There was no reason in the world to ask to be insulted, and if Blake had any sense she'd do the same.

On December the seventeenth, their last day before they closed for vacation, the place was full of regulars, PXs and PPXs, all wanting a perfect meal before they had to fend for themselves for two whole weeks.

Even though they were swamped, they got through service relatively unscathed. Everyone seemed blessed with a burst of energy, probably deficit spending from their planned weeks of slothfulness. Emily had asked everyone about their plans, and was not surprised to learn that most were planning absolutely nothing, and were damned glad about it. She was one of the few who was traveling, and she was only going to Detroit, not a big spot for the jet set. To give herself time to slide into the vacation, she was flying out on Monday morning. Tonight and tomorrow she hoped to accomplish only two things: lie on the sofa in her pajamas, and order Chinese food.

"Final ticket," Blake called out. "Ordering—fire it—one crème brûlée and one profiteroles." She slammed her hand down on the pass. "We are out."

A cheer went up, making even Blake laugh. "You can go when your station's clean, or..." She jogged to her office with an astounding burst of energy, popped inside and emerged carrying a crate. "You can help me put a dent in this case of wine."

They were going to drink together? Was this what they always did for the holiday?

"I'm ordering delivery," Blake continued. "What'll it be?"

The staff started negotiating, like they were well-used to this. Emily jumped in to vote for Thai, which won by a whisker. Blake called in the huge order while everyone started to clean, with most of them holding a glass of wine in one hand as they worked. Emily was struck by the fact that no one ever mentioned the FOH staff, and no one paused to consider inviting them in. They all worked for the same place, and they all had the same boss, but Blake seemed to look at the front of the house as a necessary evil. Even though the servers and bartenders were the public face of the restaurant, they weren't cooks.

Blake had gone into the dining room to blast some rock, and Emily later caught sight of her, lying on the floor in front of the fry station, scrubbing under the darned thing while she sang along to The Cure. How could you not respect the head chef when she shimmied under the grimiest piece of equipment in the whole operation and attacked it with every bit of her persnicketiness?

By the time the food arrived, with the delivery guy giving them a funny look when he saw he was entering a big, professional kitchen, the wine was really flowing. The kitchen was as clean as it could get, and everyone climbed atop any flat surface that wasn't still hot, balancing paper plates on their laps as they dug in.

It was the first time they'd actually socialized as a group. Hell, it was the first time they'd eaten like normal human beings. Blake made the rounds, going from person to person, chatting, teasing, pouring wine into every slightly diminished cup. But Emily noted she purposefully avoided giving any to Raven, their child pastry chef. Even during a party, she kept her eye on things.

Emily, Brady and Alicia huddled together atop a nearby counter. They'd become a real team, supporting each other and stepping in whenever duty called. Through constant feedback, Alicia was now seasoning her dishes perfectly, and Brady could speed up or slow down to keep pace when her sides were taking a little longer than usual. They were a good group, and Emily felt herself misting up at the good cheer that filled her.

Blake came cruising by, then spent a few minutes speaking to Alicia. Seeing them interact, it was hard to believe Blake had been on the verge of firing her just a few months before. Despite her temper, you had to hand it to Blake. She didn't hold things over anyone's head. She fired you or let you be. You always knew where you stood with her, which helped the staff maintain their focus. When Emily got her own place, she was going to mimic that. Be transparent.

The crowd started to thin out, all of the people with families heading home to begin the exodus. Emily and Grant walked around with trash bags, collecting all of the detritus, and when they were done, she jumped up onto a counter and took a sip of her wine. She'd been very moderate. The last thing she was going to do was get toasted in front of Blake, but she'd eaten enough to let her have another glass and still keep it together.

A loose-limbed Raven came to stand in front of her. Because she was sitting on the counter, Emily necessarily had her legs spread, and Raven insinuated herself right between them. Her colorfully decorated hands slapped onto Emily's thighs as she leaned into her. "Wanna head out?"

"Uhm…what?"

"We're on vacation. Let's go celebrate. Your apartment."

Blake walked by at that moment, and she nearly sprained her neck whipping her head around to gawp at Raven. Embarrassed, Emily put her hands on the kid's hips and pushed her away. Then she jumped down and guided her over to her usual station. "I appreciate the offer, but I've got some things to finish. I'm heading home to visit my family and I haven't even packed."

"Won't take long." The girl's dark hair had fallen into her face, obscuring her usually alert eyes. "No big thing. I think you're fun, and I *know* I am."

"Thanks, Raven, but I'm going to have to pass." Now she understood why Raven said she didn't drink. *Shouldn't* drink was more like it.

"'S'cool." Undeterred, she moved back over to the group who'd gathered near the pass. "Hey, Brady. Wanna head up to your apartment?"

Emily shook her head and laughed to herself. Raven obviously got over heartbreak really, really quickly.

Something caught Emily's attention, and she turned to see Blake waving at her from her office. Walking over, she said, "Yeah?"

"Got a minute? It's fine if you don't, but I thought we could kick around some ideas for New Year's Eve."

"Oh, shit. I guess we should." Their next morning in the kitchen would be the busiest night of the year. *Super.*

"Yeah. Just in case we need to order anything special. It has to be festive, it has to have caviar, and it has to be soaking in Champagne."

"If I didn't know better, I'd think you weren't looking forward to this," Emily teased, taking her usual chair when she entered.

"I hate New Year's Eve, but we've got to be open. The owners would have a fit if I tried to skip it."

"We can make it work. Are we doing a prix fixe?"

"We usually do. Two options for each course. Plus a vegetarian menu."

"Why don't we pare it down to one protein and one really special meatless dish for each course? That'll make things simpler."

"True…" She started to doodle, drawing a Champagne flute with tiny bubbles escaping from the rim.

Emily took a look outside. Once she and Blake had come into the office, everyone had taken off. Now just a few empty wine bottles sat on the counters. Twenty people, twelve bottles of wine, less than an hour. That was one quick party.

"What are you doing for vacation?"

A personal question? Blake was obviously still in party mode, but Emily hadn't seen her drink a drop.

"I'm going home. Detroit," she added, assuming Blake had forgotten where she was from.

"Mmm." Her posture was uncharacteristically relaxed as she leaned against her desk and continued to draw, now moving onto a rough sketch of an oyster.

"How about you?"

"Not sure." She looked up and met Emily's eyes. "Want a drink?"

"A drink?"

"Yeah."

A case of wine wasn't enough? "Uhm…sure, if you're having one."

She opened her bottom drawer, glass tinkling as it slid wide. "What do you drink?" She looked up again. "I've got more wine, or maybe you like beer." She twitched her head toward the dining room. "Hell, we've got a great bar. I could make you a cocktail. I'm told I make a killer Rob Roy."

What in the hell? "No, that's too much trouble. I'll have a little Scotch if you have any."

"Have I got Scotch," she mumbled, a cute smile tugging at her lips. Six bottles emerged, each set onto the desk with flair. "This is the real deal." She took a bottle and shook it, with about two inches splashing around. "I like my Scotch rich and floral with just a hint of peat. You?"

"Make it two."

Instead of the plastic cups they'd used for the party, Blake had a stash of nice rocks glasses hidden away. She eased a little Scotch into each glass, looked up and asked, "Ice?"

"No need. I like the warmth."

"As do I." She handed a glass to Emily, then said, "Cheers," as they clinked the glasses together.

Emily took a tiny taste, letting her palate adjust after the hearty wine and spicy Thai food. "Really nice," she said. The floral notes started to build in her mouth, with the full, rich taste boosted by a whisper of peat. She'd never been to Scotland, but could imagine being in front of a fire in the cheery warmth of a cabin in a glen. Dense fog floating past the windows. Maybe bagpipes playing a mournful tune in the distance…

"I'm sorry about Raven," Blake said, interrupting her daydream. "I should have kept my eye on her. She obviously hasn't been around liquor much."

Emily could have told her Raven wasn't lacking experience with mind-altering substances, but that wasn't something Blake needed to know. "No problem." She laughed a little. "I've had women proposition me with even less subtlety."

Dark eyebrows shot up. "Really? That doesn't…bother you?"

"Yeah, it bothers me a little."

Blake nodded, her mouth pursed, then went back to drawing. Her Champagne flute was perfect, and now the size of the bubbles rising from it varied, giving it a three-dimensional quality.

"If a woman's going to proposition me, I'd like her to use a little charm. Or at least lick her wounds for a second if I shoot her down. Did you see her move right over and try to hump Brady's leg?"

Blake put her head back and laughed. "That was good. He looked like he'd seen a snake." She took another sip of her drink, very contemplative. "I'm surprised it doesn't bother you to have a woman make a move."

Emily cocked her head. "Why would it bother me? How else am I going to find women to sleep with?"

Those eyebrows shot up again, along with Blake's body. Now she sat in her normal position, centered in her chair, back straight. "You sleep with women? Your boyfriend's cool with that?"

"Boyfriend?"

"The guy you introduced me to."

Now Emily threw her head back and laughed. "Oh, god. Chase isn't my boyfriend. He's a *dude*." She extended her index fingers and crossed them. "No go."

"You like women." Her big brown eyes were wide open. Staring.

"I do. A lot."

A bright smile settled onto Blake's face, but she didn't say another word.

The question didn't need to be asked at this point, but Emily posed it anyway. "Do *you* like women?"

"Hell, yeah. You didn't know that?"

"No. I mean… I've heard rumors, but people label every powerful woman gay. I didn't think about it much."

"Well, in my case, they're right. Not that I'm very powerful. But I'm really gay."

Emily gave her a sly smile. She was stunned they were flirting with each other, but didn't consider stopping. "You're really powerful too. You must not see yourself the way other people do."

"Maybe. You're not the first to make that observation." She gazed at Emily for a minute, with her eyes roaming all over her face. "You want to run your own place, right?"

"I do."

"You do have some power when you run your own restaurant. I assume it's clear that I love being in charge, but it's still hard."

"God knows." She laughed. What an understatement!

"Not the food," Blake said, her dark eyes filled with earnest concern. "That's easy. It's the butt kissing and socializing that kill me."

"But you're the definition of charming!"

An eyebrow rose. "Really? You think so?"

"I really do."

"Huh." She looked down, picked up her pencil and carefully drew the name Emily in bold, three-dimensional block letters. "What do you do when you want to...?" Her gaze shifted to lock on Emily's. "You know..."

She was so stunned she almost choked. Chef wasn't just flirting. She was hitting on her! *Awesome!*

"I...uhm...I've used dating sites without much luck. Now when I'm in the mood, I go to a bar and poke around until I find a server or a bartender who pings my radar. Sometimes it takes until last call, but I'm persistent."

"Been there." She looked up. "I can't do that anymore, though. I don't want to be in someone's blog."

"No, that's probably not a good idea." Blake wasn't super famous, but people in the industry knew her, and some of those people would love to be able to boast about bedding her. "Sometimes I think I ought to look for something more permanent, but I haven't had a real girlfriend since I graduated from cooking school." She let out a sigh. "I can't figure out how to focus on work and have enough energy left to maintain a relationship."

"I sure can't. At least, I haven't." She extended stalks from each of the letters of Emily's name, like they were big flowers or balloons, then drew a vase to hold them in. "So...you're not looking for a relationship?"

"I haven't been. I'm not closed off to finding a woman to love, but it's not a priority." She smiled, knowing she didn't have to add this, but doing it anyway. "Work is."

A small furrow settled between her eyes. "Can you have sex for fun? No strings?"

"I can." She stuck out her glass and Blake portioned the remaining Scotch between them. "Not a single string."

After taking another sip, Blake's voice turned soft and reflective. "I hate it when chefs use their position to get sex." She looked Emily directly in the eye. "I'd never do that. Sex and work are different worlds to me, and one has no bearing on the other. I'd fire my girlfriend—or my mother—without a second thought if she couldn't cut it."

Emily chuckled. "I think I'd give my mother a second chance. Unless she peed on the toilet seat." She made a slicing motion across her throat. "One strike for that."

A half smile showed she didn't mind being teased about her temper. "That's why you're not quite ready to be in charge. You've got to be coldblooded."

"But I'm close," she said, chuckling. "Only my mother gets a second chance, and that's just because she carried me around for nine months. I'd cut my father in a second. His contribution wasn't as labor-intensive."

Blake scooted her chair closer to Emily's, then planted her elbow on the armrest and set her chin on her hand, with their faces just inches from each other. "I like you," she said, her sexy, low voice sending shivers down Emily's spine.

"I like you, too."

"Are we going to do this?" Her breath was warm and smoky from the liquor.

"I think we are. I think we should." She leaned closer, waiting for Blake to make the first move.

Instead of coming closer, Blake locked her eyes on Emily's lips, staring at them for a few seconds. Then her gaze shifted up so their eyes met. "I'd like to kiss you," she said, her voice so sexy Emily nearly slid from the chair. "May I?"

Her mouth was dry as dust, but she managed to speak. "You may."

It took just a heartbeat. Then soft, full lips settled onto hers. So sweet! During her few, brief fantasies, Blake had been forceful, almost rough when they kissed. This was *so* much nicer. A callused hand cupped her cheek. "I need to kiss you again," she whispered. "Would you like that?"

"Uh-huh." Not the most elegant reply, but words were tough to form.

Blake's amazingly soft lips met hers again, making Emily swoon.

After breaking the kiss, Blake moved back an inch or two. Then dark eyes stared at Emily as a smile started to form. "Why don't we lie on that sofa and see what happens?"

Emily started to get up, in a very big hurry to get going. But Blake held onto her arm, her tone grave. "If you change your mind, speak up. No hard feelings if you want to bail. Promise."

Emily gave her a smile and threaded her hand into her hair, pulling her forward. Then she planted a hot one onto her succulent lips, holding Blake in place for a few seconds. "Does it seem like I'm indecisive?"

"No, Chef!" She started to laugh, then stood and pulled Emily up with her. Blake swooped up all of the samples and magazines that had gathered atop the well-used dark brown leather sofa and tossed them into the corner. Then she locked the door and turned on a speaker that was obviously hooked into the main system. Sitting down, she took Emily's hand and tugged her onto her lap. "I love decisive women," she purred before latching onto her mouth with brio.

They kissed for a long while, their enthusiasm increasing with each passing second. Now they were getting after it like Emily had pictured. This was Blake at her essence; forceful, bold, and purposeful. Unafraid to march down the path she'd chosen. Gentle hands held Emily's face still as Blake's tongue slid into her mouth., making her shiver as it darted, teasingly, wherever it chose.

With her arms draped around Blake's square shoulders, Emily hung on and opened herself to her touch. Blake was in charge, and that was just how Emily wanted it, which was slightly puzzling. Normally, she was the aggressor. But with Blake, her craving was to follow.

Once they'd gotten into a good rhythm, Emily's hands started to move, gliding up and down Blake's arms. She was surprised to hear herself murmur, "Where did you get these guns?"

A soft laugh bubbled up. "Swimming. Butterfly." Then she latched onto Emily's mouth again, suckling her tongue, cutting off any more attempts at speech. They could talk later. Right now, their bodies were screaming to be heard.

Emily soon lay half on her back, pushed up against the padded arm of the sofa. Blake was sprawled atop her, kissing her face, her neck, her ears. Every sensitive spot was caressed, nibbled on, and nipped.

Freeing a hand to unbutton Blake's jacket wasn't easy, but Emily got it done. Then she slipped inside, feeling the warm, humid heat of her body. Questing fingers found just what they were looking for. A perfectly shaped breast, heavy as a split Charentais melon. Now they were getting somewhere. Blake pushed her chest into Emily's hand as she let out a satisfied mew, just like a contented cat. She rolled them onto their sides, giving Emily both permission and opportunity, so she squeezed the firm flesh, palming it in her hand as her mouth began to water. There was nothing better than a full breast waiting to be suckled.

They wrestled, briefly, with Emily peeling Blake's tank top up to reveal a snug sports bra with a front closure. Looking up, she was rewarded with a slow, sly smile. "You look like you're about to drool."

Emily smirked when she popped the bra open and warm, soft flesh filled her hands. "I *love* breasts," she said, her clit throbbing with arousal. Every part of sex was fun, but nothing ratcheted up her desire faster than diving in and bathing all of her senses at once. The sight of Blake's pale skin, the heft of the flesh in her hands, the gentle catlike purr when Blake started to get into it. Emily buried her face between her breasts, breathing in the essence of her scent. It was *fantastic.* Almost herbal; like thyme or maybe tarragon after a long roast in a hot oven. The heat of the long day had drawn out every complex, aromatic note, making Emily's mouth water at the primal sexiness of her.

It was crazy to let herself dig in like this, but when you'd only have one shot why leave anything on the table? Like a dog on a hunt, she burrowed into her, tickling across her chest, along a prominent collar bone, then up to her throat, breathing in with her mouth open to catch every element of her compelling aroma. Her pulse beat hard, and she consciously tried to slow herself down. To savor rather than gorge.

Emily sucked in a deep breath, but every molecule of air was laden with Blake's scent, making her shiver with lust. Dipping her head, she sucked a ripe, pink nipple into her mouth. Nearly swooning, she laved it with her tongue, certain she could remain exactly like this for hours. Blake was gently rubbing her back, continually letting out soft sighs and stunningly sexy moans. So aroused she worried she'd hurt her, Emily finally broke the suction, making a loud "pop" when she pulled away.

Blake's laugh was lazy and low. "There's nothing casual about the way you have sex."

Emily met her gaze, seeing she meant that as a compliment rather than something to worry about. "If it's fun, I'm all in." She placed another gentle kiss on a hard nipple. "This is fun."

"Come up here and kiss me. Before tonight, I'd never noticed how gorgeous your lips are." Her fingers slid across Emily's mouth, making her shiver. "They're works of art."

"One minute. I've got my hands full." She grinned at the luscious breasts filling her hands. "I can't resist these spectacular beauties."

"At your leisure." Blake settled into the sofa, sticking her arms above her head, pressing the flesh into Emily's mouth. "You don't have to resist a single thing."

Emily took her at her word, caressing, suckling and enjoying her breasts like the finest delicacies, with the pulse between her legs throbbing and tingling every time she wrenched a gasp from Blake. Then a gentle hand landed on her head, stroking her, urging her on as Blake squirmed under her, clearly digging this. It was *so* hot when a woman got off on the same things that made your clit quiver.

"I love this," Blake murmured as Emily filled her mouth once again, devouring her like a glutton. A thigh pressed up against her, and Emily ground against it as she continued to fondle the trembling mounds. She could feel Blake's pulse beating, hear her breathing start to catch, smell all of the scents that clung to her clothing after a long day in the kitchen. But hidden in the mash-up of aromas was Blake's own, the one Emily had begun to know from meetings in her office at the beginning of the day, long before the kitchen bathed all of them with its liquor. That scent—the essence of Blake, the one she was savoring on such an intimate level, was truly intoxicating. Emily knew the science of it all. Pheromones and other chemicals gave every body a scent thumbprint. Emily had discovered that she was as particular about a woman's natural scent as she was about food, and Blake's hit her right on the button. Her mouth watered like it did before she took the first bite of something luscious, all because of that delightful scent.

Her head was spinning when she looked up to see Blake lying there, a peaceful, calm, open expression on her face. She was such a beauty. So ripe. So sweet. Those beautiful lips pursed to form a kiss. "Now?" she pouted, her lower lip sticking out playfully. "I've been awfully patient."

Emily moved up to lavish a dozen kisses onto her waiting mouth. They rolled over, nearly falling from the large sofa, but Blake stuck an arm down, stopping them on a dime. Emily reached over and ran her fingers down her bicep. It was perfectly normal looking, not bulky at all, but hard as a rock. *Damn!* Having arms like that with such gorgeous breasts was a double-play she'd never experienced. Her two biggest turn-ons from the same woman. *Fantastic.*

After shifting her hips, Blake had Emily on her back. Hovering over her, she licked and kissed her neck, murmuring, "What do you like? What gets you off?"

"Everything," Emily said, laughing at how true that was at the moment. "But given the time, you'd better use your hand."

"The time?" Her eyes opened wide. "Do you have to be somewhere?"

"The time of day… The distance between right now and when we showered this morning."

"Oh!" She laughed, the sound so relaxed and happy it made Emily smile. "I forgot about that. I'm not a clean freak when it comes to sex but…"

"It's been a long day."

"It has." She leaned in and kissed Emily again, her touch tender and soft. "But we're ending it with a bang."

"Give me that hand," Emily said, taking Blake's hand and urging it into her pants, which had slid half off during their wrestling. Blake's hand moved past her bikinis, quickly finding their target. "Oh, yeah," Emily hissed as the cool fingers settled onto her heated skin. "Touch me any way you want. I'm so into this you could breathe on me and I'd come."

Blake found her mouth again, kissing her and sucking on her tongue as determined fingers skimmed over her clit. It was divine. Emily had seen those hands do everything from make a silky pasta to debone a leg of lamb. She knew they could be strong and determined or teasing and gentle. But when they touched her most intimate flesh, a whole new way of experiencing them filled her. A much, much better way. Stunningly intimate and strangely soothing.

Squirming under her touch, Emily thrust her hips against Blake's searching fingers. She was so aroused it took just seconds before she felt the familiar tension in her belly, then she was over the edge, panting as Blake's fingers slowed, then stopped.

They lay together, their bodies hot and glowing with sweat. Blake kissed her throat, then moved down to nuzzle against her neck. Emily could smell herself on the hand that rested on her shoulder, her after-sex scent always making her want another tumble.

"I didn't even get your jacket off," Blake said. "That's like eating an orange with the peel on."

"Aww…" She forced her head up enough to give her a long, slow kiss. "Who told you to rush?"

"Couldn't help myself. If you were throbbing like I was…"

"At least."

"Yeah," she agreed, smiling. "I could tell you were about to pop when you were trying to swallow my breasts."

Emily laughed at that, having to agree it was true. "I know what I like." Her fingers tried to slide into Blake's pants, but they fit snug against her waist. "How about you?" Emily asked, starting to get serious about finding her way inside. The problem was that Blake didn't have the usual elastic waistband. Her pants were probably custom made, with single buttons on each side. Finally, Emily got one open and found she could move the whole front panel down, allowing her to easily get her hand inside. "Someone forgot her undies today," she teased, as her fingers slid across soft, pliable flesh.

"I wear them off duty, but I don't want to stop the sweat from rolling down my legs at work. It cools me off a little."

Emily brushed her hand across the exposed fabric, finding the waistband was lined with terry cloth. Ingenious! "Where do you get these? I want a pair—stat."

Blake took her hand and stuck it between her legs, grinning wryly. "I'd love to exchange shopping tips, Emily. Maybe *after* you fuck me?"

So typically Blake. A little bit of a smart-ass, always with her eyes on the prize. "I can't wait to feel you," Emily murmured, trying to steer them back into the mood.

"Then let's get going," Blake urged. "I'm about to slide off this sofa."

As her hand slipped into the humid warmth of Blake's body, Emily's clit burst with feeling again. It was like touching herself to let her fingers slide across sizzling hot skin, slick with excitement.

"*Nice*," Blake growled. "I can take all of that you've got to give."

"I could do this for hours. Easily." Her fingers moved everywhere, making Blake twitch. "This is a very nice place you've got here," Emily murmured as she put her mouth to her neck and took a big lick just to lock that scent into her brain again.

Blake grasped her head and held her still as she stared into her eyes. "I had no idea you were so silly." With a tender kiss, she added, "I love that."

Emily didn't say the truth. They'd never had time to goof around, and Blake had never given any indication she wanted to start. "I have many facets to my personality." She shifted down so her fingers eased into Blake's warmth. "I like to keep the ladies guessing."

"Mmm, I'm not guessing." The tip of her tongue emerged and slowly licked her lips. *So* sexy. "I'm loving this."

Emily kept pumping her fingers in and out slowly, making Blake's hips sway and buck. Then a hand pressed her fingers deep inside and held her there as Blake's fingers snuggled next to hers. With a deep groan, Blake began to gently touch herself as she pumped her hips.

"Make yourself come," Emily purred into her ear. "You're so close. So slick and hot…" She sucked Blake's earlobe into her mouth, tickling it with her tongue as the walls of her pussy started to spasm. "So sexy," she murmured, then her fingers were bathed with moisture and Blake's head moved from side to side, like she could hardly stand the sensation, yet needed every bit of it.

"Jesus, you're good at that," she moaned, a sheen of perspiration now covering her. Emily looked down, seeing her coat and bra lying open, two hands shoved down her pants, legs bent and spread. Chef was a hot, sexy mess!

"I could go again," Emily growled, clamping down on Blake's flushed neck.

"Me too. It's almost Christmas," she said, giggling weakly. "Let's have our presents early."

Who knew how much time or how many orgasms later, Emily had gotten her clothing back in order, fixed her ponytail, and made herself as presentable as possible given the circumstances. They were probably not alone. Armando, the overnight steward, came in after midnight to scrub the floor and clean the anti-fatigue mats they stood on. Even though she hadn't heard him, she wasn't about to run into the guy looking like she'd just been thoroughly fucked. "It's late," she said, taking a peek at the clock. "Time for the Sandman."

Blake had moved over to her desk chair once she'd gotten herself in some semblance of order. Then she reached out, grabbed Emily's hand and tugged her onto her lap again. As protective arms wrapped around her, Emily rested her head on her shoulder, then tilted her chin when Blake leaned forward to place a long, sweet kiss upon her lips. It was a strikingly intimate moment, the most touching of the whole night. Then Blake's hands held her cheeks, their eyes locked together for a few seconds. "I haven't enjoyed myself like this in a long, long time. No matter what Santa brings, tonight was my very best present."

"Aww." Her instinct was to say something sappy, but she got hold of herself. This chapter in their lives had been a great one, but it was over.

Instead of saying the wrong thing, she placed one final kiss on Blake's lips, sneaking another sniff of the essence she was going to have to ignore when they came back to work. Just as she was about to get up, she caught sight of the computer monitor. The little sneak had a closed-caption layout of every segment of the kitchen displayed! No wonder she knew all of their secrets! But that still didn't explain the case of the bitter Brussels Sprouts. That remained one for the ages.

"Time to commune with the night-owls," Emily said, squeezing Blake's shoulder as she got to her feet. "You meet the nicest people on the E train at four in the morning."

Blake opened a drawer and pulled out a few bills. "Take a cab. Please."

"No need. I'm used to it. But thanks."

"Sure?" She waved the money under her nose.

"Positive. I'm going to go change."

Blake met her eyes, with a hint of sadness in her gaze. Then she stood and got very close, but they didn't touch. "Are we good? Back to normal?"

"We are perfect." Honoring the distance Blake had chosen, she didn't move toward her, even though she was sorely tempted to give her yet another final kiss. "No strings." The smile Blake gave her showed just a tiny bit of relief, but Emily didn't let that diminish the high she felt. They'd had a great night, and it made no sense to regret that they couldn't have more.

A few minutes later Blake was by the loading dock, supervising a guy who was stacking crates of non-perishables.

"It never stops, does it?" Emily asked.

"No, it never does." Blake extended her hand and Emily shook it. "You did an excellent job on a very challenging day, Emily. I hope you have a great vacation."

"Thanks...Chef. You too." She smiled and moved to the edge of the dock, then jumped down into the alley. Chef? She'd just fucked a woman silly, yet still called her Chef?

The next afternoon, Emily was still in bed, checking her messages before she considered what kind of calorie-laden, inauthentic Chinese food she would fill her empty belly with. The phone rang, startling her. "Hello?"

"Emily? Blake."

"Hi..." Calling her nothing was the safe choice, so she stuck to that.

"You didn't happen to leave me any ideas for specials for New Year's Eve, did you? Like maybe a note I didn't see?"

"No, I didn't." I was too busy deep-throating your breasts!

"Okay. Well, if you get a chance you could text me."

"All right. I'm not thinking clearly right now—"

"No rush," she interrupted. "Just... Well, today would be ideal. I'm taking off and won't have reliable cell service, so I won't be able to call in an order if you think of something we don't normally stock."

Was she supposed to know where she was going? No, she was sure Blake hadn't said. Unless those fantastic breasts had been covering her ears... *Stop that!*

"I did have some ideas. We just... Time got away from us."

"Yeah," she said, sighing. "Happens every day, doesn't it?"

Did she forget what they'd spent hours doing? "I suppose it does. I'll get up and get my brain in gear. Text you later. Merry Christmas, Chef."

"Oh, right! Yeah. Merry Christmas to you too, Emily. Have a good vacation."

Emily let the phone drop to the bed. Then she rolled onto her side and gazed at the silver gray skies for a minute. It was such a god-damned shame. The best sex she'd had in years had been a one-off. Sighing, she tossed her feet to the floor and stood. Her one-off was her boss, and it was time to get back to work.

Chapter Seven

AFTER THEY PICKED HER up at the airport, Emily and her parents drove over to her sister Charlotte's new home. "Is Chuck on call today? You know I haven't seen him in over a year." She chuckled. "I don't know why people insist on having heart attacks when I'm in town."

"Charlotte said she's going to hide his phone and his pager," Carol said. "We haven't seen him for a couple of months, and they live twenty minutes from us. I don't know how they do it."

"They're hard working," Emily said. "I can relate."

"I'm not sure which of my girls works harder," Carol said. "But I wish both of them could cut back."

"Once Charlotte's finished with her residency, she'll have normal hours. There aren't many emergencies for cosmetic dermatologists. As for me…there's no end in sight."

When they pulled up into a big, wide driveway, Emily's breath caught in her throat. Her sister, her *younger* sister, had bought Versailles. Birmingham Michigan's version of it, but still… The house was massive. Truly massive. And the landscaping must have cost as much as a decent college education. But it looked so formal, so theme-parky.

A stand of tall, conical trees, each identical, separated the front lawn from the street, making it more fortress than home-like. Emily couldn't imagine living there, even if it had been located on her street in Queens. Then the image of a big, Provincial style home on her street made her laugh to herself. A new auto repair place would fit in a heck of a lot better.

Charlotte came dashing out, clad in a very expensive ski jacket and jeans. Emily only knew the jacket was expensive because she saw ones like it in store windows in TriBeCa and Soho. Her sister had become one of the upper, upper crust, but she was still her little sister, and she loved her deeply. Charlotte nearly pulled her from the car, then wrapped her in a long hug. "I've missed you," she murmured, then placed kisses on both cheeks. When she grasped Emily by the shoulders, she held her at arm's length. "You look beautiful, Em. Really, really good. Seriously."

That meant she looked overworked, tired, and pasty. Which she did.

After praising the Brazilian cherry floors, Travertine marble baths, four point five of them to be exact, and the five lushly carpeted bedrooms, Emily was led to the kitchen. It was huge, as big as the cold area at work. But this one didn't look like there were often three people standing shoulder to shoulder making desserts and canapés. In fact, it looked unused. There was also not a hint of anything cooking. Weren't they supposed to have dinner?

"Beautiful stove," Emily said, running her hand over a gleaming stainless steel model.

Charlotte beamed. "Professional grade. At least that's what the kitchen designer said."

"Yeah, I'm sure it is." She was actually sure it wasn't. You'd have to be crazy to put a true commercial range in a home. Normal gas service wouldn't be strong enough to power it, you wouldn't have a broiler, and the burners would be so powerful you'd scorch everything. But if Charlotte wanted to believe she had a pro range, what did it hurt to let her think it?

"Once I start working normal hours, I'm going to learn to cook," Charlotte said. "You can come visit and give me a few pointers."

"That's a great idea!" Emily put her arm around her sister and gave her a thump on the head. "Then you can come visit me and give checkups to all of my friends who don't have health insurance."

Despite the beautiful range and massive refrigerator, no food was to come from the kitchen. Chuck treated them all to dinner at a nice spot where the staff seemed to know him and Charlotte well. As they drank the first of what she knew would be several bottles of wine, Chuck said, "How often do you go out to dinner, Em?"

"Every Christmas, when it's your turn to cook," she teased, raising her glass.

"Come on. You live in New York, and you love food more than anyone I've ever met."

"I work six days a week, Chuck. Every week."

"But…"

"Leave her alone," Charlotte warned. She speared a bite of her appetizer, and held the fork to Emily's lips. "Why does this taste so good?"

Emily considered the bite for a moment, letting the individual flavors develop. It was like looking at a well-stocked aquarium. At first you saw only a splash of vivid color, then the fish began to stand out as separate beings. Food had always been that way for her. A wash of sensation, then a sense of clarity as each element emerged.

Once the tastes were sharp and separate, Emily said, "Well, the golden caviar starts you out with that bracing, briny taste, then you get some heat from the jalapeño. The sea bream itself is so fresh it's vaguely sweet, and the Parmesan crust gives you that salty/savory kick that lingers for a while. It's just careful layering by a cook who knows how to make flavor profiles work together."

"I wish I understood food like you do," Charlotte said. "I guess you inherited mom's palate."

"And you got dad's scientific mind. We both did well for ourselves." They might have vastly unequal earnings potential, but Emily wouldn't have changed jobs with Charlotte, and she was pretty sure her sister felt the same way.

During the drive back to Detroit, Emily's dad, who'd had just one glass of wine, spoke quietly, trying not to wake her mom, who'd had several. "You don't ever regret your decision to become a chef, do you, honey?"

He was so transparent. "I assume you're really asking if I'm jealous of Charlotte's husband, BMW, mansion and bank account?"

He shot her a worried look in the rearview mirror. "I suppose that is what I'm asking."

"No, dad, I don't." She reached forward and gave his shoulder a squeeze. "I'd love her bank account, for sure. But medical school didn't grab me like I thought it would. I'd much rather do what I love and be poor."

"I worry about you, Em. What if something unexpected happens? Your mom and I would help in any way we could, but we've got to save every dime for retirement."

"I'm doing fine, dad. Admittedly, I don't have much savings, but I can easily afford my apartment."

"We went to dinner over at the Hastings' the other night. Melinda's back home, with two kids and no job. Mike and Elaine are stuck paying off her credit cards."

"Why don't they let her go bankrupt? You shouldn't have to bail your kids out when they're over thirty."

"They're not those kinds of people." The scowl he bore showed he wasn't that kind of person either. "Melinda married a jerk who left her when her chronic fatigue got worse. It's no one's fault she's in a bind." He fixed Emily with a look. "You're keeping up your health insurance, right?"

"Of course."

"It's a good policy? You're sure?"

"I'm sure, Dad."

His gaze hit her again, and she could tell he was more worried than he'd let on. "I've held up my end of the deal we struck years ago. I've never given you a hard time about how little you earn, but you've got to maintain that policy."

"The deal's solid, dad. My policy costs ten percent of my after tax income, but it's the best available. As long as I can work, I'm good."

"Your job doesn't provide any kind of disability insurance?"

Chuckling, she said, "Charlotte's my disability insurance. If I'm unable to work, I'll come be her personal chef. She could easily afford to pay me as much as I make now."

His expression grew even sadder, touching her heart. “I wish you made more, honey. It’s just not fair to work like you do for so little.”

“If I ever get my own restaurant, I’ll do better. Not a lot, mind you, but enough so that I can afford to have just Chase for a roommate.”

The drive seemed to take a long time. Or maybe it was the worried frown on her dad’s face that made it seem much longer than it really was.

On Christmas Eve, Emily sat at the family table, surrounded by her nearest and dearest. Her mom’s sister Sarah was sitting next to her, and when the table was particularly noisy she leaned over and quietly said, “Your mom never tells me anything about your personal life. Who are you dating?”

“No one.” She shrugged. “I’m one of the many, many single cooks in New York. We should form a union.”

Now even quieter, she said, “Then who are you sleeping with? I know you’re not going without.”

Emily laughed. Having an aunt only fifteen years older than you had its benefits. Sarah had been a great resource when Emily was a teenager and had questions she was too embarrassed to ask her parents. Now? It was sometimes awkward, but she was well used to the invasive questions. “I’ve been on a pretty long dry spell.” She paused for effect. “But I had a great vacation send off on my last night at work.”

“Co-worker?”

“Uh-huh. There was a party after work, and we kept partying when everyone else left. You know how it is…”

“I used to,” she said, giving her husband a pointed glance. “I hope it’s clear I’m jealous.”

“Being single isn’t all it’s cracked up to be, Sarah.”

“Neither is being married. You know I love Mark, but I miss the variety. Any chance for more with this co-worker?”

“Doubtful. We texted the next day, and she didn’t even mention it. All business.”

Empathy filled her voice. “Ooo, are you okay with that?”

"Oh, sure. We had a great time, but it's not possible to have an affair with a co-worker when you're with them fourteen hours a day. It'd be a mess."

"But you had a *great* time?" Sarah asked, eyes twinkling with interest.

Emily thought of Blake's breasts and the way they shook as her excitement grew. "Really great," she said, sighing when she considered that she'd likely never get the chance to taste them again. That was a damned shame. Like locking the Mona Lisa in a closet.

Emily strolled into work on New Year's Eve at her usual time, surprised to see Blake pacing across the main kitchen, still in her civilian clothes, with her cell phone glued to her ear. She didn't look up when Emily passed by to go to the locker room, but Emily had studied her during her short walk from the loading dock. Blake had clearly been somewhere warm and sunny during their break. Her skin was surprisingly tan, eyes bright, even her haircut was fresh and bouncy. But she was at work super early, and was already so focused she appeared to be in another world.

Just minutes after arriving, the joint started jumping. Most everyone was in early, and by eleven they were flying around like maniacs. It was a darned good thing they were all rested, because tonight was going to be a shit show. Two hundred and fifty covers, with very few reservations before seven p.m. Strap in, hold on, and get ready to jump.

Their super-star owner Vincenzo didn't appear, but the other three partners and their wives showed up at eight. At eight oh one they sent Thierry in to ask Blake to come out. She let out a frustrated groan, but marched for the door, grumbling, "Cover me, Grant."

"Oui, Chef!"

Emily could see the smirk begin to grow. He loved the fact that Blake always tagged him to plate and expedite. But Emily sternly reminded herself not to be jealous. Why ask for more work?

Blake came barreling back into the kitchen after spending a good forty-five minutes with their PPXs. "They think the food just appears," she groused before insinuating herself back into her position. "Firing—two beef, rare, for table nine."

"Oui, Chef," Jameson said as he tossed perfectly weighed portions into searingly hot pans.

Blake was still mumbling something to herself as she reached for the next chit. The PPXs must have really gotten under her skin, and it didn't take long to find out why. A guy strolled into the kitchen like he owned it, which he apparently did. He paused in the doorway for a moment, almost getting a tray-full of dirty dishes dumped onto him when Meb, one of the commis du rang, flew in from clearing a table. The guy jumped, then nearly plastered himself to Blake at the pass.

Emily watched out of the corner of her eye, tempted to tell the guy to give Blake some elbow room. But if he had the guts to stand at the center of the action in a swamped kitchen on the busiest night of the year, he was too dumb to take a suggestion.

He was tall and thin and had the narrow-shouldered look of a guy who'd made his copious amounts of money sitting at a desk. But even though he didn't have a distinctive affect, he was no shrinking violet. "Listen," he said, talking loud enough to be heard over the cacophony of the kitchen. "I'm not fucking around. I'm sick of your blowing me off every time I ask you to do me a favor."

"I'm not blowing you off," she said, her voice gentle even through gritted teeth. "I'm working."

"Well, I need you to *work* at this festival. You owe me."

She didn't look up. Taking her tweezers, she delicately lined up tiny slivers of zucchini, then grabbed a squeeze bottle filled with zucchini puree and made a dot atop each one, making them look like a series of "i"s. With cubes of roasted potatoes placed next to them and a square portion of Kobe beef nestled alongside, everything lined up harmoniously. The fact that she'd plated the dish in less than a minute while a guy stood right behind her peering over her shoulder showed how acute her powers of concentration were.

"Pickup! Table three."

"Did you hear me?" the guy asked. He seemed like the kind of fellow who everyone listened to, whether they wanted to or not.

"Of course. But I can't afford to take off three days to go to Aspen. I'm needed here."

"This restaurant will never get to the next level if you don't market it." He was clearly frustrated with her, but Blake didn't stop or look at him. Instead she called the next order and began plating the cold lobster first course Emily had just passed her.

"Don't you care?" he demanded loudly.

Emily saw her pause for half a second, her calm, sure hands hovering over the lobster. Even though the kitchen was noisy, Emily swore she could hear her take in a heavy breath.

"I care about this restaurant more than you can imagine," she said quietly.

"Then show it! The more publicity you get, the better the restaurant does."

"Not true. The better the food, the better the restaurant. I have a very good team, but I know the quality is better when I'm here. Now if you'd like to hire a chef de cuisine and send me to every food festival in the world..."

"The restaurant's not throwing off that kind of money and you know it. So your staff's going to have to keep the place running."

She looked like she was about to snap. To take one of those heavy pans and do a replay of her Brussels Sprouts drop kick. But her voice was calm and modulated when she spoke again. "If I thought I wasn't needed here, I'd find another job. I'll go to any festival in the world, Chad, without complaint. But I'll close the restaurant while I'm gone."

He reached in front of her and snatched an oyster April had just sent to the pass. After slurping it down, he wiped his mouth with the back of his hand. "We didn't back you because of how you cook. We put up two million bucks because of your face and your..." Emily couldn't stop herself from shifting her eyes to look at him, finding his focus locked onto Blake's chest—a cheap, slimy move so blatantly offensive that she almost slapped him on Blake's behalf.

Chad tossed the oyster shell onto the floor and strode back out of the room, leaving behind a red-faced, shaking Blake. But her voice was calm and level when she said, "Refresh the oysters for table two, please." Then her steel-toed clog cracked against the base of the pass, making the whole structure shiver. Chad would never know how close he'd come to needing a cast on his shin, nor would he learn how it felt to have a bowl of seafood truffle tagliatelle dumped onto his head by a fiercely protective sous chef who'd just barely controlled herself.

They worked, without pause, until one thirty, when the last order spit out. "Order—fire—one chocolate torte." A heavy sigh left Blake's lips. "We're out."

"Happy fucking New Year," Grant panted before sliding down the length of the refrigerator behind him. He sat on the floor, splay-legged, taking up much of his work area. Jameson and Cleveland stepped over him as they started to break down their stations, neither one of them seeming to notice he was there.

"I'd grab a couple of bottles of Champagne for us, but I'm too tired to drink," Blake muttered to herself. Louder now, she said, "I'm sure most of you will go out. Just remember it's amateur night out there, people. Be careful."

"Oui, Chef," a discordant, weak reply came back.

"Excellent work tonight, everyone. Most of our guests drank too much to notice the food, but we gave them some terrific dishes."

Blake started at the prep kitchen to shake everyone out, then made her way around, finally stopping at Grant, who hadn't moved. She tapped him on the thigh, and then the shin with the toe of her clog.

"I assume your inability to get up shows you'd rather I didn't go to food festivals every damn weekend?"

"Oui, Chef. Please don't ever leave us alone."

She shook the hand he lethargically lifted, then plucked off his soggy cap and dropped it onto his lap. "Thanks for stepping up tonight,

Grant. I wasn't telling the truth earlier. I know you and Emily can run the place. It's just not fair to ask the two of you to do the work of three."

"Thank you," he said, looking up at her and offering a weak smile.

"You're welcome." She moved over to Emily and took her hand. "Good job tonight. Aren't you glad we have tomorrow off?"

"Oui, oui, oui, Chef."

"I'll see you all on Saturday," she said, waving as she went into her office, closing the door behind her—the first time she'd ever done that at end of service.

Emily cast a quick glance at that closed door. What Blake had said about drawing a bright line between sex and work wasn't BS. Emily was one hundred percent certain no one in the kitchen suspected a thing. If she hadn't been there, even she wouldn't have believed she and Blake had been bumping boots in that office just two weeks earlier. Maybe it *had* been a dream!

A January cold snap calmed traffic at the restaurant by about twenty percent. Given that none of the staff had a financial stake in the business, they enjoyed the chance to breathe a little. At ten o'clock one Monday night, Emily noted that the printer hadn't made a sound for five minutes. Catching Grant's eye, she said, "You can handle things, right?"

He nodded, looking slightly puzzled.

"Then I'm going to take off."

"Good idea," Blake said, not taking her eyes off the desserts she was fussing over. "You're putting in too many hours. Pick-up, table eight!"

"I'll text you some ideas for first courses on my way home," Emily said. "If that's okay."

"Perfect. Ordering! Two cheese plates!"

Pleased to have Blake's permission, Emily rushed toward the locker room, trying to skedaddle before a big group of hungry fish lovers wandered in, forcing her to stay.

As she hit the loading dock she started to shiver. It was bitterly cold, with the icy wind finding its way to her overheated body through her coat collar. Her sister had given her a really nice winter scarf, but she hated to have it wrapped around her sweaty neck, so she'd left it at home.

The subway was only a few blocks away, and for a change all of her fellow passengers weren't restaurant workers, musicians or cleaning crews. Tonight she was surrounded by well-dressed people who'd been to the theatre or out to dinner. Weird, but nice.

On the walk home from the subway, she stopped and bought a bottle of wine. She and Chase could spend a whole hour together before she had to crash. After dropping her things at the door, she walked down the hallway to find his door closed. Someone, not Chase, was moaning, and definitely not from pain. Smiling to herself, she snuck down the hall, careful not to make a sound. It looked like both she and Chase had ended their dry spells.

The next morning, Emily was particularly chipper when she sailed into the kitchen through the loading dock. Getting an extra hour of sleep had given her an extra bounce in her step, and she resolved to punch out early whenever possible.

She'd begun to take more initiative, starting, without getting the all clear, to work on first courses that were variations of French classics, dishes Blake always jumped on. Why wait to have the meeting if she knew the dish would be approved? She rolled up her sleeves and began to work on her mise for rillettes of duck. She thought she'd work some cranberries into the dish, maybe a compote to intensify their flavor. Lost in her work, she barely looked up when Blake passed by. But when Emily sensed her presence and stood up straight to shake her hand, both of them glanced at the empty station next to Brady.

Fuck!

Alicia was late again. Blake didn't say a word, but her expression darkened in a heartbeat, then she turned and went to her office, leaving Emily to worry.

She looked at the clock every ten minutes, silently begging the talented cook to get her butt in gear. Well after one, a burst of cold air heralded Alicia's entry. Looking like she was headed for the executioner, she approached Emily. "I'm *so* sorry," she moaned. "I swear it won't happen again. I changed the locks on my apartment to keep him out, but my boyfriend came over early this morning and caused a scene. Somebody called the police and..."

"Alicia!" Blake's voice boomed from her office.

A panicked look flashed across the young woman's face, and her cocoa-colored skin paled in seconds. There was nothing Emily could say and even less that she could do. Alicia turned and walked, lead-footed, to the office. She'd been inside for what seemed like seconds when she emerged and jogged for the rear doors, her sobs echoing against the stainless steel.

"Did you have to fire her?" Emily demanded as she found herself standing in front of Blake's desk, glaring at her.

"I did." She didn't look up from her paperwork. "You'll have to find someone new."

"By tonight?" Her voice had gotten shrill, but she couldn't temper it.

Slowly, Blake looked up, her face expressionless. "That would be a good idea. Then *you* won't have to be the entremet."

Furious, Emily stormed back to her rillettes. She'd like to take her duck legs and beat the stuffing out of Blake with them. Now she was going to have to make two first courses, then prep and cook the sides for seven entrées, all the while keeping an eye on Brady. That shit-fest would continue until she found a replacement for Alicia, which would take days, if not a week. Fuck Blake and her fucking high horse!

At midnight, Emily started to scrub her station. It had been a while since she'd had to work the line, but the work itself wasn't bad. It was actually kind of nice to get into the rhythm of cooking under pressure. Once you settled in, consistency was all you cared about, and she was justifiably proud of the fact that not one dish had come back to her, even with Blake, the super-taster, at the pass.

Even though she didn't mind cooking, she hated cleaning up. Clouds of steam bloomed in her face as she poured hot, soapy water onto the flattop and started to scrub. A tap on the shoulder made her turn her head to see Blake, one eyebrow raised. "When you're finished…?"

"Give me ten."

"No problem."

Sure. No problem for her. She could sit on her butt and relax. Hell, she could have a shot of that good Scotch and put her feet up. Emily's blood pressure rose as she continued to sulk. Finally, she finished scrubbing and got the whole station dried. Then she strode over to the office and knocked on the frame before entering. "You wanted to see me?"

"Door."

Now even more annoyed, Emily shut it and sat down. "Yes?" It sounded like she'd spit the word out.

"I know you're angry that you have to work her station, but I think you're also pissed that I fired Alicia."

"I am."

Blake leaned over a little, getting closer, dark eyes clearly puzzled. "Why?"

"Why? She's a kid who's gotten into a relationship she can't get out of. It's got to be bad if her neighbors are calling the police on the guy!"

"I didn't know that." She looked down, obviously troubled.

"How could you? You spent five seconds firing her. She couldn't have had time to explain things to you."

Slowly, their eyes met. "It wouldn't have mattered."

"What kind of attitude is that? She's a person, not a machine! Alicia's a very talented cook who needs a little time to get her life sorted out."

"That's probably true, but I don't have time for her to get things sorted out *here*," Blake said, her dark eyes boring into Emily. "I'm sorry she's in a bad relationship, but last year she had a bad roommate who turned off the alarm one morning. The next time she was late it was because she'd gone out and gotten drunk the night before." Her arms crossed over her chest, making her look even less sympathetic. "Every member of this staff has issues, but Alicia let hers take precedence. That's not fair to the rest of us."

"That's too cold-blooded for me. If this were my kitchen, I'd be more understanding."

An icy cold expression settled onto Blake's face. "Well, it's not your kitchen, is it. And one thing the rest of the staff seems to understand is that we're all in this together. If you don't pull your weight, every day, you're out."

Emily stood, her legs tingling with unspent anger. "Oh, I understand your rules."

Blinking, Blake said, "But I don't think you understand why they matter."

After grasping the door knob, Emily said, "What difference does that make? This isn't a democracy." With that, she strode toward the locker room. If she'd stayed for another minute, she'd be joining Alicia on the unemployment line.

She and Chase didn't run into each other until Thursday, when Emily came dragging in at one, clutching a bottle of Scotch. It wasn't particularly good Scotch, but it was 90 proof, plenty of alcohol to chill her out with a minimum of effort.

Tired as she was, she smiled when she heard him call out as she walked down the hall. "Do you fly in an airplane, or cook at a stove?"

Turning into the living room, she tossed her bag onto the sofa. "I feel like I use a small shovel to dig a hole for six hours every morning, then I spend my evening filling it." She dropped to sit next to him and let her head loll upon his shoulder.

He wriggled his arm to pull it out and wrap it around her properly. "Is my bestie having a bad day?"

After pulling her tote over, she tugged the Scotch out of the paper bag, opened the bottle, then put it to her mouth and let a little trickle in. Dramatically wiping her mouth with the back of her hand, she said, "Why would you ask that?"

He got up, having to move her to free himself, then stood in front of her with his hands on his hips. "I'm getting you a glass, then you're going to tell me all about it." As he walked toward the kitchen he added, "I'll get two glasses. I know you hate to drink alone."

"If I'd had this on the subway, it'd be half gone by now," she grumbled.

When he returned, he grasped her hands and pulled her to her feet. "Off with the coat," he instructed. "We're civilized adults. We can't sit in our apartment and drink with our coat on." He tickled under her chin, making her giggle.

After she dropped her coat to the floor, she reached behind herself and unhooked her bra. They didn't parade around naked, but they'd come to treat each other like they hadn't hit puberty yet, with neither one shy about acting like they would with a close friend of the same sex.

Emily collapsed again, leaning against Chase's body as he poured a finger of Scotch into each glass and handed one to her. They touched the rims of the glasses, then she eased a little of the calming balm into her mouth. "Not great, but full of alcohol."

"Tell me," he said, his voice now soft and understanding.

She slowly took in and blew out a breath, snuggled a little deeper into his body and said, "Blake fired my vegetable chef."

"She fired Alicia?" His warm breath flowed over her, making her smile. It was *so* nice to have a friend who cared enough to remember the names of your co-workers.

"Yeah. I don't know the details, but her neighbors called the cops on her boyfriend after she changed the locks."

"Oh, fuck," he said, almost whispering. "What's she going to do? Is there a women's shelter nearby?"

Emily's stomach flipped at that. "I didn't ask," she admitted. "She walked in two hours late and walked out in less than a minute. I was going to call but…"

"Call her in the morning. Before you get swamped."

Shuddering, she said, "It'll have to be before I leave the house. I've got to do her job until I can find a replacement. The agency hasn't given me a single candidate, and this happened on Monday."

"How does that work? Do they have a bunch of people in chef's coats sitting in a room, waiting for a call?"

"Yeah. Just like those goofy talent agencies in the old movies." She laughed at the image. "Where there's a guy spinning plates, and a singer running through scales, and tap-dancing triplets with a crazy mother yelling at them."

He elbowed her playfully. "Seriously. Is there a union hall or something?"

"Most places use an agency. You used to be able to call them at nine and have anyone from a chef de partie all the way down to an assistant dishwasher knocking at the door by noon. No longer."

"The agency is no longer...?"

"Oh, no," she said, shaking her head. "They're still there and they'll find me someone. But it's taking longer than it used to." She took another sip of her Scotch. "The emperor not only has no clothes, he's worked himself to death."

"Translation?"

"Fewer people are willing to work as hard as we do for as little money. When I graduated from the CIA, I had to fight to stage at a place."

"That means work for free, right?"

"Uh-huh. But people aren't fighting for jobs any more. A lot of them don't even want to get promoted. They know they won't get much more money to become a sous chef, so why not remain a chef de partie? You have less responsibility and much less stress."

"Uhm...okay, I'll bite. Why not remain a chef de partie?"

She thought about her answer for a few moments, really mulling it over. "If you love it," she said, "you want more. More responsibility, more control, more power. You can't wait until you have your own place and can create a restaurant that reflects you." She gave him a sidelong glance, finished her Scotch and settled back against his body. "I worry that the bloom is off the rose. People got into watching famous chefs on TV, thinking they could work in a kitchen and soon have legions of adoring fans. That was never true, but we've had a long spell where people thought it was."

"Uhm…what happens if you're right?"

"Quality will suffer if salaries don't go up or hours don't go down. I can't guess which will happen, but I can't see people paying twenty to thirty percent more for restaurant meals. It's already ridiculously expensive to go out to a good quality place."

"Maybe restaurants will have to get leaner and meaner. I mean, that Pakistani place we like doesn't have anything on the menu over ten bucks. And that stuff is *good*."

"Yeah, maybe," she said, sinking down a little as a wave of lethargy hit her hard. "But I don't dream of making the same ten things every night. That would just be a job."

"You're an artist," Chase said, sounding so damn sure of himself. "You'll get past this little bump in the road and get right back to loving it."

She patted him firmly as she got to her feet. "I hope you're right. If not, bury me with my knives in my hands. I want to be remembered as someone who didn't go down without a fight."

As the search for the perfect entremetier continued, Grant earned a lasting place in her heart by stepping up to prep more of the first courses. Even though she knew she'd do the same for him, Emily was touched by the gesture. On Saturday morning, bone tired and listless, she sat at the desk at nine a.m., waiting for the guy she'd just interviewed to change into his whites. His resume was solid, but she had to make sure he knew his way around a side dish, so she was going to give him a few challenges and let him run with them.

The office phone rang and she picked up. "Kitchen."

"Emily? It's Alicia."

"Hey! How are you?" A wave of guilt washed over her. She'd spaced on making the call, even though she reminded herself every night when she got into bed.

"Good. Really good. I was calling to thank Chef for getting me in over at the Oxford House."

"You're at a hotel?"

"Uh-huh. It's a union job. With benefits," she added, sounding gleeful.

"I…I had no idea she'd done that."

"I didn't ask her to. She just did it."

"That's great, Alicia. Want me to have her call you?"

"She won't want to. Just tell her I called to thank her, okay?"

"Sure. Will do. Be well." She glared at the phone for a minute. Alicia had certainly landed on her feet—with help.

After service that night, Emily knocked on Blake's door. "Do you have a minute?"

"Sure." She looked up, but didn't show any expression. "I don't need help with Monday's menu, if that's why you're here."

Emily entered and sat down. "It's not. Alicia called today to thank you for getting her a hotel job."

"Oh, good. I thought she'd fit in there." A small smile made her mouth curl at the corners. "They'll be more understanding if she's late once in a while. With so many cooks, they can cover more easily."

"Did you know you were going to help her out when I was in here the other day bitching at you?"

Her smile grew wider. "Uh-huh. I always try to help if the person's not an asshole. Why?"

"Because if you'd told me that I might not have been so bitchy."

Blake leaned back in her chair and gazed at her for a moment. "Those were separate issues." Her voice softened and she rested her arms on the desk as she sat upright. The tone she used reminded Emily of the way her father spoke to her when she'd done something particularly dumb. "When even one member of a small staff can't follow the rules, it makes the others resentful. You've never worked in a poorly managed, chaotic kitchen, have you."

"No, I guess I haven't."

"Well, I have. I went from staging at a place where you had to stand at attention, to one where you could smoke or sneak a sip of pastis at your station if you wanted to."

Emily let that sink in for a moment, then circled back. "Did you honestly have to stand at attention?"

A slow smile made Blake's eyes close. "Sure did. When you weren't actively working you had to stand in front of your station, hands clasped behind your back, waiting to jump into action."

"That's…" Emily couldn't think of a word to characterize it.

"It was the way they'd been doing things for hundreds of years. I thought that's how things were everywhere, but at my next job the inmates were running the asylum. It *sucked*," she emphasized. "I try to be somewhere between those poles. Not too rigid, but no-nonsense about the rules I think are most important. I don't bend those rules for *any*one. Every member of the staff knows them from their first day. Including Alicia."

Emily nodded. "You're right. She knew." She stood and lingered by the door for a second. "I'm glad you gave her a hand. She's going to be a good chef when she gets her personal life in order."

"I think so too. She's only twenty-two, you know. I'll bet she's got everything under control within three years." She stood and reached over to grab a very long knit scarf and start winding it around her neck. "Are you going to hire the guy you tested today?"

"Can't. He didn't have a shred of creativity. I've got to keep looking."

Her lower lip stuck out for a second, then she nodded. "We'll do fewer specials while you're on the line. I know you're about to drop."

"I'll live."

"Then come in later. Eleven's early enough."

"No, it really isn't." She smiled, touched by Blake's concern. "I get a lot of work done between ten and eleven. I can't make the staff suffer so I can get an extra hour of sleep."

Blake stood and gave her shoulder a squeeze. "I was wrong when I said you didn't understand why my rules mattered. You clearly do." She turned her and pushed her out the door. "Take a longer weekend. Come in at four on Monday. I'll take over for you in the morning and check in the deliveries, do the ordering, and come up with the first courses."

"But…"

"No buts. I don't want to see you before four."

"My mise…"

"I've prepped more mise than I care to admit. Being an entremetier for an afternoon won't kill me."

Emily turned and gave her a grateful smile. "I can't tell you how much I appreciate that. I'm running on fumes."

"We're a team, Emily. That means we succeed or fail together."

CHAPTER EIGHT

THE FOLLOWING WEEK, KERMIT, the brand new entremetier, stood next to Brady. He was a tall, muscular kid from Brooklyn, just twenty, with no true line cook experience. But both of his parents, Jamaican by birth, worked in restaurants, exposing him thoroughly to restaurant life. For training, he'd gone to one of the city's culinary arts high schools, completing several externships. Since he'd graduated, he'd spent a year as a commis at a well regarded place in Ft. Greene, then had been promoted to garde manger. That was a very quick progression, yet the chef he worked for had written a glowing recommendation, saying he thought Kermit was ready to move up again.

The kid kept up all day, and seemed to appreciate it when Emily corrected his technique. That was often tough for a young guy to accept, but he didn't appear to be overly headstrong, which was a big plus in her book.

To keep an eye on him, Emily had him help with the complicated first course she was making. It was a very fussy dish, with three different herbs resting upon a foamy emulsion enveloping barely cooked cockles. Kermit bent over the dish, using a short, ungainly pair of tweezers he'd probably borrowed from his mother's makeup kit.

Emily pulled her forceps from her breast pocket and handed them over. "If you use these, you can stand up a little straighter. Your back will thank you."

He looked so relieved she almost laughed. "I'll clean them and get them back to you as soon as service is over."

"They're a gift," she said, clapping him on the back. "You're in the big leagues now and you need professional tools."

"Yes, Chef," he said, so earnest she had to fight the urge to hug him. Working together, they finished the dish early and he once again warmed her heart when he took out his phone and took a photo. "I want to show my dad," he said, grinning.

Minutes later, Emily, Blake and Grant stood in the dining room, where Grant did his sales pitch on the specials. There was a new face in the crowd, a tall, sexy brunette. Every time Emily looked up, the woman was giving either her or Blake the once-over. Hmm...a new server who might like the ladies. Things were looking up.

As they headed back to the kitchen, Blake leaned over and whispered, "I saw her first," then let out a low chuckle. Apparently she really meant it when she said she could have sex with no strings attached. But that was cool. Nice, really. Emily started to formulate a plan for how to get the rush on the new hire. If she wound up on Blake's sofa, the battle might be lost.

Emily would never admit this to Blake, but Kermit was going to be better than Alicia. He and Brady very quickly worked out their cues, allowing them to silently communicate speed and pacing. Alicia had been good, darned good, but Kermit was going to surpass her. Emily could easily see him moving up to her job in a few years, and that gave her a boost. She'd had to hire a number of people at Henri, but Kermit was going to be the best of the bunch.

To urge both of her guys to stretch, she'd started asking them to suggest a first course or a main every day. Letting their creative instincts show through was the best way to help them progress.

Near the end of January, Emily went into Blake's office after service on Saturday night and handed over a list with three entrées and four first courses neatly written down. "For Monday," she said. "I guarantee you'll like every one of them. Not a single re-tread."

"Impressive," Blake said, after studying the list for a minute. "When did you have time?"

"I've got my guys helping out." She sat, then removed her baker's cap, something she often forgot to do until she got to the loading dock. "It's fun to watch them compete to impress me. I can see why people like to be mentors."

"It's one of the best parts of being in charge." She set her chin in her hand and let out a sigh. You could rarely tell that she was tired, but tonight she couldn't hide it. The droopy eyes and pasty pallor were a dead giveaway. "Are you hungry?"

There was a transition period between work and life, and it often took Emily a few minutes to start noticing things like fatigue or hunger or thirst. She was slightly surprised when she found herself nodding. "I really am. Did we eat today?"

"No," Blake said, with a wry smile. "Grant got behind because of that damned quiche that didn't set right, and he never had time to make the family meal. One of us could have stepped up, but he's too proud to ask for help." She leaned back in her chair and let out a loud yawn. "By the time I noticed, it was too late to get anything together."

"And I was too busy to notice I hadn't eaten. I should have remembered when I saw Kermit gulping down a burrito he must have gotten at a bodega." Emily stretched out, sticking her legs in front of her to relieve some of the stress that always settled in her lower back. "When I tell people I'm a chef, they always say they'd be fat if they were in a kitchen all day. They don't realize we usually only lick the backs of spoons as food passes by us."

"I didn't lick one spoon tonight, so I'm more hungry than usual." Her voice took on a dreamy quality as her eyes lost their sharp focus. "I used to crave protein at the end of service, but lately I've wanted something rich. I must need calories."

"I think you've lost a few pounds." Emily didn't want to say how often she'd checked her out when she bent over to pick something up.

"You could use a few calories yourself." She pointed at the mini refrigerator in the corner. "Open that fridge and see what we can liberate."

Ooo! The sacred stash! Emily yanked the door open and started to remove a couple of paper-wrapped packages. "We got some great stuff from our cheesemonger yesterday. I meant to think of a way to show these off, but time got away from me."

"Screw it," Blake said, her eyes dancing. She pointed at the cheese in Emily's left hand. "If that's what I think it is, I might eat the whole wheel. You can put everything else back."

Emily slapped a two pound wheel of cheese on the desk. "Goat's milk. Cave aged—"

"From Île de France," Blake said, looking like she'd drool. "The farm is surprisingly close to Paris. I've seen the goats myself."

"I just bet you have."

Blake jumped to her feet. "I need honey and walnuts for this one. Be right back."

"A couple of glasses of ale wouldn't hurt," Emily called after her.

"Done. Get your taste buds ready."

It took Blake a few minutes to find everything, but she returned with cold bottles of Scottish ale, a bowl of walnuts and another with honey pooled in the bottom. "I can taste it already," she said, excitement bubbling from her.

"This is half the reason I became a chef," Emily said as she placed chunks of the cheese on the extra plate Blake had carried in. "I love to feed people, but I really love to eat with people who crave good food as much as I do."

"Same here. Some of the best times of my life have been hanging out with other cooks, ripping through the larder at some late-night spot."

Nodding, Emily said, "The guys at Henri liked to get together and eat every once in a while, but people here are all about drinking."

"I've noticed that. Maybe they're just at that age." She picked up a wedge of cheese and dropped it into her mouth. Emily watched her jaw move up and down slowly, then her head fell to the desk. "I'm sure goats aren't crazy about being milked every day, but I appreciate their sacrifice. God damn, Emily, this is epic."

Emily put a piece into her mouth and let the layers of flavor bathe her taste buds. She didn't realize she was groaning with delight until Blake started to laugh.

"There isn't much difference between sex and food, is there."

"Not when they're both top notch." After dipping a walnut into the honey, she let it rest on her tongue for a moment. "Good, good, good. It pulls out some flavors I missed before."

Blake slugged down a hefty amount of her beer. "Great idea about the ale. I don't drink beer very often, but when it's the right choice, it's truly the right choice."

"You'd better have been teasing when you said you might eat this whole wheel. I will fight for this shit." Emily popped another hunk into her mouth, shivering with pleasure. "Cheese is my favorite thing in the world. I'd give up just about anything before cheese—alcohol, chocolate, even French fries."

Blake chuckled. "I love French fries too. Twice cooked. Preferably in lard."

"Mmm…lard." She grabbed another piece of cheese. "Now I want something cooked in lard. Stop putting ideas in my head!"

"Drink up," Blake said, starting to wrap up the cheese. "We're going to go get a real meal."

"We are?" Emily gulped the rest of her beer, then slapped a hand over her mouth to partially cover a burp. "Where?"

"Mmm…" Blake's eyes were half-closed in thought. "I know just the place."

Emily didn't ask for details. She hurried for the locker room to shed her chef's clothes, then got back into a heavy sweater and jeans. When she came out, Blake was in her usual—jeans and a crisply pressed blouse, this one blue plaid. A thin, slim-fitting, black down parka seemed too light for the weather, but the wool scarf wrapped around her neck in the perfect French style would help. "I'll pay for the cab," Blake said as they exited the restaurant and she locked up.

"No subways close to where we're going?"

She chuckled. "I don't even know all of the subway lines. There might be one right next door." When they got to the street, she stuck her arm into the air at the first cab whose white light was on. He pulled over and they got in, with Blake giving the guy the cross streets she was looking for.

"That's four blocks from here," Emily said quietly. "Do your legs work?"

"Only in the kitchen." Given the journey was so short, Blake leaned back and stretched out, clearly assuming she didn't need to supervise the driver like she had last time.

They arrived in minutes, and when they entered a dark, quiet bistro, Blake headed for the rear of the building. Emily watched, stunned, when she strode right into the kitchen through swinging doors. Moments later, Blake's laugh rang out, then another, deeper laugh joined hers. She emerged with her arm around a young guy, both of them smiling like old friends. "Emily, this is Gustavo Gallegos. He had your job two years ago, and now he's the chef de cuisine here, feeding cooks until the wee hours."

"Good to meet you, Emily," he said. "Blake's got our number. We're open 'til two, and I'd bet half of our late night diners are cooks and servers." He looked up as the hostess approached. "Put these two near the kitchen so I can come out and talk."

As they moved to a table, Blake said to the woman, "Sorry I blew past you. Sometimes I forget to be polite."

"No problem," she said, probably well used to the eccentric behavior of cooks. "Can I get you something to drink?"

"Do you have a hearty ale?"

"We do. Two?"

"Why not?" Emily said.

By the time their beers came, they were spreading marrow onto crunchy French bread. "I'm going to regret this in the morning, but this is so good I'm not going to think about the repercussions," Emily said.

Blake took a big bite, and spoke around the food that nearly filled her mouth. "Are you saying it's not a good idea to gulp down cheese and beer and marrow at one in the morning?"

"I don't think the surgeon general includes any of that on his list of healthy choices. But I got my vegetables by licking the back of a spoon a hundred times tonight." She burped again, not bothering to hide it. "I have a pretty hearty constitution, but rich food isn't always my friend."

At Blake's raised eyebrow, she added, "Sometimes it leaves the premises quickly."

"Ahh. I must have convinced my digestive track not to screw with me. I can put just about anything down there and have it stay the proper length of time."

Emily almost followed up with more details, then decided it might not be a super idea to talk about digestive troubles with someone you wanted to sleep with again—like in the next hour.

A server appeared with plates piled high with French fries, a strip steak and a bowl of mussels. "I've got your vegetable right here," Blake said, snatching a fry so hot steam was coming off it. She popped it into her mouth and blew around it so she could chew. "Damn, that's good. Potato, fat and salt. A trio you can't beat."

"Ketchup?" the server asked.

"No!" they said, in unison, both breaking up as the server shrugged and walked away. Emily grabbed a fry and ate it quickly so it burned her mouth the minimal amount of time. "I don't understand why you'd smother a perfectly cooked potato in ketchup."

"Don't look at me. I like ketchup on some things, but not if it's too sweet. I make a good one in July and August when I can get local tomatoes."

Emily carved a bite of steak off and slid it into her mouth. "Mmm-mmm. We should use Gustavo's purveyor. This is excellent."

"We do. Gustavo does these sous vide, then fires them just long enough to develop a crust. We could do that too, but not many people want a simple steak from us." She cut a piece for herself. "Simple is better." Winking at Emily, she added, "Don't tell our guests."

"Shove that bowl of mussels over here, or I'll rat you out to the whole town."

Blake had a very pleased smile on her face as she slid the bowl across the table. "I love eating with someone who loves food."

"If you can find someone who loves food more than I do..." Emily trailed off and shook her head. "Can't be done." She slurped a mussel into her mouth. "Mmm...good aioli."

Blake reached over with her napkin and wiped a bit of broth off Emily's chin. "I wouldn't have bothered, but I didn't want that to drip on your sweater. Personally, I like to watch someone eat with such gusto that the food flies."

"You should meet my mom. I'm joking when I say I love food more than anyone else. My mom's easily my equal."

"Really?" Blake asked, gobbling down a mussel.

"Oh, yeah. Sometimes we look like we've been in a food fight after a good meal. Then my dad and my sister are sitting there, neat as pins, staring at us."

"I'm the only one in my immediate family who loves food," Blake said. "Well, my mom might, but I think she closes her mind to a lot of the things she loves. You can't have a love affair with food if you're more concerned with the calories than the taste."

"I was blessed with a good metabolism," Emily said as she worked on freeing another mussel. "If it looks good, I shove it into my mouth."

"Standing for twelve to fifteen hours a day might have something to do with how many calories you burn. I don't know about you, but my metabolism wouldn't be happy with me if I had a desk job. I'd probably gain five pounds a week."

"We'll never have to find out," Emily said, pointing a crisp French fry at her. "You can't cook at a desk."

They ate so much Emily had to unbutton her jeans. "I wish I could learn to be just a little moderate. But if I'm hungry and there's good food…"

"I'm the same. But if the food's bad, it doesn't matter how hungry I am. I'd go days without eating and not complain."

"I'd complain," Emily joked, "but I'm not willing to eat bad food, either. Not when good food's so easy to make."

"Tell that to the millions of people who don't know how to turn on their ovens. They're missing out on one of life's great pleasures."

Emily stretched, then settled back into the booth like a contented cat. "Maybe they're too busy sampling life's other great pleasures to bother."

"Doubtful," Blake said. "I've never met anyone who was good in bed who didn't like food. All of those pleasure centers are connected." She'd ordered another beer and was sipping it slowly. Over the last few minutes, she'd started to send off some signals that Emily couldn't, and didn't want to, ignore. Blake's eyes were trained on her mouth, a mouth she'd said was particularly sexy. It was about time to hit that sofa again.

"I'm all about the pleasure centers. We wouldn't have them if we weren't supposed to use them."

"Hear! Hear!" Blake held her bottle up and Emily clinked hers against it. Then Gustavo emerged from the kitchen and dropped heavily onto the seat next to Blake. He lifted the beer from her hand and drained it, sticking his elbow up to push her away when she tried to grab it back. Those kinds of hijinks would never happen in Blake's dining room, but it was after two, and the vibe at Gustavo's was much more laid-back.

"May I have one of these?" he asked, waving the empty bottle at the server who was clearly trying to get out of there. "And another round for my guests?"

"We can go somewhere else and get a drink," Blake said, giving the server an apologetic look.

"It's fine," Gustavo insisted. "I'll send the servers home. We can clean the dining room tomorrow."

Emily watched as Blake slammed her mouth shut. It must have killed her to have one of her proteges not have learned her most important lesson. Cleanliness always came first. But she happily accepted another drink, clearly able to ignore a mess that wasn't in her own domain.

"Heard about your favorite sous?" Gustavo asked, his mouth curled into a smirk.

"I love the one I'm with," Blake said, giving Emily a fond glance. "Emily's as good as anyone I've worked with in America."

Emily felt a blush rise to her cheeks, then she considered the geographic narrowness of the compliment. Oh, well, America was a big country.

"You know I mean Scott Williams," Gustavo continued. "He's a personal chef for some billionaire. Splits his time between the Upper East Side, the Hamptons and Palm Beach."

Blake's hand hovered mid-air, with a juicy bite of meat resting on her fork, then it clanked off her plate when she quickly lowered her hand to the table. "Are you shitting me? After he busted my chops for two years trying to get me to let him create a tasting menu?"

Gustavo obviously loved having knocked her off stride. He roared with laughter, finally dropping his head to his chest, where it bounced a little. When he looked up, he met Emily's gaze. "Scott and I were paired for about a year. Like you and Grant," he added. "At least once a week he proposed a tasting menu, with all of his precious little creations filling it. Drove Blake crazy."

"That's not a difficult task," Blake said, shaking her head as she picked up the fork and slid the bite of steak between her teeth. She chewed thoughtfully, then said, "I hope whoever he's working for is up for eight or nine courses a night."

"I've often wondered why we don't have one," Emily said. "Not that I'm pushing for one. I was a line cook at two places that had them and they made my life *so* much worse."

"Try expediting when you've got half of the restaurant getting nine courses, and the other half happy with three. It's a mindfuck," Blake said. She took a big slug of her beer, like she was trying to get a bad taste out of her mouth. "I'm not opposed to tasting menus, but I don't love 'em."

"They're food porn," Gustavo said, his mind clearly made up.

"Not always," Blake said. "But every time I have one, everyone at the table focuses exclusively on the food. It's coming at you every ten minutes, so you almost have to. I prefer kicking back and conversing with the people I'm eating with."

"I just want bigger portions," Emily said, making both Blake and Gustavo laugh. "It's true! If something's great, I want a lot of it."

Blake made a fist and gave Emily a playful punch on the shoulder. "See why she's my favorite? She can not only cook, she loves to eat as much as I do."

At three, Emily stood on the step in front of the restaurant, eye-level with Blake. Both were a little tipsy, and if Blake's belly wasn't about to burst, she had a different make-up than Emily.

"I hardly notice the cold," Blake said, her cheeks pink and rosy. "The food and alcohol have heated me up thoroughly."

"I must not be drunk enough." Emily burrowed down into her coat. "It's friggin' freezing!"

Blake gazed at her for a few heartbeats, not even trying to hide her interest. Those dark eyes lingered on Emily's lips much longer than you'd normally do with a co-worker. Emily was sure they were going to hop into a cab for that long four blocks back to her favorite sofa, but Blake shook her head like she was knocking an idea out of it. Then she held up her arm and waved for a taxi.

"Take the cab," she said as a cab cut across three lanes of traffic to squeal to a halt in front of them."

"Nah. No one wants to go to my neighborhood. They whine and bitch if you make them."

"Then let me order you a car." She pulled her phone out and clicked on an icon. "I hate to think of you on the subway at this time of night."

It took a Herculean effort to hide her disappointment, but Emily exerted all of her abilities to do so. "You really don't need to. The subway's right across the street."

"Is that *your* subway?"

"No, but I can change at Grand Central."

Blake was standing very close, but she didn't move an inch closer. Emily was stuck, wanting to kiss her, to take the lead and suggest they hook up again. She'd do that—without a second thought—for any other woman in the world. But not tonight. Since Blake was the boss, she had to lead.

"Are you sure?" she asked as her cabbie tooted his horn.

"Of course. I should probably walk home. I won't be able to sleep if I don't digest some of this food."

"Can you? Walk?"

Chuckling, Emily said, "You *really* don't know where Jackson Heights is."

"No, I don't, but I know cars go there." She twitched her head toward the waiting cab. "Let me ask this guy if he'll take you and not bitch about it. Actually, I'll go with you and he can have a huge fare when he brings me back."

"It's all yours." Emily squeezed her shoulder and started for the sidewalk. "Thanks again for dinner. I owe you one."

"Oh, I'll get a meal out of you someday." Blake gave her a final grin, charming in the extreme. "Be safe, Emily. I'd have a hell of a time replacing you."

As she crossed the street, Emily reflected that she might have made a mistake or two during the evening. Stuffing yourself with rich food after declaring you had a tough time holding onto it wasn't the best pick-up strategy. She could be such an idiot! Or maybe the truth was that Blake simply wasn't interested in a repeat. It sucked not being able to cut to the chase and make an overture. But that's what happened when you mixed sex with work. Maybe that's why everyone in the world warned you not to do it.

Chapter Nine

CONSISTENTLY REFUSING TO GO out with the staff wasn't a good idea. You needed to bond, and cooks bonded in bars. But after that first hangover, Emily had made it a habit to only go out on Saturday. Having Sunday to recuperate was a must, no matter how moderate she was. Gone were the days she could stay out all night and bounce into work a few hours later, bright-eyed and bushy-tailed.

After service that night, she, Brady and April closed up shop and went over to one of their favorite haunts. Grant and the pastry chefs would follow along once they'd closed the kitchen. Kermit was still underage, but he didn't seem eager to join them anyway, which made Emily even more confident that he had a good head on his shoulders.

Emily was on her second drink when the door opened and Grant led not only Lorelei and Raven, but most of the front of the house staff inside. In minutes, Grant had the new server, the one both she and Blake had an eye on, cornered by the juke box. Emily didn't pay much attention to them, instead concentrating on stopping Brady from ordering another round for her. The kid could easily drink her under the table, and she was bound and determined to remain upright.

Minutes later, a warm presence settled at her side and she looked up to find the pretty new server standing there.

"How do I convince Grant I'm not going home with him?"

Emily looked at the playful expression on her face. A flirty expression. "You could sit on my lap." She twirled her stool and slapped at her thighs.

The woman laughed and leaned close to make herself heard. "You move quickly."

"Move? Me? I'm just trying to be helpful."

"I'm Michaela," she said, putting her hand out. It was soft, silky really. Not like a cook's hand at all.

"Emily."

"I know all about you," Michaela said. "When I started, the guys went down the whole list with me. They pouted when they told me you were gay." Her smile grew. "I didn't."

"I'm not pouting either," Emily said, "About you, that is."

"Want to play pool?"

"Sure. But…" She craned her neck to see across the dim space. "There's a line."

"The sofa's open. Why don't we go sit down and talk?"

"That was going to be my next line…I mean…suggestion." She made her grin as charming as she could muster, took Michaela's elbow and led her over to the sofa. As they passed Grant, he gave Emily a sour look, but she forced herself to be mature and not stick her tongue out at him. If she was lucky, she'd soon have better things to do with it.

Emily's luck was running hot. After she and Michaela talked for a while, she kicked things into gear, pinning the clearly receptive woman into the corner to begin kissing her with deadly intent. It didn't take long for them to slip toward the horizontal, with Michaela giving off nothing but "go" signs. The thought ran through Emily's head that maybe she should be more discreet, but she'd seen far worse from Grant. Actually, she'd seen a world famous chef in the corner one night, blatantly humping a woman young enough to be his daughter. Once you punched out for the night, propriety often stayed at the restaurant.

Her pants buzzed, diverting Emily's attention for a split second before she decided to ignore the call. Sometimes Chase called if he wanted to meet up, but he always understood if she ignored him while chasing a good lead.

Given that Michaela responded so quickly and enthusiastically, Emily kicked it up a notch, boldly sliding her hand between their compressed bodies, maneuvering it until it was high on Michaela's thigh.

Jackpot! Michaela purposefully opened her legs and Emily's fingers slipped down like heat-seeking missiles, with her nails running up and down the seam of her jeans until she began to squirm.

After letting out a sexy laugh, Michaela tilted her head until her lips brushed against Emily's ear. "I think you want to get into my jeans."

Emily began to push herself upright. "I do. Right now," she decided, ready to rock.

"Where do you live?"

"Queens."

"Me too. Laurelton. Two hundred and twenty-seventh street."

"I'm closer." She had no idea where Laurelton was, so she had to be closer. When they stood, both a little shaky, Emily took her phone from her pocket. It was very rare for her to blow her budget on a car, but every once in a while thirty bucks didn't seem like much money at all. "One sec," she said, trying to focus on the overly bright display. "Shit," she muttered. "There was a big storm in the midwest and I've got a flight attendant in my bed. We'll have to go to your place."

The news didn't seem to bother her a bit, and they continued weaving their way through the crowd to reach the door. "I share a one-bedroom," Michaela said when they met again after splitting up briefly to maneuver around a group. "Is it okay if we're not alone?"

Emily stopped at the door and blinked at her, thoroughly confused. "Are you asking what I think you're asking?"

Michaela returned the stare, head cocked. "We'll have to use the sofa in the living room. What did you think I meant?"

Don't admit you thought she was proposing a three-way! "That's exactly what I assumed. It's private, right?"

"Right." They went through the door and passed around the smokers to reach clean air. "Unless my roommate gets up to use the bathroom. You have to go through the living room to get to it."

Emily grasped her by the hips and held her still. "Could you talk your roommate into taking the sofa?"

"Not again," she said, a pout forming. Shining brown eyes shifted toward the door. "Bathroom?"

Emily pondered the question for a minute. Michaela was really, really cute. Sexy and responsive too, which made her even more attractive. But doing the deed in the john of a dive bar crossed some kind of line. The "I've stopped giving a fuck" line that she wasn't ready to breach. If she worked in kitchens much longer she'd eventually cross every line known to man, but she wasn't there yet. "Let's do this another night. I usually have a room all to myself."

As she sighed, Michaela's shoulders rose and fell. "All right." She took another look at the entry door. "Sure?"

"Yeah," Emily said, regret making her resolve waver slightly. "If it doesn't smell great in there I couldn't get into it." Her eyes lingered on the old wooden door, layer upon layer of black paint flaking off. "I'd be amazed if the place was even marginally clean."

"You're probably right," she said, disappointment showing. "But I can ignore a lot when I'm turned on."

"I can too. But my nose controls my libido. Sex smells are great. Other ones…not so much."

Her head tilted slightly, probably surprised that Emily was actually going to turn her down. "Want to ride home together?"

"I do." Emily buttoned up her coat as they started down the icy sidewalk for the subway. She wasn't going to spend thirty bucks on a car just to sleep alone.

Michaela wrapped her hand around Emily's arm, letting her take the lead in clomping through the frozen snow that packed much of the sidewalk. Emily leaned close so she could be heard over the bracing wind, and she sniffed Michaela's sultry perfume into her lungs one more time. She bet there wasn't another person in that bar who would have refused Michaela's offer to join her in the john for a quickie. She also had an inkling she wouldn't be asked again.

On a cold, dreary Sunday morning in February, Emily woke with a hangover, even though she hadn't gone out or had a drink when she'd returned home. This was a work hangover. The kind that made your head, shoulders, lower back, legs, and feet ache. As she shuffled into the kitchen to make coffee, she had to acknowledge that her body ached every single day. But some mornings it grabbed her attention and wouldn't let go. She was tempted to pop a couple of ibuprofen with her coffee, but she was strangely averse to pain relievers, worried they might hurt her stomach. That didn't stop her from using alcohol as an analgesic on a regular basis, but she never claimed to be overly consistent.

Chase emerged from his room with a pretty redhead in tow. "Got any extra coffee?" he asked, approaching Emily for a hug. "This is Natasha," he added, moving to drape an arm around the woman.

"It's good to meet you, Emily. Chase talks about you constantly."

"Same here." She tried to assess this new addition to Chase's life in the few seconds she could stare at her while remaining polite. He'd said she was pretty, and she was, but not in the style that appealed to Emily. Natasha had that clean-cut, open, Midwestern affect, exactly the kind of girl she'd been surrounded by at her prep school. But she'd always preferred a more dramatic, exotic look, particularly if that look included the probability of the woman being gay. But when Natasha flashed an easy, bright smile you couldn't help but like her.

"I'm happy to make coffee for you guys," Emily said. "Want breakfast?"

They were both wearing Chase's clothes, even though Natasha had to hold the sweatpants up with a hand. Obviously she wasn't at the point of stashing clothes in Chase's room.

"No way." Natasha went to the refrigerator and started poking around. "Chase and I will cook for you." That sweet smile settled onto her face and stayed there for a few moments. "There's no way I'd let a chef cook for me on her one day off."

Stunned, Emily met Chase's buoyant grin. That might have been the first time in her life someone had turned down an offered meal. Natasha rocked!

After breakfast, the lovebirds settled on the sofa in the living room, while Olivia and Ray, their peripatetic flight attendant pair, lay on

Olivia's bed, watching something on her laptop. Poking her head in the room, Emily said, "I don't think I've ever seen you two here at the same time."

"Storm in Denver," Olivia said. "We're stuck until tomorrow. Wanna squeeze in and watch 'Fright Kings' with us?"

"Nah, but thanks for the offer."

Going back to her room, she pried the window open to check the weather. It was a day custom-made for staying inside; leaden gray skies, brisk wind, maybe a trace of snow...no, that was just particulate matter raining down on the neighborhood from a nearby factory.

Despite the gloomy day and her aching joints, she decided to go out. Over the years, she'd learned that her battery needed activity or variety to recharge. Lying in bed simply didn't cut it. By the time she'd made up her mind, however, Natasha was in the shower. After taking a look in the mirror, Emily decided she could wash her face in the kitchen and defer her shower until night. It took a minute to properly bundle up against the cold, then she bade everyone goodbye and took off for the city.

A group of people from Defarge, the place she'd worked before Henri, almost always gathered at a bistro in Soho for Sunday brunch. It was an ever shifting group, with their numbers expanding and contracting during the hours they hogged a group of tables. Must have driven the servers nuts, but they tipped well, so there were no hard feelings.

She got off the subway at Spring, one stop before the usual one for work, and headed south. Sixth Avenue was a little quiet, given the time. Everyone was probably jammed into the more popular, touristy places near Broadway. But cooks tended to seek out the spots where you didn't have to wait for a table. For people who made their livings preparing top-notch meals, many cooks were surprisingly tolerant of uninspired offerings, choosing marginal grub so long as it was paired with inexpensive drinks. Truthfully, most of them would have accepted poor quality food if the drinks were *very* inexpensive. But The Angry Rooster's food was above average, and they had a killer bloody mary.

Just as Emily stepped onto the stoop to enter, a figure shot out of the noodle shop next door.

"Chef!"

Alarm shifted to amusement as Blake gave her a half-smile. "Good afternoon, Emily. Ça va?"

"I'm good." She took a close look at her boss. If she'd had to guess, she would have put money on the fact that she'd been up fewer than fifteen minutes. Her hair, while presentable, was flat on one side, her curls having decided to remain lifeless. On further inspection, Blake's eyes lacked their usual sharpness, and a pink line down her cheek might have been from a pillow case. "How about you?"

"Hungry." She shook the bag she carried. "Groggy. Lazy." With a shrug, she added, "About normal for a Sunday."

"I read you. Ten hours of sleep barely put a dent in it."

Blake yawned, trying to cover her mouth with a gloved hand. "I'd give a lot for ten hours. I got roped into dropping by a party after work, and now I'm paying for it."

"Udon?" Emily pointed at the bag.

"Yeah. I'm not sure a steaming bowl of noodles will help, but it couldn't hurt."

Suddenly feeling awkward, Emily turned her gaze toward the door she stood before. "Some people from Defarge hang out here on Sundays."

"The Angry Rooster, huh? I don't think I've been inside."

"Do you live...?" Doh! Don't ask personal questions. She clearly likes her privacy.

"Yeah, I live," she said, a smile creeping onto her lips. "Today I'm about half alive, but I'll take it."

Emily slapped her on the shoulder. "You probably want to eat your soup. I'm holding you up."

"I've got a microwave." Her smile grew in intensity as her eyes took on a glimmer of interest. "If you were going to hold me up, you should've come by at about four thirty. I could've used you then."

She's flirting!

Emily's stomach started to flutter. Flirting was one of her favorite things. "You've got my number. I'll pick you up any time you need a hand."

"Pick me up?" Those expressive eyebrows lifted dramatically. "Are you trying to pick me up?"

"No!" Emily gasped, then realized Blake was screwing with her. "Well, yes, I guess I am. Do you mind?"

"As you once said, I'll mind when women stop trying." Her expression turned almost wolfish. "Have you eaten?"

"A little. Why? Do you want to cook for me?"

"Yeah," she said, chuckling. "That's exactly what I like to do on Sunday. No, I thought you might like some noodles. We could go to my apartment and eat. Or something…"

Her spine tingled at the thought of getting her hands and mouth on Blake again. "Let's do both. What did you order?"

"Tsukimi. I thought the egg would help."

"Be right back." She ducked into the noodle shop and ordered the same thing. If they were going to be swapping spit, it was smart to have it all taste alike.

They took the same route Emily used to get to work, but veered off a few blocks north of the restaurant. For a minute, it appeared they were heading for the on-ramp to the Holland Tunnel, but they stopped at Watts, a little street she'd never been on. Blake led the way into a blocky building that could have passed for a warehouse, murmured a hello to the doorman, then went to press the elevator button. "We could walk up, but I'm too tired."

"I'm jealous you live so close," Emily said. She'd worked for a catering company for extra money when she was new to the city, giving her a peek at a few Tribeca/Soho apartments. But she'd never actually known anyone who could afford to live within miles of either neighborhood.

Blake shrugged. "It's okay. It took almost every dime I had, but I wanted to live close to work. I had a nice, almost unique place on the

Upper West Side, but once I got the restaurant I knew I'd hate spending half an hour getting home every night."

The elevator pinged, and after they entered it rushed them all the way to the third floor. "Here's my luxury penthouse," Blake said as she opened the door.

They entered, passing a large, white marble bath and a couple of doors that must have hidden closets. After a slight turn they were in the living space. It was…underwhelming. The TriBeCa homes Emily had seen possessed soaring views, double-height ceilings, and dramatic lighting. This little nook overlooked the snail-like entry to the Holland tunnel, and had just one window. But it was a big one, and was clearly double-paned, given they couldn't hear the cars snaking along right below them.

The ceilings were surprisingly tall, maybe ten feet, and the floor was a wide-planked dark wood that didn't show a speck of dust. A Murphy bed took up much of the living space, but when it was put away the room would have been good sized. Two modern, white leather chairs were pushed against the wall, along with a glass topped coffee table. Floor to ceiling bookshelves bracketed the bed, with each stuffed with hardbound books and framed photos.

Even though it was just a pale grey box, the place was strangely soothing due to the plentiful art on the walls. Big, modern, impressionistic pieces, all very colorful and vibrant.

"I love your art," Emily said, moving over to stand in front of a particularly beautiful piece, gorgeous blues and greens suffusing it.

"They're only prints, but I like them. I found a couple in France." She pointed to two of the larger pieces. "The rest I picked up here and there. Hungry?"

"I am." Emily handed over her bag and Blake took the food into the kitchen, which was located behind the wall that created the entry hallway. In seconds, the soup was poured into a big, white bowl and began to spin around inside the microwave.

"Let me take your coat."

After going to the hall to hang up the coats, Blake returned to the living area and flipped the bed back into its nook. Then she pulled out and closed ingenious, hidden doors that covered it. It took only two more minutes to put the furniture back where it belonged, since the coffee table rolled on industrial-style wheels, letting her get it right where she wanted it with a minimum of effort. That was *very* Blake. Now that the furniture was arranged, the place did look pretty big. And neat, of course. There wasn't a thing out of place.

Blake headed back to the kitchen when the microwave dinged and Emily followed her, noting two guitars, one electric, one acoustic, resting on stands in the corner of the living space. "I was going to ask if you play, but then I heard how dumb that sounded," she said, laughing a little. "I guess I should say I'm impressed that you play. I'm jealous of people with musical abilities."

"Thanks," she said, adding nothing.

Before Blake opened the microwave, she thoroughly washed and dried her hands. Some habits were not to be broken.

Then they sat on the very comfortable, ergonomically perfect chairs, slurping their noodles. Pointedly looking around, Emily said, "Even though I'd give a lot to be able to live close to the restaurant, if I worked at a place near *my* apartment, I'd be slinging hash for the guys at the car repair shops."

"I know I've been fortunate," Blake said, looking a little… Shy? Embarrassed?

"Hey, don't apologize for being a success. I'd love to copy that."

Her brow furrowed and she shook her head after sucking in a few stray noodles. "I wish I earned enough to afford this." She took a look around, her dark eyes critically assessing the place. "But I don't. I inherited a chunk of money from my grandmother and blew it on the apartment. Even the common charges are a little steep for me."

"Oh." Her stomach flipped. She was going to be sharing a place in the outer boroughs for the rest of her natural life.

Blake pointed at Emily with her chopsticks. "I'm never going to be rich, but I don't mind. I know from personal experience that money can't buy contentment, much less happiness."

"No, but being poor can buy unhappiness," she said, adding a wink.

"This is true." Blake wolfed the rest of her food down, then went into the kitchen for a refill. "More? I can top you up again."

"No, please. Finish it."

"Sure?" The kitchen was very modern, with dark grey lacquered cabinet fronts and high-end stainless steel appliances. There was very little on the counter, made of white marble with grey veining, but what was there was tidy and utilitarian. All of her serving utensils, spoons, ladles and spatulas were in a big, black ceramic container. Next to it was a black silicone trivet—and that was it. Nothing else had the nerve to poke its head out.

"Positive."

As she watched her work, Emily's nerves started to act up. It was disconcerting to be in Blake's home, her private sanctuary. But Blake seemed just like herself. The self she presented when she entered and exited the restaurant. The self she'd shown when they'd had dinner at Gustavo's place. But it was the other self, the one that took over from noon until midnight that Emily felt most comfortable around. And work Blake was absent today. This more relaxed woman was the one she was going to get to sleep with, and she tried to get her emotions to catch up.

"I'm starting to feel better," Blake said as she sucked another bunch of noodles into her mouth. "Salt and broth and carbs are my lifesavers." She was looking perkier, with her eyes losing some of their puffiness and the color returning to her cheeks.

"Did you at least have a good time at your party last night?"

Blake's bowl was empty, so Emily got up and took it into the kitchen.

"No." She crossed one ankle over a knee as Emily scoped out her outfit. Expensive-looking ankle-length brown boots, dark jeans and a baby blue fleece turtleneck. Nothing fancy, but she looked well put-together, even hungover. "It was a work thing. Eric Van Leuwen has a new cookbook out, and his publisher hosted the book launch at his restaurant after they closed."

"Are you—friends?"

"Yeah, we are." She wrapped her hands around her knee and pulled. Probably working out some stiffness in her back, the constant battle-wound of every cook. "I wouldn't call him if I needed to borrow money, but we've worked together on a few things."

Emily finished putting the bowls and utensils in the dishwasher. "I bet he's got plenty of money to lend. How many restaurants does he have now?"

Blake shook her head, her eyes rolling around like she was stunned. "I don't know… A dozen? I've heard the new one in Vegas is a piece of crap. Apparently it's hard to find a good chef de cuisine in Sin City."

"I don't know much about Vegas, but I've heard you can get away with haphazardly prepared, overpriced food there. Try that here and you'll be out of business in six months."

"Six might be optimistic." Blake stuck her legs straight out in front of her, continuing her stretching routine. "Are you tired?" she asked, stopping to cock her head.

"Always," Emily said, laughing a little at such a silly question. "Why?"

"Would it sound strange to propose a nap? I'm as full as a tick and nothing sounds better than lying down for a while." Her eyes grew wide. "But only for a while. Then we can get to something a lot more fun."

Emily's heart skipped a beat at the adorable look on her face. Completely unguarded. Open, trusting. "Sunday afternoon… Bellies full of good soup noodles… A peaceful view of the Holland Tunnel." She paused, making sure Blake took that the right way. "A nap sounds great."

It was weird. No two ways about it. They kicked off their shoes, and when Blake reached under her shirt to shrug out of her bra, Emily mimicked her. Then they lay down on the surprisingly comfortable platform bed, keeping a respectful distance. Apparently they had to have sex before they could touch.

"Is an hour too long?" Blake asked while setting the alarm on her phone.

"I'm a half hour girl. I'll set my own alarm." She turned to meet Blake's puzzled gaze. "Sleep as long as you like."

"I'd like two," she said, a half grin tugging at her lips.

"Then set it for two. I'm perfectly content to lie here and dream up some specials."

"Are you sure? I could…"

Emily wasn't in the mood to let Blake set the emotional tone for their day. She leaned forward and kissed her, tasting the rich broth on her lips. They were just an inch from each other now, and she could see her eyes brighten as she smiled.

"I'm positive. Now get busy sleeping. Your eyes are half-mast."

"Full mast," Blake said, closing them and turning onto her side. "Or I guess that should be no mast."

Emily's alarm made the pillow vibrate. Automatically, she slid her hand under and turned it off without having to look at it. Then she let her body sink back into the mattress and the warmth at her back. What…? It took a few seconds to orient herself, then realize whom she was lying next to. It wasn't too strange, sharing a bed, fully clothed, with your boss, who'd pushed you to the edge of the bed by grinding her butt into your hip.

Lying there quietly, Emily forced away her unease and tried to enjoy the experience. The bed was nice, much nicer than her own, it was a lazy Sunday, with nothing but what would undoubtedly be a fun sexual encounter on her agenda. But if she shifted so much as a knee, she'd fall to the floor. Blake hogged the bed unlike anyone she'd ever known. Even asleep she had to be in charge!

Emily got up, with Blake immediately gobbling up the space she'd abandoned. But that left the other side of the bed empty, and Emily decided to stay horizontal while dreaming up recipes.

Lying on her back, one ankle propped onto a knee, she guided her mind to the coming week. She let her palate fantasize, considering ingredients she knew were readily available in February. Blake murmured a few indecipherable words, then flopped onto her belly, with an arm settling atop Emily's middle. A few menu ideas eventually floated into her head, but when she realized all of them revolved around well known aphrodisiacs Emily decided she was wasting her time. Might as well get ready for the second act.

Lifting Blake's arm, she snuck out of bed and went to explore. She'd been wrong about those two doors being small closets. They were, instead, two doors to a single, generous closet. And the bathroom was bigger than it should have been. The architect had stolen a little space from the next apartment, letting Blake's spacious bath extend beyond the plane of the front door. It was all decked out in pearl grey marble and gleaming chrome, with the kinds of fixtures that Emily's sister would choose. Very top-of-the-line stuff.

Giving into a loathsome habit, an unnatural desire to check out other people's medicine cabinets, she poked around, finding nothing particularly interesting. Just a surprising number of hair-care products. Apparently, the rock-star waves took a little effort. While she freely admitted snooping was a disgusting trait, Emily had once found a fresh bottle of lice killer right before she got into bed with a stranger. Ever since then…

She was in the middle of shaving her legs when a soft knock preceded a naked Blake partially entering. "Want company?"

"Sure. I hope you don't mind if I use your razor."

Blake slid into the enclosure, eyes still half closed but a lazy smile in place. "I'd rather have a dull blade than a rash from your stubbly legs rubbing against my shoulders." Her grin turned lascivious. "That's gonna happen, by the way." She slipped her arms around Emily's waist and gave her a long, sensual kiss. "I dreamed of sex," she breathed, making Emily shiver in anticipation. Then she removed the razor from Emily's hand, propped her leg on a thigh and quickly finished the job, frowning in concentration just like she did when plating food.

Emily leaned against the wall, her hands resting lightly on Blake's shoulders. Damn, those were scrumptious shoulders.

In clothes she looked thin, thinner than she was. It dawned on Emily that all of the civilian clothing she'd seen Blake wear hid her curves. Her wardrobe of tailored cotton blouses and roomy sweaters had to have been chosen intentionally, probably to hide her body, given everything she did seemed planned, considered.

In fact, the woman was built like a sleek Italian coupe, gentle curves and lurking power. She must not have wanted to reveal her body to her employees, which was a damned good idea. Neither Emily nor any of the guys would be able to concentrate if Blake made a show of her assets.

As Blake turned to place the razor on a built-in shelf, Emily ran her hand over her side. "Let me see that."

Arms lifted, and Blake presented her body for inspection. A lovely, carefully wrought image of a cow decorated one side of her chest, a pig on the other. They were relatively large, with the heads of the animals near her waist, their tails at her ribs. "These are lovely," Emily said, drawing her fingers down the art. "I've seen renderings like these before, but they usually have butcher's cuts on them."

"Yeah, they're not uncommon. These are from paintings, though, not the standard butcher's charts."

"Mmm, yeah, I can see that. French?"

"Of course," she admitted, chuckling. "The paintings, that is. I had the tattoos done here. I didn't have enough money to buy a croissant when I worked in France." She turned and let Emily see the colorful salmon at the base of her spine. "I got that one in Japan," she said, patting the space. "Do you know Yuri Katsasuma?"

"Only by reputation."

"Nice guy. He took me to his favorite tattooist when I visited him last year. I was torn about using color, but I'm glad I did."

"They're all nice." Emily ran her hands over the delicate art work. "The tools of our trade."

"More than that," Blake said, her voice growing sober. "I often think about the animals we slaughter for food. If I couldn't afford to use humanely raised protein, I'd get out of the business."

"I can't see you doing anything other than running a restaurant, so I'm glad you can afford the good stuff."

Still unsmiling, she said, "I visited every single supplier before I made my decisions about who to buy from. There are a lot of us who feel the same way and we share information. It's not rare for one of us to visit a farm unexpectedly to make sure quality stays high."

Emily smiled at her, finding her strong opinions a turn-on. "I can tell you respect the animals we use. I've never seen you angrier than the day Alicia was helping Brady out and lost track of a branzino she was poaching. I'll bet her ears are still ringing."

A cute half-smile settled onto Blake's mouth. "I think she got the 'this animal made the ultimate sacrifice and you treat it like a rock' speech."

"Something like that. But she never ruined another fish." Emily couldn't keep her hands off Blake's torso, continuing to slide her fingers along her skin, which pebbled despite the warm water raining down on them. "I thought you were the one chef in New York without ink."

"I don't like it to show. It's more personal this way." She took Emily's arm and turned it, considering the dark stripe than ran down the underside of her forearm. "I've never seen your bare arms. Is this *your* knife?"

"Uh-huh. My Yanagiba. It just fit."

"I like it. It marks you as a cook."

"So does this." She turned the other arm and showed an old-fashioned hand beater that took up the same amount of space as the knife.

"I know you don't cook with one of these, although it'd be handy in a blackout."

"I don't now, but I used to. When I was little, we had an elderly neighbor who used to let me help her bake. My job was always beating egg whites." She laughed at the memory. "I don't think she needed half of them, but she let me beat them to keep me entertained."

"Is that when you got the bug?"

"Yeah. I was over there all the time. Mrs. Bing belonged to a big Baptist church in Midtown Detroit, and she must have been their designated baker. Her sugar and butter bill had to be through the roof."

"No cooking with your mom?"

Emily shook her head. "Not really. My mom can cook, but she admits she's better at making reservations than dinner. How about you? Did you learn at mommy's knee?"

"Ha! I got a peanut butter and jelly sandwich or boxed macaroni and cheese at five, then my mom put whatever she'd bought at the gourmet shop into the oven twenty minutes before my dad came home at seven. He taught me how to make a perfect Rob Roy, though. My only home cooking lesson." Blake slipped her arms around Emily's waist and pulled her close. "This is fun," she said, a gentle smile curling her mouth. "Every time we get to talk, I really enjoy myself."

"Me too. But..." She didn't want to put a damper on things, but they had to be smart. "I don't want anything to interfere with work."

Just the mention of work made her stiffen. "It won't. No strings, remember?"

"I do. And I agree. Getting involved with someone you work with can be awkward."

Her smile was starting to come back. "I haven't gotten close to anyone in a while." She took the shampoo and started to lather her hair. "You're the first woman I've had over."

"The first?" Her heart skipped a beat.

"Yeah. I've only been here for three...three and a half years, but..." She shrugged, her tattoos stretching out as her shoulders rose. "I don't like many complications." After she rinsed her hair, an eye opened and cast a questioning gaze. "Hey, did you get anywhere with Michaela?"

"This close." Emily thought of the sexy server who, predictably, had never made another overture. "We were ready to pull the trigger, but didn't have anywhere to go. Roommate trouble." Seeing the smirk that covered Blake's face, she said, "I have a feeling you didn't have that problem."

"I've got a sofa in my office," she said, letting out an evil laugh. "The only true perk of having your name on the building."

Emily finished before Blake, deciding to leave her alone in case she needed some privacy. After wrapping herself in a big, white towel, she went back to the living room, checking out the place more thoroughly. On a shelf in one of the bed-flanking bookcases, she noted a gleaming silver bowl. First place in a very prestigious international cooking competition, dated the previous year, along with the place—Tokyo. *That's* why she was over in Japan getting tattoos. The owners probably had to hold a gun to her head to make her enter, so she'd gone and won the thing.

Emily neatened the sheets, fluffed the pillows and drew the light grey shades to shut out the oppressive, dark sky. Then she switched on some lights, making the room glow with warmth. Blake came up behind her and bent her head to nibble on Emily's neck.

"I don't know what your perfume is called, but it's fantastic," Emily murmured. She loved few things more than a freshly showered woman ornamented with judiciously placed hints of perfume. Subtlety was the key. Her nipples hardened as Blake's body enveloped her own. "This is going to be fun."

"Not a doubt in my mind." Blake turned her and placed a delicate kiss upon her lips. Then she followed up with a more forceful, hungrier one. Emily let their bodies mold together as her towel slipped away and their skin touched along their lengths.

"We'd better move over to the bed, or you're going to have to carry me. I am ready to *rock*."

Smirking, Blake effortlessly bent and swept Emily into her arms. Their faces nearly touched and when Emily looked into those dark eyes she could have swooned. "I don't think anyone's ever picked me up. I may never walk again." She lifted a hand to squeeze Blake's well-defined shoulder. "You're so hot it's criminal."

Laughing, Blake deposited her a little forcefully onto the bed. "I have short bursts of strength." She held her arms out, showing that both of them were shaking from the effort.

"Come down here and join me." Emily grasped her hand and soon they were lying next to one another. "This is so nice. I could spend every Sunday like this." As soon as she said it, her stomach flipped. She didn't mean with Blake...

"That'd be nice wouldn't it? We just have to find women who demand next to nothing of us, and don't mind seeing us only on Sundays. What are the odds of that?"

Thank god she hadn't taken that as a sign of neediness. "Slim and none. We'd better make the most of a rare opportunity."

"Maybe rare for you," Blake teased. "I'm one of America's rising young chefs."

Emily rolled onto her side and propped her head up on her hand. "Does that lure the ladies in?"

"In the last year, I've had two guests on my office sofa, so, no. But it'd be nice if it did."

"All the more reason to get our fill today." Emily draped a hand over her shoulder and started to pull her close.

Blake didn't reply with words, but her heated kiss showed she felt exactly the same.

Emily let her body rest against Blake's, feeling her head spin from her delightful scent. Sexy, feminine, delicate, with a touch of spice. You could make billions if you could bottle it, but then it wouldn't be uniquely Blake. Emily nuzzled against her neck, breathing in the scent. Thank god she didn't wear it to work. Someone—probably Emily—would be so distracted they'd cut off a finger.

Touching each other in the shower had warmed them up, and now, lying next to each other, they got serious. Emily continued to slide her hands across and along Blake's body, thrilled by her womanly contours. The tattoos had been a surprise, but they were so well done they were like small canvases hung from her torso. She licked the cow's ears, then followed along its back. A ninety degree turn let her slide her tongue across Blake's chest. Her breasts were the main event, and Emily had always been the kind of person to save the best for last.

She'd thought she'd enjoyed playing with Blake's breasts when they went at it on her sofa. Now those quivering mounds of tender flesh smelled of the mild soap Blake used, fresh and delicate. Emily was able to put both hands around one and lick it like an ice cream cone, keeping that up until she'd filled her mouth. As her lips grasped Blake's hard nipple she could feel her pulse beat, strong and sure. Determined to make it pound, Emily feasted on her body, licking and kissing and sucking on that trembling flesh until her head began to spin.

Her desire for Blake's breasts was so strong she backed off for a while, worried she'd hurt her if she gave in to her instincts. Trailing her tongue down to her side again, she spent a minute tracing the outline of the tattoo. As she kissed her way across Blake's hip, she was able to detect her scent. Very delicate, just a hint of sex. Her mouth started to water at the thought of diving in, but she held back, teasing her with kisses and nibbles as Blake started to squirm under her. Nothing in the world felt as good as this kind of gentle foreplay. Everything was possible. Her world pulsed with promise.

Hands trailed along her scalp, with Blake trying to maneuver her into position. But Emily stayed the course, teasing herself as well as Blake. When she really looked forward to something, she liked to make herself wait. And she was really, really looking forward to nestling her face between Blake Chadwick's legs.

They wrestled, briefly, with Blake laughing as she tried to climb on top. But Emily flipped her onto her back once again, and submitted to her poorly disguised attempt to direct the action. She settled down in between her legs and rested her chin at the top of a smooth thigh. "You already know how much I love food," she purred, "but it's a tossup between a good meal and this." She closed her eyes and trailed her tongue all the way along Blake's glistening skin. "Fantastic," she murmured as more goosebumps chased along strong, silky-smooth legs. "This is gonna be so much fun." Taking in the complex mix of notes that lingered on her tongue, she wasn't sure which of them would enjoy it more. But she knew—without question—that Blake's natural perfume was easily as appealing as the French scent she'd probably spent a day's salary on.

There was no need to look at the clock. No place she had to be. And there were hours to kill before she had to go to bed. What a great day. One of the best she'd had in months.

Blake was out cold, her hair curling against her pillow, an unguarded, peaceful expression on her face. This was just about the only time Emily had ever seen her perfectly still. Just as she had the thought, Blake's eyes started to twitch underneath her lids. Even in sleep she was moving.

It would be nice if they could do this on a regular basis. If nothing else, it was a great way for both of them to blow off some steam. But she couldn't ask, and she was certain Blake wouldn't make the overture. Hell, she'd probably try to erase Emily's memory so she didn't recall where she lived. Reaching out, she tenderly moved some stray strands that threatened to tickle Blake's nose. Then she gave in and turned onto her side, keeping a good bit of space between them, starting to build up the wall that had to separate them. Another nap wouldn't hurt. It was Sunday.

The quiet "bong" of a computer powering up woke Emily. She patted the bed next to her, then murmured, "Is it morning?"

"It's a long way from morning. Only six o'clock."

"Oh, good." Emily stretched lazily and forced herself to sit up. Blake was dressed in a roomy pair of blue plaid flannel pajama bottoms and the same fleece she'd had on earlier. "When did you sneak out of bed?"

"A few minutes ago. There's no need to rush if you're tired. I've just got some things to catch up on..."

Emily set her feet on the floor, then realized she'd have to fetch her clothing from the bathroom—naked. Blake had seen, touched and licked every part of her body, but it was still embarrassing to parade across the room naked when your sex partner was fully clothed.

As she scooted by, Blake reached out and grasped her hand, stopping her. Emily put her other hand on Blake's shoulder and gazed down at her.

"I had a great time today," Blake said, eyes clear, a darling smile brightening her expression. "If I didn't have to catch up on this stuff I could go for another round."

"You wouldn't have to work too hard to talk me into it. You know exactly how to punch my buttons."

The smile grew warmer, making Emily shiver. Blake had the prettiest mouth she thought she'd ever seen.

"Your buttons aren't very hard to push. You're the definition of responsive." After putting her laptop onto the table, she tugged Emily onto her lap. They looked into each other's eyes for a moment, with Blake shifting her gaze away after a few seconds. "I'm really attracted to you," she said, sounding adorably embarrassed.

"Me too. A lot." She twitched her head in the direction of the bed. "Another tumble?"

"Aww, why not?" Her grin showed how eager she was to start "I deserve a full day off." They were soon lying face to face. "And *you* deserve another orgasm. That last one wasn't up to par."

Emily weakly slapped at her chest. "Only because the previous ones had sapped the life out of me."

"You've had a nap, so you should be raring to go."

"I'm raring to get these clothes off you." Blake sat up and Emily whipped her turtleneck off. "You should be bare from the waist up. All of the time." Her hands glided over her shoulders, down her arms, then back up to gently tickle her breasts. "You might get cold, but I think it'd be worth it."

"I'll consider it, but only if you stop wearing pants." Reaching down, she grabbed Emily's ass, really getting a good grip on her flesh. "World class."

Emily kissed her gently, staying close after they broke apart. "You can compliment me to your heart's content. I have an unlimited appetite for praise."

With a lecherous grin, Blake said, "Let's use our mouths for something other than talk. I know!" She pushed Emily onto her back, then started to scoot down the bed. When she got into position, she lightly rested her head on Emily's belly. "I'm going to visit one of my favorite neighborhoods. Let me know if I overstay my welcome."

Emily lay back onto the pillows, perfectly content. "I've got to be at work at ten in the morning. Since we're so close, you can stay right there until 9:45. Knock yourself out."

Their threats didn't equal their actions. Just an hour later Emily went back to the bath to rinse off and get dressed. By the time she returned to the living room, Blake had her computer on her lap again, giving the screen her usual intense focus.

Emily walked over to her and ran a hand through her hair, neatening it up a little, even though she loved bed-head. "Thanks for a great day."

Blake looked up, a gentle smile making her look young and nearly innocent. "I'm really glad we ran into each other. Doing budget projections with a hangover wasn't something I was looking forward to."

"How are you feeling now? You seem perfectly fine."

"I am," she said, her smile growing. "I've got a new hangover cure. But if I publish it, your phone's going to be ringing off the hook."

Emily bent over and gave her a peck on the cheek. "Let's keep it between us. Feel free to call next time you're seeing double."

"I will," Blake said, sounding entirely sincere. She took Emily's hand and held it in front of her face for a few seconds, inspecting it. Then she closed her eyes and gently kissed it. "See you tomorrow."

Emily pulled away, maintaining eye contact as she walked backwards to the door. "Bright and early. Don't stay up too late."

"I won't." With a final smile that warmed her heart, Emily slipped out into the hallway and leaned against the door, thoroughly satisfied but also a little down. If they could do that even once a month—once a quarter—she'd never have to settle for another dodgy pickup. When you met someone you had such great chemistry with, didn't it make sense to make it a regular thing?

She pushed off the door to walk to the elevator. Her argument would have been stronger if she hadn't just avoided using Blake's name. Besides not having done so yet, she didn't want to get into the habit. It'd be too easy to slip at work, and that was something they couldn't allow to happen.

The elevator arrived and she pondered the situation on her very brief ride. Sleeping with the boss with any kind of routine was dumb, and trying to convince herself otherwise wasn't going to work. She was too realistic to believe they could fly under the radar if they made this a habit, but it was a damned nice fantasy.

The next morning, they met in Blake's office, completely back in business mode. One of Emily's worries had been that Blake might distance herself, maybe even stop their morning meetings. But here they were, same as usual, not a single thing having changed.

Amazing.

After Blake suggested a few ideas that Emily added a minor twist to, the menu for the day was set. Proposed menu in hand, Emily got up to deliver it to the printing firm that ran it off for them. Her hand was on the knob, and she was just about to open the door when Blake got up and stood right behind her. A firm hand held the door closed, then lips bent to whisper into Emily's ear. "My nipples ache," she murmured, using the low, sexy tone she generally only pulled out when they were actively having sex.

Despite having had her tank topped up to full, Emily was ready to hit the sofa again. She turned to face her and was tempted to at least offer a kiss. But they were at work, and no good could come of that. "Don't distract the cooks," she said, inching away from Blake's compelling aura. "You don't have a very deep bench."

Chapter Ten

DESPITE HER BEST EFFORTS to prevent it, Blake had begun to get under her skin. During the day, Emily was able to focus all of her energies on her job, treating Blake exactly like she'd treated her previous bosses. But at home she'd started to idly dream of her in bed, images of her dancing around the corners of her mind as she tried to fall asleep. There were so many images, each of them touching her in a way she found more and more troubling.

They weren't starry-eyed young women just trying to figure out who they were. Both of them had been at this for a decade, both of them prioritizing their careers over all else. That had been a conscious decision, at least on Emily's part. So why was she mooning over a woman she knew she couldn't have? More than that, a woman she didn't want.

That was the puzzling part. She was both tremendously attracted and mildly repelled at the thought of spending more time with her. They'd developed a very good working relationship, and Emily was learning exactly the things she'd hoped she'd be exposed to. This was important stuff. Stuff she couldn't afford to ignore. But she was so damned attracted to her! It was hard to find someone you got along so well with in bed, someone who made your knees weak with a suggestive glance. But she had to be clear-headed about this.

Nothing meant more to Blake than her restaurant. Her staff was a team, and knowing the boss was sleeping with a player would invariably harm their cohesion. No matter how well they clicked, she knew in her heart that Blake would never do anything to screw up the restaurant. So even though they were cold comfort, Emily was forced to rely only on her fantasies, a poor substitute for the reality she'd had just a tiny taste of.

One cold, snowy night in late February, they sat in Blake's office, idly tossing around ideas for the next day's entrées. Blake was on a roll, her creativity sparking as she suggested one fantastic sounding dish after another.

"I've got to stop thinking about food," she said, starting to laugh. "My stomach thinks my throat's been cut."

"You didn't eat today?"

"Not much. I got up late, and only had time for a bowl of cereal before I came in. Then I got involved with Thierry and had to eat the scraps leftover from the family meal."

"We've got enough ideas for tomorrow. Go get yourself something to eat."

"Mmm." A slow grin transformed her face, making her look like a kid choosing an ice cream flavor. She tapped at her lips with a finger. "What do I want?"

This kind of playfulness was rare, and without taking a second to dissuade herself, Emily jumped in with both feet. "What's your norm? Do you usually grab something quick on the way home? Or do you like a real meal?"

"Ideally?" She leaned back in her chair, rocking a little as she thought. "I'd like a meal, but I'm too lazy to cook for myself. There are plenty of places open at this time of night, but I won't go to a restaurant alone." She let out a tired-sounding laugh. "I know that's weird, but it's the truth."

Emily's heart started to beat faster, her palms suddenly damp. Blake was practically daring her to offer a suggestion. "I owe you dinner, you know. How about Korean food? I know a great place."

Blake's head tilted while she regarded Emily for a full minute, a sly smile covering her face. She was so cute when she was being playful. Eventually, she was gazing at Emily through her dark eyelashes, practically batting them. "You owe me dinner, huh?"

"I do. You paid when we had that fantastic steak and those fries that should have been illegal."

"I guess I did." Her flirty, playful side continued to emerge, like the sun breaking through after a storm. "What do you have in mind,

Emily?" The way she said it made it seem like she was expecting an invitation to head straight for bed, but Emily had been having some stern talks with herself about sleeping with the boss, having decided it was a losing bet. But maybe there was a way to have a little something outside of work. Just a friendship with someone she really liked.

"There's a great twenty-four hour Korean spot in Queens that I truly love. It's super casual, and they can make anything."

"*All* Korean?"

"Uh-huh. All good." She could see Blake adjusting her tastebuds, seeing if Korean food fit her mood.

"How far?"

"Far," she said, having to be honest. "The last stop on the 7 train."

"Okay." Blake stood and started to unbutton her jacket. "You pay for dinner, I'll pay for a car."

"This place is so inexpensive, I might be getting the better end of the deal."

Blake picked up her phone while raising an eyebrow. "Address?"

"Hold on." Emily checked her own phone, mumbling, "What did we do without smartphones?" She found the entry, saying, "150-51 Northern Boulevard, in Flushing."

Blake shook her head, saying something about tennis while she typed. "Five minutes." She looked up and shooed Emily from her office. "Go!"

The best time to take a car out to Flushing just happened to be midnight on a Wednesday. Their driver, a guy who didn't seem to have the ability to tolerate a moment of silence, drove a Camry he must have cleaned with a toothbrush. Emily wasn't sure what his ethnicity was, but he had everyone else's down pat, rattling them off as they drove. "This was all Italians and Greeks," he said, pointing at nothing in particular. "Still some Russians hanging on," he added as they swiftly cruised down a commercial strip dotted with stores bearing Cyrillic characters on their signs. "I figure the Chinese will take over the whole borough soon enough."

"Have you lived in Queens long?" Emily asked, having to carry the conversational load, given that Blake had her attention glued to the window, looking like an enraptured tourist on her first trip to the big city.

"Yeah. My pops moved here in the seventies, but my mom's people have lived in Douglaston forever. How about you? You don't live in Flushing, do you?"

"Jackson Heights."

"What's in Flushing?" he asked. "It's kinda late."

She loved having a chatty cabbie who didn't have any boundaries. People said New Yorkers weren't friendly, but she'd never found that to be the case. You just had to reframe intrusion as friendliness. "There's a food court I like out there."

He turned around and gave her a puzzled look, almost drifting from his lane as his attention flagged. "The Korean place?"

"Yeah. Do you know it?"

"My mom's Korean," he said, grinning at her in the rearview mirror. "Every time I'm around there, she makes me stop and get stuff for her."

"Cool," Emily said, not sure why this little bit of connection resonated. "You should park and eat with us. Especially if you speak Korean."

"No can do." He took a glance at his watch. "My wife's on the late shift at Long Island Jewish. I've gotta get home and watch the kids."

"Want me to run in and get a snack for you? It won't take a minute."

He looked into the rearview again, this time catching Blake's eye. "You've got a good one there, Chief. Hold onto her."

Blake beamed a smile at him, then put her hand on Emily's shoulder. "You're a very good judge of character…" Emily could see her lean forward to read the guy's name on his license. "David."

"I call 'em like a see 'em. When you find a nice girl, don't screw it up."

"Words to live by," Blake said, giving Emily a wink. "And I'm not even going to tell you how well she can cook."

A few minutes later, Emily stood on the sidewalk, freezing her butt off while Blake tipped David. As Blake put her wallet back into her tote bag, Emily moved close and said, "We must look extra lesbian tonight."

"What?" She was scanning the big sign atop the one story building, even though it was in Korean.

"We weren't touching or anything, but David assumed we were together."

Blake turned and looked at her for a few moments. "Aren't we? I sure hope so, since I'd *never* get back to Manhattan if you dumped me out here."

"Not a chance," Emily said, relieved David's inference hadn't freaked Blake out. "Once you realize how good I am at ordering, you won't let me out of your sight."

"I won't let you out of my sight once I get inside." She ran for the entrance, her breath making little clouds of fog. "Queens is colder than Manhattan!"

After they'd burst through the doors, Emily stopped and unwrapped the scarf she'd looped around her face. Blake wore only her remarkably thin black jacket and gloves, daring the cold to give her frostbite. Shivering, she said, "Is this a restaurant or a supermarket?"

"Both." After Emily removed her gloves, she led the way deeper into the market, the normally jammed aisles mostly devoid of customers because of the late hour. "If it's Korean, they've got it. On a Sunday afternoon, it's a madhouse."

"It's nice now," Blake said, following along compliantly.

"Sure is. Especially since I'm starting to smell some of my favorite things," she said, vaguely singing the words. "The Snack Corner awaits us."

"Mmm, the smells are making my stomach gurgle."

Emily paused, closed her eyes and took in a deep breath. "I don't know the name of hardly anything, but I can smell some of the stuff I've ordered before. Excuse me if I drool." Starting to walk again, Emily rubbed her hands together, partly in anticipation of their meal as well as an attempt to warm them. "I like everything I've ever had here," she said as they approached a small counter with an expansive menu posted above. "Want a couple of big dishes or a bunch of little ones?"

"Uhm..." Blake met her gaze. "Both?"

"My kind of eater. Mind if I order for us?"

"I don't like organs that still look like organs." Her eyes half closed as she thought. "And I don't like feet. Any kind. Other than that, I'll eat it."

There were a couple of older men in front of them, asking many questions and negotiating with each other about what they should eat. Emily used the time to not only look at the menu and try to recall what she'd had before, but also check out what other people were eating. When it was her turn, she pointed, as discretely as she could, at a dish on a nearby table. "I want some of that."

The guy behind the counter nodded. "Budae-jigae. One?"

"Yeah. And some of those noodles with perilla seed."

"Yes, yes," he said, making a note. He raised an eyebrow. "Modumjean?"

"Is that the pancakes?"

He nodded again. "Very good."

"Definitely," Blake said, leaning over Emily's shoulder. "I love anything with a pancake."

"I think we need some kimbap," Emily said.

"I love kimbap," Blake said, pressed into Emily's back, clearly having trouble not having her vote counted.

Emily took another look around, checking out a tray that a kid carried to a nearby table. "How about one of those," she said. "It looks like a hot dog."

The guy shrugged, either not agreeing, or not having an alternative to compare it to. "This is enough," he said, after taking a long look at both of them. "If you need more, get porridge."

"Fantastic. What do I owe you?"

He toted up the numbers. "Thirty-two dollars."

Emily whipped out some bills, then left a few bucks in the tip jar. As they moved to the seating area and settled across from each other on benches, Blake said, "That's an awful lot of food for thirty bucks."

"Lots of competition around here. Keeps the prices down."

They'd barely removed their coats when a young guy brought out the first dish. "Ooo, the budae-jigae," Emily said. "I'm sure I don't pronounce it right, but I love this stuff."

First, the guy placed a portable burner on the table, then settled a small pot atop it. He started to leave, then pulled a packet of instant ramen from his apron, tossed it onto the table and hurried away to fetch more food. "*Instant* ramen?" Blake asked, clearly suspicious.

"We don't need it. There's plenty in here to keep us happy." She took her hand and cupped the steam that rose from the pot, drawing it toward her. "Smell that kimchi?"

"Set me up," Blake said, bouncing around happily on the bench. "You can't put food in front of me and dawdle."

Emily ladled some of the stew into a bowl and set it in front of her. After poking at the ingredients for a second, Blake said, "Spam?"

"Uh-huh. And bacon and slices of hot dog. Eat up," she said, taking her first bite. "Ooo," she moaned, her eyes rolling around in her head. "Is there anything better than a spicy, meaty stew on a cold night?"

"Good, good, good," Blake said, slurping the stew down like she hadn't eaten in weeks. "Go get more of this. I could eat three of these."

Their server returned while she was speaking, this time with a big bowl of noodles. Blake once again poked at them, clearly trying to guess what was floating around. "Why are they stained orange and red? I'd guess beet and carrot, but I'm out of my depth here."

"Try some."

Blake abandoned her stew to slurp a mouthful down, pausing to chew, her brow furrowed. "I think I'm right."

"You are."

"It's a nice combo."

"Do you like the wild sesame?"

She took another bite, then met Emily's eyes. "Who wouldn't? How'd they make it so creamy?"

She took an experimental taste. "I'm not sure if it's the sesame or the dough. Whatever it is, it's good, isn't it?"

"Really good," Blake nodded. "Creamy, doughy, a nice rich broth, hints of beet and carrot." She met Emily's gaze, with a lazy, contented smile seeming to make her fatigue evaporate. "These people care about food."

"Too true." She took a big bite of the noodles, savoring their delicate goodness. "I have tons of respect for someone who cooks the same classic dishes every day. You've got to care to do it well when you don't have new stuff to break the tedium."

"Do you do this a lot?" Blake asked. "Hunt for places like this?"

"Nearly every Sunday. If Chase is around, we go out together. Sometimes we'll take the train until we see the signs on stores change to a different language, then we'll jump off and look for crowded places. They're never hard to find on a Sunday." Her eyes lit up thinking of a recent expedition. "We wound up in Little Quito not long ago and had some awesome food. Well worth the trip."

"I don't do this," Blake said. "I love different kinds of food, but I don't have the energy." She sucked another bunch of noodles into her mouth, shaking her head as she chewed. "I'm missing out by ordering from the same few places all of the time. I've got to get out more."

"Hop on the 7 train and come on out. Queens is probably the most diverse place in America. Where else can you try Dongbei cuisine?"

"I don't even know what that is."

"Northeastern Chinese. Really good. You'll like it."

"I'll happily give it a try," Blake said, an impish smile on her face. "But I'll get there in a car."

They nearly had to roll out of the market, their bellies full to bursting. But Emily couldn't resist stopping at a tent located just outside the main entrance. "Gotta have a donut," she said, with Blake following along.

"A donut? Really? After Spam and bacon and hot dogs and noodles and that corn dog thing and deep fried meat patties and kimbap?"

Emily batted her eyes at her. "Are you implying we ate too much?"

"Can we split a donut?" She watched carefully when the vender drizzled brown sugar syrup over flat, golden dough. "I definitely want a bite, but if I have my own, I might die."

Emily handed the guy two bucks and took the still hot oval of dough wrapped in waxed paper. It was colder now than it had been earlier, with a bitter wind blowing their hair around. She held the donut up and Blake leaned in a took a bite, while Emily moved forward at the same time. Their faces were two inches apart, each of them taking a big bite of the delectable, insanely sweet treat. "Oh, damn it," Blake murmured, grinning. "I need my own."

Emily put a hand on her arm to stop her from ordering another. It was the first time she'd touched her all night, and her fingers tingled from the sensation. "We can come back another time. Let's share this one and live to see tomorrow."

With a pout, Blake turned back and took another bite, this one ridiculously huge. "I got more than half," she said, trying to speak around the ball of dough in her mouth.

"You're taller. You've got more room for food."

"Our car should be here in a second," Blake said, scanning down the busy street. "Sure you don't want another?" She gazed longingly at the guy who was frying up his wares for a bunch of shivering customers, all of them ignoring the cold and the biting wind.

"I've got to get up in…" She took out her phone and looked at the time. "Six hours. I think I'd better stop while I'm ahead."

"Six hours? What kind of awful job do you have that makes you work such crazy hours?"

"I've got the best job in town," Emily said, smiling when she realized how much she meant that.

Blake returned her smile with one easily as wide. "That's great to hear, because I couldn't be happier with my sous."

The car arrived moments before they froze, and they hopped in and shivered for a few seconds. The driver knew Emily's address from the app, and he didn't give any indication he wanted to hear another word out of her. He pulled away from the curb in a hurry, snapping her neck back.

Turning, she saw Blake staring at her, big, dark eyes nearly boring a hole through her body. "Hey," she said, with a frown settling between her brows. "When Grant leaves, I could hire someone for your job, and you could switch over to his."

"Is he leaving?"

"It's been two years this month. He's a short-timer."

"Uhm..." She stared back, trying to guess what Blake was getting at. "I'm kinda happy to be rid of scheduling."

"Oh. Right. Well, those are just details." She nodded, looking happier. "I was just thinking that if you came in at noon, our hours would match. We could grab dinner after service. You know...talk about the next day's specials and stuff." Suddenly, she seemed hesitant. "That's only if you want to. I mean, you might like going right home. I just thought that—"

"That would be kinda awesome," Emily said, with chills running up her spine. "Now that Chase has a girlfriend, I'm usually alone when I get home. I find myself thawing a bagel just so my stomach stops rumbling enough to let me sleep."

"I don't normally mix business with pleasure," Blake said, a huge understatement. "But we deserve a damn meal, don't we?"

"We definitely deserve a meal. God knows we're not going to get one at work, so we can basically have a business lunch—at midnight."

"I like the way you put that. We'll start as soon as Grant moves on to claim his empire."

"It's a deal," Emily said, reaching over to shake Blake's hand. "I'll think of some places that won't break the bank, but aren't as far away."

"This is cool," she said, leaning back to relax now that she was confident she'd gotten her way. "I like seeing the parts of New York I've ignored for all of these years. It's like moving to a new town—while being able to sleep in my own bed. Feel free to hook me up with some Dongbei food out here in the wilds of Queens."

Images of future meals filled her head as they raced down the unreasonably crowded street. Just because they couldn't have a sexual relationship didn't mean they couldn't hang out. While Emily would have always preferred being horizontal with a stunner like Blake, having a fellow food addict to wind down with at the end of the night was nearly as compelling. Despite having established a good relationship with Grant, she suddenly couldn't wait for him to leave.

Chapter Eleven

MARCH WAS RIGHT AROUND the corner, but February had its ice-cold tentacles wrapped around New York City and wasn't about to let go. Emily had her scarf wrapped around her face, the hood of her coat tied close to minimize the biting wind.

Stepping from the sidewalk cutout to cross the street, her boot caught—then slipped. Every muscle tensed as her leg shot out from under her. Instinctively, she threw her bag aside, anything to help her fight gravity. Time slowed… Her equilibrium tried, hard, to keep her upright. Arms flailing, her head dipped past horizontal, the battle lost. Slush flew into the air as she crashed to the street. Then a swath of bright colors filled her vision as a stabbing pain bore into her skull.

A stunningly bright light was trying to drill into her eye. Lifting a hand, she tried to push it away, but her coordination was sluggish.

"Good morning," a brisk voice said.

"What?"

"You're in the hospital." The light clicked off and a blurry face took its place. "Do you remember falling?"

"Falling?"

"Yes. You fell and hit your head."

"My head." Both hands raised to grab and hold the broken pieces of her skull together. Instead of a mass of parts, it felt the same as normal. But it couldn't have been. An intact skull couldn't possibly hurt like this.

"Can you tell me your name?"

Annoyed at the questioning, she gritted her teeth against the pain. "Emily Desjardins."

"Good." The man, who was getting a little clearer, made a note. "Do you know what today is?"

"Saturday." A burst of panic hit her. "I'm late for work!"

The doctor nodded. "Are you a waitress?"

"I'm a cook and I'm late!"

He put a hand on her shoulder to keep her from sitting up. "That explains why you kept begging the ambulance team to call the restaurant." He laughed a little. "That had them scratching their heads."

"I have to call right now! I'll lose my job!"

She wasn't getting through to this guy. He barely looked up as he made another note. "We got your emergency contact from your phone. Someone will be here to help you out."

"I need my phone," she insisted, her pounding pulse making her head hurt worse. As though that were possible.

"We're going to send you for a CAT scan." He probably thought a brisk pat to her leg showed sufficient empathy. He was wrong.

Time wasn't moving along at its usual rate. Days couldn't have passed, but when Chase appeared, anxious and out of breath, Emily would have sworn she hadn't seen him since Wednesday.

"God damn," he panted, leaning over her. "They wouldn't tell me anything! I threw up on the subway."

"Where am I?" she asked, grabbing his cold hand and holding on tight. "No one will talk to me."

"St. Matthias." He leaned close and inspected her face. "What happened?"

"Don't know." She had to close her eyes to stop his image from splitting in two. "Fell." Her pulse picked up again. "Call work!"

"Okay. Okay." His hand, now warmer, glided over her cheek. "I'll take care of it, Em. Do you have your phone?"

"I don't have my damn pants, Chase! All of my stuff is gone."

"I'll find someone who can help. Don't go away."

A few minutes…or a few hours later, he was back. "Got it," he said, holding the precious device up. "What's the number?"

"I don't know. It's in my contacts list."

"Right." He dialed, then pursed his lips. "Voice mail."

"Leave a message. Tell them where I am. I'm not sure if I can get there by service…"

He gave her the look he usually reserved for people arguing with themselves on the street. "Right. I'll tell them you might be late." He cleared his throat. "I'm calling for Emily Desjardins. She's at St. Matthias. We're not sure what happened, but she's got… I'm not sure what's wrong with her. I'll call back later. Oh. This is Chase, her friend." He hung up and winced. "I don't think I did a great job, but I'm freaked out!"

"Shh…" She begged. "Quiet. Please be as quiet as you can possibly be."

His gentle hand settled on her forehead. That didn't hurt. But it didn't help the pain. "What can I do, Em?"

"Do you have headphones?"

"Yeah. Right here." He pulled red muffler-style phones from around his neck.

"Can you put them on me and turn on something soothing? There's so much noise."

"I can do that." It took a second, but he finally got the headphones settled onto her ears and soon a piano concerto replaced the noise that had been more annoying that she could fathom. Then Chase took her hand, put it up against his chest, and held it tight.

X

The floor must have been made out of craggy boulders. How else could the gurney bounce around like they were off-roading?

They finally pulled into the holding pen for all of the people who'd gotten to the point where you'd seen a doctor, but weren't ready to go on your way. Chase took her hand again and leaned close. "Blake called. She's freaked out."

"I don't blame her. She's going to have to cover for me."

"That's not why, Em. She's worried."

"Me too." For the first time that day, Emily couldn't hold the tears in. She wasn't going to work. That was out of the question. Now she had to wonder if her head would ever be the same again. It sure as hell didn't feel like it possibly could.

Chase had gone to get something to eat, and he returned right when a harried young doctor appeared. "Ms. Desjardins?" He somehow managed to pronounce both of the esses.

"Yes?"

"I think we're going to have to keep you." He held up a black and grey image of a head, probably hers. With a pen, he circled a spot that looked the same as every other part. "This might be nothing, but there's a chance it's a slow bleed."

Her heart started to pound in her chest. Brains and bleeding were a very bad combo. "Will I… Surgery?"

"I don't think so," he said, almost scoffing, which made her feel immeasurably better. "But a skull fracture isn't anything to toy with."

"Fracture?" Chase gasped.

"Yeah. Right here." He pointed to an area next to the possible bleed. "It doesn't look too bad. It's a linear fracture. They're usually nothing to worry about. How'd you fall?"

"I don't know. Ice…"

"Yeah. We get a lot of those at this time of year. You must've hit the curb or something. It normally wouldn't crack at this spot if you'd fallen flat onto your back." He patted her on the leg, a technique they must have taught during your residency. "You'll probably be fine."

"Can I have anything for the pain?"

"Mmm… Not yet. But soon." Another dismissive pat and he was gone.

"I'm so sorry, Em," Chase soothed. "It must be killing you."

"Let's not use that word for a while, okay? Use nice words. Happy words." Then she closed her eyes so she didn't have to see the fear in his.

They would have let Chase stay, but Emily couldn't take his worried, fretful gaze another minute. After thanking him a dozen times, she lay in her uncomfortable bed and tried to sleep. At midnight, her phone rang, so shrill it was like a fire alarm. Seeing the number, she answered, "Hi." She still wasn't comfortable using her name.

"Jesus Christ, I've been so worried about you!" Blake said, her voice tight and strained. "I inspected every piece of fish we sold tonight, but I couldn't tell you what they were. All I could think about was you." She let out a breath. "Are you all right?"

"I don't know." She fought against it for a minute, but couldn't hold out. Her emotions took over and she was bawling like a baby in the blink of an eye.

"Shh... It'll be all right, Emily," Blake soothed, her voice slow and soft and gentle. "Come on now. Tell me what happened."

"I don't know," she sniffled, trying to get herself under control. "I was almost at work and I guess I fell. My memory's really hazy."

"It'll come back. You'll rest for a day or two and be back to your old self. Is it okay if I hop in a car and come see you?"

That shocked the hell out of her. "I think it's past visiting hours."

"Visiting hours?" Emily was sure Blake hadn't meant to shout, but it hurt like hell just the same. "You're in the hospital?"

"Uh-huh. I've got a fractured skull and they're concerned about a spot that might be bleeding."

"God damn it," Blake murmured. "Are you at St. Matthias?"

"Yeah."

"I'll be there in fifteen minutes."

That simple sentence was like a balm, soothing her jangled emotions. "You don't have to do that. Chase was with me all day, and my mom's coming in the morning. I'm not very good company, anyway."

"I don't want to hang out, Emily," she said softly. "I just don't want you to be frightened."

"Thank you." She started to cry again. "That's very nice of you." She sucked in a breath and tried to speak clearly. "I'll probably be fine. If my brain's not bleeding, I'll be in on Monday."

"No way. I believe you'll be fine, but you'll need to rest for a few days. Do what the doctors tell you."

"But you'll have to do my job..."

"I did it for three weeks before I hired you. Grant and I handled everything just fine."

"So you don't need me?" she asked, trying to joke.

"You know we do. But your head's worth more than this whole restaurant."

"Thanks. That means...a lot."

"Sure you don't want company? I'll raid my office fridge and bring you some cheese."

"You have some, and then go home. I know you're beat."

"Will you try to get some rest? You'll feel better if you can."

"It's hard to sleep with someone hitting you on the head with a sledgehammer, but I'll try."

"I'm really sorry, Emily. Truly."

"Thanks. I'll let you know when I'll be back."

"I'll call you tomorrow. Take care of yourself."

Emily hit the "end" button and tried to let Blake's concern soothe her. It helped, it definitely did, but some extra-strength pain relievers would have been a heck of a lot better.

Chase and her mom each held onto an arm and tried to guide her up her stairway. It was a fairly wide one, but it wasn't made for three people. Emily would have tried to get up on her own, but the vertigo came and went, and she was filled with dread at the thought of falling again. All her life she'd been notably sure-footed, but the accident made her doubt each step. That would take a while to go away.

They got up to the apartment, and she headed for her bedroom like a shot. With great care, her mom got her undressed, then pulled a T-shirt over her head and tucked her in. Kisses rained down on her poor, aching head, then a tender hand started to glide through her hair with whisper-soft care. Tears leaked out when her mom started to sing a favorite lullaby from her childhood. Emily rolled onto her side and tangled her arm around her mother's waist, relishing the comfort. It had been nearly thirty years since she'd been tended to like a baby, but it was just as welcome today as it had been then.

A soft voice woke Emily and she tried to figure out why she was imagining her mother in the room. Then she fought through the cobwebs to hear her say, "She's very dizzy, unsure on her feet, and much more emotional than usual. But they say that's to be expected."

Hmm…it wasn't her dad. That wasn't the tone they used when they talked.

"I'm not sure when she'll be back, but I know she'll try to return before she should." A quiet laugh filled the room. "Yes, she's hardheaded, but not as hardheaded as I wish. My poor girl's in a lot of pain. She doesn't complain, but I can see it on her face."

Emily closed her eyes and put a pillow over her head. Hearing your mom talk to your boss about you was freaky. And not in a good way.

The next time she woke, Carol said, "I talked to Blake."

"I heard you. Next time you complain about my being hardheaded, I'm going to remind you that you wished I was even worse."

"Ooo," she cooed. "You're getting your sense of humor back."

"It started to come back when I learned my brain wasn't bleeding. It'll be all back when my head stops hurting…if it ever does."

"I have some good news."

Emily opened one eye. "I could use some. What've you got?"

"Blake said she was going to pay you while you're out."

Both eyes shot open, then closed when the pain made her want to vomit. "What? She said that?"

"She did." Even though she couldn't see her, Emily knew her mother was happy. You could hear it in her voice.

"No one does that. No one."

"She said she wasn't going to replace you, so there was no reason not to keep expenses the same." A gentle hand landed on her knee. "I think she really likes you, honey. You're obviously doing a great job."

"Yeah, she likes me," Emily said. "But she's also a nice person. As long as you don't pee on the toilet seat, or serve old Brussels sprouts, she's got your back."

For three days, Emily did no more than go to the bathroom and lie in bed. It hurt to have the lights on, it hurt to watch TV, it hurt to listen to music. Not that she could have concentrated enough to do any of those things, even if she hadn't been in pain. All of the synapses in her brain must have been reorganizing, not yet able to process more than the most rudimentary commands. The only thing she enjoyed was having her mom or Chase read to her—softly. It didn't matter what they read, since she couldn't follow anything complex. But having someone she loved speak in a rhythmic cadence calmed her and made her able to nap.

The first time she'd been able to go to the bathroom on her own she gasped when she steadied herself in front of the mirror to take a look. No one had told her she had two gruesome black eyes, swollen and mottled skin that turned her stomach to look at. God knew what other secrets her caretakers were hiding, but her head hurt too much to even think of asking.

By Thursday, she was able to sit up and watch a movie, and that night she actually had an appetite. A bowl of chicken soup sat on a tray in front of her, but… She put her nose right over the bowl and breathed in. Nothing. How could that be? She'd watched her mom make it. Another breath. Still nothing. A tentative bite. Nothing. Somehow, neither the chicken, the onion, the carrot or the celery threw off a single flavor.

Looking up at her mom's anticipatory smile, she demanded, "Taste this!" and shoved the spoon at her.

Clearly puzzled, she did. "It's great. Adding that chicken stock you had…" Her eyes grew wide. "What's wrong, Emmy?"

"I can't taste it. I can't taste it!" She sniffed furiously, moving her head as fast as she could without getting dizzy. "I can't smell anything." Grabbing her mom's hand, she sniffed it. "I can't smell the onions. Or the chicken. Nothing!"

"Calm down, baby. I'll call Charlotte. Maybe this is…something that happens when you hurt your head. It'll pass. Don't worry."

Charlotte was swamped, but she finally had time to call back. Carol handed Emily the phone. After she put it to her ear, she said, "Charlotte?"

There was a long silence, then Charlotte cleared her throat. "I wish I didn't have to tell you this, Em, but it's possible…" She took in another breath. "It's probable that you've lost your sense of smell."

"Lost it? How can I have lost it? Charlotte, I make my living with my nose!"

"I know, I know. I put in some calls and found a guy who'll see you tomorrow. He's a top notch neurologist, Em. He'll be able to figure this out."

"Lost it?" she murmured, her dizziness returning with a vengeance.

The next afternoon, Emily and Carol sat in the consultation office of a Park Avenue neurologist. He'd examined her, and was now studying her CAT scan. Emily's guts were in knots, and she was squeezing her mom's hand so hard she knew it must have hurt. But she couldn't moderate anything. Not even her shaking hands.

The doctor turned around and gave her a sympathetic look.

Fuck!

"I wish I had better news, but I'm afraid your anosmia might be permanent."

She closed her eyes and let her head fall into her hand.

"The olfactory nerve sits right here," he said, although she didn't bother to look up. "When your brain jostles around that nerve can run over this bone structure and tear…or sever. I can't see the nerve, but this is a common result of a traumatic brain injury."

"Will it come back?" Carol asked. Ever the optimist.

"Maybe. At least partially. It might take six months or even a year, but you might have some improvement."

"I'm a chef," Emily said, finally lifting her head to look at him. "I make my living with my sense of smell."

"You still have your sense of taste," he said, clearly trying to cheer her up.

She fixed him with a glare. "Do you really think that's the same?"

"No, it's not." He stood up and extended his hand. "But your brain seems in perfect shape other than that. Trust me, it's better to lose your sense of smell than your ability to speak, or your vision. If you had any idea of how many people die from falls just like yours…"

"I'm grateful for that," Emily said, getting up to shake his hand. "And I'm very grateful you took the time to see me."

"I'm glad I was able to." He walked them to the door, adding, "You can try Vitamin B-6. And some people claim a steroidal nasal spray helps."

"But it doesn't, right?"

"A severed nerve can't fix itself, Emily, but an awful lot of people wish it could."

It took a load of convincing, but Emily finally got her mother booked on a flight home on Saturday morning. They spent their last few minutes together standing in Emily's room, holding each other.

"You'll never know how it feels to have your child lose something so dear," Carol murmured. "I'd give you all of my senses if I could."

"I know, mom. I know." They broke apart and she kissed her on the cheek. "It's been wonderful having you here. As good as Chase is, he doesn't hold a candle to the way you take care of me."

Carol held her at arm's length and gazed at her, clearly worried. "You're not…you're not feeling depressed, are you, baby?"

"Of course I'm depressed, but I think I'll bounce back."

"You haven't had any thoughts of…"

"Killing myself? God, no. I'm shaky now, but I'll be all right. Once I get back to work and…" She caught herself. "If I get back to work."

"You will," Carol said, not a single note of doubt in her voice. "You're a very resourceful girl."

"I know. But resources don't make up for not being able to taste what you cook. I just pray I can work by sight and memory. If not, I guess I'll..." She shook her head mournfully. "I have no idea what I'll do."

Chase had stayed at Natasha's while her mom was in town. If Emily had been as thoughtful as she'd like to be, she would have called him to tell him he could return whenever he wanted. But a pulsing need, a burning desire she couldn't begin to resist, kept her from touching the phone.

She was finally alone. No one to gaze at her with eyes brimming with solicitude and sadness. No one to look up anxiously when Emily simply got up to go to the bathroom. No one to try with all of her might to make a dish that would awaken Emily's sense of smell. It was remarkably freeing not to have to worry about anyone else, not to have to try to be cheerful, not to have to see the disappointment in her mother's face when yet another meal couldn't resuscitate a lifeless nerve.

But she was also lonely. Achingly lonely. Having to be sociable had given her something to focus on. Now she was left with the awful sense of loss, the worst she'd experienced. Even though she knew there would be far, far greater struggles in her life, this one had devastated her. Had made her doubt the safety and reliability of the very ground she walked on.

Lying on her neatly made bed, she bunched up a pillow and cried into it; great, heaving sobs that made her ache. She hadn't just lost something that gave her such pleasure, she was probably going to lose the job she loved with all her heart. She had just two days to get her head on straight and come up with a plan to keep it. The problem was, she didn't know where to start.

On Monday morning, Emily got ready early and started her walk to the train. Nothing tickled her nose. No exhaust, no burning rubber, no eggs frying at the Columbian diner. There was now an invisible barrier between her and the aromatic world. A permanent, impenetrable barrier. She'd never thought of it this way, but her sense of smell was her main portal to the world, such an important part of the way she experienced life that she found herself unable to believe it was gone. But her subconscious must have believed, since it made her burst into tears dozens of times a day. Her emotions were all over the place, as the doctor said they would be for quite a while. But crying silently the whole way to work was a new and very unpleasant experience, one she couldn't afford to lapse into once she was in the kitchen.

After pushing her way through the loading dock doors, she stood stock still, tears rolling down her cheeks when the kitchen smelled like absolutely nothing. Her home away from home, the place she loved to immerse herself in, would never be the same.

Emily worked her way through the day's deliveries robotically, and when she got to the final box she stared at a sample their cheesemonger had sent. A slice of a sheep's milk cheese she loved rested in her hand. It was a chameleon—sometimes pungent, sometimes bordering on sweetness. It all depended on the time of year and what the sheep had been grazing on. Taking a knife, she scraped off a corner and stuck it into her mouth. Great mouth-feel, creamy and thick. But the flavor? Nothing. Not a single element. She opened her mouth and breathed in as deeply as she could. Eyes closed, she sucked the air in again, forcing it over her palate.

A hand landed on her shoulder. "I don't know which sight is more welcome," Blake said, smiling down at her. "You or that cheese."

Emily tilted her head, letting Blake see the obvious damage.

"Whoa! Did you get into the fight before or after you fractured your skull?"

"Side effect." She probably should have used makeup to cover the purple, green and yellow bruises that lingered under her eyes, but the heat would have made anything she tried run down her face.

Blake took the knife and cut off a bite. "Mmm. The cheese is fantastic, but…seeing you, even with your multi-colored eyes, takes first place." Resting her hand on Emily's head, her voice gentled. "How does it feel?"

"It's still tender. Right here." Her hand lifted to touch the spot, still noticeably swollen and hot to the touch. "But I'm not dizzy any more."

"Are you sure your doctor said you can work?"

"He did. No restrictions." Just the inability to taste a God damned thing!

"I'm…we're very happy to have you back." Blake patted her shoulder, then went into her office. "Come on in and let's discuss the menu."

That she could still do. You didn't have to smell to create. Just to execute.

✗

Service was a mess. A true mess.

A dish's smell changed subtly right before it was cooked to the proper point. She'd never realized she used that slight change to instinctively know when to put the sides up on the pass, but her timing was off so many times it finally dawned on her. Of course, she'd known food gave off different compounds as it cooked, but she'd honestly never thought about it to any degree. It was simply a reflex she'd honed. Now she had to find a way to compensate for not being able to recognize that.

Good fucking luck.

For the third time, Blake send a dish back down the line. "Salt," she snapped when a turnip puree came back. Kermit was a good cook, and had progressed in just the week Emily had been out. But like most novices, he was inconsistent in his seasonings. She'd worked with Alicia for months to get her up to speed. How would she give Kermit any feedback? Everything tasted the same. Like gruel.

Once the turnips had been rejected, Blake began to taste everything from Emily's side of the pass. The last time she pushed a pan back, she glared hotly. "Have you run out of pepper?"

"No, Chef." Hurriedly, she moved down to Kermit. "You've got to kick it up. Don't be afraid to season."

"Oui, Chef," he said, clearly embarrassed. "I'll pay more attention."

He'd better. Both of their jobs were on the line.

Things calmed down around ten, but Emily stuck it out until end of service. The scowls, puzzled looks and outright glowers she'd earned would have to be dealt with. As soon as the last order came through, Blake headed for her office, with Emily right behind her.

"What in the hell was that all about?" Blake demanded, taking her apron off and throwing it to the sofa. "Is your head…bothering you?"

"No, no, I'm just off my game. I guess it's going to take me a while to get back into the flow."

Gazing at her with concern, Blake said, "We don't have a while, Emily. You need to bring it. Tomorrow."

The next day, Emily and Grant were hurriedly preparing the specials for the presentation to the front of the house staff. She was making a terrine, with Kermit working away next to her. Blake came by, stopped and stuck a spoon into the creamy leeks he was making. A scowl settled onto her face, making Emily's heart race.

"Taste," Blake demanded, sticking the spoon into her mouth like she would with a baby.

The faintest vegetal aroma came in. It wasn't specific, but she was pleased she could at least tell it was some kind of plant. An unspecified plant experienced through a pair of wool socks. "Yes, Chef?"

"What does it need?" Those dark eyes bore into her.

"I'm not sure, Chef."

Fuming, Blake turned and added something, then stuck the spoon into Emily's mouth again. *Hurrah!* She got a taste. A real taste! Brightly, she smiled and said, "Horseradish. You added horseradish."

"No," she grumbled. "I added crème fraîche, which rounded out the flavor, letting you taste the horseradish that was already there." Kermit was bent over his pans, trying to act like he was invisible.

Suddenly, Emily was being dragged into the office by the shoulder of her jacket. After Blake slammed the door, she stood just inches away, staring at Emily like she was an imposter. "What in the hell has happened to you? You've…lost your talent."

"No, I haven't." She couldn't look at her. She just couldn't. Her head dropped low, and her voice was shaky, but she got it out. "I lost my sense of smell. The accident…"

Blake dropped into her chair, hitting it so hard the metal groaned. "Oh, my god."

Emily lifted her head to see her face. It was ashen.

"I still have my sense of taste…"

"You've only got bitter, salty, sweet, sour and umami? That's it?"

"That's all I have. Probably all I'll ever have."

Blake dropped her head into her hands, which were shaking. "Oh, my god." With a heavy sigh, she lifted her head and met Emily's gaze. "That's worse than losing a hand." Her eyes were brimming with compassion. "How can you go on?"

"I'm not sure I can." She collapsed into her usual chair and began to cry. Soon, great, heaving sobs poured from her. She'd been holding back, trying to look on the bright side, trying to be happy she hadn't died, or lost her sight, or her ability to think clearly, or remember things, or speak. But she hadn't allowed herself to grieve, and her body picked that second to start.

Blake sat, helplessly, in her chair. She looked like she wanted to help, to do something, but didn't have a clue what to offer.

It took much, much too long, but Emily finally got herself under control. The sleeves of her jacket were wet with her tears, and her nose continued to run, but she'd stopped wailing. Looking up, she caught Blake's expression. Emily knew her well enough by now to read every element in that look—sympathy, concern, compassion, a little bit of despair, and a cold-blooded realization that Emily was no longer the talent she'd come to rely on.

"I don't know how to work around this," Blake said quietly.

"I don't either. I guess…I guess I'll quit."

"No. Don't do that." Blake's strong, confident voice was back in place. "You're very, very good, Emily. You're a great asset to the restaurant. We'll figure something out." She put her fist up to her mouth, her brow deeply furrowed. "We'll tell Brady you've got some allergy problems and can't taste the sides. He's got a good palate."

"That can work. For a little while. But not permanently. When he's cooking four things at once, he can't let himself be interrupted."

"No, it can't work permanently." She folded her arms and let her head drop to rest on them. "I don't know what will."

Emily worked as hard as she ever had, trying to be on top of everything at once. She arranged each order, just like she normally did before placing it on the pass. When Brady had a second, they switched places, and she tended the fish station as he carefully tested each of Kermit's sides. "Thyme," he barked, sending a pan almost flying. She'd never seen the guy show even a hint of anger, but he'd also never been right next to Blake at the pass. The pressure was tough to take even when you'd been cooking for nine years.

At the end of service, Brady was toast, baker's cap wet with perspiration that ran down his pink cheeks. "That was awful," he grumbled.

"Knock off," Emily said. "I'll clean your station."

He paused for just a second, then nodded and headed for the locker room. He must have really been trashed to let his boss, who'd just come back from a traumatic brain injury, clean up after him. She didn't blame him a bit.

Brady took up the slack for the rest of the week, but on Saturday afternoon Emily found herself sitting in Blake's office, both of them contemplative. Blake was doodling, drawing a series of dark, disturbing images. Skulls, knives, even a pool of blood next to a crumpled man.

"We've got to come up with a permanent solution," she said quietly. "Brady says he can't keep up."

Oh, damn. That hurt. Going over her head to complain sucked. "I know. It's impossible to fire six fish while you're trying to..." She struggled for the word. "Uhm...the sides." Words were missing, lost in the mush that used to be a smooth-running brain.

Blake caught it. She caught everything. But other than a slightly raised eyebrow, she didn't comment. She was too focused on getting her point across. "We need to come up with something. By Monday."

Emily looked at her blankly. "I don't have any ideas."

"I've got one." She cleared her throat, then slowly met Emily's eyes. "You and Brady can switch jobs. He's close to being ready to move up, and with your help he'd have an easy transition."

Emily gulped, trying to swallow around the knot in her throat. "He's twenty-three."

"I know. But you've learned age isn't what matters." Their eyes met. "You have to be able to do the job, Emily. On a slow night, I can handle tasting. But on a Saturday? You know I rarely have time to plate, much less taste." She looked down and continued her gloomy drawings. "I need two strong sous. That's just not a negotiable point."

"And I'll never be back to normal."

Looking up, Blake said, "You know how to season fish with your eyes closed. I know it's not what you want, but being chef de parti isn't a demotion. It's..." She bit at her lip for a second, clearly at a loss. "Okay, it's a demotion, but it's the only way you can cook at this level."

"I know that," she said quietly. "I figured that out the night I realized my sense of smell was gone."

"We'll tell everyone the truth. They'll understand you're not being demoted. You're just switching to a job that suits you better with your... disability. They'll sympathize," she said, obviously trying to put a good spin on it.

Emily waited until their eyes met again. "Would you want your coworkers' sympathy?"

Her expression grew dark. "No, I wouldn't."

Standing, Emily said, "I'll find a replacement for Brady. If you could keep me on for a few days, I'd appreciate it. That'll let me get a new poissonnier in and spend time showing Brady how to do the ordering and the time cards. The transition will be easier this way."

"Take a week." Blake's voice was gentle, soothing, but she didn't meet Emily's eyes.

"If I have to. But a few days might be enough. You can tell Brady he's moving up."

Blake finally looked up and gazed at her for a few seconds, like she was hesitant to say what was on her mind. "What will you tell people? Why will you say you're leaving?"

Her hand was sweaty where it rested on the doorknob. "I don't know. Can I think of a story before you talk to Brady? Ideally, I'd like to have something lined up before I announce I'm leaving."

"As a poissonnier?"

"That's all I'm qualified to do, Chef."

"But you won't do it here."

Emily looked at her, praying for understanding. "No. I have to work where I have people's respect, not their sympathy."

Blake stood and they locked gazes for a minute. "I'll make some calls. I'll get you placed." Reaching out, she squeezed Emily's shoulder gently. "You'll be an excellent poissonnier. I'm certain of that."

"I am too," she sighed as she opened the door, "since I was excellent three years ago."

They made the announcement on Wednesday, during the lull before service. Brady was congratulated, seemingly sincerely, but every head kept shifting toward her, wondering what was going on.

Blake put her hand on Emily's shoulder and forced a smile onto her face. "Emily's leaving us to move uptown. She's going to help Le Lapin add another Michelin star to the two they already have."

A murmur of excitement rumbled through the room. Only Grant gave her a quizzical look.

"I want to thank Emily for her contributions over the past six months," Blake continued. "I've greatly enjoyed working with her, and I know you all have too."

Polite applause moved around the room. But it wasn't the kind of sound you'd hear for a real promotion. Blake hadn't said exactly what Emily was going to be doing, and that was an omission everyone noticed. As they broke apart, Grant made a bee-line for her.

"You're going to be sous at Le Lapin? I didn't hear about an opening. Who are you replacing? Herman or Klaus?"

"Neither. I'm going to be poissonnier."

His head cocked. "Why?"

She hadn't been able to come up with a believable story, but telling the truth wasn't an option. If there was any way she'd ever get her own restaurant, no one could know she had no sense of smell. That would make her radioactive. "I think they're close to getting another star. I thought I could be in the mix, making an impression. Then, when there's an opening, I'll be a known commodity."

"Those two are lifers," he said, openly suspicious. "Do you really think you can jump over them to be chef de cuisine when Daniel Lillianthal leaves?"

She gave him the slyest smile she possessed. "You never know."

Everyone was friendly, maybe even a little too enthusiastic in their goodbyes. But no one invited her out for drinks. That wasn't surprising. When someone left under curious circumstances, people kept their distance. Like you had something they might catch.

Emily wrapped up her knife roll, put all of her odds and ends into a colorful bag her mom had given her, and headed out. Blake was meeting with Grant in her office, so she passed by quickly, trying to avoid further questions. She'd jumped down from the loading dock for the last time and had just started down the alley when she heard a sharp, "Emily!"

The familiar voice caught her right in the solar plexus. It was going to suck not having that warm, confident presence at her side every day.

Blake came loping down the alley, just in her whites, frigid air clouding from her mouth as she spoke. "I hate to see you go. Out of everyone, every sous I've ever had, you were the one I knew could replace me."

Charmed, she shook her head. "I'm nowhere near as good as you are."

Smiling that cocky grin, she said, "I didn't say you were, but you could easily replace me. The quality of the restaurant wouldn't suffer one bit, and the morale would rise."

"Thanks," she said, about to choke up. "That means a lot. I'm very appreciative you got me on at Le Lapin. I'm not looking forward to working the line again, but it's still cooking."

"Take care of yourself." Blake clapped her on the shoulder. "And if your sense of smell comes back…"

"You'll be the first to know. Actually, you'll hear me shouting with joy." Her mood darkened. "But that's not going to happen."

Blake stood there, clearly not wanting to leave, despite the cold. "Take care," she said, repeating herself.

"I will." She gave the best smile she could summon, then turned and started to walk.

"You're good, Emily. Really good. Don't let this ruin it for you."

"Oui, Chef," she said, letting the tears fall as she shuffled down the alley, heading for the subway.

Chapter Twelve

ON HER FIRST DAY AT her new job, Emily entered the locker room and put on her new chef's jacket. "Le Lapin" was embroidered in rose above a delicate outline of a rabbit. She snapped the jacket into place and took a look at herself in the full-length mirror.

The changing room was much bigger than Blake's, with long lockers for at least forty people, each labeled with names. And this was just for the back of the house staff. The FOH had their own space. Her locker was fifth in the row, behind Daniel Lillianthal, the chef de cuisine, Helmut Langer, the sous chef for the meat side, and Klaus Klum, the sous for fish—her boss. John Morrow, undoubtedly the rôtisseur, was fourth. With a moment of regret, she realized she'd be third if she were still at Blake's. Angrily, she tried to slap some sense into herself. Where you lined up wasn't a big deal. Who'd complain about coming in at two in the afternoon to make two dollars an hour more? Looking at herself critically for a few seconds, she had to admit she was the fool who'd complain. She'd much rather be sous than chef de parti, even at a more prestigious restaurant. But she'd made the best of a bad situation, with Blake's help, and was determined to attack her new job with gusto.

After leaving the locker room, she passed into the main kitchen. The ceilings were higher, air moved more freely, and, even though twice as many people filled the place, it was quieter. That was probably due to acoustics, but it still felt odd.

She'd spoken to both Daniel and Klaus when she'd interviewed, and she recognized Klaus by his bald, shiny head as he bent over to arrange something on a plate. Approaching from the side, she said, "Klaus? I wanted to check in and let you know I'm here."

He nodded, not looking up as he very delicately placed currants around a piece of fish. "Very good. Welcome, Emily. You know what to do, right?"

"Set up my station and butcher some fish."

"Perfect. Talk to Fernando, your entremetier. He'll tell you how we do things."

"Great."

The hot side of the room was much bigger than she was used to, with far more cooking stations. But a guy stood on the left of the pass, weighing portions of beef, so he had to be the rôtisseur. That meant she was on the right. Just like at Blake's. As she studied the layout, she noted nearly everything was like it had been at Blake's, which was a little odd. None of the other restaurants she'd worked in had been similar, each of them using the space they had to optimize the layout. Here, as at Blake's, it seemed the kitchens had been arranged according to a shared plan.

Fernando was very helpful, showing her around with a casual, but professional attitude. Once she'd learned where the walk-in was and how big their portions should be, she got to work, butchering four styrofoam containers of whole fish in an hour. Now she set to work on knocking larger pieces of fish into portion sizes. Given that their focus was fish, she had a lot more product to work through than the rôtisseur. But she was cool with that. It was actually nice to focus on something she was supremely confident of. Her foundations had been shaken those last few days at Blake's. Being unable to taste was so disorienting that she questioned every single one of her competencies. Maybe Le Lapin would help her build them back up again.

Her first dinner service was...interesting. Things had gone smoothly, the way she suspected they always did. Most of the cooks had been there for a long time, and most of them were lifers, with no interest in moving up or out. That was very good for a restaurant, but it took away the high-wire act you got at a place with lots of turnover.

Emily got into a groove after the first hour, shaking pans on the flattop, concentrating with every bit of her focus. One of their main courses was a pike that she finished with a dollop of crème fraîche and a spoonful of golden caviar. She'd run out of caviar and called down to the garde manger, "Hey, Rudolph, can I have a tin of…" She had no idea what the word was. Images of round, golden balls, shimmering in the bright light filled her mind, but the word was nowhere to be found.

Rudolph kept turning his head, waiting for her to finish her request while he worked on his cold appetizers. A wave of panic washed through her. First taste, then words? Finally, she dashed over to Rudolph and showed him the empty container.

"More?"

"Golden or black?"

"Golden," she said. That's it. It was golden…

Fuck!

She ran back to her station and started to fire the next order that Daniel called out. Then she thought of her visit to the neurologist. He'd asked, several times, if she was having trouble thinking of names and words. At the time she'd brushed it off, but she wasn't taking the question lightly now. *God damn it!* At least she'd made the right choice to drop out of medical school. You'd freak a patient out if you told them the thing in their chest that beat and pumped blood around was on the fritz. In a restaurant, not being able to think of words would just make the other guys assume you were hung over.

Chase and Natasha were in the living room, eating ice cream while they watched the end of a movie. Emily started to tiptoe past them to get to her room, but Chase hit the pause button and gave her an outraged look. "We waited up for you, only to have you try to sneak past us?"

"I'm not sneaking," she said, walking over to take the pint from his hand. He offered up the spoon, and she put a bite of…whatever…into her mouth. But it was sweet, she was sure it was sweet.

She was standing close to the back of the sofa and Chase grasped her hand and brought it to his nose. "How many cats followed you home?"

"Oh, shit." She held her hand to her nose. Nothing. "Is it bad?"

"No," Natasha said, giving Chase a reproving look. "He's just being funny."

Emily handed the ice cream back and walked around to sit on an upholstered chair. "Were you really waiting up for me?"

"You don't think we had to watch 'Road House' one more time, did you?"

Emily shrugged. "Maybe you're big Patrick Swayze fans."

"How was your first day?" Natasha asked, gazing at Emily like she was waiting for her SAT results.

"It was fine. People were pretty friendly, they've got so many interns they're always running around trying to help you out, and everyone is well seasoned. No rookies screwing things up."

"That sounds good," Chase said, clearly wanting more.

"It was fine. Really." She kicked off her running shoes, very glad to have, hopefully, put her winter boots away for the year.

"I don't see much enthusiasm bubbling over there," he said, looking at her even more carefully.

The perky attitude she'd failed to sell drained away in a second. "It's routine, Chase. There's nothing wrong with that, but I've been used to more. A lot more. The job's easier, and I make more per hour, but it's… routine."

"I get that," he said, clearly trying to show empathy. "But you can't seriously want to work harder. You were killing yourself, Em. Working only seven or eight hours will let you have a life outside the restaurant. Once you've found some things to fill up your free time, you're gonna be relieved you moved. Guaranteed."

"You're probably right," she said, standing, then moving over to the sofa to kiss him on the cheek. She didn't know Natasha well enough to kiss her, so she gave her a friendly pat on the shoulder. "Even though I didn't kill myself, I'm still beat." She headed for her room, saying, "Thanks for waiting up. I appreciate it."

As she entered her room, she went straight for the bed, lying down fully clothed. It was wonderful to have friends who cared. But neither of them truly understood. She lived to cook. It wasn't something she did—it was who she *was.* Only being able to execute a routine was going to drive her nuts. It was still cooking—but not really. Not being able to smell the fish in the pan, or tell if the onions had been sitting too long and had gotten too strong… There were a million things a good cook did, and she wouldn't be able to do most of them. She was going to have to figure out a way to make her job more interesting or she was going to have to… After several seconds, she had to admit there wasn't another thing in the world she was qualified for, or wanted to do. She was a cook who couldn't taste, and that was like being a singer who'd lost her voice. It wouldn't kill you, but it sure did take a big, nasty bite out of your pleasure center.

Her first two weeks at Le Lapin moved along as smoothly as a Swiss watch. It was barely midnight, and she was already in her pajamas. Chase and Natasha were in his room, leaving her to channel surf to relax enough to sleep. She'd run through the whole lineup twice, not finding anything to land on. Then her phone rang, and she picked it up without looking at the display. "Yeah?"

"Emily? Blake."

"Yes, Chef?" She sat up straight, like she was in Blake's office.

"I wanted to see how you are. How are things at Le Lapin?"

"Things are fine. I think I'm fitting in."

"Good. Good." She didn't say another word, but Emily could hear scratching. She was probably doodling. Sometimes she lost track of a conversation when she was concentrating on a figure.

"How's Hernando working out?"

"Hernando?" A surprisingly long pause. "Oh, the new guy. He's fine. You did a good job in finding him. I like having a guy around who isn't hoping I die so he can take over."

"So Grant's well?" she teased.

"Yeah, he's fine. He's…Grant. One of my first jobs was working under a guy just like him. It took me a while to figure out not all cooks were angling to move up."

"Just most of them. Where was that? Your first job, I mean."

"France. You know I trained there."

"Where…specifically?"

"The first place I staged? Nice. My grandmother knew a guy who took me on."

"Your grandmother?" What in the hell? Whose grandmother got them a cooking job? An unpaid cooking job in a foreign country, no less.

"Yeah." The scratching grew louder. She must have been shading something in. "I wanted to learn to cook, and she wanted to help me out. A guy who ran a restaurant near us had a brother who owned a place in Nice. Room, board, and Sundays off." She chuckled. "I was thrilled."

"Was that after…" She had no idea if Blake had gone to college or cooking school.

"After I threatened to take off on my own."

"Uhm, let me know if I'm prying, but I have no idea what you're talking about."

"Really? I'm not being clear?"

"You're opaque. When was this?"

"Oh…" She chuckled softly. "You want a timeline."

"Yeah, I guess I do."

"It was the end of my sophomore year."

"Mmm. I know a lot of people who left school after two years. Once you have to declare a major—"

"Not college. High school."

"What?" Emily wished she could pull that last word back in. She wasn't sure, but she might have shouted. But Blake took it in stride, not even commenting on her volume.

"Uh-huh. Things were… I had some trouble and threatened to take off. You know."

Emily did *not* know. In her group of friends, you were a bum if you didn't finish graduate or professional school. "You moved to France when you were still in high school. Alone."

"No, not alone. My grandmother went with me. She stayed for a couple of weeks to make sure everything was on the up and up."

"Was it?"

"Yep. When she saw that Chef Lomelle was running a respectable operation, and I had a decent place to sleep and was getting fed—she took off."

"And you stayed for how long?"

"Mmm..." A crackling noise replaced the scratching. That sheet must have been filled. "I've been here for four years, and at Jean-Michel's for two. That means I was in France for eight."

She didn't need to add Jean-Michel's last name. Everyone knew the great man.

Wait!

"How long?"

"Eight years. Nice, Eugénie-les-Bains, Bordeaux and Paris."

"Damn, you'd seen all of France by the time you were twenty."

"Not really. I didn't get paid until I hit Bordeaux. And the pittance I got there limited my travel options. I was only able to poke around a little, mostly by going to visit co-workers' families."

"Weren't you scared? I went to science camp when I was fifteen and almost called home to beg my parents to come get me."

"Nah. It was intimidating, but I wasn't afraid. I'd rather be challenged than bored any day of the week." A funny noise came through the phone, then Emily heard her chew. "Sorry, I was so busy today I haven't eaten a bite." Her voice grew low and playful. "After everyone left, I snuck into the walk-in and stole some cheese."

A sense memory of layers of flavor hit her like a punch to the gut. It had been weeks, but she still woke in a panic most mornings, sure something was horribly wrong, unsure of what. It always took a few seconds for her heart to stop pounding after she envisioned herself falling through the air—knowing she was going to hit the pavement and lose a part of herself.

"Damn, I miss cheese."

"No improvement, huh?"

"Mmm..." She thought of how to describe her current state. "I think my sense of taste has started to sort itself out. Like salt is more predominant than it used to be, so I try to avoid it. Sugar's more reliable. I can almost always tell if something's sweet, even though I don't get any nuance." She let out a brief laugh. "You should see my refrigerator. Nothing but vanilla ice cream."

"You won't have a Vitamin D deficiency. Of course you'll probably drop dead from a heart attack." She waited for a second, then said, "Is it okay to tease you?"

"Yes," Emily said decisively. "People are treating me differently, and it's annoying."

"Yeah? Like how?"

"Like my mom. We used to talk about food all of the time. She'd tell me about a new place she'd reviewed and we'd really get into it. Now she just talks about my dad and my sister."

"Wait. What do you mean, places she reviewed?"

"My mom's a restaurant critic. Didn't you know that?"

"I had no idea! Tell me more."

Blake had never sounded so excited about something so ordinary. "She's been reviewing restaurants since before I was born. It took me a while to realize everyone's mom didn't go out to dinner five nights a week."

"My mom went out a lot, but no one paid her."

"I don't know what she earns, but I don't think it's much. That doesn't bother her though. She'd probably do the job if all she got were the meals."

"She must have been a big influence," Blake said. "Here I thought your...who was it? A neighbor who taught you to cook?"

"Yeah. I guess I don't give my mom enough credit. Her work clearly influenced me. Going out to dinner with her let me see you could cook at a high level and make a decent living at it."

"That is so friggin' cool." She sounded absolutely delighted. "I've never met anyone who grew up with a restaurant critic. Did you go to a lot of places with her?"

"Hundreds. Literally hundreds. My sister and I tagged along all the time, but Charlotte thought of it as cutting into her TV time. For me, it was like church."

"I can't believe I didn't know something so cool about you."

Emily cocked her head, puzzled. How would Blake know anything at all about her or her family? They'd cooked together for six months, had two meals together, and two bouts of sex. None of that required much backstory.

Lying on her back, looking up at the cracks in the ceiling, Emily said, "So you left Le Cordon Bleu after one term?"

"Yeah." She let out a big yawn. "Sorry. Uhm, yeah. I'd already learned more staging than I did at school. My grandmother was willing to pay for me to get a certificate, but it seemed like a waste."

"Well, it hasn't hurt you. No one much cares what your education is. They just care if you can cook. And you can."

"Sometimes I feel like I'm losing my edge. But I'm having to get more creative again. Brady can't keep up with you. He keeps offering up recycled dishes, thinking I won't notice."

"Ha! I should have warned him. You've got a mind like a steel trap." She wasn't sure why she brought this up, but she said, "My mind's not quite what it used to be."

"Your mind?"

"Well, my brain. I've got some…fuck. What's the word for not being able to think of a word?"

"I have no—"

"Aphasia," she declared triumphantly. "I've got it, and it's been kicking my ass."

"From your fall?"

"Uh-huh. I checked on the internet, and lots of sites say it might be…what's the word for something that doesn't last long?"

"Brief?"

"No, another one. Something with a 'T'. Transitory," she said, immensely relieved every time her brain stuttered and she successfully retrieved a word. "Thank god I'm not an air traffic controller."

"You can cook without having to talk," Blake assured her. "I worked with a guy in Paris who was born deaf. He could speak, but he didn't like to. He was one of our best cooks."

"Thanks," Emily said. "It's nice to know I could lose another sense and still make a living."

"A missing sense or two won't stop Emily Desjardins." She yawned again. "I'd better get home." A rustling sound crackled over the line. "Damn! It's three thirty!"

"I guess it is." Emily started to sit up, then fell back onto the cushions. There was nothing wrong with sleeping on the sofa. It was right there…

"It was nice to catch up."

"Yeah, it was. Take care." She clicked off, then pondered their very long interchange while she scooted around, trying to get comfortable. Why had Blake called? Apparently, just to talk. Maybe they'd wind up being friends.

The next Saturday night, Emily was poised on the front step of her apartment building when her phone rang. It was stupid cold for April, still glove weather. Pulling off the right one with her teeth, she managed to slide the button to answer. "Yeah?"

"Emily?"

That silky smooth voice was as warm as a hug.

"Yes, Chef?" It was so stupid to call her chef! But that's how she thought of her. That was her identity.

"How are you?"

Time to get inside. Blake might be in a chatty mood. Emily always had her keys in her hand as she walked, letting her get into the vestibule quickly. "I'm okay. How about you?"

"Good. I'm good. Okay." She sounded so…flustered. What was going on? "Would you ever like to get a drink or something?"

"Sure. I still drink."

"Great. When?"

"When would you like to?"

"Uhm…now?"

Damn, nothing like being direct! "I'm already home…"

"You want to, right? You can tell me if you don't. No hard feelings."

"No, I want to. Really. It's just the thought of walking back to the subway…"

"Oh." She sounded relieved. Proof that everyone had some level of self-doubt. "No problem. I'll come out there. I don't know how long that'll take, but…"

She thought for a moment. "How about meeting on the Upper East Side? We can both get there in about the same amount of time."

"Great. Do you know a good place?"

"Hell, yes. I'm a cook, aren't I? Cooks can ferret out a good bar like a bee can find honey."

Despite taking the time to shower, shave her legs, put on a nice shirt and clean jeans, Emily beat her to the spot. Blake was probably trying to find the "E" train after not being able to grab a cab. Finding one at midnight in TriBeCa was as bad as five p.m. in Midtown. Emily wasn't sure why she hadn't taken to routinely using a ride service. Knowing Blake, she liked to be able to scope out the driver before she got in. She was all about control.

A little while later, Blake's head popped in, then those piercing eyes scanned the crowd. A sweet smile lit her face when their eyes met. That was a very, very welcome sight. "Hi," Blake said when she approached. They hugged, briefly, slightly awkwardly. "Sorry that took me a while. I must have had a sign around my neck that said 'Blow past me.' Finally had to call a car and pay congestion pricing. The thieves," she grumbled softly.

"No problem." Emily jiggled her glass. "I'm with a friend."

"Oh-oh. I'd better catch up." She made eye contact with the bartender and he bustled over. "Scotch. Do you have anything interesting?"

Gruffly, he picked up a cocktail glass and shook his head. "No."

"Then…Scotch. Neat."

As he moved away, Blake leaned over and whispered, "I can see why you like it here."

She laughed. "I didn't say it was nice. I said it was good. No crowds. Cheap drinks."

Blake's drink was delivered, and she clinked her glass against Emily's. "To cheap drinks. The lifeblood of cooks everywhere."

It was warm in the bar, and Blake slipped her jacket off. A crisp white blouse caught the juke box's blue light, making it glow. "You look nice," Emily said. "I'd never guess you'd been at work for twelve hours."

"Fourteen. Brady's good, but he's no Emily Desjardins." She tilted her head, leveling her gaze. "I wish he were. I mean, I wish you were still around."

"I do too. I thought I'd be able to pick up some tips from Chef Laurent, but that's not going to happen."

"Is he ever there?"

"If he's been there, I haven't seen him. Do you know his chef de cuisine?"

"I know his name, but that's about it."

"Nice enough guy, but he's not as involved as you were. He works through his sous, mostly. He's more of a manager."

"Mmm…a clean coat."

"Right," Emily agreed, chuckling at the description. "He's always clean."

"You might as well wear a suit and tie if you're not going to cook. I can't imagine being in a kitchen and not tasting the food…" She stopped abruptly, then Emily could see her swallow. Her gaze was locked on the bar when she said, "I'm so sorry. That was insensitive."

Emily put a hand on her arm and gave it a squeeze. "No, it wasn't. You don't have to tiptoe around me. Just be normal."

"I'm a chef," she said, a charming grin lighting her face. "I don't know how to be normal."

After a second drink, they were both a little buzzed. Drinking at two a.m. seemed to make you sillier than the same amount of alcohol earlier in the evening. Emily didn't know anyone in the place, but Blake had gotten a few pointed stares which she didn't seem to notice. Emily wasn't sure if she was oblivious, or simply didn't mind being whispered about.

Blake leaned over and murmured into her ear. "You know what would be fun?"

"I've got a few ideas," she said, catching the lusty look in Blake's eyes. "What's on your list?"

"I think it's a good night to see Queens. Where exactly do you live?"

Smirking, Emily said, "Jackson Heights. You were in the car when the driver dropped me off after our Korean eat-off."

"Truth? Only Manhattan registers with me. Everything else seems foreign. But I've always wanted to see Jackson Heights. Is there a tour I could take…?"

"Yeah. There's a tour." She got up and started to put her coat on. "Let's go. The tour bus doesn't run very often at this time of night."

"We can take a cab…"

"Maybe you can, but cabs aren't in my budget."

Blake stood there for a moment, clearly indecisive. Then she grasped Emily's hand and pushed the door open. As her arm went up, a cab skidded to a stop in front of them. "There's only a slight extra charge for an additional passenger," she said as she held the door open. "Be my guest."

For some reason, the cabbie hadn't complained in the least about taking them to Queens. Maybe he'd thought Blake was with the Taxi Licensing Commission, given the way she kept leaning over the seat, checking his route.

Luckily, there wasn't a flight attendant anywhere near her bed, but Emily wasn't ready to use it yet. They hadn't even kissed, and going right to bed seemed too rushed. Leading Blake to the sofa, she sat close, but not close enough to touch. "Want another drink? I've got something a little better than what you've been choking down."

"It wasn't bad." She put her hands around her knee and stretched her back out. "I don't think I need any more alcohol. I'm starting to relax."

Her eyes were still bright, with her body giving off an electric energy that seemed more like someone who'd been up an hour or two rather than fifteen or sixteen. She leaned over and snuck an arm around Emily's shoulders, pulling her close. "I've really missed having you around," she murmured into her ear. "We'd just gotten into a good groove." Leaning back, she met her gaze. "Don't you think?"

"I do." Sighing, she let her head rest on Blake's shoulder. "But I had to leave. It would have been too weird to move down the line."

"I know." They sat there, neither one talking, for quite a while, while Emily tried to figure out why they were there. Blake hadn't given off much in the way of sexual vibes, but she also wasn't very talkative. Did she…was she there simply to hang out? Maybe she was a lonely insomniac.

"Have you been seeing anyone?" Blake asked.

"Not a soul. You?"

"I haven't been looking." Shrugging, she added, "I guess I've been too busy." She shifted a little and leaned close, with her sexy voice now in play. "This morning, I woke up ready for sex. All day long, I've been extra sensitive. Once I finished up I decided I wanted to…you know. I'm really glad you were free."

"I am too. I'm glad you're here."

"Maybe you could show me around. There's a room I'd really like to see…" Her wolfish smile was too cute.

Blake was probably uncomfortable starting anything in the living room, given Emily's plethora of roommates. Time to fix that.

Emily got up and took her hand, then led her into the bedroom. It wasn't lavishly decorated, but she'd taken some care to make it homey and personal. Blake immediately went to the desk and picked up a photo.

"Mmm, mmm. I would have finished high school if you'd been in my class."

"That's college," she said, chuckling, "Although I'll admit Chase and I look like we haven't hit puberty yet."

Her head nodded briefly. "I forgot you went to college. I remember reading your resume, but I only paid attention to where you'd worked."

She moved to stand beside Blake. "Not going to college wasn't an option. My dad's a chemistry professor."

"No kidding!" She looked amazed. Like she'd never met an academic.

"Yeah. I was going to become a doctor, but I bailed after a year."

"A doctor? You went to medical school?" If her eyes got any wider, they might fall out.

"*Started* medical school. It took me a year to find I didn't have the drive or the passion or the desire that the other people did. So I upset the hell out of my parents by dropping out to go to cooking school."

"I'm glad you did," Blake said, slinging an arm around her shoulders. "Even though you could be one of my investors if you'd become a rich doctor. That'd be cool."

"I doubt we'd have met. That'd be uncool." She turned to regard her, loving the way her eyes twinkled in the dim light.

"I really like you, Emily." Blake held her face in her hands and placed an achingly gentle kiss on her lips. "It's so rare for me to meet someone I get along with this well." Emily closed her eyes as she tried to take it in. First kisses always gave her a big boost, sparking her libido. But this time that rush of feeling didn't appear. No burst of sensation made her tingle.

It was working for Blake, though. Her lips pressed firmly against Emily's, then she started to move them toward the bed. Emily lay on her back, her fingers tangling in Blake's hair as she was kissed with increasing drive. It was unnerving! Like being kissed through plastic. She concentrated on the suppleness of Blake's lips, and the feel of her body, but without her scent the experience didn't get inside. Nothing clicked.

Even though she tried to go along and respond like she normally did, Emily wasn't pulling it off. Slowing down, Blake's lips moved to her ear. "What's wrong? You're not…you don't seem into this."

She sat up, with her stomach clenching from nerves. "I am. Of course I am. But…"

God damn it!

Standing on shaking legs, she told the truth. "Nothing's right. Every damn thing I do has a damper on it."

"Everything…?" Blake looked up at her, clearly confused.

It all started to come out. The frustration, the confusion. "I don't even *think* about sex any more. Everything that used to make me perk up is gone."

"Everything?"

"Everything," she stressed. "I used to smell a woman's perfume when she passed me on the street. That one little thing would make me start to feel sexy. Stuff like that all added up to give me a sex drive." She grabbed Blake by the shoulders and stuck her face up against her neck. "I can't smell you!" Swiping her tongue along her neck, she added, "I can't taste your damn skin, which was fucking awesome." Flopping down beside Blake, Emily slapped her hands over her face. "I get off on smell, on taste." She wanted to cry, but reined herself in. "I will always remember the first time we kissed."

Blake put a hand on her leg, sharing a sad smile. "I'll remember it too."

Emily focused, recalling exactly how she'd felt. "We'd both been working all day, and I could read your skin and your hair like a map." She stuck her nose into her hair and breathed in. "Nothing!" She was so distraught she wanted to scream. "My turn-ons are gone, Chef. The things that made me wet have been taken from me, and I'm never, ever going to get them back." The finality of the loss kicked her in the chest. Her favorite things in the world were eating and having sex, and both had lost their allure.

"I'm so sorry," Blake soothed, gathering Emily into her powerful grip and holding her tightly. "I'm so sorry," she whispered again. "You lost something vital, Emily. Something you'll never replace. I can't imagine how it feels, but I know it's devastating."

That was it. No "It'll get better." No "Think of something else." No "Maybe your other senses will get sharper." No "I don't have a good sense of smell either." That was the worst one. The one that made her want to deliver a quick punch to the speaker's face. But Blake didn't push the platitudes or try to diminish the loss. She simply had empathy, which took a good-sized bite out of the isolation that had been building up inside. Having someone validate her loss instantly made it feel less harrowing.

They remained in that tender embrace for a long time, and when they broke apart Blake gently touched the spot on the crown of her head that was still vaguely sore. Emily nearly burst into tears again, deeply touched that Blake recalled exactly where the fracture was. She'd forgotten Emily's neighborhood, and hadn't recalled her year of med school, but she was spot-on with the important things.

"Are you hungry?" Blake asked, her voice still gentle and sweet.

"I should be, but..." She *wasn't* going to dwell on this. No one wanted to hear you whine every two seconds.

"You're losing weight," Blake said when her hand slid up under Emily's shirt and gripped her waist, now noticeably thinner. "Is your appetite screwed up?"

She nodded, not needing to add details. "There's a decent diner not far from here. If you want to go, I'll get something too." The sexiest woman who'd ever crossed her threshold had come for sex, but they were going to eat food that wouldn't taste like anything at all. Was that a kick in the face, or what?

Blake was staring at her, eyes focused sharply in concentration. "How are you with spicy food? Do you get any sensation from heat?"

"Don't know. I've been making peanut butter and jelly sandwiches for lunch every day. That at least gives me crunch and sugar."

"Think that bodega down the street is open?"

"Yeah. It's an all-nighter. Why?"

"I'll be back in a few minutes. Get some pans out. We're going to have breakfast."

Standing next to Blake at the counter, each of them quietly working, almost made her burst into tears. They'd never have this again. This easy camaraderie while working to feed people, to provide sustenance for a crowd. They couldn't work together, and they wouldn't have sex again. No one wanted to be with someone who couldn't get aroused. Especially a sexy beast like Blake. But chopping jalapeños and tomatoes and onions was soothing, even if she only knew they were onions by the tears dotting her cheeks.

Blake did all of the work after that, whipping up a spicy salsa, then making breakfast burritos with eggs, cheese and chorizo. Emily's mouth watered from the memory of the taste, then she took a bite, looking into Blake's lovely, expectant face.

"Heat," she said, trying to force her taste buds to get back in the game, if only to make Blake happy. "I've got a burn in the back of my mouth. And a little…a *little* something from the chorizo."

"Good. You've got to mix things up, Emily. You can't live on ice cream and peanut butter."

Her concern was almost palpable. Emily put a hand on her arm and gave it a squeeze. "Thanks for this. I appreciate it."

"I hope so, because I'm about to choke!" She wiped tears from her eyes with the back of a hand. "I love hot, spicy food, but I don't eat it often. One of my first chefs convinced me you burn out your taste buds if you get too fiery, and that's made me wary. Now I think he might have been right!"

Emily leaned up against her. "You're a good person. I just wish I could really taste this." She held the burrito up into the air. "A Blake Chadwick original, with a broken palate that can't appreciate it."

"You're not broken," Blake said, with a sober expression on her face. "You have what you have. Now you have to figure out how to live with what you've got." She held her nose closed with one hand, then took a bite of her food, eyes shut. "I get a certain richness from the chorizo, and some good mouth-feel from the egg." She frowned, clearly trying.

"Maybe that's all you can get. But you can find *some* pleasure in food. Maybe you'd do better with vegetables."

"Maybe. I'll try to be more creative."

Blake popped the last of her burrito into her mouth, then put her hands on Emily's shoulders. "You're very creative. Use that gift to give yourself texture and crunch and mouth-feel. If ice cream tastes good you're probably getting some pleasure from fat."

"Yeah, I guess I do."

"Exploit it. Use whatever you can to stimulate your senses. Darn it," she grumbled. "I should have done something with pomegranate. I bet you'd notice the burst of the seeds. You might get some of the sour taste, too."

"You're being awfully sweet." She tried hard to emphasize how touched she was. "I'll try to kick-start my limited palate."

"It's your only palate, Emily. Exploit it."

"I will." She got up and moved over to the sink to clean up. "Do you want to stay over? I bet you're tired."

Her head cocked like a startled puppy's. "Do you want me to leave?"

"Of course not. I just thought..." Embarrassment colored her cheeks. "I'm not much of a sex partner any more."

Frowning, Blake said, "You know, for a really creative woman, you're not looking at this the right way." She moved to the sink and took Emily's hand, then grabbed a towel and dried it. "We can clean later. Let's go make some progress on this little problem."

"It's not a little problem, Chef."

Blake stopped and gave her a half-smile. "You don't have to call me chef anymore."

"That's how I think of you." She swallowed, thoroughly embarrassed. "But I'll try to get past it if it makes you feel funny."

Blake bent and gave her a long, soft kiss. "If you want to call me Chef, I'm perfectly fine with it. I've been called worse."

They returned to the bedroom, and Blake sat down. Then she took Emily's hands and studied them. "I'm not, in any way, dismissing or trying to minimize how this has affected your sex drive." Their eyes met. "But sex is about more than scent. You have to shift some of your attention over to sight and feel. It won't be the same… I know that. But you can enjoy sex again. I know you can."

"I'll try. I will."

"You make this sound like a job." Their eyes met again, revealing Blake's puzzlement. "A job you don't want to do."

"No, I do. I *really* do. But…" She was so embarrassed she wanted to cry. But she had to get this out. "I'm not who I used to be. I don't feel sexy, and I'm sure I don't put out the same energy I used to. So you don't have to…" Her gaze slid to the bed. "I appreciate how kind you're being but—"

"Whoa!" Blake jumped to her feet. "This isn't sympathy sex! Your nose isn't working, but from my perspective you're just as sexy and pretty and bright and inviting as you were the first time we kissed. I'm into you, Emily, and I'm happy to slow down and go at your pace until you get back in the groove. Because you're going to," she said firmly. "I know that."

"I wish I could be as confident as you are. I just don't think you understand how important smell was to my sex drive—"

"I'm sure I don't. Everybody has her own things. But you can see and you can hear and you can feel. All of your nerves work except one, right? Are you going to let one nerve ruin your sex life?"

"I don't want to…"

"Then don't." Her eyes were blazing as she grasped Emily by the waistband and pulled her close. "Let me show you exactly what I find sexy about you. That might help you get back into the mood."

Gazing into Blake's eyes, so full of determination, gave her an emotional boost she desperately needed. A few graceful movements had Emily's shirt sliding from her shoulders, then her bra followed. Her chin tilted down, and she watched her nipples begin to harden. The room was lit by a small lamp on the desk, the multi-colored glass shade tinting her skin gold and amber. "Look at those," Blake soothed. "As ripe as a raspberry." She sat on the bed and pulled Emily to herself by the hips. Then her warm mouth captured a nipple and sucked it inside. Emily closed her eyes and let the increasing warmth pervade her body.

"That's nice," she murmured as her hands instinctively moved to glide through Blake's curls.

"Look at them," Blake urged, running her thumbs across the nipples. "Watch my face. See how I get off on touching you."

Their eyes met again, with the intimacy of the look hitting Emily in the chest. Those gorgeous brown eyes were locked onto her own, a slight smile covering Blake's mouth as she gently suckled. Then her eyes fluttered closed and she grasped Emily by the hips and pulled her in tightly. Her mouth opened wider when she started to suck lustily, enveloping the pale flesh. Soft, sexy sounds emerged, clearly reflecting her growing pleasure.

Emily's fingers stopped stroking, now gently holding Blake in place. A tingle started between her legs as she took in the enjoyment Blake got out of touching her, feeling through her body how much she was digging this.

Hands rested on her hips, now turning her toward the mirror. "Look at your breasts," she murmured. "That curve is perfect." A finger slid down her flesh, then glided up to brush across the hardened nipple. "And look at this." Arms encircled her to lower her zipper and push her jeans and bikinis to the floor. "So nice," she purred. "Just like I remember." Fingers tickled down her belly. "Look at how smooth and soft your skin is. Have you ever seen anything prettier? It's like marble come to life."

Blake was full of it, but it was working. Chills chased down Emily's spine as those warm fingers glided up and down her sides, always returning to her breasts. "I can't get enough of these." A low growl came from deep in Blake's chest. "More." She turned Emily again, then leaned close and sucked as much of the tender flesh as she could into her mouth. Emily watched, transfixed, as Blake's mouth moved slowly, sculpted cheeks drawing in as she licked and tongued every inch. Strong hands grasped her ass, kneading the flesh possessively while her breast was sucked hard, making her knees so weak she had to hold on to Blake to keep from tumbling over.

When she finally lifted her head, Blake sounded half drunk. Eyes smoldering, she murmured, "I would *love* to fuck you."

"I was just about to beg you to."

"Do you have…?"

"I do," she said, nodding vacantly. This was going to be good.

As Emily leaned over to open her bedside drawer, Blake stood and started to peel off her clothes. She'd been at work, so she wore her usual sturdy sports bra. As her fingers popped the closures, she said, "How do you feel about underwear?"

Emily stood, one hand holding her sex toys. "I feel good about it. What do you mean?"

"I was just wondering if underwear turns you on. It doesn't do a lot for me, but a lot of women like it."

"I like it kind of a lot," she admitted. Looking at Blake's breasts, she smiled. "But what's inside matters a lot more."

"Good to know. It's a nice garnish. Not a requirement."

Blake reached out and took the toys from Emily's hand. "Nice one." A smile quirked one corner of her mouth as she dexterously stepped into the harness and settled the toy in place. Emily usually pitched, but she prided herself on her versatility. Now, looking into Blake's burning gaze, she was damned glad she liked being on the flip side, because Blake looked like she'd never caught a day in her life. She was a pitcher, through and through.

Blake moved to her, wrapped her in a snug embrace and murmured into her ear, "We'll go slow. I want you to talk to me. Tell me how you feel."

A tendril of anxiety grabbed hold of her heart. Her confidence was so damned shaky. "I will. But I'm not sure I'm turned on enough yet. I'd better get some lube out—"

"I know how to tell." Blake gave her a gentle push, chuckling when Emily dropped to the bed. Then her knees were in the air, with Blake dropping to the floor in front of her. A gentle finger traced a line down her sex, and chills broke out as it traveled. "Your mind might not be connecting to your body the way it used to, but you're as slippery as an eel." Their eyes met again, with a sly smile making Blake's mouth quirk. "Can't be too sure, though. I'll take a closer look." Her head dipped and she used her warm, wet tongue to paint every part of Emily's skin, quickly making her purr with pleasure. She gripped Blake's shoulders, feeling the taut muscles as she moved. Those shoulders alone made her wet, but when they were matched with Blake's powerful, curvy body, her head spun.

After Emily nearly squirmed off the bed, Blake knelt next to her and pulled her up a few feet, handling her as effortlessly as she picked up a sack of potatoes in the kitchen. Returning to kneel at the foot of the bed, she sat back on her heels and placed Emily's legs over her shoulders. The expression on her face was beyond sexy. Confident, sure, determined and sizzling hot.

"Want to see how ready you are?" she asked, clearly playing a little game.

"I do."

That sexy grin grew wider. Then she slid her fingers inside Emily's body as she murmured, "You could hardly be wetter." Slowly, she eased her fingers in and out slowly, a satisfied smile covering her face. "Your body wants to be fucked." Their eyes met again. "Is your brain into it?"

Emily grabbed her hand and pulled it into herself, grinding on it. "What do you think?"

"I think every part of you is ready to go." Blake looked down, gripped the toy and slipped it inside, going so slowly Emily wanted to force her to move. When it was all the way in, Blake grasped her hips and started to move her, effortlessly grinding her against the toy at an excruciatingly slow, steady pace. She'd never had anyone fuck her like this, but in seconds Emily was biting her fist to stop from waking the neighbors. It was so deliberate, so dominant, so in control that Emily could let herself go. She could experience her own body in a completely new way, entirely under Blake's care.

The gorgeous creature filling her vision, golden in the warm light, was enough to make a statue swoon. Straining muscles shifted and flexed as they worked Emily's body against the pressure that completely filled her. Blake's luscious breasts swayed as she worked, slowly, carefully, unceasingly. Emily had never been fucked so methodically, or with so much pleasure. A sated, contented smile had settled onto Blake's face, making her look like she was having the time of her life. Knowing her, knowing how little bullshit she tolerated—made Emily believe. She could feel Blake's desire, could share it, join in it, be nurtured by it.

Gazes locked together, an intimacy that stunned her built with each thrust. It was like looking into her soul, with Blake unafraid to show her own need, her own desire. Emily had rarely felt so exposed, but an aura of perfect safety cosseted her. In Blake's warm, gentle hands she knew she was deeply cared for.

Emily reached down and clamped her hands around Blake's forearms, better able to take in the sensations when they were more connected. Everything was going to be fine. Sex was all in the mind, and she was a believer.

Blake lay on her back, legs and arms spread out. "Can you open a window?" she asked, her words sliding together.

"Too tired. But I'll fan you." Emily took the sheet and wafted it over her glowing skin. "I thought you were going to combust there for a minute."

"*Good* orgasm," she said, making a funny face. "Not that I've ever had a bad one, but that was one for the record books."

"I'd have to say you look satisfied."

"I'm not the only one." She grabbed Emily and pulled her roughly onto her body. A big smile was firmly affixed to her face as they rubbed noses. "For a woman who was ready to give up sex an hour or two ago…"

Smirking, Emily said, "I'm going to give it another chance. I might have been hasty."

"Yeah, you might have been." She snapped her wrist, making Emily yelp at the sharp slap to her ass. "You're a firecracker, and you know it. One missing sense isn't going to keep you down for long."

"It was strange," she said, rolling off to lie next to Blake. She started to play with her hair, making some of the damp strands curl exactly the way she wanted them to. "I'm not going to lie and say it was the same for me. I truly missed being able to taste you. But I was able to concentrate a little better than usual. All of my focus was on you."

"Whatever you did was a stunning success." She reached over and gave her another, gentler slap. "Now I've got to get moving."

"What?" She searched for the clock, then picked it up from the floor. One of their flailing legs must have kicked it. "It's six a.m."

"I know. If I get going, I might be able to get a good nap in."

"A nap? What am I missing?"

"Didn't I tell you what I got roped into?"

"No ropes have been mentioned."

She nodded, then moved to pick her jeans up off the floor. "I've got to go to some stupid celebrity chef auction this afternoon. If I win, and I'm definitely putting that in air quotes, I get to make dinner at some stranger's house."

"Tonight?"

She chuckled, shaking her head. "A future date to be negotiated. But it'll have to be a Sunday, my one damn day off."

"Why…? How…?"

"You met Jessica, Alan's wife, right?"

"Mmm, not exactly. But a woman came in once and you looked like you wanted to kill her. Is that her?"

"Probably. My homicidal urges come and go with the partners. Lately they've been on high alert. She's been after me to do all sorts of charity things, and this was the least horrible."

"Going to a stranger's house on your day off to cook is the least horrible?"

"Uh-huh. Now try to guess how bad the other things were." Shaking her head, she grumbled, "Not pretty."

Emily slid out of bed and wrapped Blake in a tender hug. "You were wonderful tonight. Sweet, caring, sexy—everything."

"It's not like I was giving blood, Emily." She bent and kissed her gently. "I had a great time."

"But you went out of your way to make me feel better. Don't act like you didn't."

"Okay, I did. But that was pure self-interest. When you find someone you get along with, someone who turns you on so much, who's not only sane but isn't clingy—you'd be stupid to give up easily."

"Thanks for not giving up." With a quick hug, she released her. "If you win, and I hope you don't, I'll come prep for you."

Blake gave her a warm, bright smile. "Then I hope I win. I'd love to cook alongside you again, even on a Sunday.

Chapter Thirteen

ON MONDAY AFTERNOON, EMILY was busily setting her station up, preparing for service. The pace, while intense, was nothing like it had been at Blake's. No more juggling a bunch of balls in the air, always trying to squeeze in a few minutes here and there to send a text or use the bathroom. Here, she was a cook. It could be boring, but sometimes the simplicity of the task was welcome, letting her focus every bit of her attention on the fish.

A presence at her back made her turn her head. "Good afternoon, Chef." Daniel Lillianthal, their chef de cuisine, stood behind her, ticking things off a checklist. He had different colored clipboards for things, the color key known only to him.

"Everything good?" he asked, not looking up. He was a funny mix. In some ways he seemed like an accountant, very concerned with portion control and waste. But he was also fairly laid back. She'd heard he was from Colorado, and she could easily see him hanging around a lodge, sipping cocoa, après ski.

"Fine. Hey, I've got some geoduck clams left over from service last night."

"Still perfect?" His head cocked.

"Yeah." She'd had the guy with the best palate in the whole kitchen smell them, just to make sure. "We have enough for about fifty starters."

"Mmm. I'll make a note." He looked at one of the big clocks up near the ceiling. "We don't have time to do anything complex with them."

"I've got an idea." She'd never been asked to contribute to menu creation, nor had Klaus, her boss, near as she could tell. But Daniel didn't seem like the kind of guy who minded help, so why not try?

"Hit me."

"We don't have anything with an Asian influence today. I'd make a geoduck mousseline and work in some edamame."

"That's it?" He made a note, then looked up, waiting.

"I'd round it out with wasabi..." She considered the heat, knowing she had to keep it delicate for their less adventurous guests. "Maybe a creamy wasabi sauce to temper it. And lime."

"We'll smoke the edamame," he said, jotting that down. "That'll give it more depth. I'll asked Manuel to make the wasabi sauce. Spicy, but not hot."

It was *so* nice to work at a restaurant with a saucier. Manuel had been whipping up savory concoctions since Emily was a girl, and there was nothing the guy couldn't do—and do perfectly.

Daniel tapped the clipboard with his pen. "Do you like creating dishes?"

"I love it. That's where the fun is."

His lips pursed for a second, as if he was about to ask a question. Then he reeled it back in, his expression blank. "Let me know any time you have an idea."

"I will. I've been treading lightly, trying not to step on any toes."

"That's not an issue here."

"I wouldn't be going over Klaus's head?"

"Not at all. Klaus's job doesn't include menu creation." He gazed at her for another few seconds, then reiterated, "I'm happy to hear any suggestions you have." Then he dashed away, clipboard clutched tight.

By the end of the month, Daniel was a regular visitor. A few minutes after she arrived in the afternoon, he'd stroll by and cock his head. That was his signal. *Hit me with whatever you've got.* That encouragement made her voluntarily come in a little earlier to see what they'd gotten in from their purveyor. Their guy always knew what and how much to send for the mains, based on a list he received a day or two before, but he often threw in something special if he came upon a fish he thought they might like. It was never much, sometimes just a few pounds of something they rarely saw, but she loved helping to showcase something unique. Luckily, Daniel seemed to love her input.

Being creative helped her mood, which helped her enjoy her job more. Much more. By the time spring came, which to her meant a day where she didn't wear her winter coat, she'd started to look forward to going to work. That was huge.

It had been weeks since Blake called, and when her name showed up on Emily's display surprisingly early on a Sunday morning, she clicked the button and said, "Yessss?"

"Hi, there. What's up?"

"Not much. You?"

"Busy. Super busy. I've been traveling a little."

"Traveling? When do you have time to travel?"

"I don't," she said, a wry laugh echoing through the phone. "Three weeks in a row now I've had to go over to Teterboro after service on Saturday night and get on a plane. It sucks."

"Ooo, I hate small planes."

"I don't. Not anymore." Her laugh now sounded more genuine. "It sucks because I'm never going to want to fly commercial again. I was treated like a princess."

"You *are* a princess. So…?"

"So… I thought we could get together. If you want to."

"Ooo. So I don't have to if I don't want to?"

A warm laugh made goosebumps break out across Emily's body. The thought of a day full of sex made her mouth start to water, which surprised the heck out of her. Despite having reacted so powerfully the last time they were together, her sex drive had gone into hiding when Blake walked out the door that morning. But if it could come back when summoned, that wouldn't be the worst thing in the world.

"You're pretty spritely today," Blake said. "I like it."

"Why don't you come over and I'll show you something else I know you like."

"I'm hailing a cab. Right now."

"Cabs and private jets. Now that sounds like you."

Blake looked gorgeous, but exhausted. Dark smudges had settled under her eyes, which were bloodshot. And her posture wasn't as erect as usual. Even her laugh was slow and muted. But she was dressed like she'd been dazzling all of New York. A snug, short, black leather jacket covered a fluffy black turtleneck, and black leggings showed off every well-defined muscle in her long legs. Black riding boots, shined to a mirror-like finish, made her look like she could have led a grand parade.

"I don't know where you've been, but I'm glad you wound up here."

"Are we alone?"

"No one in the hangar," Emily said as she led the way into her bedroom, "but Chase and Natasha are in his room."

"The hangar?"

"They're flight attendants, so that's what Chase and I call their room."

A slow smile crept onto Blake's pale face. "You could come up with a good fantasy about hot flight attendants winding up in your bed by mistake."

"That's Chase's fantasy. Or it was until Natasha arrived on the scene." They hadn't yet established how much or when they were allowed to start touching each other. Emily normally waited for Blake to signal that the barrier was down, but today she looked so weak Emily couldn't help herself. She slipped Blake's jacket off, then caressed her cheek with a hand. "How much sleep did you get last night?"

"None. Why? Do I look as bad as I feel?"

"You don't look great," she admitted. "Why'd you call so early? When I saw your number I assumed you'd butt dialed me in your sleep."

A weak laugh made her lips curl up slightly. "No, I called on purpose. I was out until dawn." She yawned, heartily. "I started to play some music to relax, hoping to ease my way into bed, where I planned on sleeping the entire day away. But construction crews showed up at seven, fixing something in the tunnel, I guess. I knew I'd never get to sleep, so I thought I might as well have some fun." Her smile was wan but sincere. "You're fun."

"I appreciate that you waited until nine to let the games begin."

Blake let out a soft chortle. "Even when I've got my eyes on the prize, I'm polite."

"Here's your prize." She playfully pushed Blake onto the bed, giggling when she looked up, clearly surprised. "Time for a nap."

"Really? I..." She looked around, then shrugged her shoulders. "Are you sure?"

"Positive." Blake's boots and leggings slid off with ease. When Emily climbed onto the bed and tugged her sweater over her head, then unhooked her bra, she leaned over and placed a kiss on each breast after addressing them. "You two are going to get a workout later. Rest up."

Blake pulled her close and nuzzled against Emily's neck for a few moments, like a cat. "I need sleep more than I like to admit. Are you going to nap too?"

"Maybe. We'll see if it's contagious." After tucking the sheet up around Blake's shoulders, Emily sat back against the headboard and rested her computer on her lap. Then she slipped her fingers into Blake's hair and massaged her head until she drifted off, minutes later.

Blake slept like a child, dead to the world, splayed out as though she needed every inch of the full-sized bed.

After catching up on her email, Emily picked up the limp arm that lay across her thighs, then settled it onto the bed. Wandering into the kitchen, she found Chase rummaging through the refrigerator.

"Whatever it is, we don't have it," she said.

He peeked over the open door. "Hello, stranger. Who are you holding captive?"

She reached out and grabbed his nose. "Right now? You." Closing the door, she gave him a quick hug. "My former boss has crashed like a two-year-old."

"Ooo." His eyes danced with excitement. He was more interested in her love life than she was. "You were very, very quiet. We didn't hear a thing."

"Is Natasha asleep?"

"She is. Obviously, you and I have more stamina than our…what is Blake anyway?"

"A phantom," she said, chuckling. "She pops up, then disappears."

Concern filled his eyes. "You're okay with that?"

"Uh-huh." Emily started looking through the cabinets, finding very little of interest. "I could call her if I wanted to, but we've kind of established this routine…" She turned and leaned against the counter. "We've only hooked up a few times. It's not like we're exclusive."

"But you like her."

"Yeah." She smiled, thinking of how attracted she was. "I do. And I know she likes me too. But she's clearly stated she's not in the market for a real girlfriend."

"Are you? I can never tell."

"Not sure. I guess it depends on the girl." Clapping her hands together, she said, "I'm going to cook. Tell me what you want, and you'll have it."

"Anything?"

"Anything at all, as long as they sell the ingredients at the bodega."

"I want…" His face scrunched up in thought. "Some kind of soup. Or stew. Something hearty. Chicken?"

"I can do that. Want to go with me?"

"Yeah. Let me put my pants on."

It wasn't until that moment she realized he was in his boxer shorts. When you lived with a guy for a long time, you stopped registering details.

Blake stumbled out of the bedroom at five, her eyes almost closed, hair askew. She stood in the kitchen doorway, swaying. "Did you slip something into my drink?"

Emily got up from the table and led her to a chair. "You didn't have a drink." Blake's hand was unnaturally warm to the touch. "Are you all right? You look shaky."

"Just tired." Sitting down, she extended her hand across the table. "Blake."

"Natasha. It's good to meet you." She jumped up and went to the cabinet. "I'm getting you a bowl. The chicken and dumplings Emily made is *so* good."

"I was lying there dreaming about chickens," Blake said, her brow furrowed in thought. Her eyes met Emily's. "I really was. The smell must have penetrated my dreams."

Emily bent over to pick up the napkin she'd dropped when something caught her attention. From that angle, she saw that Blake's neck was flushed a deep pink. "Are you really okay?" she said, speaking quietly.

"Uh-huh. Hungry." When Natasha put a bowl in front of her, she thanked her, then dug in, eating like she was being chased.

Both Natasha and Chase watched, enthralled, as she kept her head down and demolished the stew. Finally, she looked up, clearly trying to find the person who was in charge of the chow. "More?"

"Sure." Natasha got up again and filled the bowl almost to the brim. Now Blake ate slightly more slowly, but with just as much concentration.

"So good," she murmured, her first comment.

Chase caught Emily's attention with his wide-eyed stare. She shrugged, trying to show she was just as puzzled as he was by Blake's single-minded quest to eat everything she could get her hands on.

"Damn, that was good," she finally said. Turning to Emily, she asked. "Did you make that?"

"Yeah." She smiled, meeting Chase's gaze. "I used to cook something substantial every Sunday, then we'd nosh on it all week. I'd lost interest but…" Returning his big grin, she said, "I'm going to do it again."

"Can I come over every Sunday?" Blake asked, a very weak smile covering her face.

"Sure. You too, Natasha. Having an appreciative crowd always makes cooking more fun."

"If I appreciated this any more," Natasha said, turning her empty bowl up for Emily to see how clean it was, "I'd eat the spoon."

Blake sat quietly for a moment, staring at nothing. Then she picked her head up and looked at Natasha. "More?"

After eating a whole lot more than a normal human being should have, Blake let herself be led back to the bedroom. Natasha and Chase had offered to clean up, and Emily thought she'd better leave them to it, since she liked things done her way and didn't want to be a nudge.

Blake started to take her sweater off, but Emily stopped her when her head was still inside. "Hold on." Her hand glided over Blake's back. From the base of her salmon tattoo up to her shoulders, it looked like she had goosebumps, with the skin flushed bright pink. Emily traced the rash along her sides, where it stopped.

"What's wrong?"

"You're covered in a rash."

Blake's head popped out of the sweater. "Oh, shit." She slumped down onto the mattress, her body limp. "I was afraid of that."

"Of what?"

"I must have a fever. Sometimes I get a rash." She put the back of her hand to her forehead. "I can't tell."

Emily went into the bathroom and came back with a digital thermometer, which she slipped under her tongue. "This works better than a hand." Blake looked up at her, eyes glassy. You didn't need a thermometer to see she was sick, but Emily was curious about the number anyway. If her temperature was high, she was going to drag her to a nearby drugstore clinic.

When the device beeped, she withdrew it and checked the display. "One oh two. Not good, but not dangerous."

"Shit," she grumbled quietly.

"Let me get you out of these clothes." With a slight bit of help, she managed to get the leggings off again. Then Blake turned onto her side and curled into a ball—at the foot of the bed.

"Don't you want to scoot up a little?"

"Yeah," she whispered, that one word sounding like it took an effort. "Gimme a minute…"

Emily watched her twitch a few times, then settle down. Her instinct was to caress her. To rub her body to get the feel of it into her senses again. But that wasn't what they did. Their intimacy was sexual—purely sexual. Avoiding the temptation to treat her like a girlfriend, she placed a pillow under her head, covered her with the sheet, then went out to the living room, hoping to engage Chase and Natasha in some power TV catch-up. Their DVR had to be about full.

"Emily?" A weak, confused-sounding voice called out from the bedroom.

"The patient speaks," she said, jumping up to go to her.

By the time Emily entered the room, Blake was sitting on the edge of the bed again, still naked. "I'm *so* sorry I came over."

"I'm not." Emily sat next to her and tucked an arm around her waist. "You're too sick to be alone. You never would have gotten anything to eat."

"That soup was really good," she said, still vacant. "But I haven't been very good company."

"You're usually super good, so you get a free pass." Taking her hand, she tried to pull her toward the head of the bed, but Blake had enough strength to resist.

"Got to go home."

"Oh, I don't think that's a good idea. You sleep right here and I'll take the sofa."

"No, I've got to go. I've got…stuff to do."

She had to laugh at her determination, even though it was like watching an ant try to move a boulder. "You're not in any shape to go home. Come on now. Sleep another twelve hours and you might be able to go to work."

Her eyes opened wide for the first time in hours. "I've *got* to go to work!"

"I know. Believe me, I know." Blake was undoubtedly harder on herself than she was on her staff, and god knew she was hard on them. "But you're shaky and weak." Fuzzy eyes blinked up at her. "You need to sleep."

"But I'm in your room…"

"It's fine. Really. I can sleep on the sofa or in the hangar."

"Are you sure? I could call a car service and be out of your hair in a few minutes."

"Go to sleep." Now when she tugged, Blake went along, then dropped like a rock. Emily covered her again and went back to the living room. With any luck, Chase and Natasha had paused the show they were watching. If not, Chase would entertain her with a careful, detailed summary—which would be longer than the five minutes she'd missed.

Emily woke when she sensed someone near. "Chase?"

"Blake." She settled on the arm of the sofa. "I was leaving you a note." She spoke quietly, like Emily was still asleep.

"Are you any better?"

"I think so." She put her hand down and gently stroked Emily's head. "Thanks to you."

"I just let you crash. No big deal."

"It *was* a big deal. You wouldn't let me be hardheaded. I barely remember last night, but I know I tried to leave."

Emily fought with the blanket that had her trapped against the back of the sofa. Then she sat up and tried to get everything working. "How bad do you feel?"

"Pretty bad, but I'm hoping I rally." She had her work face on. The no-nonsense one. "I'll have Grant and Brady plate tonight so I can just expedite. I don't want to pass this on to a guest if I'm contagious."

Emily didn't mention the fact that she'd probably give it to her co-workers. That was expected in a restaurant. Viruses jumped from one person to the next all year. "Can I make you some coffee? Breakfast?"

"No, but thanks. I'm going to call a car and go home. Maybe I'll go in late."

"Sure. That's a good idea." It also wasn't going to happen. But Blake could have her little fantasies. Emily stood and walked her back to the bedroom, then helped her into her lightweight jacket. Standing in front of her, Emily looked up and settled her collar. "If you see anyone you know, duck."

"That bad, huh?" A smirk covered her face. She could take teasing better than most.

"You're not at your best. Try to get another nap if you can."

"I will." She started for the door, then stopped. "Did you say you'd go to the Barstow Awards with me?"

Emily almost plowed into her. "What?"

"The James Barstow Awards."

"I know *which* Barstow. I'm…no, I didn't. You didn't ask me."

"I meant to. I dreamed I did." Chuckling, she said, "I had some crazy dreams. You didn't bring a live lobster into the room and let it crawl on me, did you?"

"Yeah," she said, straight-faced. "I keep a pet lobster in the tub. I thought you might like to play with him while you slept."

Chuckling, Blake said, "My head's so muddled I'm not sure if you're teasing." She put a hand on the door. "Are you going with me? I've got to send my response in."

"Is it on a Sunday?"

"It is."

"Then I'm in."

"Good. Have you been before?"

"Never, but I've always wanted to go."

"Now's your chance. Too bad I didn't know you last year. We could've been introduced." She shrugged, opened the door and started down the stairs. "We'll still have fun though." She looked up when she was halfway down the first flight of stairs. Her hair hadn't been combed, her eyes were slits, and her grin didn't have its usual wattage. But she was still so pretty Emily's heart started to race. "I always have fun with you."

Emily closed the door, then raced to her computer. Finding the awards website, she noted that Blake had been a finalist for Rising Star the year before. Words poured out of her mouth, even though no one was awake to hear them. "She's under thirty years old!"

Blake was probably dozing in the backseat of a car, but Emily couldn't stop herself. She texted her, saying, "Rising Star? Should I have IDd you before we had sex?!?"

A few minutes later a reply showed up. "Made it under the wire. I turned 30 last month." Then she added an emoticon of a person sticking his tongue out. Well, that was slightly better. Emily was only two years older than a person who'd always have more experience, be more accomplished and undoubtedly more famous.

Rats!

The Barstow Awards were the highlight of the American culinary year, recognizing achievement by chefs, restaurants, writers, TV personalities, even bloggers. There were dozens of categories and various small ceremonies held over an entire weekend every spring. But the big deal, the Academy Awards style event, was what she and Blake were going to. Nearly every notable chef in the country attended, and Emily was looking forward to meeting some of them. And being with Blake. That was no small part of it.

Emily hadn't been to a black tie event in four years. Actually, that was the *only* formal event she'd ever been to. She'd been vaguely gay in high school, too gay to go to prom with a boy, but too unsure of herself to ask a girl. And by college she'd turned a little hippieish. You couldn't have paid her to wear a fancy dress back then. She'd dropped the hippie look for a cook's utilitarian wardrobe when she'd moved to New York eight years earlier, but even though dressing up had never been her thing, she was really looking forward to pulling out the stops for the awards.

They'd agreed to meet at Lincoln Center, easier for her than having to go to Blake's and backtrack. Emily arrived early, just to hang around and see who she might recognize. It hadn't dawned on her that there would be a crowd of spectators. Having so many celebrity chefs all fighting for time on TV had clearly changed the game. It was funny how many people thought they wanted to cook, given the low pay and backbreaking hours, but it felt like every third person dreamed of grabbing a knife and getting busy. At least in their fantasies. Most would change their minds after their first fifteen hour shift.

A barricade had been set up to keep the fans from the stars, and she stayed on the fan side, poking her head through the crowd to catch sight of some celebs. At 5:45 her cell phone rang and she pried it out of her small purse.

"Hi."

"Hey there. I'm here. Are you close?"

"I'm in the crowd, watching people go in."

Chuckling, Blake said, "We have tickets, Emily. *We* can go in."

"I'll try to free myself from the scrum. Meet you by the fountain."

She broke away from some very enthusiastic fans who were vying for autographs from a guy who looked famous, but she couldn't imagine why. It took a minute to get into the plaza, but when she did she was richly rewarded. Blake stood in front of the dramatic fountain, with bursts of water shooting fifty feet in the air, whooshing up, then splashing loudly as they crashed. Emily's heart started to boom as she took Blake in.

She looked six feet tall, even though she was a couple of inches below that. But her slate grey suit, made of some vaguely shiny material, fit her form so beautifully it made her legs look extra long and lean. Her hair was extra rock-star cool, too, gentle waves framing her gorgeous face. A bright white tuxedo-style blouse, top button open, was crisp and elegant, especially where the French cuffs emerged from her sleeves. No heels for Blake Chadwick. Patent leather flats were as far as she'd go in the fashion footwear race. As Emily got close, she noted dark socks with some form of decoration. Ahh… Toques. The perfect touch for a big, chef-centered event.

"I haven't been inside yet, but you're the prettiest woman here," Emily said, sliding into Blake's embrace.

"No way." She gripped Emily by her arms and held her out for inspection. "I had no idea you wore dresses." Her eyes glimmered with interest. "We need to go out again—soon—and you have to wear that dress. I'd like to spend the whole evening concentrating on how fantastic you look."

"Aww…thanks. This is the only dress I own." She grasped the full, platinum-colored skirt and shook it. "My bridesmaid's dress from my sister's wedding." Her hand went to Blake's lapel. "We match really well tonight. Lucky accident."

Blake's dark, interested eyes hadn't stopped scanning her. "You've never done that…thing with your hair. I love it."

"Just a chignon."

"Chignon du cou," Blake said, her appreciation evident. "Nape of the neck. Yours is well worth showing off." Her fingers traced along the gold pendant Emily wore, and her voice dropped to a sexy register. "Would you mind if I kissed it?"

"It depends on *how* you're going to kiss it," she said, letting out a soft laugh. "You've been known to get a little adventurous."

"I'll behave." When she leaned forward, Blake's silky hair was nearly in Emily's face. She longed to smell it, to detect one of the hair products she used, or maybe even a hint of the sensual perfume she sometimes wore. But she was left imagining it. A poor substitute, but at least her imagination was vivid. When soft lips barely touched two spots, both very sensitive, she felt a wisp of moisture. Now she didn't have to use her imagination. She could let the warm feeling run down her arm, making it tingle.

"I've really been looking forward to this," Emily said. "Now I'm hoping the whole thing's over in ten minutes. I need to get you alone."

"We won't stay late," Blake said, grinning impishly. "You didn't happen to bring a change of clothes in that tiny bag, did you?"

"That seemed a little presumptuous."

A sober expression covered Blake's face. Leaning close, she looked into Emily's eyes and said, "No, it's not. When we have the chance to get together, I'd like time alone with you. As much time as you have to spare."

Well, that was surprising. Then the precise words she'd used reached Emily's brain. Blake was simply saying that having sex was always part of the deal. "Okay. Next time, I'll pack for an extended stay."

Blake held her arm out, a smirk now affixed to her face. "Let's make our entrance."

Surprisingly, they were immediately surrounded by young people in black, wearing headsets, speaking quietly. "Right this way," a guy said, herding them into a chute. A woman in a very dramatic dress was twirling for the cameras, then she sauntered off. "You're next," another guy said, giving them a slight push. Walking down a red carpet was a bit outside Emily's experience. About as far out as you could go and stay in the solar system. But Blake seemed perfectly at ease as flashes burst when they stood on the indicated X's. A woman announced, "Blake Chadwick, last year's Rising Star finalist, and guest." Grinning, Blake leaned over and said, "Next year I'd like to hear Emily Desjardins and guest." The flashes popped when her lips were close to Emily's ear. She knew Blake had an impish grin on her face, she always did when she used that tone. Emily was going to find out how to get a copy of that photo, if only to remind herself of the spark of excitement she felt at that moment. Blake was the star. No two ways about it. And it wasn't just her cooking that was exceptional. It was her style, her personality, her charisma. You needed the whole package to show up on the radar, and Emily didn't think she'd ever have it. But she was happy with the status quo. As long as she and Blake were whatever they were to each other she'd get to glimpse this other side of the cooking biz. That was enough.

The awards were pretty typical. A large auditorium, hokey jokes from the presenters, most of them celebrities or nearly so, recipients whose speeches ranged from terse and cool to those who completely lost it, veering off into emotion-laden gushing that embarrassed everyone. After one guy, a chef from Texas who wore a black leather cowboy hat, won a regional award, Blake leaned over and whispered, "I was afraid he was going to thank his horse. I think he got everyone from pre-school on in."

"I think he mentioned the horse first. He kept thanking Miss Daisy, and he never specified she was human."

"You didn't bring any food, did you?"

"Food?" She held up her purse, which could barely hold her Metro card, twenty bucks and the keys to her apartment. "I don't have room for mints."

"I keep smelling food. My stomach's rumbling."

"It'll be over soon. They're almost at the West Coast."

"They'd better have real food. I need something to chew."

"I'll take you out for a burger if they don't. Or we can drink enough to not care."

"Oh, right," she said, her laugh gaining volume. "I forgot they have a full bar."

The woman in front of them turned around and glared. Emily put her finger to her lips and tried not to laugh. Then Blake grasped her hand and rested her head on Emily's bare shoulder, occasionally tilting her head to kiss the skin. Like they were longtime girlfriends. What in the heck was going on with her? With them?

Emily had only seen Blake put on her charming act a couple of times when she was trying to impress guests or the owners. Each time she'd seemed pretty much like herself, but with extra personality. Tonight, around fellow chefs, most of whom she knew to some extent, she showed a different side. A side Emily found not only compelling, but adorable. Blake glided around the reception, tasting food from every station she could get to, chatting up the proud, mostly young chefs who provided it. Then she'd take whatever she'd wrangled, and share it with Emily before dragging her to the next open spot.

It was a crazy way to feed people, more like a food fare than a dinner, but it let dozens of cooks get a little notice while allowing the foundation to squeeze a lot of paying guests in.

Once Blake's hunger had been partially slaked, she relaxed and found her friends. She had a *lot* of them. Many more than Emily would have thought. But when she considered she herself had run into six people she'd worked with during her years in the city, she realized that only made sense. Chefs composed a relatively small band, at least chefs at Blake's level. They went to the same schools, apprenticed at the same top restaurants, and made their bones in the same kitchens. Those bonds, however fleeting, lasted. It reminded her of former pro athletes. When they got together, they knew something of the struggles the other guys had gone through, even if they hadn't been on the same team.

They'd been chatting with a woman who Emily saw on the food channel every time she turned it on, finding her just as engaging and entertaining as you'd expect a TV celebrity to be. As they turned to leave, she heard Blake say, "Bonsoir, Laurent. Ça va?"

Stunned in place, Emily made herself smile. She hadn't considered the big boss would be there, but he was a very prominent chef. Of course he'd go to the Barstow Awards.

"Blake," he said, enveloping her in a hug. "I was just talking to Jean-Michel about you."

Her head swiveled. "Is he here? I haven't seen him."

"Oh, yes. He was saying you should have won last year. He thinks Jason Greene's food is a bad joke."

She laughed, then put her hand on Laurent's shoulder. "I can't say I agree with him, but..." Her voice lowered. "I agree with him."

"You should! You, my friend, will win best New York chef one day. I have no doubts."

"Laurent, do you ever actually cook at your restaurant?"

"In New York?"

"Yeah. In New York."

"I don't have the chance. Why?"

"I was wondering why you didn't recognize your new poissonnier," she said, making Emily almost choke. Blake's arm slid around her bare shoulders. "Emily Desjardins. Stop by and see her next time you're around. She's going to make her mark, Laurent. I bet she'll win best New York chef before I do."

He looked a little embarrassed, but put on a very debonair smile and took Emily's hand, then kissed the back of it. "I must apologize for my bad manners, Emily. I'm sure we've met."

"Actually, we haven't," she said, mortified. "Daniel hired me just a couple of months ago. You've been traveling…"

"Ah! That explains it." He smiled at Blake. "I thought I must be losing my eyesight. It is rare for me to forget such a beautiful face."

Blake elbowed him. "She's not my sister, she's my date!"

As Emily tried to find a hole to climb into, Laurent burst out in laughter, then tossed his arm around Blake's shoulders. "You haven't changed. You're the same silly girl I met in Nice." Winking at Emily, he added, "Has she told you her stories?"

"Not many of them," Emily admitted.

"Oh, you must make her talk," he insisted. "I had just been made chef de parti when this child was left in a basket on our doorstep. Of course, we took her in and fed her." His hand went to her cheek, which he pinched. "How could you abandon such a sweet child? It was criminal!"

Emily stared at him, unable to think of a reply. What in the hell was he talking about?"

"Pay no attention to Laurent's odd sense of humor," Blake said. "He's just a few years older than I am, but he acts like he's my grandfather."

"I met you when you were a child," he insisted, "and I'm very pleased to see your taste in women has matured as you have."

"What was the name of that saucier we fought over that first summer? Adéle?"

His raucous laughter made nearby guests turn to stare. "No. Aimée. She chose the sous."

"That's right," Blake said, shaking her head. "They always chose the sous."

Laurent took Emily's hand again. "It looks like I've won this time." He scowled, leaning over just a few inches in front of Emily. "Don't let her try to take you back."

She figured she might as well join the game. "My days of working for Blake are over. I'm perfectly content at Le Lapin." When she said that, she realized it was true. Her job had turned out far better than she'd hoped. And not working for Blake had an added bonus. Chef never would have kissed her sous' neck in public.

There were dozens of after-parties at restaurants all around the city, and Blake had formal invitations to seven of them. She and Emily stood in the corner of the reception area, deciding which to attend. "I have to go to Jean-Michel's, even though it's always jam-packed," Blake said thoughtfully. "We'd probably have something good to eat at Mark Lartner's place. Last year he went big. And the drinks at Come Ça are phenomenal. What do you think?"

"Do you want to stick to one place?"

A smile lit up her face. "I don't. Let's do them all. We can walk to Mark's place. It's on…Seventy-Third, I think."

"Let's do it." It was nine o'clock, they'd only eaten single bites of food, and both of them had to go to work the next day, but Emily wasn't going to cut the night short. Seeing Blake in her element was way, way too much fun.

At two a.m., they stood outside Jean-Michel, the exalted temple to French gastronomy. Emily still glowed from the affectionate way the master had fussed over Blake, repeatedly kissing her on both cheeks and speaking in rapid-fire French that she seemed to easily understand.

Blake had slugged down quite a few drinks, but was still steady on her feet. "How can I entice you to come to my apartment?" Her arms slid around Emily's waist, pulling her so close her eyes crossed.

"Mmm…" It was a tough decision. She knew they'd have fun in bed. Each time had been game-changing. But it was really late and she'd have to either go home afterwards or take the subway ride of shame in the morning, wearing her fancy dress on the trip back to Queens. "I want to. I really want to…"

"Too far?"

"No, distance isn't the problem. But your clothes won't fit me. I'd have to go home to change before work."

"Mmm. I understand. We're a little discordant borough wise."

"Big words for a woman who's close to hammered," Emily teased.

"I think I'm past hammered. Damn," she said, shaking her head. "We had wine and Champagne and vodka and…what did we have at Il Piccolini?"

"Grappa. That's what put me over the edge."

"Why did we have grappa?" She held her head, moaning, "That's what we'll regret tomorrow. I mean, later today."

"I won't regret one moment." She pulled Blake close and gave her a long, heartfelt kiss. "I had the nicest time. Really. The nicest."

"I did too." She tightened the embrace, looking deeply into Emily's eyes. "And I'd *really* like you to come to my apartment. I guarantee you'll enjoy yourself."

She almost forgot the logistical problems. Almost jumped at the chance. But Blake could just as easily have come to her apartment, and she hadn't offered. Emily didn't believe in playing hard to get, but she also didn't want to be the one who always gave in. She put her hand on Blake's cheek and caressed it, continuing her gentle touch when Blake closed her eyes and leaned into it. "I'd like for you to come home with *me*."

A lazy smile settled on those pretty lips. "I was hoping you wouldn't suggest that. Am I a jerk for not wanting to have to come back to the city in the morning?"

"No. You're just as practical as I am."

"Okay," she said decisively. "Next Sunday. Bright and early." Shrugging, she added, "Early for cooks. We'll spend the day at my place, where we'll be all alone, then I'll take you home. It probably won't be on the subway, but I'll take you home."

"You've got a deal. I love a woman who can compromise." Blake took her hand and they started to walk. "Where are we going?"

"We're going to the Empire Hotel. I can see the address to put it into my car sharing app. I don't want to worry about some guy drooling on you on the subway."

"You're a very good date, Chef. Very good indeed."

Blake stopped, put her arms around Emily and gave her a long, tender kiss. "I will deny this to anyone who ever asks, but I love it when you call me Chef." Then, with a self-satisfied smirk, she took Emily's hand and escorted her to the hotel, amid the clatter of the city serenading them with honking horns, jackhammers, and the occasional siren. Easily as pretty as a symphony.

Chapter Fourteen

EMILY HAD JUST CHANGED into her whites the next afternoon when Daniel caught her eye and signaled for her to come into his office. She hadn't entered the room since the day he'd hired her, and her stomach did a flip when he gestured. No matter how secure you were, when your boss called you into his office unexpectedly, your body prepared to run.

"Sit. Please," he said.

She did, then waited, expectantly.

"By the time I made it across the room last night, you'd gone."

"Oh! I didn't see you."

"Well, I saw you and I'm glad I did." He smiled at her, like he knew a juicy secret.

"I'm glad you did too."

"Now I understand."

"You understand…"

"Why you left Blake's. I assumed you had a drinking problem, or maybe even drugs. I wouldn't have hired you, but Laurent pressured me."

"Uhm…thanks?" What were you supposed to say to that?

"It was smart of you to leave when you two got involved. Really smart."

"Oh, yes," she nodded, ready to go along with anything he assumed.

"I've seen a lot of careers go up in flames because people let gossip undermine their authority. That was a good choice. For both of you." He leaned forward and tapped his mouth with his fist, clearly still thinking. "But why'd you settle for working on the line? With a good recommendation from Blake, you could have easily had another sous job."

"Yes, I'm sure I could have." If I had a sense of smell! Why wasn't she better prepared for these kinds of questions? "Uhm…I…well, everyone knows Le Lapin is the best seafood restaurant in the country. And I've never worked in a Michelin starred place. I thought I was at the point in my career where it wouldn't hurt me to take a half step back to learn from the best." That sounded pretty good for winging it.

"You know," he said, leaning back in his chair before pulling a drawer out and bracing a foot against it, "some people say women aren't assertive enough. But I think they confuse assertiveness with blind ambition. Some of the women I've worked with have taken steps that puzzle men, but turn out to be good tactical choices. I think you've made a good one in coming here."

"I think I have too." He seemed like he was finished with her, so she stood to leave.

"No ideas for tonight?"

"Oh, sure, I've always got some." She sat back down and riffed on a canapé they'd had at one of the parties they'd hit the night before. It paid to notice the details.

Just two days later, Emily sat in Laurent's office, so nervous her knees were knocking. A very efficient young man followed him around wherever he went, making notes and checking details on a tablet he carried. When he'd stopped by Emily's station and summoned her, just after she'd arrived, she felt like she'd been called to the principal's office. Now she was just puzzled.

Laurent breezed in, wearing a very luxurious v-neck emerald green sweater and black slacks that made him look thinner than he already was. The joke was to never trust a skinny chef, but most of the good ones she'd worked with were on the thin side. "Emily," he said, extending his hand to shake.

"Good afternoon, Chef."

"How are things for you here?" He sat down, with his ergonomic chair barely making a sound as it absorbed his weight. He tossed his head, banishing his shoulder length chestnut hair from his eyes.

"They're very good. I'm learning a lot."

A slight smile lifted the corner of his mouth. "What have you learned?"

Doh!

"I've learned…there's nothing more important than quality. And that excellent technique really matters." She sucked in a breath, thinking of something…anything she'd learned. "And how important teamwork is…"

"Hmm." His gaze pinned her in place. "Did you not know all of this before? I know Blake well. Her standards are second to none."

She could feel her cheeks coloring. "No, Chef. This is nothing unique. But being in another restaurant, one with a bigger budget and a larger staff, has cemented those things for me."

"I see." He looked like he was about to call her a liar! "All of those things are important, as you say. But I don't believe you are learning anything that will help you—or me. Daniel tells me you have the mind of a chef, not a cook."

"They're the same—"

"That's not true and you know it. Now." He stood, then moved around his big, modern desk to sit on the edge. They were so close their knees almost touched, but she wasn't going to move since he'd chosen the distance. "Here is a proposal. I am opening a restaurant in Las Vegas. We've been working on it for almost two years, and it will open in September. It *must* open in September."

She looked up at him, seeing how closely he watched her. Was she supposed to speak? Instead of rushing in, she waited, hoping he'd continue.

After a brief nod of his head, he went on. "Time is very short and my sous chef is…gone. I want you to go there and take his place." She swallowed as the weight of his words sank in. "You will help us make our opening."

"You want me to help open a restaurant? But I've never done anything like that."

"The job will be challenging, but it will be nothing you cannot manage."

"What makes you so sure I'm competent?" she asked, then almost bit her tongue off when she heard the words come from her mouth.

He moved back to sit in his chair. Steepling his hands together, he stared at them for a moment. "Blake would not hire you for herself, or recommend you to me, if you were not very capable. It is hard to gain her trust. You have it."

"I agree that's true. But…we're involved. She's not unbiased."

"Were you involved when she hired you?"

"Of course not! We'd never met."

"Then my point remains. Think about it. Let me know your decision. Perhaps by Monday?"

"Yes, Chef." She stood when he did, shook his hand and went back to her station, hoping her nerves didn't make her cut a finger off.

On Sunday morning, with morning technically only lasting fifteen more minutes, Emily stood in front of the doorman in Blake's lobby, waiting for him to get permission to send her up. When he did, she got on the elevator for the short ride. Blake was standing in her doorway, freshly showered, her hair wet and just starting to curl. Little bits of it turned in every direction, the waves having minds of their own. "Good morning," Blake said, her voice husky and low.

"Good morning to you." Emily leaned into her and gave her a brief kiss. "I brought bagels and smoked salmon."

"We make a good pair. I brought my appetite." She took the bag, then closed the door after Emily entered. "Throw your umbrella anywhere."

Ha! That was a trick! Emily hung it in the coat closet, finding every item on identical hangers, all facing in the same direction. Then she went into the kitchen and took a seat at one of a pair of stools that sat under the counter separating the kitchen from the living area. "I bought the plain one for me and the poppy for you."

"Plain? Really?" Blake sliced one of the bagels in half and slid it into the toaster.

"I can't taste the seeds, so why have them stuck in my teeth?"

Blake came over and stood behind her to rest her head on Emily's shoulder. "No improvement?"

"A little. I had a cold a couple of weeks ago. A bad one. My nose was really stuffy and I realized I could taste even less than normal. Good news."

"That's good news? How..."

"I think I'm getting a little back, since there was a decided change when I couldn't breathe."

"I guess that's good news," Blake said, clearly not convinced.

"It is. Really. Right after the accident, I could hardly taste salt from sugar, but I can do that reliably now. So taste is pretty solid, and I've got at least five percent of my smell back."

"Five percent isn't much," Blake said, sounding so sad Emily was ready to change the subject.

"It's not much. But I woke up the other day and smelled something really acrid. Then I saw guys tarring a roof next door."

Blake stood and went back into the kitchen. "I'd rather you could smell a rose than a roof."

"Me too. But if I get a little back I'll be able to smell things like a gas leak or a fire. It'd be nice to be able to save my life in an emergency."

Blake didn't respond to that, but she met Emily's eyes, her empathy so vivid it was too much to take this early in the day. Blake must have thought so too, since she dropped the depressing topic, opened the waxed paper bundle and took a sniff. "Want some salmon? It smells great."

"Yeah. I can sometimes get a little saltiness from it."

They sat next to each other, drinking coffee and eating their bagels. "I've been looking forward to seeing you," Blake said. "When I was dragging yesterday, I thought 'Emily will come tomorrow to play.' That cheered me up."

"Aww...you think about me at work?"

"No," she admitted, grinning. "On my way to work. Once I'm there..."

"All business." She put her hand on Blake's shoulder and pulled her close for a hug. "I need to talk about business with you."

"My business?" An eyebrow rose.

"Mine." She gathered her thoughts for a moment, then said, "Laurent wants me to go to Las Vegas and help open his new restaurant."

"Las Vegas?" Her eyes opened as a big smile settled onto her face. "That's great! I knew it wouldn't take long before he'd realize how talented you are."

"He wouldn't know me from the night steward," she scoffed. "He admitted he hired me because of your recommendation. Plus, I'm sure Daniel told him I'm pulling my weight."

"Laurent wouldn't put you into a demanding job if he didn't believe you could do it. And you do more than pull your weight. Much more."

Emily shrugged off the compliment. "Yeah, I guess. But I think it's mostly because he trusts you. He said as much."

"Then I'm glad I raved about you. When will you start?"

Emily sat back so she could get a look at her face. "I'm not sure I'm going to accept."

"What? This is a fantastic opportunity!"

"Yeah, yeah, I know." She stood and walked over to the coffee pot, freshening her cup. Then she topped Blake's off too. "But I don't want to live in Las Vegas, and even more important, I'm not sure I can pull it off. He wants me to be sous chef."

Blake's expression was filled with certainty. "You can do this, Emily. You can. Will you have the same menu as Le Lapin?"

"God no! I'd never make it at Le Lapin. The new place is a bistro. Much simpler food than I'm used to cooking."

"That's good." She nodded emphatically. "Very good. If your dishes are true bistro style, they won't be as delicate. Precision won't be paramount. If you under-season moules-frites a tiny bit no one will notice."

"I suppose that's true." She bit at her lip, unable to say what was holding her back.

"It's also a chance to get into the Las Vegas scene and make an impression. If you can be sous for two years, you'd be ready to be chef de cuisine."

"There are hundreds of expensive places in Vegas. Hundreds! And I'd be just one more anonymous sous. Why would anyone take a chance on me?"

Blake grasped Emily's hand and pulled her close. Quietly, she spoke, her conviction touching. "Because you're good. Very good. You know how to put utterly delicious food on a plate, Emily, and that's something you either have or lack. Talent wins in this game." Her arms tightened around her body. "You have talent. Loads of it."

"But I can't taste my own food. Someone will find out and I'll be toast."

"There's no reason anyone will find out. You can finesse this. I know you can."

Emily held Blake away from her body, needing to look into her eyes. "You didn't say that when I had the accident. You said, very clearly, that I'd never be able to be a sous again."

The skin at the base of Blake's throat moved when she swallowed, but she didn't say a word.

Emily couldn't let it go. "Now you want me to take a job working for someone you respect? Someone who respects you?" She let that hang out there for a minute, seeing Blake's gaze shift to the floor. It was impossible to tell what was going on in her mind, and she didn't rush to make her thoughts heard.

Finally, she spoke, quietly, with her certainty reflected in her voice, if not her eyes. "I think about this all of the time, mulling over what happened. Especially when I look at Brady. You know he's competent. And he has the right personality for the job. But he doesn't have your talent. Food doesn't speak to him like it does to you. Your talent can make up for your inability to taste, Emily. I believe that, and I want you to believe it too."

"Cooking is half tasting, Blake. Don't act like that's not true."

"It is. I admit that. But composing is *all* hearing, and Beethoven was deaf. If he could get over that, you can get over your disability."

"How?" She wanted to believe. She really did. But...

"You find someone who can taste. Someone you know has a good palate and isn't afraid to step on toes. Make him responsible for fine-tuning the dishes. Push that element of your job down a level, then make sure to shine in every other way."

"I'm not sure that can work, since I have no idea of how they're planning on setting the system up." She sighed. "And I *really* don't want to live in Las Vegas."

Blake held her, then rested her chin on her shoulder for a minute. "I didn't want to go to France, so I know how you feel."

"But you love France!"

"I do. But I'd just turned sixteen when I went. Leaving home and my friends and everything I was used to was tough." She pulled back and looked into Emily's eyes. "Even though I was afraid, I went because I thought it would let me reach my goal faster than if I stayed home." She nodded decisively. "I was right."

"Las Vegas isn't Nice," Emily grumbled.

"No, it's not. But it can be a stepping stone." She took a deep breath. "I was too hasty in letting you leave. I made a mistake. Now that I've had time to think about it, we should have restructured to accommodate you." Grasping her by the hips, Blake moved her back and forth a few inches, punctuating her point. "Don't let my mistake ruin your dreams."

"Maybe I should try to find a sous job here. Poke around until I find the right situation."

"I don't think so," she said, a frown lining her face. "You're stuck with Laurent for a while. It would look bad if you left so quickly. Besides, he definitely wouldn't like it, and you don't want to make him dislike you. It would come back to haunt you."

"Maybe I could..." She sighed, acknowledging she was stuck. "I don't want to go." She gazed into Blake's eyes, seeing they were filled with sadness. Was that because she felt responsible for forcing Emily out? Or because she would miss her? There was no way to know, and she didn't have the guts to ask.

Blake got up to clean the small amount of mess she'd made in the kitchen, while Emily went to the window to look out. It had turned into a nice, late spring day. The grey clouds had disappeared, replaced by big, white, fluffy ones. Blake came up behind her and wrapped her in a hug.

"Want to go out?" she asked, her low voice tickling Emily's skin. "We can if you want." Her teeth nibbled along an ear, covering Emily's body in goosebumps. Blake had learned the key to nibbling was subtlety.

Emily turned in her embrace and gazed into her dark eyes. "What would you do if I weren't here?"

"Nothing. I'd still be in bed."

"Do you really do nothing on your day off?"

She grinned unrepentantly. "Is playing my guitar doing anything?"

Emily stared at her for a minute, assessing how serious she was. "I suppose that depends on how much energy you expend when you play. Show me."

Blake's brow lifted. "Show you?"

"Yeah." She went to grab Blake's acoustic guitar, then handed it to her and sat down to watch. "Knowing you, you're deadly with that thing. I want a demonstration."

Slightly skittish, but game, Blake looped the strap around her neck and spent a few minutes tuning the instrument. Her eyes, half-closed, were focused on something in the distance, her head cocked slightly, clearly paying rapt attention to the sound. Once she had it right, she started to strum, not playing anything in particular. Probably just getting loosened up. "What would you like to hear?"

Emily gave her a knowing smile. "You're like a jukebox? I name a tune and you bang it out?"

With a tiny nod of her head, she said, "We could try that, but I was thinking you could give me a range of things you like."

Not needing a moment to think, Emily said, "I like singer/songwriters. Mostly women."

"Women, huh?" An eyebrow went up. "Amanda Palmer? Courtney Love? I know a Hole song."

Emily made a face. "I'm more Indigo Girls than Hole. You don't know any folky, acoustic stuff? I'd think a woman who plays a guitar would know songs by women who write them."

Shaking her head, Blake let a sly smile bloom. "I taught myself to play on this guitar because it cost under thirty bucks." She started to strum again, hitting the strings harder and harder. "But as soon as I had some money, I bought the electric. When I play, I like to *play*. I'm a head-banger, through and through."

"You've got nothing to please my delicate little lesbian ears?" She wasn't much of an eye-batter, but she gave it her best shot.

"Hold on," Blake said, grabbing her computer and tapping her fingers across the keys for a few moments. "I can do this," she said, her confidence back in place. She had to re-tune, but that only took a minute. Then she played a few chords and nodded. "After I bought this, I found a 'teach yourself guitar' book at a used bookstore. When I finished my shift, I'd sit outside on a vegetable crate and play until my fingers bled." She shrugged, her smile now a little shy. "It was either too hot or too cold where I slept, so it was almost always nicer outside. This is one of the first songs I taught myself."

Emily was so charmed by both her story and her affect she almost told her not to bother. She'd learned all she needed to know. But Blake put her foot up on the chair and carefully plucked out the tune. She played it slower than the original, and had dropped it down to a more manageable key, but she sang it with heart. "Somewhere over the rainbow, way up high…"

The choice of song stunned her for a second, then Emily leaned back and let Blake's sweet voice wash over her like a gentle wave. In a flash, she could see her, young and earnest and lonely, sitting on a crate, playing a cheap guitar while simply trying to stay warm. Emily had to fight to keep tears from falling, but it was hard! Hard to think of her, working her fingers to the bone for no money at all. Having to learn the language on the fly. Having to acclimate to an entirely different culture. No parents to guide or encourage her. How in the hell had she done it?

Blake's eyes were closed now, her voice sure and strong. The song was achingly sad, but the way she sang it brought out the lightness, the optimism, the certainty that she could fly wherever she wished. "When happy little bluebirds fly beyond the rainbow… Why, oh why, can't I?"

Then she flicked her thumb across the strings, ending with an adorable smile as her eyes opened as she locked her gaze on Emily.

With goosebumps covering her, Emily stood, turned and made for the bathroom. "If you ever have a dry spell, play that damned guitar and you won't be able to stop women from diving into your bed. I'll be back in two minutes. Be naked."

When she returned from the bathroom, Blake had the bed set up and was already horizontal, the sheet covering her as she smiled seductively.

"Tell me specific songs you like, and I'll learn them." Her hand poked out from beneath the sheet and she patted the bed. "Said the spider to the fly."

Emily quickly removed her clothing, then pulled the sheet back to slide in. As the fabric pulled away from Blake's body, Emily's mouth dropped open. "Jesus! Where did you get those?"

Blake was wearing a beautiful black bra, designed to make her already gorgeous breasts look like they were about to break free of their confines, and very snug, black satiny bikinis.

"I picked them up on the way to work yesterday." Her grin grew even more seductive. "I told you I was thinking about you."

Emily normally would have started to get wet at the mere thought of Blake in sexy lingerie, but this time only her eyes got in on the action. Her chin quivered as a few tears slid down her cheeks. "You did that for me?"

In a second, Blake was on her feet, padding around the bed. Then she was next to Emily, with her arms wrapped around her tenderly. "Of course I did. You said you liked nice underwear, and since you're having a tough time figuring out how to get into sex again…"

"You're so sweet," Emily sniffled as she buried her face in Blake's shoulder. "You're so kindhearted."

"Hey," she soothed. "This was no big deal. I didn't do it to make you cry."

She stood up straight and wiped at her eyes with the backs of her hands. "I'm much more emotional than usual. They say it takes six months to a year for a…" She fought for the word and managed to pull it out of her wonky brain. "Traumatic brain injury to heal fully."

"That's such a good term for it," Blake said, standing to enfold her in another embrace. "It was traumatic. Very traumatic."

Emily looked into her concerned gaze. "This might be the worst way to start a day in bed. Can we relaunch?"

"Sure." She smiled and sat down on the bed. "You start."

"Let's slide into this." When Blake lay down, she got in next to her. "Each time we've been together, we've been chasing orgasms. I've noticed some things that caught my attention, but I've never taken the time to ask about them." She took Blake's right arm and ran a finger down a long, thin line. "What's this from? It looks like a series of dots."

"Oh, that was a bad one," she said, shaking her head. "I was in Bordeaux, and a kid who was staging was making caramel. He was moving a pan to make room for me, and the dope held his spatula over my arm." She leaned over and looked at the scar carefully. "You can see the biggest drop was here, then they get smaller as they go down." She rubbed the scar, as if it still hurt. "I've worn long sleeves in the kitchen ever since, even though they're a hell of a lot hotter."

"I've got a good one here," Emily said, pointing to the wide red welt at the base of her left wrist. "I was putting something into the salamander and some jerk ran into me from behind. If I'd had my knife in my hand, I might have stabbed him."

Blake laughed. "A jury of cooks would have acquitted you. It's bad enough when you hurt yourself. Having someone else do it makes me homicidal."

Emily ran her fingers over Blake's perfectly smooth skin. "Have you ever noticed how many cooks don't have any hair on their arms?" She put her arm right next to Blake's. Both as smooth as newborns. "I swear I had a normal amount before I started cooking, but I've burned it off so many times it's gone forever."

"We're the walking wounded. That's why we should only date each other." She carefully traced a dark pink line that ran across Emily's index finger. "This is a battle scar you earned while learning your trade." She kissed it tenderly. "I respect your wounds."

Emily shifted until she could reach Blake's mouth. Then she kissed her, sliding her tongue into her mouth and probing until Blake broke away, panting.

Emily looked into her eyes, seeing a depth of understanding, of shared experience and goals. "You're the only person I've ever... You get me," she added, shying away from characterizing their relationship as a relationship.

"I do get you," Blake said, her gaze burning in its intensity. "And I respect you. I don't say things like that lightly, Emily."

"That makes it all the more special." Emily wrapped her in a tender hug and nestled against her body, feeling cared for and understood in ways she could never recall experiencing. It was good. So good. And ending very, very soon.

A cab waited outside her apartment, the engine growling in the still night. Blake had walked her to the door, as promised, but was going to head right back home. The cabbie had been confused, but she reasoned he'd seen far stranger things than a woman riding from TriBeCa to Jackson Heights and back.

They'd had a great day, even though there had been an undercurrent of sadness. Or maybe lost promise. She wasn't sure Blake was as down as she was, but there had been glimpses of pain in her eyes. Like the sad smile she'd given her right before they'd left the apartment. They hadn't spoken of it, though, both keeping things light and optimistic.

"I'd better go," Blake said. "If that cabs leaves, I'll never get another one."

"You didn't pay him. He'll stay all night."

Chuckling, Blake nodded. "You've got a point. But I've got to be up by nine."

"You get going then." Emily draped her arms around her neck and pulled her down for a long, leisurely kiss. "I had a great time today."

"Me too. Call me and let me know what's going on, okay?"

"Of course. I'll give you a call tomorrow after I talk to Laurent's assistant."

"I want an assistant," Blake said, sticking her lower lip out in a pout.

"Can't help you there, Chef. But if this doesn't work out, I might be available. Cheap."

Laurent was emerging from a Town Car just as Emily got to the door of the restaurant the next morning. She'd come in four hours early just to make sure they had time to talk, but she was so nervous she wished she'd spoken to him during prep, when they'd barely have time to exchange a word.

His head cocked, a question in his eyes as she scooted under his arm when he held the door. "You have good news for me?"

"I..." She wasn't willing to have this discussion in the middle of the dining room. "Can we go to your office?"

His gaze was playful, but she had a feeling he was being perfectly sincere. "If you have good news, yes. If it's bad, tell me now."

This was going to be her new normal. It would take some time to get to know this guy, but if Blake liked him, he had to be okay. "I have good news, but we need to agree on some details."

His smile made him look awfully proud of himself. Like he'd worn her down. Maybe it would be less smug after they talked.

Going directly into Laurent's spacious office, Emily waited for him to divest himself of his supple leather jacket and paisley scarf. Who wore a jacket and scarf in New York in June? He looked at his phone with half of his attention, giving her the other half. "Tell me what details you need."

She almost waved her hands in front of him to garner more of his focus, but she was only going to get the portion he had left after frowning at his phone. "I don't want to move to Las Vegas, but I'm willing to go there to help."

"Fine. Fine." Now he started to look at the mail that was lying on the middle of his desk, already opened and organized for him.

"That means I'd like you to keep looking for a permanent sous while I'm there."

His eyes shifted up to meet hers. Then they narrowed, briefly. "All right." She really had his attention now. He stared at her for a few seconds, then said, "Since you will not be working for him permanently, I will admit that I doubt Felix's skill in hiring. He hand-picked the sous who left, but they had nothing but problems." His head cocked as his gaze gentled. "Can you hire people?"

Gulping, she said, "I've only hired seven."

Laurent let out a frustrated sigh. "Emily. You must be better at saying good things about yourself. Now." He placed his hands on the desk, looking like a school teacher. "Let's try again. Can you hire people?"

"Yes." She tried to look confident. "Everyone I've hired has worked out, and two of them have been promoted."

"Then you will interview everyone, and let Felix speak to only those you approve of. Yes?"

"I can do that. But I can't afford to live in Las Vegas."

A frown flitted across his handsome features. "I understand you want to return when the restaurant opens. You may."

"No," she said, trying to be clearer. "I can't afford to live in Las Vegas *now*."

He blinked a few times, shoved his chair away from his desk and gave her his full attention. "Explain this to me?"

"I can't stick my roommates for my rent in New York, and I can't afford to maintain two places." She tried to temper her words with a smile. "I'm not complaining about my salary, but it's not enough for that."

His puzzlement swiftly moved to pique. Or at least that's what it looked like when he picked up his phone and hit a button. "Michael? Where can Emily live?" A few seconds passed, then he snapped, "For *free*." His face contorted in a variety of looks, none of which she could clearly identify. "That will work." His broad shoulders shrugged, as though Michael could see him. "You'll have to find another place for me. The hotel will work with you. Don't worry so much. It ages you."

Then he hung up and gave her a quick smile. "You will live in the room the hotel provides for me."

"But..."

"That is all that I have. It will be good for you."

Thinking that having her squatting in his room might lead him to keep his promise to let her return, Emily extended her hand to shake.

"This will be good. For both of us," he said, his mind made up.

"I hope so. When would you like me to start?"

"Mmm." He looked at his phone again, paging through something that captivated him. "Wednesday, I think. No later."

Her stomach performed a major flip. "Two days from now?"

"See Michael about your travel," he said, his focus having moved on.

She stood there, stunned, until he dialed a number and started to talk. *Wednesday?*

That night, Emily sat with Chase at their kitchen table, eating a fiery chicken curry she'd picked up at a late night place near the subway. At least Chase said it was fiery. Emily was happy to be able to taste a hint of curry and enjoy the tingles in her mouth.

"What am I going to do without you for the whole summer?" he moaned, chin resting on his hand. "No one else likes to wander around Queens on a hot summer Sunday, eating things they can't identify."

She popped him on the head with her fork. "That's my biggest contribution? The fact that I'll eat anything?"

"I'm teasing about that. I'll miss the hell out of you." He reached over and took her hand for a moment. "Not that we see each other much any more."

"Hey, don't apologize for finding a girlfriend with a better apartment than we have. If I could crash at Blake's, I'm sure I would have done it."

He played with his food for a few moments, then said, slightly tentatively, "This is bad timing for you, isn't it?"

"Pretty bad. Yeah." She took another bite of her chicken, chewing while she thought. "We're nearly at the stage where I might have hoodwinked her into girlfriend mode. Now, it'll be just as easy to drift apart and lose contact."

"Aww, that's not true. Not given how she acted when you were so down."

Shrugging, she said, "I know she likes me. She's not the kind of woman who'd hang out if she didn't. But I think she'd have been exactly like that with anyone she slept with." Their eyes met and a smile settled onto her face. "She's got a very kind soul."

"But you're awesome!"

"I'm not sure she knows that yet," she said, allowing his outsized view of her to go unchallenged. "Every time we've been together has been great, but it's just been a few times. I'm worried that some new bartender or server or sous chef will show up and make her forget all about me."

"Have you told her you're going?"

"No. I thought I'd do that right now."

As she got up, Chase caught her and pulled her close, resting his head on her hip while she trailed her fingers through his hair. If she could have ever convinced herself to fall for a guy, he'd be the one. But she'd never had the slightest interest in the weaker sex, as she and her sister referred to men. But just because they weren't intimate didn't mean she wasn't going to miss him like crazy. She looked down at his closed eyes, seeing he was close to tears. As she pulled away, she bent and kissed his cheek. Neither of them put words to the possibility, but she wouldn't have been surprised if he made the move to Natasha's while she was away. The important people in her life were going to go on with their own plans—while she languished in a city she had no interest in.

She was feeling so glum Emily barely lifted her feet as she went into her room and dialed Blake's cell phone. "Hi," Blake said when she answered. "Can I call you right back?"

"Sure. I'll be up for hours."

Ten minutes later, the phone rang and Emily picked it up. "Catching you at a bad time?"

"No, it's fine. I was just poking around, checking on things before I locked up. I'm walking home now."

"Guess who's going to Las Vegas in thirty-one hours?"

"What? Why so soon?"

"Because Laurent's determined to open on Labor Day weekend. And he doesn't trust his chef to make good hires."

Blake let out a stream of air, almost, but not quite, a whistle. "Damn, that's a tough one. Maybe it's Laurent who didn't do a good job of hiring. If you don't trust your chef to bring in the right people…"

Chuckling, Emily said, "I didn't think it was my place to point that out. Even though I thought it."

"You're more polite than I am."

"And I didn't spend a summer chasing girls with him. You have a history."

"Yeah, I guess." She let out a sigh loud enough to carry over the line. "I don't envy you, Emily. Getting a restaurant open is awfully hard work."

"Uhm, isn't this the point at which you should be encouraging me? Maybe even telling me you're sure I'll whip the place into shape with weeks to spare?"

She started to laugh, but she sounded really tired, too. "That's a given. I know you'll do a good job. I just hope you can get along with Felix. I only know him by reputation, but I've heard he likes to do things his own way."

"What chef doesn't?" She paused for a second. "Except you, of course. You don't have strong ideas about hardly anything."

Blake let out a soft chuckle. "Your sense of humor will help you get along with Felix. Make sure you pack it."

"Ugh. I'd better get started on that. I've never moved with just two suitcases."

"That's all you'll need. Whites, pants, underwear, clogs, toothbrush and a comb. You'll be so busy you won't need another thing."

"Thanks for the pep talk," she said, laughing. "Now I'm really excited."

Seriously, Blake said, "I know you'll do very well, Emily. I was looking forward to spending my Sundays with you this summer, but…"

"Yeah. Me too." She wasn't sure how to follow that up. "I guess I'll see you when I get back. Hopefully in September."

"Keep in touch, will you? I'm interested in how everything sorts out."

"Will do. Take care of yourself, and don't let anyone drip caramel on you."

"I won't. Oh! My lucky number's thirteen. Play that for me."

"Oh, sure. I'll have plenty of time to be down at the craps table, playing for you with *my* money."

"Roulette, Emily," she said, her laugh tired but genuine. "You'll be looking all day for a thirteen on a craps table. On second thought, you'd better stick to cooking. You know what you're doing in the kitchen."

"I hope so."

"I know so. And so will Felix. And Laurent. And the rest of Las Vegas." The background noise changed, and Blake said, "I'm going into the elevator, so I'd better hang up. I'd say best of luck, but you won't need it. You've got talent."

Chapter Fifteen

EMILY HAD NEVER BEEN to Las Vegas, so she wasn't sure why she was so certain it wasn't for her. But she was certain it was in the desert, and sand just wasn't her thing. She was a greenery girl, through and through. Of course, Jackson Heights wasn't exactly verdant and she was perfectly, or at least reasonably happy there. She was clearly laboring under preconceived notions, and that wasn't fair.

After catching a cab from the airport, she spent the next few minutes marveling at the size of the hotels and casinos on the Strip. She'd seen pictures, of course, but nothing had prepared her for the gargantuan nature of the place. Everything was outsized; signs, streets, buildings, women's breasts. She'd thought she'd seen a lot of silicone in New York, but she'd been mistaken. This was the home office for plastic surgery. Every third woman made Blake's lavish breasts look like they could have been contained by a training bra. This place was going to take some getting used to.

The hotel staff treated her with a good deal of brisk hospitality, and soon Emily was riding up a glass elevator to near the top of the tower. Laurent hadn't gotten the penthouse, but he was only off by two floors. The room, the nicest, biggest hotel room she'd ever been in, had a bedroom, a small dining room, and a big living room, all with glass walls that allowed you to view miles of desert with hills or maybe mountains in the distance. It was hard to tell how far away they were, making it impossible to gauge their height. The other side of the hotel must have provided a view of the action on the street, but this was nicer. She tipped the guy who'd brought her bags and showed her where all of the amenities were, then snapped a few pictures of the big space, which she promptly texted to Chase and Charlotte.

Then she turned off her phone, stuck it into her pocket and grabbed her room key. Taking the garment bag that held nothing but her chef's clothes and clogs, she headed down to the restaurant.

It was strange having to cut through a gambling floor to reach your job. She'd been to a few casinos, but only ones in and around Detroit. This was another kind of thing. A much bigger, brasher, noisier thing. Right before she reached the aisle that led to the fine dining restaurants, a roulette wheel caught her eye. It took a few minutes to have a patient patron explain how and when to bet, with the guy doing it for her when it became crystal clear she had no idea how to follow his instructions. A few seconds later, she was a winner. She was fairly sure thirteen hadn't come up, but the guy told her black had hit, and four whole dollars said he was right. Maybe this was her…or Blake's lucky day.

Excitement, anticipation and anxiety always filled her on the first day of a new job, and today anxiety shot to the top of the mix. She got a few puzzled looks when she ducked behind a facade made of plywood, heralding the fall opening of Laurent Bistro. More looks, this time from construction workers, when she pushed past stacks of drywall to enter.

The dining room had barely been laid out, with tradesmen wandering around, their toolbelts hanging low on their hips, dirty, sweat-stained T-shirts showing their efforts. Electric saws, clouds of sawdust, and banging hammers assaulted her as she picked through the chaos to find the kitchen. Thankfully, it was in better shape than the dining room—missing only the ovens. The one piece of equipment she'd need to test cooks. But it was big. The biggest kitchen she'd ever been in.

At the rear of the space she found an office, nicely appointed. A guy about her age, with dark hair and stylish stubble sat at the desk, his feet braced against the wood as his chair leaned back at a dangerous angle, knees high in the air. He had to be the chef, but she'd never, ever seen a chef wearing a golf shirt, khaki shorts and leather sandals. Nor had she seen one with a glowing bronzed tan, save for his feet, where socks had left them oddly pale.

Chef or not, this guy seemed either bored or angry. It was hard to tell which with a stranger. When he looked up, his dark eyes scanned across her face. "Server?"

"Chef." She put her bag on a spare chair. "Sous chef. I'm Emily Desjardins."

His brows rose, and those dark eyes brightened briefly. "Great. I knew you were getting into town today, but I didn't expect you to come down." He stood and extended his hand to shake. "Felix Doumani. I'm glad to have you."

"I'm glad to be here, Chef. Where should I start?"

With a relieved smile, he handed her a pile of sheets from a printer. "Resumes. Pick through them and come up with a list of people you want to interview."

"How many are we hiring?"

"Give me a minute." He searched around his desk, then pulled a sheet from the pile. "Here's the list. I've got pastry already."

Great. He'd hired one person and they needed over thirty. "Where should I work?" His office, while good sized, had only one desk and one phone.

He made a face that made him look a little like a cat. Like he was playing with her, and enjoying it. "Didn't Michael set you up in Laurent's room?"

"He did."

"If I were you, I'd use it. There's no space down here." He shrugged. "Besides, it's too noisy to hear."

She hefted the pile of papers. "Do you want me to run with this? Or do you want to be consulted?"

A half smile made him seem both content and doubtful. "If you can fill this place with people who know what they're doing, I'll be happy. I only want to talk to any sous you find. The rest of them are…" He shrugged. "Cogs in the machinery."

"Do we have a budget?"

"You bet." After going through his file cabinet, he pulled out a purple folder. "It's all in here. Everything comes down from New York. You've got to beg to spend an extra dime."

"I don't like to beg, so I'll try to follow the budget."

"Good luck." He sat down again and let out a wry laugh. "You'll need it."

Ensconced back in her room, Emily briefly considered ordering room service. But Michael had made it clear her expenses were her own. So she went out to the Strip and walked until she found a good-sized mini mart. It was tough finding much that wasn't merely salt and fat, but she managed to grab a few things that probably wouldn't give her an instant heart attack. One small benefit of losing most of her ability to taste was that she could eat unripe fruit and limp vegetables and not notice much difference. That dulled sense would probably come in handy if this turned out to be her grocery store. She'd thought her local bodega in Jackson Heights had poor selection and high prices. *Ha!*

For some reason, Laurent Bistro did not use many French terms, even though Le Lapin used the full compliment. Emily was charged with hiring two sous chefs, along with two cooks for each of eight stations: sauté, fish, roast, grill, fry, vegetable, cold appetizer, and hot appetizer. They'd also need two swing cooks who could fill in at any station, and six prep cooks. Not to mention all of the people who would clean and keep the place tidy. Of course they could use as many interns as she could gather up. Free help was mandatory when you had a tight budget.

Going through the pages of information New York had sent, she finally saw that the restaurant would have two hundred seats—bigger than Le Lapin. Not only was the restaurant significantly bigger, it was open more than twice as long, with daily lunch and weekend brunch service added to the mix.

Not sure where to begin, Emily sat down and started going over resumes. She'd need more. Lots more. She was going to call Felix to ask what agency he'd used when she realized she hadn't gotten his phone number. And he hadn't asked for hers. Talk about hands off!

Emily sat by the pool on Sunday morning, trying to get some fresh air while it was still only eighty-five degrees. It would be hotter soon. Now she was beginning to cement her hunch that she didn't want to live in Las Vegas. Besides her distaste for sand, scorching heat sucked.

Her phone buzzed and she picked it up and took a look at the screen. "Hello there," she said, a zing of excitement hitting her when she saw Blake's name.

"I'm hoping no news is good news."

Emily's breath caught as she searched her brain. Had she said she was going to call? Had Blake asked her to? "I was going to call you today." That wasn't truly a lie. She *had* been thinking about her.

"Beat you to it. So? Are you ready to open?"

"I'm ready to open a vein," she moaned. "This place is going to be huge! We need a much bigger staff than I'm used to, then we have to double it to cover all of the shifts. A four hour lunch every weekday, and five hour brunches both weekend days. Dinner seven days a week, too. It's insane!"

"It's a darned good thing the menu is going to be simpler. There's no way you could be open that long and be cutting edge."

"I don't think anyone's looking to cut any edges here. Every single decision comes from New York."

"Really? Felix isn't doing the menu?"

"Nope. I get the impression we're not even going to have specials, or at least not many." She blew out a breath. "You wouldn't work in a place like this for more than a day."

"Maybe not, but you can't make any real money with a restaurant like mine. Last year our margin was less than five percent."

"Damn," Emily said, letting that tiny number really sink in. "That's criminal. All of that work for so little."

"That's the game. I could make a lot more if I owned a burger joint, but I wouldn't enjoy it as much."

"I'm with you. I'm willing to do this for a while, but the cooking isn't going to be unique—it's pure volume. I'm dealing with things I'd never be exposed to in New York, though. Like working with the casino and hotel staff, figuring out how to get paid back for all of the comps they want us to offer." She laughed, thinking of some of the demands. "They act like we're the school cafeteria. I tried to tell them we can't simply throw another bag of beans into the soup pot. I guess I'll have to get Felix involved."

"How's that going? Is he as tough to work with as I've heard?"

"You rat! You didn't tell me you'd heard that!"

Blake's laugh was a little tentative. "Uhm…well, it was just gossip. You know how cooks gossip. I didn't want to worry you—"

"I'm busting your chops. We're getting along fine."

"That's great, Emily. I'm really happy to hear that."

"Yeah. I've found he's very easy to work with if you do all the work." She lowered her voice, even though she was nearly the only person by the pool. "I have no idea what he does all day, but he's always on the phone when I go down to see him."

"Go down? You're not on the same floor?"

"I work out of my hotel room. There's only one office, and he doesn't want to share. It's been weird, Chef, but I'm enjoying the work."

"That's a relief. I've been worried that you might hate the whole thing."

"No, no, I'm finding I've got a knack for negotiating."

"That's because you're charming," Blake said, sounding like a proud parent.

"I'm not sure that's true, but it's been fun. We're getting our stove put in this week. As soon as we're running, I'm going to start interviewing people. I've got twenty-eight cooks to hire and train. Along with another ten people to wash dishes and clean. Thank god I don't have to hire the servers. The dining room manager's going to do that—if Felix ever hires one."

Blake whistled, a low, soft sound that made Emily smile.

"You've got a great whistle there."

Her voice took on its sexy timbre. "I have a lot of talents you haven't gotten to sample. Maybe I can show you some of them when you get back."

"I'd like to see what you've got. For the first time in my life, I think I'll be looking forward to the end of summer."

Laurent visited every week, showing far more interest in the details than Felix did. The more Emily got to know Laurent, the more she enjoyed working together. It didn't hurt that he quickly and decisively approved all of her plans for hiring and organizing the work shifts and stations, but more than that, he listened and responded. That was huge.

By the end of July, she still hadn't hired a soul. That was anxiety-producing, but not odd. Good cooks were already working, and having a proposed opening date that was a month away was too speculative for most people to give notice. So the hiring would have to happen just under the wire.

There were still plenty of things to do. She was working on the layout of the various stations one night when her phone rang. A satisfied smile lit her face as she saw the number. Blake hadn't called since her first week, and Emily had consciously decided to wait her out. Everything she knew about her indicated she hated clingy women, and Emily was never going to fall into that category.

"Hi there," she said, checking the time. "Done for the day?"

"Yeah. Pretty slow night." Blake yawned. "So why am I more tired than I would be if we'd been busy?"

"I don't know, but that happens to me too. Are you walking home?"

"Uh-huh. Can you hear the road work?"

"Yep. Some people get crickets and bullfrogs as nighttime noises. We get pile drivers, jackhammers and, road graders."

"I'm glad to hear you say 'we.' I've been thinking you might have changed your mind about living in Vegas."

"No, it's not for me. Of course, that opinion is as well thought out as people who come to Times Square for a few days and whine about how horrible it would be to live in New York. I haven't seen a real neighborhood since I've been here. Off the Strip might be fantastic."

"You don't have a car, right?"

"Right. I have to take a bus to the grocery store, but I make myself do it so I'm not stuck with junk from the nearby mini-mart."

"Ahh, the glamorous life of a chef," she said, laughing. "I can see why everyone wants to go to cooking school."

"I'm glad they do. Gives me more bodies to pick from."

"I'm almost home. Thanks," she said, obviously talking to her doorman. "Have a good night." Then the background noise changed. "Hold on a second. Got to get my keys out." Emily waited patiently, wondering why she stayed on the line. Before, she'd hung up when she got into the elevator. "Okay. Home again. Do you mind if I make myself something to eat?"

"Feel free." It was like being twelve and talking to a friend from school.

"I was thinking," she said as cookware rattled in the background. "Maybe I'll come out to Vegas, if I wouldn't be in the way. Like on a Sunday. I haven't been there for a few years, and I'd like to see your setup."

Emily blinked in surprise. Her setup? Was she interested in the restaurant, or her? "You wouldn't be in the way. Felix never works on Sunday, so that would be good. But it's a long trip for one day."

"Yeah, I guess it is." Her enthusiasm was dropping fast.

Trying to amp her back up, Emily said, "August in Vegas. What could be nicer? I've got to go to Detroit this coming weekend, but any time after that would be good. "

"Detroit? What's going on there?"

"It's my sister's thirtieth birthday. Her husband's throwing a huge party."

Blake's snack preparation was making a heck of a lot of noise. And she obviously couldn't talk while she cooked—even for herself. But then the noise stopped and she took a bite. "Sorry," she said. "I'm just so hungry."

"It's all right. God knows I understand. I've been making something for myself around seven each night. I'm not sure how I'll ever get back into my night owl routine."

Blake circled back to the previous thread. "Your sister's having a party, huh?"

"Yeah. Chuck, her husband, made it for Sunday since I was still in New York when he planned it, and he knew Charlotte would kill him if I wasn't there. I think he's invited a hundred and fifty people."

"Would a hundred and fifty one screw things up?"

So stunned she gasped, Emily quickly recovered her ability to speak. "You want to go to Detroit?"

"Well, no, but I'd like to see you and Detroit's closer than Las Vegas. I could fly out on Sunday morning and come home on the last flight back." She took a bite of whatever she'd made. "But only if that works for you. If you'd rather go alone…" She paused just a second. "Or maybe you already have a date."

"No, I don't. I'd love to have you," she said, letting her enthusiasm show. "I'll send you the details."

"Great. Uhm, should I get a hotel room? For us, I mean."

"Hotel room? Aren't you going back the same day?"

"Yeah, I'll need to, but I'd like some privacy. I don't want to uhm… disturb your family."

Damn, she was nearly tongue-tied! "They live in a modern condo. Two master suites on different sides of the unit."

"Great," she said, her voice now free of whatever had made her sound so unsure of herself. "I'll let you know when I can schedule a flight. Talk to you soon."

"Sounds good. Nice talking to you."

"Same here, Emily. See you."

She clicked off and sat there, unmoving, for several minutes. What was going on?

Emily's Pacific-time body clock didn't nudge her out of her Detroit bed until one o'clock on Saturday afternoon. Stumbling out into the living room in her pajamas, she dropped onto the sofa. "I'm so sorry for sleeping the day away." Her head fell back against the squishy cushions. "When I have a day off, I go a little nuts."

Her mom was sitting on a chair that sat at a right angle to the sofa, which allowed her to reach over and pat Emily on the cheek. "You need your rest, honey. It's fine with us if you sleep most of the time you're here."

"But I want to talk to you, and I can't do that if I'm out cold."

Carol stood and started for the kitchen. "Let me get you some coffee."

"Don't bother. I've stopped drinking it."

Halting abruptly, Carol turned and stared. "You've stopped drinking coffee? You've been gulping it down since you were in high school!"

"I know, but I can't taste it very well. I started to get all of these odd notes…" She thought for a second. "It was starting to taste sour." Making a face, she said, "Really nasty."

"How about tea?"

"No, I decided to kick the caffeine habit. It's only been two weeks, but it's been easier to get to sleep at night."

"Apple juice?"

"Okay, but just a little. An ounce or two in water would be great." She could hear but not see her mother in the kitchen. "Where's dad?"

"He went over to help Chuck set up." Carol returned, handing Emily a glass.

"Do they need help? I'm pretty darned good at getting things organized."

Waving a hand, Carol said, "They might, but it's stiflingly hot. I thought we could stay inside and talk." Laughing, she added, "Does that make me a bad person?"

"No, not really. Selfish? Yeah." She laughed as well, knowing her mother wouldn't take offense. "I'd much rather talk than work, so I'm selfish too." She cleared her throat and dove in. "I'm bringing a da… guest tomorrow."

"You are?" Carol's face lit up in a smile. "Is Chase able to come?"

"No, Blake is."

"Blake?" She looked like Emily had said she was bringing her postal carrier. "Why… Are you *seeing* her?"

"Uhm..." This was the tricky part. "I guess. We've hung out a few times."

"You guess?" Carol didn't follow up. She was good at waiting you out, making you spill things you had no intention of revealing.

"It's odd, Mom. Like I said, we've gone out for a couple of meals, and spent a Sunday or two together. That's it. So I was really surprised when she said she'd like to come."

That explanation didn't fly. Emily could see her mother's agile mind dismiss it. "Why would you invite her, honey? I mean, if you're not really seeing each other it seems strange to expect her to travel for a party."

"I didn't invite her. She invited herself."

Frowning, Carol said, "Your former boss picked up the phone and announced she was coming to your sister's birthday party?"

"No, no, we were talking, and she offered to fly to Vegas to see the restaurant. I said I was available anytime after this weekend, and when she asked what I was doing, she said she'd tag along." Boy, that sounded dumb!

Clearly becoming more puzzled by the moment, Emily watched her mom try to make sense of the whole thing. "So you've been out a few times and she's interested in seeing you more. Maybe she's trying to get to the next level with you."

You couldn't admit to your mother that there weren't many more levels for the types of things they did together. "No, that's not it." She stretched out on the sofa, hoping she'd be able to think more clearly if she relaxed. "She made it clear she doesn't want a relationship. Very clear," she stressed. "That's why this threw me. It came out of left field."

"Well, if you were starting to see each other in New York, your going away might have stirred something in her."

"I doubt that, Mom. We've talked twice since I've been gone. If she missed me, she'd at least text." They weren't going to get anywhere trying to figure Blake out. Emily was sure of that.

On Sunday morning, Emily sat in her mom's car, waiting in the cell phone lot for Blake to land. It was 7:30, and her internal clock was all screwed up, but she was too nervous to be tired. After her chat with her mom, she'd spent much of the day trying to figure out why Blake was coming. They were fuck buddies. Nothing more. But why would a fuck buddy fly halfway across the country to go to a birthday party where she didn't know the guest of honor?

"Touchdown!" Blake's text said, chirping.

Emily swallowed and started up the car. This was going to be interesting. Or enlightening. Or something.

Emily caught sight of her at the curb. Jeans and a sky blue t-shirt, with a messenger bag draped across her body. The poor thing looked like she'd been up half the night. "Hi," Emily said as Blake settled herself in the small car, then leaned over and offered a kiss. Emily couldn't taste it, but the nicotine gum was present. Blake's shifting jaw muscles gave it away. "Good flight?"

"Not bad. Thanks for coming to get me."

"I was happy to. We'll have the whole day together this way."

"Yeah. That's why I came so early. I wanted a full day and the next flight would have gotten me here at 2:30." She gave Emily a funny look. "That's why I thought it might be smart to get a room. Then we could…you know…have some privacy."

Oh, shit! She'd come only to have sex! Stupid, stupid, stupid! "It would look pretty funny if we got a room at this point." Wincing, she added, "I guess I screwed up."

"No, you didn't. I just…" She bit at her lower lip, nervously. "I always feel funny when I stay at other people's houses. You've got to follow their schedules." A shy grin peeked out. "I'm not great at following other people's schedules."

"You look tired." Emily took her hand and kissed it. If they were going to go to family parties together, she was going to let herself be affectionate outside of the bedroom. "When did you get to sleep?"

"Mmm." She stretched as well as she could while stifling a yawn. "Two? Two thirty?"

"And when did you get up?"

"Four thirty. I should have just stayed up, but I thought a couple of hours was better than none."

Cocking her head, Emily asked, "Think you were right?"

"Nope." She leaned her seat back, let her mouth drop open and stuck out her tongue. "I couldn't have been more wrong."

They got close to the building, with Blake looking around curiously. "When you said you were from Detroit, I imagined you living in one of the suburbs. I think I was wrong."

Emily tried to ignore the familiar sights, and view her city the way a stranger would. There was no denying Detroit had fallen on hard times decades ago, and hadn't been able to boost itself back up very far, but it was her home and she had a load of affection for it. "Very wrong. Both sides of my family have been Detroiters for generations. My dad's family moved to the 'burbs in the 70s, but my mom's parents refused to flee, even when the crime rate was off the charts."

"Your parents have lived in the city since they've been together?"

"Uh-huh. My mom wouldn't budge when they got married, and they're still here."

"Interesting. My family hasn't been near a city since…" She pondered that for a moment. "I might be the only Chadwick to have ever lived in a city."

"We lived in a pretty big house in University Heights when I was growing up, but my parents moved to this condo when Charlotte went to college. My mom hates to bang around a big, empty house."

"Does your dad work close to home?"

"Very. He can walk if it's nice out." She pulled up to an automatic door and waited a second as it rose. "Wouldn't it be nice to have a car and a garage?"

"I can hardly imagine," Blake said, smiling.

They left the car in its assigned space, then took an elevator to the third floor. "This place was a printing factory," Emily said. "I think the developers spent a ton to convert it, but it never really took off. My parents paid for their apartment in cash." She let that sink in. "And they don't have a lot of cash."

They exited and walked down a hallway that still had an industrial flair to it. "Edgy," Blake said, nodding in approval.

"I often think of what this would cost in Manhattan."

"A converted factory with inside parking?" She let out a laugh. "Some of our customers would be able to afford it. But not many."

Emily slipped her key into the door, and they entered, standing in the entryway for a second. "Check out the ceiling height."

"Damn, a loft with parking? All of the people you know put together couldn't afford this if it was in Manhattan."

Carol walked in from the living room. "It's nice to actually meet you," she said, putting her hand out to shake. "I'm so glad you could come for a visit, Blake."

"I'm glad to be here. Thanks for having me."

"Come on in," Carol said. "Could I make you some coffee?"

"I look like I need it, don't I," Blake said, smiling that charming grin.

"Blake's running on fumes, Mom. Would you mind if she took a nap?"

"Of course not," she said, sympathy showing in her pale eyes. "I don't know how you girls work the hours you do. Get her set up in the guest room, Em."

"Uhm… I thought I'd hang out with Blake. I could use a nap too."

Carol's eyes opened wide, but she was obviously trying not to show she was surprised. "Whatever you two want to do is fine with me."

"What time do you want to leave for the party?"

"We don't have to leave until noon." She was clearly flustered, and trying not to show it. "If you're not ready then, I can have your dad come back and get me. Then you can have the car and come over when you're ready."

It was barely eight thirty. "I think we'll be ready long before noon. Thanks, mom." Then she headed for the guest room, with Blake right on her tail. Emily closed the door and leaned on it. "Awkward!"

Falling to the bed, Blake said, "I'm glad I wasn't imagining that. Your poor mom looked like she didn't know what to say."

"There's only one guest room, so she knew we were going to sleep together." She made a face. "I guess she didn't expect us to sleep together at eight thirty in the morning. It's been a long, long time since I brought a girl home. We're both out of practice."

Blake kicked off her shoes, then stood and started to undress. She was neatly folding her jeans when she said, "How long ago was that?"

"College. No. Med school. I was dating someone from Ohio and we spent Thanksgiving here."

After taking off her T-shirt and bra, Blake stretched her body out, displaying her awesome curves without the slightest bit of unease. "In your mom's defense, she handled it really well. That might not happen at my parents' house."

"No sleepovers at your place?" Emily couldn't resist. She stood next to her and slipped her arms around Blake's waist, purring with satisfaction as all of that warm skin enveloped her.

"None. Ever."

She looked into Blake's eyes, searching them for information. Her tone had been matter-of-fact, but the words had been so decisive. "Are they religious?"

"My parents?" She chuckled. "They go to church once in a while. Like Christmas and maybe Easter, but I think that's for the music." She reached down and started to unbutton Emily's shirt. "I'm just guessing at their reaction. For all I know they'd be happy to have me visit and bring a woman."

"What do you mean, for all you know?"

Her smile grew as Emily's clothing fell to the floor. "I've never had anyone to take, so I can't say one way or the other."

"Wait." Emily put her hand over Blake's, stopping her from unzipping her slacks. "What do you mean?"

She spoke patiently, but her eyes showed she'd much rather continue her quest. "I've never had a girlfriend, so they've never had to learn to deal with one."

"But they know you're gay."

"Everyone knows I'm gay," she said, her grin turning sly. "But they've been able to ignore it." Her head cocked slightly. "I've told you that."

"No, you haven't. I'd remember."

"Huh. Well, they don't know much about my life, and they don't ask." She finished her task, then sent Emily's slacks to the floor, quickly followed by her underwear. "Boy, that bed looks nice," she said, grinning. "It'll look even nicer with you in it."

Letting herself be distracted for a moment, Emily pulled down the comforter and sheet. When they both got in, Blake hissed out a long, pleasured sigh. "Does anything feel as good as a nice bed when you're exhausted?"

"No, I guess not." She lay on her side, holding her head up with her hand. "When you say you've never had a girlfriend, you mean in the U.S., right?"

"Nope." Blake pulled Emily close and placed a soft kiss on her lips. "Never."

"Not in France?"

"Nope." Another, longer kiss.

She pushed her away, determined to get this straight. "You've never had a girlfriend."

Obviously seeing this was an issue, Blake sat up and faced Emily. "I don't think you understand what it was like for me in France."

"You've never talked about it, so you're probably right."

She settled against the headboard, then brought the sheet up to cover her breasts. "Sure I have."

"Nope. Not a word."

Her head cocked curiously. "Are you sure?"

"Yes, I'm sure. You've told me what cities you worked in. That's it."

"Right. Right." She nodded. "I guess I thought you'd just know."

"How would I know? You're the only person I've ever met who took your path."

"Got it." Nodding again, she said, "Well, I wasn't sure I was gay when I went to France, but after a few fumbling encounters with boys in meat lockers, it became clear I was."

"Meat lockers?"

"I lived in a converted barn on the chef's property, Emily. With his older daughter and another cook. We all shared a big loft."

"Oh, shit!" She laughed, thinking of Blake smuggling a date home in that situation.

"Yeah. I was in Nice for two years, knowing I wanted a girl, but not being able to bring one home. So I got used to…making do."

"In meat lockers?" she asked, chuckling.

"More like alleys or a bathroom in a restaurant or a dark club."

"Ooo, that must have been tough."

"Nah." A slow smile formed. "It was fun. Sneaking into a club, or meeting a girl who lived at home and had to be very discreet made things exciting. I didn't have sex lying down until I was…" She thought for a minute. "Twenty."

"Did you ever have your own apartment?"

"Not to myself. No way could I have afforded a place alone. So I always had roommates, people I worked with." She shuddered, as though she was reliving a traumatic event. "I learned early on not to let your coworkers know too much about your private life. So I went to a woman's apartment if she had one, or got carried away and made do." Shrugging, she added, "It worked out. And never interfered with work."

Ahh… That was the key. Even as a kid, work had been paramount. And that hadn't changed one bit.

Emily was able to enjoy herself, even though her mom was just one room away. Her sex drive was still more of a memory than a reality, but going without for a while was obviously the key to losing some of your inhibitions. But Blake was much quieter than usual, going so far as to cover her face with a pillow when she was close to climaxing. Given that she was already very quiet, that seemed like a big overreaction. Emily pulled the pillow away, and chuckled at Blake's pink face. "I don't want to have to perform CPR on you, Chef. You've got to breathe."

"I'm breathing. I just filtered the air." She wrapped her arms around Emily and pulled her atop her body. "That was worth the price of the ticket." After raising her hand, a comically alarmed look flitted across her face. "I was going to slap your ass!"

"It's okay," Emily soothed. "I've had sex here before and my mom didn't stroke out." She chuckled. "I've never excused myself first thing in the morning to get at it, but I think my mom handled it fine. Trust me. She's got headphones on, or she's already left."

"Have you ever heard them?"

"Having sex?" When Blake nodded, she said, "No, but Charlotte did." She started to laugh, thinking about her sister's histrionic fit. "It was always hard to rattle Charlotte, but she almost climbed onto the roof and jumped when she heard my parents going at it. She was right at the point where they told the kids a lot of details in sex ed, and I guess it was just bad timing. I can still get her to shiver when I remind her of it."

"If we catch your mom on the roof…" Blake's words were teasing, but her usual smile was missing.

"How about you? Did you ever catch your parents?"

Emily had learned Blake's facial expressions very well over the months they'd worked together, and she was certain she wasn't going to answer. But she put her hands behind her head and stared up at the ceiling for a little while, then said, "I caught my mom."

Chuckling, Emily said, "Just your mom?" She made a face. "Oh, no! You caught her masturbating?"

"No, no, it wasn't that."

"But your dad wasn't—"

"No, he wasn't," Blake said soberly. "She was with a guy. In her bedroom. I'm still not sure who the guy was, but he seemed vaguely familiar, like I'd seen him at the grocery store or in town. Maybe even at my pre-school," she said thoughtfully. "Maybe he was some kid's dad."

Now sorry she'd brought it up, Emily rolled onto her side and carefully scanned Blake's features. She didn't look upset, but she sure wasn't smiling. "What did you do?"

"I just stood there in the doorway, unable to move."

"Oh, you poor thing. How old were you?"

"Young. Four, maybe?"

"Shit. What did your mom do?"

"My mom's damned hard to rattle. She got up, covered herself with a pillow, and walked over to me. Then she bent over until she was right in my face and said, 'Go play.' I took off like a frightened cat."

"That's it?"

"Uh-huh. I'm telling you, she's not the kind to lose it. She'd be a good spy."

"Did the guy run out five seconds later?"

"If my memory's right, he was there for a long time. I guess they got back to it and finished."

"Fuck!" Emily sat up, staring at Blake. "You caught her red-handed and she finished?"

"Think so. She's not very excitable, Emily. Cool as a cucumber."

"God damn, Blake. That must have freaked you out!"

She seemed very contemplative for a few minutes, the time ticking by as Emily studied her.

"I don't think that's the right term. After the guy left..." She let out a wry chuckle. "I was in the front yard and I remember him waving when he walked to his car. A little while later, my mom called me in and sat me down at the kitchen table. After she put the cookie jar and a glass of milk in front of me, she said, "I don't want you to tell anyone about the man I was talking with upstairs. Do you understand? No one. Not daddy, not grandma, not your friends."

"Oh, damn, having secrets like that isn't good for a kid."

"It worked out okay. I got to eat cookies until I was sick, something I never, ever got to do." She sighed, looking wistful. "And it was kind of cool to share something with my mom. We didn't have much, even back then."

"Did you tell anyone?"

"You're the first," she said, smiling sadly.

Emily gazed at her profile, waiting for more. But there wasn't any more to come. Blake might have thought that was a little mother/daughter bonding time, but she was wrong! Having secrets like that put a kid in a very bad position. As they lay there, Blake closed her eyes, fatigue finally catching up to her. But Emily couldn't sleep. She kept thinking of a sweet-natured child, grasping at a tendril of connection to her mother, having to be satisfied with holding onto a lie she was pledged to keep.

That afternoon, Emily watched Blake charm the pants off every guest she encountered, while looking as pretty as Emily had ever seen her. The epitome of casual, preppy-chic—with an androgynous flair. Her slim-fitting cotton slacks were the color of ripe watermelon flesh, and a green and white checked blouse, sleeves rolled up to expose her arms, complemented them perfectly. Even though they'd already enjoyed each other thoroughly, Emily was ready to take another bite. Watermelon had always been a favorite.

Blake wandered across the lawn, a hungry grin on her face, two Sea Breezes in her hands. There should have been some kind of law against looking that good. It truly wasn't fair to the rest of the world.

Emily's aunt had come up behind her, and she said quietly, "If Mark ever looked at me that way, I could die happy."

Stunned, Emily shrugged off her embarrassment and forced herself to regard Blake with as much detachment as she could. She really did look like she wanted to ravish her. But when she thought about it, that wasn't odd. They clearly had something special when it came to sex. But was there anything *behind* the desire? How could you tell with someone so enigmatic?

Emily took the offered drink and they clinked their glasses together. "I don't know about you, but I'm having a fantastic day," Blake said, her eyes not leaving Emily's face as she lifted her glass and took a long drink.

"I am too. I'm really glad you came."

Then, as if she'd just noticed her, Blake shifted her gaze to Sarah. "Blake Chadwick," she said, showing her most winning smile as she stuck her hand out to shake.

"Sarah Michaels. Emily's aunt," she added.

"Oh, great," Blake said, nodding happily. "I've been looking forward to meeting Emily's family."

Sarah snapped her fingers and pointed, making Emily's younger cousins give up their chairs under an umbrella. "Let's sit down and get out of the sun for a minute."

"Good idea." Blake set her drink down, then started to swiftly move around the table. Both Sarah and Emily grabbed seats before it dawned on her that Blake had been going to hold her chair. Strangely gallant, and unexpected. But then they'd never had a sit-down meal at a table, just a booth. Maybe that was part of her front of the house restaurant training.

Sarah looked all too interested, and Emily wished she'd prearranged for her sister or her mom to rescue her if they were trapped. The whole family knew once Sarah got her hands on you, your secrets were a thing of the past.

"So, Blake, Emily's been keeping your relationship all to herself. We had no idea you two were dating. How long have you been going out?"

Blake's mouth opened. Then closed. Firmly. Her eyes shifted and landed on Emily.

Two choices. Both bad. Lie about a relationship that didn't actually exist, or tell a truth that would lead to more questions. "We're..." She snapped her mouth shut too, weighing the options for a moment.

Blake broke in. When she led with that easy, full grin you could easily lose track of the question. "Cooks don't date," she said, a gentle laugh floating away on the breeze. "You need free time for that." She tucked an arm around Emily, a heavy metal watch hot where it touched her forearm.

"That's what my kids always say," Sarah said. "If you ask me, guys just don't want to have to pay for dates, and girls are letting them get away with it."

"Well, there's that." Blake laughed, sounding so relaxed and comfortable that Emily studied her for a moment. No gum since they'd left the condo. She must have been as calm as she looked. "Cooks have no money, either."

"So you don't go out," Sarah said, gnawing on the issue like a dog with a juicy bone. "How long have you not been going out?"

"We met a year ago, so we've not been going out for at least that long, right?" A playful wink showed the interrogation didn't bother Blake at all, which let Emily relax.

"Yeah. It's been a year since we haven't been going out. I guess I should add the thirty one years before that, since we didn't go out then either."

"Only twenty nine for me. But I was in France for eight years, and we *really* didn't go out then." Blake met Sarah's gaze and added, "I could tell you about the women I didn't go out with in France." Kissing her fingers, she acted as though she was going to swoon. "Fantastique!" She took another long drink, with both Emily and Sarah studying her with various degrees of intensity. "Have you been to France?"

"We had our honeymoon there," Sarah said, sounding a little wistful. "In the Loire Valley."

"Where did you eat?" Now Blake was engaged. Fully engaged. No more playing around or teasing. Sarah had thrown a fat fastball right into her wheelhouse, and she was salivating at the chance to hit it out of the park.

Blake and Carol sat at a shady table, with the afternoon sun having passed over them long ago. They leaned in toward each other to be able to hear over the DJ, who was cranking out Charlotte's favorite pop hits. Emily would have been happy to have never heard a nineties boy band again, but it was her little sister's birthday, and she deserved to enjoy the music she liked.

Charlotte had the entire weekend off, letting her have a couple of drinks—a rarity for her. So she was a little buzzed when she said, "What do you think they're talking about? Mom looks like she wants to lean over and kiss her."

"What?" Open-mouthed, Emily stared at her sister.

"Well, she does. Look at her."

Emily forced herself to look, even though she really, really didn't want to think of her mother lusting after women—especially her date. "You've lost your mind," she said, confident in her assessment. "They're talking about food. Look at how Blake's using her hands. She always does that when she's interested in something, and the only thing she's really interested in is food."

"And you," Charlotte said as she put her arm around Emily and pulled her close for a kiss on the cheek. "She's got excellent taste."

"I'm not so sure about that. I mean, I know she likes me, but we don't spend much time together."

"She looks at you like she's crazy about you," Charlotte said, the sharp spark that usually filled her eyes missing. Now her more tender, emotional side showed through. The side that Emily was always drawn to. "And she's clearly trying to impress Mom."

"I don't think so. That she's trying to impress Mom, that is. They both love food and that's enough for Blake." She put her arm around her sister and returned the hug. "I hope you're right about her being crazy about me, though, because I'm crazy about her."

Charlotte stared at her, clearly surprised. "You are? Damn, Em, you haven't admitted to being into a woman in *years*."

"I've never met a woman like Blake." She gave her sister another robust hug, murmuring, "I'm not sure what we mean to each other, but I'd give a lot to make this into something." Releasing Charlotte, she headed for the table, where, as expected, Blake was talking about food.

She glanced up at Emily, nodded and continued. "No, no, you can't ignore the trends, even though there are times you'd like to."

"Restaurants get into such ruts," Carol said. "I eat out three or four times a week, and I might see the same appetizers for an entire season. Do chefs call each other and decide everyone's going to have beets with goat cheese over arugula?"

Blake looked up, a cute grin tugging on her mouth. "How many times did we serve our version of that?"

"It was on the permanent menu when I was there. Did you take it off?"

"Finally. Now I let the regulars order it if they insist." She shrugged. "People love that salad. I'm not sure why, given it's so easy to make at home. I guess most people like to eat things they're familiar with."

"Not me," Carol said. "That's why I'll head out to a Vietnamese place seventy-five miles from home if I hear it's good."

"You're like your daughter." The smile Blake showed as she looked up again did, Emily had to admit, make it seem she was pretty crazy about her. "She loves variety."

That was true. Or at least it used to be. Now? Emily wasn't sure that was accurate any longer. At least when it came to women.

They took off before Emily's parents, getting back to the apartment at six. Thankfully, they'd have the place to themselves until Blake had to leave. Her mom was pretty chill, but Emily thought her dad might be uncomfortable if she and Blake were in the bedroom in broad daylight, even if they were only sleeping. He wouldn't say anything, but she just didn't want to have to deal with his discomfort.

Blake's flight was at nine forty five, and she looked so tired Emily hoped she could sleep until eight thirty, then they'd hustle to get to the airport.

When she fell onto the mattress, Blake let out a burst of air. "Can I stay right here until Tuesday? Actually, Friday would be better. I'd be rested by then."

"Fine with me. You charmed my mother so thoroughly I know she'd be happy to keep you."

Blake rolled onto her side and let a sweet grin show. "I like her too. She'd be fun to hang out with."

"She is. I used to love going out with her to try a new restaurant. I liked it best when my dad and Charlotte didn't come, then we could tear into the food and not have to worry about having a real conversation."

"I can see you doing that. Even as a kid."

Emily went into the bathroom to brush her teeth, fully expecting Blake to be asleep when she returned. But those big, dark eyes watched her as she crossed the room. Emily moved to sit on the bed, with her hand gliding over Blake's face. She blinked in surprise when Blake sat up, tucked her arms around her body and kissed her, clearly aiming for a repeat of their morning. "Really?" Emily asked when she came up for air. "You're not too tired?"

"I'm exhausted. But we've got the chance..." For a second or two she seemed torn. Like she wanted another kiss but thought she'd better not. "Am I pushing too hard?"

Emily fussed with her hair, playing with some of the curls the humidity had created. She'd never known she'd be fascinated by curly hair, but she couldn't keep her fingers from playing with errant strands every time they were together. "Of course not. I'm just surprised you have the energy."

Now starting to look more sure of herself, Blake said, "I've got the energy to do anything that's important to me."

Emily grasped her by the shoulder and pushed her down, keeping up the pressure until they were lying on the bed, nose to nose. "This is important to you?" Her pulse picked up, hoping Blake was going to say something about how she felt.

Soberly, she said, "It is. This is working so well for me, Emily. I don't think I've ever been with anyone who knows me like you do."

"You feel like I know you well?" That was a funny way to put it.

"Yeah." A big smile forced Emily to return it. "I think we make a great pair."

"I do too. But I wasn't sure you did."

Blake took a nibble of her neck, burrowing her face into the skin. "Being with a new woman's such a crap shoot. With you, I don't have any worries. You're not going to get all possessive or start making demands." She leaned forward and placed a quick kiss upon her lips. "Since we're on the same wavelength, sex with you is always rejuvenating."

"Then let's get at it. We could both use a boost." Emily pushed her onto her back and covered her mouth with a long kiss. But her mind wouldn't shut off like it usually did. She felt foolish for thinking Blake was going to express some pent-up feelings for her. There was nothing —nothing she'd ever said that would lead her to assume those feelings existed. They were fuck-buddies. Good ones. But fuck-buddies only.

They'd fallen asleep after sex, but hadn't slept long enough to feel refreshed. Emily was groggy when she started to drive, but Blake was back in gear, rattling off the things she had to do when she got back to New York.

"You've got more energy than anyone I've ever met," Emily said fondly, taking a quick look at her surprisingly clear eyes.

"Really?" She pursed her lips for a few seconds. "I'm not sure I have that much energy, but I never mind doing things I enjoy. Like work." She put her hand on Emily's leg and teasingly ran it up and down. "And you."

"I'm not going to have to think about sex for a couple of weeks." A short burst of laughter bubbled up. "You filled my tank."

Blake's hand stilled, then slid up Emily's thigh, where it tightened. "What about then?"

Puzzled, Emily turned and met her eyes. "When?"

"What will you do in a couple of weeks?"

It took a second for the question to register. "Nothing. I'm not looking for sex in Vegas." Laughing softly, she added, "I might be the only person who can honestly say that."

"I'm not either." Her hand started to move again, her touch almost possessive. "Michaela's been dropping hints, but I'm not interested."

"Really? You didn't have fun with her?"

"Yeah, I did. But like I said earlier…" She shrugged. "I like being with you. Why look for trouble?"

Emily spared a second to take a look at her profile. Blake seemed entirely content. Calm. Happy. Emily had never considered her prowess strong enough to lure an exhausted woman half way across the country for sex. She must have been massively underselling her charms.

When she returned to the loft, her mom was busy putting away leftovers from the party. "Hi there," Carol said, looking up. "Did you get Blake dropped off?"

"I did. I don't have to go back to the airport for another nine hours."

"Do you have time to give me a hand? I'm finishing up a review for a place I went to in Grosse Pointe. Would you give it a read?"

"Glad to." They went into the seating area, where dim city lights cast a glow through the large windows. "Was it okay that I had Blake come for the day?" Emily shifted her weight, her nerves making her unable to get comfortable. "I mean… I hope it wasn't weird when we disappeared this morning."

Carol wasn't the type to reply to any sensitive question before thinking through her answer. She was more professorial than maternal in that way. She took a sip of her water, then nodded. "It's never comfortable to know your kids are having sex. If I had my way, both you and Charlotte would be above the fray." She chuckled at her comment. "I'm sure neither of you share that feeling."

"I can't speak for Charlotte…" She reached across the narrow space between their chairs and took her mother's hand, giving it a fond squeeze. "You've always made me feel relaxed about being here with a girlfriend, even though I'm sure it was tough for you at first."

Shaking her head, Carol said, "We had a couple of years to mentally prepare ourselves for you, but when Charlotte brought that boy over when they were just freshmen in high school…" A dark scowl settled on her fair features. "That little jerk couldn't keep his hands off her!"

"I was jealous," Emily said, recalling how outraged she was that her little sister was dipping a toe in the pool before she did. "I would have had sex much earlier if I could have found a willing partner. I just couldn't find a taker until I got to Michigan."

With a sly smile, Carol said, "That's why we sent you to such a small high school. We wanted to reduce the possibility of your finding an acceptable lesbian."

"I thought the revolving door principal factored into your changing your minds about my going to the magnet school. Nice to know it was a lesbian preventative." She gave her mom another hearty pat on the shoulder.

"Blake seems like a top-drawer lesbian." A delighted smile lit her face when she added, "She put on a charm offensive, didn't she? I could easily see her with her own television show if she wanted one."

"She can certainly be charming," Emily agreed, chuckling at her mental images of Blake trying to make every guest like her. "Meeting strangers isn't her favorite thing, but she was putting out quite an effort."

"For you." Carol gave her a level gaze. "She didn't act like a woman who didn't want a relationship."

Emily scooted down to let her head rest on the back of the sofa. Staring up at the big, old windows above her head sometimes let her clear her thoughts. "I don't know what to make of her. She says she likes me mostly because I don't make any demands." Her head tilted as she met her mother's gaze. "But she also made a point of telling me she's not seeing anyone else and doesn't have plans to." She thought for a moment, then swallowed her unease and spit it out. "Our relationship is mostly sexual, but it's ridiculously intimate. More intimate than I've been with some of my actual girlfriends."

Carol took her hand and held it tenderly. "I wish I had more experience with relationships, honey. But when you marry your second serious boyfriend…"

"You'd have to be a mindreader to figure her out." Letting out a frustrated sigh, she said, "It's hard for me, Mom. I'm not able to be as casual as she is. I want more." There. She'd said it out loud. She wanted more, damn it.

Chapter Sixteen

BY THE MIDDLE OF August, Emily had a pretty good tan from having breakfast outside each morning, and a great big bunch of employees waiting to start work. Twenty-nine of them would arrive on the twenty-eighth, leaving only three days to train the whole group as a team. Not much time, but she hadn't expected she'd get much.

They were going to do a stress-test for Sunday brunch on the thirty-first, invited guests only. Laurent had put out a call through his extensive mailing list, trying to fill the place with people who didn't mind paying to, in essence, be guinea pigs. Emily hoped Felix or the front of the house person he'd hired were in charge of that list because she had her hands full running the back of the house—just about single-handedly.

Now that she had bodies for all sections, she had to make the critical choices; four sous chefs and four sauciers. Since she couldn't taste what they prepared, she was going to have to rely on Felix. Hopefully, having people cooking would lure him out of his office.

On Monday morning, Emily went down to the kitchen early. It was her first day wearing her whites, making her feel like she was putting on a favorite pair of pajamas. Once she was dressed, she paused in the locker area and checked herself out. Her hair had gotten longer and blonder, now looking very much like it had when she was a kid. And the kitchen pallor had left her cheeks after nine long years of being inside most every day. She actually looked younger than her age, losing that "somewhere between thirty and fifty" look so many cooks had.

Heading for the loading dock, she found a few boxes of staples along with the meat, fish and dairy she'd ordered. She hadn't bought much. Just enough to run her sixteen candidates through their paces.

When she'd considered how to winnow the sixteen down to eight, she'd decided to have all of them cook at the same time. The kitchen was big enough to handle them all at once, and it would probably freak them out a little to be working together. That was her goal. The competition would help show which of them worked best under pressure.

A little after ten, all of the candidates were getting organized and starting to prep. Emily sauntered around the kitchen, watching carefully as they worked. Her years of cooking and tasting had refined her palate to the point she could almost always tell if a dish was going to work without tasting it. You learned the notes each element brought out and used your experience to know if those flavors would pair well. Still, she could easily be tripped up by improper seasoning. Too much garlic, not enough onion, too much of any number of fresh herbs, and too much salt were all land-mines for her. Especially salt. That was her real nemesis. Her sense of taste had either sharpened to be able to detect minute amounts of it, or she tasted so little of everything else that it jumped out at her. Whatever the reason, she had no ability to tell if a dish was over-salted, a real problem.

Each dish had a short shelf-life, so she called Felix out to taste each dish the minute it was ready. He probably thought the whole process odd, with her quizzing him pointedly, asking about seasonings to see if her guesses had been correct. They were okay—but not great. One guy looked like he was really on top of things, and he cooked with precision and decisiveness. But when Felix came out to taste, he made a face. "Over-salted mussels. And way too much hot sauce in this." He pushed the bowl away like he couldn't stand to look at it.

"That's perfect," the guy said, the red in his cheeks growing. "I've been making that jambalaya the same way for ten years."

Dismissively, Felix said, "Then you've been making it wrong for ten years. We don't want to beat people over the heads with the food."

"It's right as it is, but I can tone it down if you want me to," the guy said, clearly perturbed but willing to bend.

"No thanks. If you think that dish is right, your instincts aren't good." He turned and went back to his office without another word.

"That's it? That's all I get?" The guy glared at Emily. "You taste it." He picked up a fresh spoon and handed it to her. She couldn't detect any of the layers of flavor a good jambalaya had, but her tongue and the back of her palate burned. "Maybe you've been cooking for people who like a lot of kick. Here we're going for just enough to give the food flavor. Las Vegas diners aren't very adventurous."

"I shoulda stayed in Baton Rouge," he snapped, picking up his stuff and storming out.

The other cooks, still working away, all looked a little spooked after that. Emily didn't mind. It was good to look over your shoulder. Someone was probably gaining on you.

By the end of the day, they had their chefs. Four sous and four sauciers. Four women and four men.

All four of the guys gave off that "just happy to bang it out" vibe. With their menu, that's the kind of cook they needed. But two of the women seemed like they might want to advance over time, which was cool. One, who could have posed for a pin-up in the 1940s, had a very laid-back vibe, just the kind of person for a kitchen as busy as this one was going to be. The other, Katrina, was the oldest of the bunch, and had started cooking professionally just a few years earlier. Emily was certain she was too old to have young kids, but she'd made a comment about day care during her interview. Maybe she was raising her grandkids. Whatever her reasons for getting into cooking later in life, Katrina seemed talented as well as no-nonsense. With their big staff, the chefs were really going to have to stay on top of people.

After seeing everyone off, Emily went to Felix's office and waited outside until he got off the phone. The whole place was strangely quiet, with only a couple of guys cleaning the mess the cooks had created. As she paced in the hall, Emily heard Felix's voice rise.

"The judge said I get him every other Monday and Tuesday," he hissed, "and I don't give a fuck if that's convenient for you or not. Have him ready to go on Monday at ten o'clock or your next visitor's going to be a process server." He must have hung up, since calling someone a "fucking, lying whore" wasn't the way to get her to agree to your request.

"Come in," he said, sounding way past irritable.

"Another time?" she asked, not entering fully.

"Like there's ever a good time." He gestured with his hand, and she walked in and sat down.

Consulting the notes in her spiral-bound pad, she said, "I'm happy with our hires. A couple of the sous are still green, but they're full of energy, and that will help a lot." She looked up at him, annoyed that he was swiping left on his phone, his focus locked in. "Felix?"

"Yeah." He still didn't look up.

"How many hours a day do you plan on expediting?"

"Huh?"

She was ready to knock off for the day, but she had the tenacity to repeat her question, verbatim, until he listened. "How many hours a day do you plan on expediting?"

Now his puzzled gaze slid across her face. He must have figured out she was gay. When she'd first started, he'd been just a little flirty, but now he seemed unable to keep his eyes on her for longer than a split second. Or maybe her sexual orientation wasn't the problem. Maybe he simply didn't like women who were more competent than he was.

"What do you mean?"

"I mean exactly what I asked." She could have given him more, but he didn't deserve it.

"I'll expedite during service."

She batted her eyes, hoping to annoy him. "You're going to be standing at the pass for fifteen hours a day?"

"Of course not. You'll take breakfast and lunch."

"Okay. I can do that until I go back to New York."

"Great." He stood up and whipped off his jacket, revealing his usual brightly colored polo shirt. He walked over to a hook on the wall and hung his jacket up, his flip-flops letting her see those oddly pale feet. He'd clearly taken the job for year round golf and mornings off to play it. She just wasn't sure he was going to have that wish fulfilled once she left. Someone was going to have to be in charge, and it was going to have to be him.

She made him flinch when she added a final thought. "I'm probably only going to be here a week or two after we open, so you might want to get another expediter on board soon."

"A week or two?" His dark eyebrows shot up as his mouth dropped open. "Laurent said you'd be here until we were running smoothly. That'll take at least six months."

"That wasn't the deal I struck with Laurent. I'm just here to help you open."

"We'll see about that." He checked his big, shiny watch. "I'd call New York now, but I'm going to be late for an appointment."

"Call whenever you like," she said, with a mere hint of a smile on her lips. "But I'm going back to New York after we open. *Soon* after we open."

Emily had put in over four solid hours of work by the time her phone buzzed. "It's Felix," he said. "Come down, will you?"

"Be right there."

She entered his office, noting how flushed his cheeks were. Playing golf in the August heat must have been brutal, even if you started really early, which he hadn't been able to today.

"What's up?" she asked as she took a seat.

"How much money do you have left for salaries? I've got to hire a fucking expeditor, and I'm tapped out." He flopped down into his desk chair and started to power up his computer.

"I've got almost nothing left." She could have left it at that, but she wasn't in the mood to be respectful. "You only had to hire the front of the house manager and a head chef. Where'd all the money go?"

He gave her a look that was just short of murderous. "You pay attention to your budget, and I'll pay attention to mine."

"I did," she said, trying not to gloat. "That's why I'm fully staffed with a little leftover in case I need to pay more for a last-minute replacement."

"Well, I didn't get lucky like you did. Giorgio insisted he needed more money to hire the servers. He ate up the whole damn budget."

She stood up and started for the door. "I can find you an expediter, but I can't pay him or her. You're going to have to get a bump from Laurent." She snuck out the door before he had a chance to complain.

At nine a.m. on August the twenty-eighth, the kitchen was full for the first time. Everyone from sous chefs to a few interns right out of trade school were standing around; with all of the vets relaxed, and most of the newbies visibly anxious. Felix was supposed to be there, to welcome the staff and kick off their training, but he'd called to say he was still in New York, meeting with Laurent.

Emily resisted the impulse to bitch about his lack of interest. Instead, she took over his office, clearing his papers away to substitute her laptop and the notebook she'd used all summer to keep track of things. There was a mirror on the back of the door, and she checked to make sure her new jacket was crisp and professional. One of the things she'd always admired about Blake was how sharp she looked. It gave you a certain confidence to see your chef give off the clear signal that cleanliness and order were paramount.

She'd never worn a colored jacket, and wasn't crazy about wearing one now. But pale green was the primary color of the restaurant, and Felix wanted to highlight it. How the laundry was going to keep the jackets clean without using bleach was a question they'd figure out as they went along. At least the color looked good on her, making her pale hair stand out.

Taking a breath, Emily went into the kitchen and surveyed the troops. "Good morning," she said, cutting off all conversations. "Thanks to all of you for getting in so early." She specifically let her gaze fall on the dinner cooks, who were gathered in a group. "I know many of you had to rearrange your schedules and child care to get in at nine, and I promise we'll do our best to make sure these 'all hands' sessions are infrequent." She handed out a sheet with cell phone numbers for Felix, her and the sous chefs. "One of the first things we have to get straight is the policy on attendance. You already know we have no tolerance for being late. But if something unavoidable happens that prevents you from getting in on time, or if you need to call out, you *must* call your supervisor in advance of your shift. No surprises." She let her sober gaze travel around the room. "No excuses." Okay, maybe she was modeling herself on Blake. Why not go with a winner?

Burning through top quality food wasn't a good idea for the budget. But she needed to have her staff cook together to make sure they all understood her standards and optimal workflow. To get the job done, Emily had struck a deal with the hotel catering department. Her staff would do all of the cooking for one of their major events, in return for the hotel paying for the food. It was a great deal for the hotel, and let her conduct three days of training while only having to pay salaries. Now every station was bustling, preparing a big, fairly opulent lunch for a convention of garage door salespeople.

The sauciers were making three complex, delicate sauces and she asked each sous and each line cook to repeatedly taste them. Finally, she had a clear vote, with everyone agreeing each was perfectly seasoned. Going on a hunch, Emily called the ten commis over, saying, "I want each of you to taste the sauces for the fish, duck and beef. Then let me know your thoughts. Privately." That earned her a number of puzzled glances, but she had her reasons for talking to them separately. Young cooks only wanted to please, and she thought they might be intimidated if their peers didn't see things the way they did.

It took ten minutes, but she finally had all of the votes. Eight of them wanted to add or subtract something, with the majority of them finding the sauces too salty. That was a common mistake for a young cook to make. Without the main course to balance it, many sauces seemed too bright. But two of the commis said they were just right. One of them, a gangly kid with a southern accent, wouldn't hold his ground when she strongly suggested the bordelaise sauce was missing something. He would have agreed to put sugar in it if she'd forced the issue. But the other, a short, chubby guy named Wyatt, wouldn't budge.

"It's perfect," he insisted when she tried the same trick. "I wouldn't change a thing."

She called the two kids, Tyler and Wyatt, over. "You're early shift, right, Tyler?"

"Yes, Chef."

"You're late, right?" she asked Wyatt.

"Yes, Chef, but I can switch if you want."

"No, thanks. This is perfect." She put a hand on each man's shoulder. "Here's what I want you to do…"

A few minutes later she asked for everyone's attention. It took a few seconds for the whirling noise to settle down, but it gave her a buzz to be able to halt the work of so many people so quickly. "I'm going to try something different." An undercurrent of grumbles started. No one liked surprises mucking up their routine. "Since we're going to be pumping out orders like crazy, it's going to be nearly impossible for the sous chefs to taste all of the food and plate it. So I've asked Tyler and Wyatt to be our official tasters. I think this will help them develop as cooks, and free the sous up a little bit." She looked out on her staff and paused a second to let that sink in. "Questions?"

"No, Chef," they said, seemingly unconcerned since the change didn't make any of them do more work.

"Great. If the sous want to adjust seasonings they're welcome to, of course. But Tyler and Wyatt are going to be able to notice problems earlier, which should help keep things moving. Okay!" She clapped her hands together. "Let's get cooking."

Watching as the group got busy, Emily let her imagination take her away for a few seconds. If Blake had been able to come up with the designated taster idea a few months ago, Emily would still be in New York, working her way up. But she hadn't, and that disappointment had paved the way for this very real opportunity.

Felix arrived on Saturday afternoon, just as the last day of training was coming to a close. He walked around and met everyone, showing a flash of interest and charm that Emily hadn't known he'd kept in reserve. But that only made sense. Laurent wouldn't have hired a total zero.

When the last of the crew left the room, Felix walked over to Emily, his expression difficult to read. "I've got forty thousand dollars," he said. "You've got to get someone in here to expedite for that."

"Forty?" She knew her eyes were bugging out, but couldn't avoid staring in disbelief. "You want an experienced expediter who can work six days a week, covering both breakfast and lunch for forty thousand? Including overtime?"

"That's all I've got," he said, turning to walk away.

Emily stood there for a moment, thinking of all of the candidates she'd been holding in reserve. Not one of them would do the job for that kind of money. She was going to have to get creative.

/

The cold opening didn't start until ten a.m., but Emily had been at work since six. Even though they weren't officially open, today would set the tone for the whole operation. If she had to cook, clean, serve, then dance on the tables to please customers, she was going to do it.

She looked up at six thirty to see her favorite of the sous, Katrina, walk in and head to the locker room. Fantastic. She wasn't due until eight, and coming in early was exactly the kind of dedication Emily was longing for. Things were looking up.

By eleven a.m., Tyler, the commis with the good palate, had been nicknamed "the Nose." In their first hour of service, he'd tested every kind of brunch dish that wouldn't show a missing bite. She noticed that Katrina, who was, in fact, a grandmother raising two young kids on her own, had initially double-checked everything that slid by her, but as they got busier she stopped. She wouldn't have done that if she'd noticed any errors. Score for Tyler!

Emily was expediting, laboring under the heat lamps as she managed the ballet of dishes coming at her from both sides. She'd never expedited for a whole shift, and today was really putting her feet to the fire. Having watched three good chefs do it at her past jobs, she had a solid grasp of how to do it well. She merely needed practice. And practicing at brunch was a good trial. People were much pickier about breakfast than they were about dinner, with a quarter of the orders calling for something added or omitted from the standard.

By noon they were swamped, with so many orders flying through her head was swimming. But she was keeping up. And so were her sous, who were plating dishes with efficiency and flair. A tap on her shoulder made her jump, and she turned to find Felix, dressed in his green chef's coat. "Laurent is here," he said. "He wants to see you. I'll take over."

"Table forty," she called out, finishing the chit in her hand. "Fire one Florentine, extra spinach, no hollandaise. One scrambled with truffles. Hold the potatoes." She stepped back and let him pick up the next order. "I'll be back soon."

"No rush. I'd like to expedite for a while to get a feel for the morning staff."

She moved away, thinking he could have done that by showing up for some of the training. But she not only wasn't going to change his habits, she wasn't going to remain in Vegas much longer. It was easier to disengage when you were going to split.

Since she hadn't been cooking, Emily's coat was still clean, but she'd been sweating up a storm, so she went into the big staff bathroom to wash her face and resettle her ponytail. After putting on a dry jacket, she went into the dining room, amazed at how huge it appeared when full. They'd reserved the tables by the windows for their VIPs, so she headed over there to search for Laurent. He was facing her and gave a discreet wave when their eyes met. As she got close, the person opposite him turned, and she gasped when Blake's beaming grin came into view.

"I brought a friend," Laurent said, his eyes dancing with delight.

Blake got up and opened her arms, and Emily settled in for a hug, then a brief kiss. "I had no idea you were going to come!" In the seconds she had available, she fought to sort out her feelings. It had been four weeks since they'd been in Detroit. Other than a missed call, Blake hadn't reached out once. But she was here now, and coming all the way to Vegas just to be at the opening was a very thoughtful gesture. Why look this pretty gift horse in the mouth?

"I'm not a VIP, but I didn't let that stop me," Blake said, still grinning.

"Sit with us," Laurent said.

Stunned, Emily couldn't get her hips to bend and let her comply. She'd never, ever considered sitting at a table during service. But when the boss told you to sit, your butt should land on something horizontal. Blake jumped up at the same moment Laurent did, both of them grabbing a chair to pull it out.

"I've got this one," Blake said, giving Laurent an impudent smile.

"I will not argue…this time." Turning to Emily, he said, "You will eat with us, yes?"

"Eat?"

Chuckling, Blake said, "It's been a long time since you've cooked, Laurent. Emily can't relax and enjoy herself. She's at work."

"I am," she agreed, pleased that Blake could read her expression. "Why don't you let me make you something special?"

He put on a pout. "I wanted this to be a surprise. I thought you could enjoy letting the kitchen impress you."

"I say we let Emily choose," Blake said, giving her an encouraging smile. "Do what feels right."

She stood, then leaned over and kissed Blake on the cheek. "I'd like to make you something off the menu. Are you feeling adventurous?"

"I am," Blake said, looking up at her with thinly veiled lust. "Amazingly adventurous."

It took some effort to find a place to cook, but when she said she was making an off-the-menu dish for Laurent, space miraculously appeared. She considered a few concepts, quickly settling on an idea. After lining a muffin tin with puff pastry, she filled the cups with whipped eggs and popped the tin into the oven while she made the sauce. When the eggs were fully set, she drizzled them with a rich béarnaise, knowing Blake would get the joke.

Emily could have delivered her creation herself, but she let a server run it out. When the plates came back completely clean, with "Merci!"

written across the china by an artistic use of condiments, Emily felt a burst of pleasure, but didn't take long to bask in the praise. Felix had disappeared, and she had to keep stepping into various spots on the line to keep things moving. Timing was critical at brunch, and she wasn't about to allow a slowdown.

When the pace of orders lessened, she went to the door to check up on her guests. Blake hadn't budged, sitting right where Emily had left her, reading her phone. Laurent, however, was making his way around the dining room, thanking people for coming and generally being his charming self. Blake was obviously going to wait for Emily to finish, but she had to supervise the end of service meeting and the kitchen cleanup, and she couldn't cut corners just because the cutest chef in New York was waiting for her.

It was almost four when she peeked out again, finding Blake and Laurent back at their table, along with a couple Emily didn't know. The rest of the room was empty, save for busboys who were readying it for lunch on Monday, their official opening.

Not wanting to disturb them if they were conversing, Emily went into the locker room and changed. She'd dressed nicely, trying to set a good example, and was glad her extra effort paid off. Blake would appreciate her freshly laundered clothes before she whipped them off her. Then she wrote a note and sent a busboy to deliver it. A few minutes later, Blake walked in, let her gaze slowly move across the vast kitchen, pursed her lips and whistled. "You're in the big time, Chef."

"It feels like it," Emily said. "Everything is big."

"Done for the day?" An elegant eyebrow lifted.

"I am."

Blake moved toward her, putting her hands on her hips before bending to place a soft kiss on Emily's lips. "Why don't you show me your room? I've heard it's really nice." She reached out and ran her fingertips down Emily's cheek. "You look so damn good. I've never known anyone to open a restaurant while getting a tan. What's your secret?"

Emily took her by the hand and led her to the service exit. "It's easy. All you have to do is open a restaurant in a desert, in the summer, and head outside to have breakfast before you start your day."

They started to walk through the casino, heading for the hotel guest elevators. Emily pulled to a stop in front of a roulette table. "Want to play your lucky number?"

A wolfish grin settled on Blake's face. "I'm going to be as lucky as a woman can get in about five minutes. Why waste time?"

That was a darned good answer.

When they reached the room, Emily opened the door to let Blake enter. Once again she stopped and let her gaze slowly travel around the space. "Good lord!" she said under her breath. "You're never going to want to go back to Queens."

Chuckling, Emily moved past her. "I think Laurent would like his room back. If I was going to stay, I'm sure I'd be looking for a roommate to share some crappy place out in the middle of nowhere." She hooked her fingers in Blake's belt loops and pulled her close. "How about a kiss?"

Blake didn't respond at once. Instead, she put her hands on Emily's face and gazed at her for a few seconds. Right there. That was the look that confused the hell out of her. Those dark eyes were filled with tenderness, maybe even love. But then she went for weeks without bothering to call.

"I've missed you," Blake said, her unblinking gaze making Emily's heart clench with feeling.

"I missed you too. I'm so glad you came." She reached up and pressed her hand to the back of Blake's head, pulling her down so she could place a gentle kiss on her lips. "It was awfully nice of you to spend your day off traveling."

A smile curled one side of her mouth. "Don't give me too much credit. Laurent called yesterday to say there was an extra spot on some bigwig's jet. We flew all night, but my seat was so comfortable I was able to sleep."

"Yesterday?" Emily barely held herself back from snapping off a snotty comment. She was heartsick at the thought of so little planning or interest on Blake's part. Would she have even called to congratulate her if Laurent hadn't dragged her along?

"Yeah. I forgot this was the opening weekend." She released her hold, then walked further into the room, kicking off her shoes as she went. A tired sigh made her sound exhausted. "I honestly forgot it was already September."

Emily went over to her, and with a gentle push Blake fell onto the purple velour sofa. She blinked, looking up as Emily sat next to her.

"I thought we might have lost touch."

Eyes widening, Blake said, "Are you seeing someone? I guess… I should have made sure before I showed up."

Emily stared at her for a moment. What was going on in that impossible to read head? "You've asked me that several times. Don't you know me well enough to realize I'd say something if I didn't want you here?"

"I guess I do," she said, frowning. "But you're very polite."

Emily put a hand on her cheek and turned her head so they were facing each other. "I'm not that polite. And if I *was* dating someone, I wouldn't have you up to my room." She tapped her nose with a finger. "I don't think you're interested in being friends."

"Yes, I am," Blake said forcefully. "I like you, Emily. A lot."

"Mmm. Yeah, I can see that you like me. But we don't even bother to call each other. That's indicative of something, isn't it?"

Concern filled her expression. Tenderly, Blake put her hand on Emily's cheek, then slowly let her thumb drift up and down. "Have you wanted to talk? I'm always happy to listen."

"No," she said, admitting the truth. "I could whine about all of the things that frustrate me through the day, but I don't like to do that." Sighing, she rested her head on Blake's shoulder.

"I feel the same. When I'm finished at the restaurant, I like to watch TV or read. I'm done talking."

Emily let her gaze shift up. Blake looked like she'd just eaten something sour.

"Yeah, I get that."

"You're coming home soon, right?" She pulled back and gazed at Emily with concern. "You're not going to stay, are you?"

"No, I'm not going to stay. Vegas isn't for me, even though it has been nice to sit outside every morning, knowing it'll be sunny."

Blake's voice lowered and grew soft. "You look awesome with a tan." Her hands moved up and swiftly removed the band that held Emily's hair back. Then gentle fingers threaded through it, a look of utter delight on her face. "Your hair's such a beautiful color. Is it lighter than it used to be?"

"Uh-huh. Skin's darker, hair's lighter."

Leaning close, Blake whispered. "I hope you have tan lines. I love tan lines."

For the first time in weeks, her libido started to flutter to life. "I've got a line or two. Want to see?"

"I really do," Blake breathed, her lips right next to Emily's ear.

They stood, then headed for the bedroom. Emily started to unbutton her shirt, but Blake's hands moved in and pushed hers away. "Let me," she murmured, already concentrating on her task. In just a few seconds, the cool air wafted over Emily's bare skin.

After Emily returned the favor, Blake started tugging her toward the bed.

"Let's shower," Emily said, trying to put the brakes on.

Smiling seductively, Blake kept pulling her toward the bed. "We'll have to shower later. Let's get good and dirty first."

Swallowing her discomfort, Emily told the truth. Her voice came out as a whisper. "I can't smell myself any more." It made no sense to be embarrassed about losing a sense, but she was. Very embarrassed. "I don't know how I smell, so I've been showering so often my skin's getting dry."

Blake pulled her close, then let her nose hover over various spots on Emily's body. "You smell great," she murmured. "Your natural scent is really, really appealing. It's a turn-on for me." Her chin tilted up and their eyes met. "If you need to for your peace of mind, go ahead and shower. But if I get a vote, we'll hit that bed right now."

Touched by her tenderness, Emily gripped her hand and moved toward the bed. "You definitely get a vote. Let's get dirty."

Emily lay on her back, hanging onto the minuscule amount of space left from Blake's sprawl. It was late, and she was still buzzing from her last climax. They'd skipped dinner and the promised shower, leaving bed only to go to the refrigerator for water. The jet was taking off at two a.m., allowing Blake only an hour to nap, but she'd steadfastly refused Emily's suggestion they wrap things up early. Studying her face in the dim light, Emily had to admit she was more puzzled by Blake every time they were together. She was so connected, so open. They shared something deeply intimate in bed, with the sex they had much more like lovemaking than a friendly hookup. And then they didn't speak for a month. What in the hell could that mean? She had no earthly idea.

Their first true breakfast went great. That was likely because most people didn't know about them yet, added to the fact that eight a.m. was when many people were nursing hangovers, not craving omelettes. They had two hours before lunch, and Emily decided to make herself scarce, giving the staff the clear signal that Katrina, the morning sous, was in charge. After going up to her room to fetch her computer, she headed for the office, hoping to get a little work done while Felix was playing golf. But he was already in, on the phone as usual, but present. That was a nice surprise. He motioned for her to sit, and she did, waiting patiently.

When he hung up, he pulled a plate close and cut off a bite of his omelet. "Hungry?" he asked, pointing his fork toward the kitchen. "Katrina just whipped this up for me. Want one?"

She'd never worked in a restaurant where the chef had the cooks make a special meal for him, and she didn't like it. "No, thanks. I ate before my shift."

He nodded absently, then spoke while chewing. "I think yesterday went great. How about you?"

"I was happy. We had a few slowdowns, and got in the weeds a couple of times, but that's normal."

"Laurent seemed happy when I was out there. Did he say anything to you?"

Emily shifted her gaze when something flickered in the hallway. "Good morning, Chef," she said as Laurent glided into the room. He was staying for the week, mainly so he could personally welcome his many fans and friends during the bistro's opening days.

His smile froze when he spied the plate on the desk. After picking it up, he held it close to his face, inspecting it like it was something truly fascinating. "Smoked salmon and caviar?" Placing it back onto the desk, he looked directly at Felix, his voice showing his displeasure. "Did you make this yourself?"

"Yeah. Why?"

Emily almost choked. Felix was not only lying, his tone was close to rude, showing none of the usual respect most people had or at least faked for their head chef.

"Because I don't want the cooks spending their time cooking for the staff."

Ouch! Calling Felix staff was pretty rude, too. Emily's grip tightened on the arms of her chair, waiting to see if there would be another round.

Felix stood down, shrugging as he took another bite. "If I'm going to be here fifteen hours a day, I've got to eat."

"Wonderful. Make yourself some eggs. Add some cheese or vegetables or ham if you like." His tone grew dark. "But the salmon and caviar is for guests. Not employees."

Felix's mouth opened and Emily stared at him, amazed at how poorly he was handling this. Laurent had more sense, and knew it wasn't a good idea to fight before an audience. Before Felix could reply, Laurent turned to Emily and said quietly, "Do you have time to have breakfast with me?"

"I'm expediting lunch, but I'm free until 11:30."

"Excellent. I'll be out in a moment. I need to finish here."

"I'll be in the kitchen. Whenever you're ready."

As she exited, she heard Felix grouse, "She told *me* she'd already eaten." Wow. The guy was going out of his way to be a jerk, and everything she'd learned about Laurent told her that wouldn't fly.

Emily found Katrina in the produce walk-in. "I'm going to a meeting, but I'll be back well before service. If you need anything, Felix is in his office."

"Got it. I'm just double-checking that we're staying on top of the vegetables. I hate to waste such nice product."

"Good instinct. Let's think of a special to get rid of this eggplant," Emily said. "We can't afford to let this sit another day."

"Yes, Chef." Katrina's pen hovered above her clipboard for a second. "Are you going to do that, or should I?"

"Do you have an idea?"

"I can come up with one," she said, sounding completely confident. "I'll see what else we have too much of, and design something."

"Great. After you decide, go into Felix's office and let him know." She was certain Katrina hadn't spent any time at all with their head chef, but she needed to. "I've only been sous at three places, but each one of them was different. Very different. Some chefs consider their sous an apprentice, and they do their best to train them to move up." She considered for just a second whether she was being disloyal to Felix to give her opinion on him, then decided her primary loyalty was to Laurent and the restaurant. "From what I can tell, Felix isn't that kind of guy. You're going to have to absorb things by watching and figuring them out for yourself."

"I think you're right on that one," she said, a slight frown making her look very serious.

"But that's not all bad. He'll let you do as much as you want. You just have to take the lead. If I were you, I'd push until he told me to hold back."

"Good advice," Katrina said. "I'm used to finding my own way."

Emily clapped her on the shoulder. "Do the things he doesn't want to do. It might be annoying, but you'll learn more that way."

Laurent poked his head into the walk-in. "Are you ready?"

"I am," Emily said. "Katrina was just thinking of how to burn through this eggplant. I know we weren't planning on having specials, but the eggplant parmigiana didn't sell like we thought it would."

He picked up one of the fruits and weighed it in his hand, gazing at it thoughtfully as he spoke. "We will not have specials?" He said it casually, like he was asking a simple question. But Emily knew him well enough to see that he was pissed.

"I thought the menu was fixed in New York. No?"

"Daniel and Felix and I made a menu that will be easy to…" His eyes narrowed and he gave Emily a quick glance. "What's the word I want?"

Her aphasia struck, as it did often when she had to think of a specific word under any kind of pressure. Thankfully, Katrina yanked one out.

"Reproduce?"

"Yes," he agreed, nodding. "We need good dishes that we can reproduce many times. Classics." He turned the eggplant over in his hands as he continued to study it. "But you must have specials to use your surplus. It is a waste in every way if you do not do this." His eyes met Emily's. "Meet me in the dining room in ten minutes. I'd like to leave the building."

"Yes, Chef." She had a pretty good idea who was going to get his ass chewed for exactly ten minutes. And Felix's lazy butt deserved it.

Right on time, Laurent walked into the dining room. He pointed toward the front entrance, and they left together, moving past the dinging slot machines to exit the hotel. He turned to the left and started to move through the sparse crowds, not speaking. She couldn't tell if he was angry or simply didn't have much to say, but when they reached a nearby hotel, Laurent perked up again. Leading her over to a bank of elevators, he said, "You don't mind room service, do you? I hate to wait for a table."

"No, that's fine." Slightly confused, she watched as he swiped his card on a reader and the elevator whisked them up to the thirty-ninth floor. Looking at the panel, she saw the top floors indicated they belonged to one of the best hotel brands in the world. "A hotel on top of a hotel?"

"It's odd, but I think it's working out for both brands." The doors swooshed open and they went down the hall, where his key once again opened the door. "I like a very light breakfast, but feel free to order whatever you want." He handed her a menu, then went to wash his hands, talking the whole time he was fussing in the bathroom.

"Once I'm back in my room, I'll be able to keep some bread and jam and not have to wait for it to be delivered." He came back in and sat down, giving her a grin. "But I can wait. I'd like for you to stay as long as you will."

"I'll just have some orange juice," she said, returning the menu to him. "I have a lovely room with a refrigerator, so I'm able to have breakfast before I leave for my long commute."

He smirked, but didn't comment. After a brief conversation with room service, he turned his full attention to her. "I had a long talk with some investors yesterday," he began.

"Investors?"

"Yes. They were in town to see how well we'd done." His smile grew wider. "They were impressed."

"I'm glad to hear that. It was only brunch, though…" A flare of anxiety shot through her. "We'll have to see how the rest of service goes today."

"Are you going to be there?"

"Of course. I'm expediting both breakfast and lunch this week, but I'm going to stay close during dinner prep. I want to make sure everyone knows their part."

He leaned back against the cushy sofa and linked his hands behind his head, gazing at her reflectively. "You might not think I know this, but I saw your fingerprints all over the restaurant. The staff, the organization, the training, even the way you've set up the walk-ins. Everything was very well organized, Emily. I worry…" His brow knit in thought. "I worry things will not be so good with you back in New York."

"But I need to go home," she said firmly, trying to make it crystal clear she wasn't amenable to persuasion.

"I realize that." Leaning over slightly, he fixed her with a sober gaze. "Would you feel the same if I made you chef de cuisine? The salary is very good, Emily. You could have a nice life here."

If she spoke, she knew she'd stutter. After taking several long breaths, she was confident she could spit out a sentence. "Take Felix's job?"

"Yes. It is no surprise to you that I made a mistake in hiring him. I'd like to correct that mistake by having you take over." As he sat up straight, a smile grew. "I would be able to sleep without worry."

"I want you to sleep," she said, "and I truly appreciate your confidence in me—"

"You don't want to be so far from the many beautiful things New York has to offer," he said, sighing dramatically. "Like Blake."

"That's part of it, of course, but this isn't the kind of cooking I want to do, Chef. It's too…"

"Routine. You would be bored."

"I'd also be challenged, which would be great. But the challenge would be operational, not creative."

"True. I know this is true." He sighed again. "That is why I hired Felix. I thought he would be competent, without too much drive." His expression turned sour. "I didn't realize his drive was absent."

"I think he saw I could do a lot of things and he let me run with them. Once I'm gone, he'll have to get more involved."

"You think I should keep him?" His eyebrow rose.

"He's here," Emily said, probably the least enthusiastic performance review ever. "It wouldn't look good to fire him so soon."

"This is probably so." He nodded, his gaze turning feral. "You may return to New York as soon as you'd like. Go today if you want. Felix will succeed or fail on his own."

"Let me stay this week. I owe that to the people I hired. I want them to feel secure before I take off."

"I would like to have several of you, Emily. One here and one in New York." He spoke slowly and thoughtfully, as if thinking something through. "You know you can be a good chef and not be a good manager. Being careful and thorough and precise are not always traits you find with people who are very creative." Solemnly, he nodded. "You have those traits. You have done a very, very good job here. My restaurant would not look like it does or function like it does if you had not been in charge."

"Thank you," she said, beaming with pride.

"Come back to New York whenever you want. But I will not have you cooking fish. You have too many other skills to limit yourself."

"But..."

"Blake and I talked about this yesterday. We both think you're something unique." He chuckled softly. "Maybe for different reasons. But we agree you must be challenged."

"But I love to cook," she said. "I couldn't be happy being only a manager."

"You will cook...along with other duties." A pleasant gong rang out and he got up to answer the door. After signing the bill, he brought the juice to her. "I'm not sure how we will work things out, but I want to use more of your skills."

"All right." She lifted her glass toward him. "I'd have to be crazy to argue with that."

By Wednesday, Emily was desperate to leave town. She'd worked straight through from six a.m. until the dinner crew came in at four. During that time she had prep chefs working like mad, getting the product ready, cooks laboring under the hot lights, back waiters flying in and out of the swinging doors, and orders flying out of the printer in bursts that were hard to fathom. Every person in Vegas wanted to try out the new spot, and they all seemed to want some special order that took an extra bit of care. On top of that, she was still trying to find a dirt-cheap expeditor.

She looked up from her spot in the corner of the kitchen, where she was gulping down a bowl of French onion soup before she'd go back to her room to finish the day's paperwork. A short, stocky, dark-skinned Latin woman stood just inside the swinging doors, looking around speculatively.

Emily jumped to her feet and walked over. "Coco?" she asked.

"Yeah. That's me."

"Good to meet you." Emily wiped her hand off on her pants and extended it. "Sorry if my hands are a little greasy. We had an epic spill this afternoon and it's taken us an hour to clean up. Tough to do while you're banging out orders."

"Tell me about it."

When she smiled, Emily noticed a prominent gold canine, and tattooed lip liner, filled in with lipstick the color of a ripe plum. The look kind of worked for Coco, whose sharp gaze made her look as bright as Emily hoped she was. "I don't really have anywhere private to talk, but we can use the head chef's office."

"Let's do it."

They went into Felix's space, and Emily cleared off his side chair before she took a seat. "I was impressed by your resume," she said. "You were moving right up until you stopped working…what was it? Five years ago?"

"Yeah," she said, not flinching when she added, "I was in jail for almost a year, then in prison for three."

Emily gulped, having assumed the gap in service wasn't because the woman had been lying on a beach somewhere. But she'd hoped the hole in her resume had been because she'd taken time off to have a baby or two. "I see," she said. "Uhm…"

"My husband treated me like shit," she said, her dark eyes flashing with anger. "But that's on me, 'cause I didn't stop that shit the first time it happened." She shrugged. "One night, I hit my limit." She looked down, then raised her gaze to meet Emily's. "I stuck him with a knife, but he deserved it. You couldn't send me to jail long enough to make me feel bad about doing that." After clearing her throat, she added, "But it was hard for my kids."

"Did you kill him?" Emily bit at her lip, realizing she'd never had to ask a person if they'd committed murder.

"Nah. He's too mean to die. But I don't care about that any more. He moved back to Arizona. He saw his kids once last year," she added, with a disgusted look on her face. Her voice gained strength when she said, "I need this job. My kids are old enough to know what's going on now. If I want them to have more than I did, I can't afford to play around."

"I can only pay twenty an hour," Emily said. "Can you make it on that?"

"I make eleven fifty now," she said. "Twenty would let me move out of my grandmother's house."

"Can you come in tomorrow? I'll have you expedite breakfast. If I like your style, you've got the job."

Coco graced her with a luminous smile. "Oh, you'll like my style," she said, full of confidence. "Ain't no doubt."

Emily did, in fact, like Coco's style. She was focused, spoke little, kept her cool, and did some really fancy footwork to the songs that she was clearly playing in her head. Emily watched her work, smiling every time Coco got a big order right and did a little salsa, clearly unable to keep her satisfaction at doing a good job under wraps.

When the rush slowed down, Emily pulled Coco aside and said, "I'm sold. When can you start?"

"Tomorrow. I work four to eleven now, but I can do both jobs until they replace me."

"Are you sure? We could wait until Monday."

With a fiery look in her eye, Coco said, "I don't want you to change your mind. I'll be here by seven tomorrow."

"We don't fire our first order until eight," Emily said, laughing at her determination.

"Then seven forty-five." She took a look at Emily's green jacket. "Do I have to wear that?"

"Yeah. That's the uniform."

"Damn," she said, shaking her head. "I'm gonna have to go buy some new lipstick. That is *not* my color."

Emily watched her go back and seamlessly take over to finish out the shift. She was going to be a good one. As Blake had taught her, a person's potential was worth much more than their past.

That Friday morning she spent an hour going over all of her impressions of the staff and their strengths and weaknesses with Felix. He took a lot of notes, but she could tell he wasn't paying as close attention as he should have. "I'm going to have to hire someone to replace you," he said idly when she finished up.

"Someone? Like what kind of someone?"

"I need someone to do the things you've been doing." He picked up a piece of paper and started to fold it, quickly making a paper airplane. It went sailing over her head, landing in the hallway by the locker room. "Besides expediting, of course. That girl you brought in yesterday seems good."

"I think she's going to be. I got her cheap because she's never worked at a big place. But if you want to keep her, you're going to have to give her a raise in a few months. She'll find out how much the other expeditor's making and she'll want—and deserve more once she's proven herself."

"We'll see," he said, circling back. "It's your job I'm worried about."

"Yeah." She took a breath, trying to decide how blunt to be. "You're going to have to squeeze a good bit of money out of Laurent for that. You don't have a dime to spare—as I'm sure you know."

He nodded, having to agree with her point. She'd gone to the wall to make sure she'd hired the best possible cooks, cutting corners everywhere else possible. While he thought, he made another airplane, fussing with it to make it a little more aerodynamic. "I think you're overpaying the sauciers. The prep cooks, too. If I had a few thousand from each of them…"

Ooo, that was such a shortsighted view. A dumb, shortsighted view. "I paid them well because I think they're the backbone of a good kitchen. Those are your lifers, Felix. Don't try to cut corners there."

He looked up, giving her an annoyed glance. "Then where am I going to get the budget for an assistant?"

"I guess you'll have to talk Laurent into letting you go over budget on salaries and head count." *Good luck!*

"He'll agree when he sees how well we did this week." After picking up his cell phone, he played with it for a minute, thumbing through messages. Almost as an afterthought, he said, "What are you making, anyway? You're not on my list."

"Not enough," she said, starting to get irritated. "I've been doing at least two jobs. I'd want fifty percent more to keep going. And even then you'd be getting a bargain."

He shook his head. "I don't think I'll have to pay more than you're getting. Now that we've got another expediter, all I need is someone to keep an eye on the little things." His gaze traveled up to the ceiling where it stayed for a few seconds. "Maybe I could get a commis to do some of the stuff you've been doing."

She couldn't even form a word. Her lower lip was locked between her teeth to keep herself from reaming him a new one.

"That kid you have tasting the food at dinner service seems sharp."

This was a waste of her time. She stood up, snapped her papers into order and moved toward the door. "Fabulous idea." She stopped, turned and extended her hand. "I'm sure you'll figure everything out." Then she went to her locker to clean it out, mumbling under her breath, "You're gonna need a load of luck, you lazy jerk."

CHAPTER SEVENTEEN

ON SUNDAY AFTERNOON, EMILY sat at The Angry Rooster with some of her friends from Defarge, where she'd been poissonnier. She held the floor as morning turned into afternoon, telling tales of new kitchens, new hires, and life in her tiny section of Las Vegas. As each new wave of cooks and servers arrived, Emily found a fresh drink in her hand. By three, she was on the verge of making a fool of herself, and knew she'd better leave to avoid being pushed over the edge.

Once outside, she stood on the corner, swaying slightly. She'd intentionally not called Blake to tell her she was home, but her resolve to let her make the overture was short-lived. Taking out her phone, she texted: "Want a blow job?"

Seconds later, the response came in. "Huh?"

"Is there a term for women?"

The response stayed the same. "Huh?"

"I'm close by. Want sex?"

"YES!"

Smirking, she tried to get the phone into the back pocket of her jeans, but missed. It started to slide down her leg but she caught it before it fell to the pavement. Not bad. She was still sober enough to have some motor skills.

The day was warm and breezy, more like August than September, but the sun was at that weird angle that let it hit you right in the eyes. Fall sucked. Even the sun couldn't make itself perk up and stay at a good angle.

On the walk to Blake's, she sobered up a little. Just enough to regret texting her. On the flight home, she'd thought of their relationship, or the lack of one. The only thing that made sense was to pull back. That would make Blake chase her if she really wanted to. But she was so damned appealing! It was like turning down a slice of fabulous chocolate cake because you knew it was bad for you. Sure, that was the smart thing, but who could turn down great chocolate cake?

The doorman announced her and she leaned against the wall of the elevator, wishing Blake lived much higher up. Another few minutes delay might have made her a little sharper. But the bell dinged after just two floors, and when the doors opened Blake was right there, with a big, silly grin on her gorgeous face.

"I'm so glad you're home!" Reaching in, she grasped Emily by the hand and tugged at her, pulling her out as the doors started to close.

"Me too."

Blake tucked an arm around her shoulders and led her down the hall. "Did you just get in?"

"Yeah. Friday night."

That put a hitch in her gait, but she didn't comment. Emily saw her head turn and could hear her take a sniff, probably confirming that the eighty proof smell wasn't imaginary. When they entered the apartment, Blake went to a shelf on her bookcase and grasped a small package. Then she extended it, her grin still in place. "I got you a welcome home present."

"Really?" Emily opened it, finding a metal rendering of the Chrysler Building. "This is so cute," she said, beaming a grin at Blake.

"When we were running around town after the Barstow Awards, we passed it and you said it was your favorite building. I thought I'd get you a small reminder of what you love about New York, in case you're ever tempted to leave again."

"Aww…" She threw her arms around Blake and held on tightly, realizing her feelings were going to come out, no matter how much she wanted to stuff them down. Tears choked her voice as she murmured, "Would you miss me if I left?"

Blake grasped her by the shoulders and held her at a distance, looking carefully at her face. "Of course I would. How many times have I told you how much I like you?"

"A few," she admitted. "But I don't think we want the same thing." She couldn't stop them. The tears were going to fall.

"Hey, come on," Blake soothed. "Talk to me." She led her to a chair, then grabbed the other and pulled it close. Their knees touched as Blake leaned in, clearly ready to listen.

"You don't…" Emily sucked in a shaky breath. "You don't want any attachments. I do."

"You do?" Her voice was so gentle, so soothing.

"I love having sex with you, Chef. I really, really do." She wiped angrily at her tears, trying to stop them by force of will. "But I need more than that."

"What do you need?" She put her hands on Emily's knees, merely resting them there. "Tell me."

"I'm not sure. But I need more."

Leaning over even further, Blake placed a kiss on the crown of her head. "How can I give you what you want if you don't know what it is?"

"I don't know."

"Come on," Blake urged, moving around slightly to catch Emily's gaze. "Tell me what you want."

Her lower lip quivered as she forced herself to be honest. "I want more than sex. I want to *know* you. To know you care about me."

"But I do," Blake said, her voice still soft but insistent. "Can't you feel that when we're together?"

"Yeah, yeah, I can. But I don't feel it when we're not having sex. And that's most of the time."

"All right." Blake stood and walked over to the window, spending a few moments looking out at her god-awful view. "Tell me how I can show that I care about you." She turned and faced Emily, her eyes filled with sadness. "Because I do. Deeply."

Sighing, Emily said what should have been obvious. "You'd call once in a while. You'd ask me about my day. We'd have a meal or go to a concert together." Closing her eyes in frustration, she said, "Do you really not know?"

"No, I don't," she said, moving back to her chair. "But I can follow orders. Tell me how often to call. Every day?"

Now she felt stupid for being so needy. "No, not every day. Just when you think of me or you want to hear my voice."

"Okay," she said soberly. "I can do that. I *will* do that."

"But if you don't think of me for a month or two, act like you have. It's okay to tell me you've thought of me even if you haven't."

"Ohh," Blake murmured, running her hands from the tops of Emily's shoulders to her wrists. "I think of you all the time. All of the time."

"Then why'd you ignore me almost all summer?"

Blake stood, grasped Emily by her elbows and pulled her to her feet. Then she sat and maneuvered her to settle onto her lap. When they were snuggled so close to one another Emily felt impervious to harm. Like Blake would take care of everything that bothered her.

"How can you say I ignored you? I spent over a thousand dollars for that last minute flight to Detroit." She let out a soft laugh. "I don't normally pay that kind of money and lose a night's sleep to go to a stranger's birthday party. A party I wasn't even invited to."

"That was just to have sex," Emily grumbled.

Blake gripped her chin and turned it so their eyes met. "I hate to brag, but it's not hard for me to find someone to have sex with. Right in my office. No travel involved. I wanted to see *you*."

"You wanted to have *sex* with me," she insisted, certain of her facts. "You made it clear that's what you wanted."

Blake gazed at her for a few moments, her eyes narrowing slightly. She acted like a woman partially conversant in Emily's language, but having to struggle with a translation delay since it wasn't her native tongue. "I *do* like to have sex with you. There's no doubt about it. But that's because I like you. I'm sure I could find someone with an equally talented tongue, but it wouldn't be in your head." She tenderly kissed her head once again, letting her lips remain there for a few seconds. "That wasn't very poetic, but it's true."

Emily lifted her head and gazed into Blake's eyes. "I can't figure you out. When we have sex it's *so* intimate, but then you disappear for weeks at a time. I'm not used to that, and it confuses the hell out of me."

"I didn't..." She trailed off, clearly puzzled. "I was working. You were working. I didn't disappear, Emily. I didn't." She looked not only confused, but insulted.

"Four weeks," Emily repeated. "Not one call."

"Doesn't your phone work?" Blake's careful, skittish look had gained some heat. "If talking on the phone is your thing, you've got to tell me that."

"I shouldn't *have* to," Emily said, frustrated at Blake's inability to see this building block so elementary to a real relationship. "When you're into someone, you want to talk."

"I *do* want to talk! When we're together, I love to talk to you. But when I've been at work for twelve hours, and just want to shove some food into my mouth and get to sleep, the last thing on my mind is making a phone call." She gripped Emily by the shoulders and held her tightly. "That's not a knock against you. That's just how I am."

Emily slipped from her hold, mostly to get her thoughts in order. Thinking clearly was tough to do with Blake glaring at her with those big, dark eyes. "I've never been with anyone who lets time pass like this, Chef. No one has ever put me into a holding pattern without a word."

"One, I didn't put you into a holding pattern. And two, I don't know how to do this right." She shook her head, clearly frustrated with either herself or Emily. "I told you I've never had a girlfriend. This is why."

"Wrong! You haven't had a girlfriend because you haven't wanted one."

"That's only partially true," she insisted. "It's also because I don't know how to be one." She bore such a vulnerable expression that it felt like a slap. "I invited you to the Barstow Awards, didn't I? I introduced you to my friends, my mentors. I was trying, Emily. Trying to get closer. Obviously I suck at it, but you can't say I wasn't trying."

"You were?" Her heart skipped a beat at the fragile look on her face.

"Of course I was. And I wanted to come to Vegas to see you, but I got roped into working every single Sunday this summer. I've been to the fucking Hamptons so often I could find the damn place with my eyes closed."

"You've been working on Sundays?" She asked, tenderly trailing her fingers down Blake's face.

"Every fucking one. I was supposed to do another celebrity chef thing last weekend, but when Laurent called, I cancelled. I was so excited to see your place and see what a great job you'd done." She pulled away, letting Emily see her confused expression. "Couldn't you tell how proud I was of you?"

"Yeah. Yeah." Her head was starting to hurt, and she felt more confused by the moment. "I could tell you were happy to see me."

"I couldn't get enough of you," Blake emphasized. "It felt so good to hold you in my arms and touch you. Damn!" She pulled away again and cocked her head. "Do you think I'm some out-of-control sex addict? I don't normally keep going all night when I've got to be at work the next day. But I missed you, and touching you made me happy." Sighing, she asked quietly, "Doesn't it make you happy?"

"It does. Always." She put her hand on Blake's shoulder and spent a moment looking into her eyes. "We've got to work some things out, Chef. We've got to learn to talk more."

"I say what's on *my* mind, Emily. I don't think that's true for you."

"Then tell me what's on your mind. How would things be if you could have exactly what you wanted? Describe a perfect...whatever you want to call this."

"Okay." She closed her eyes, clearly thinking. When they fluttered open, Emily could see she was confident of her response. "We'd see each other when we had a day off and felt like being together. For me, that'd be every Sunday." Her brow narrowed. "I'd want to have sex, but I could easily skip a week or two if you weren't in the mood." Nodding decisively, she said, "That'd be perfect."

"I could work with that." Nuzzling her face into Blake's neck, she said, "That's pretty much what I want too."

"No, it's not. You want me to call you. You said so."

"Yeah." She nodded. "When we can't see each other for a while, I'd like to know you've thought of me. Or that you miss me."

"So...you don't need me to call when it's just an average day and I want to get to bed?"

"No, I don't need that. I..." She swallowed and forced herself to be frank. "You've made it clear that part of the reason you've avoided being in a relationship was because you don't like having a woman make demands on you. That makes me leery of asking for much."

A quizzical eyebrow went up. "Where is it written that I'm in charge? You need to say what you need and see if I agree. We negotiate so we're both happy." Those dark, penetrating eyes seemed like they could go right through her. For a woman who'd never had a girlfriend, she had some damn good instincts.

"Yes, Chef. That's exactly what we need to do. And as soon as I sober up, I'm going to give you my wish list."

Emily woke, tangled in the sheet, confused and groggy. While trying to get her leg free, a soft voice said, "Are you awake?"

She turned to see Blake sitting in a chair, computer lying on her lap.

"I think so. Water? Please?"

With a smirk, Blake got up and went to get her a glass. On the way back, she asked, "Aspirin?"

"No, I'm okay. Just thirsty." Emily accepted the glass and downed it in a few big gulps. "Better." Then she flopped onto her back again, drained from simply sitting up. "Why do I drink in the afternoon? I've never had a good outcome."

Blake sat on the bed and pulled Emily's head and shoulders onto her lap. "I'm no psychologist, but you might have gotten a little smashed to help you get up the nerve to tell me what's been bothering you."

"I don't think that's it. I had no intention of calling you."

"That's kinda mean," Blake said, tracing the planes of Emily's face with a finger. Idly, like she was drawing. "Or manipulative."

"I didn't mean to be," Emily said, growing more embarrassed as they spoke. "But I can see why you'd think it was."

"Stuff like this is part of the reason I haven't had a girlfriend. It's a heck of a lot easier to just have sex when I need it. No misunderstandings."

Emily shifted to look at her. "But you're willing to put up with me anyway?"

She smiled, then tickled all around her ears. "I want to see you more often, and I want you to be happy with how things are between us. I can adjust."

"Do you want my list now? It's really, really long," she said, trying to sound dramatic.

"I do. Should I get my laptop to take notes?"

"No, I think you can remember this." She took a breath. "Basically, I want what you want. I'd like for us to see each other regularly." Their eyes met. "I don't need a major commitment, but I'd like to be exclusive. Is that something you can do?"

"Sure," she said, nodding agreeably. "No problem."

Lifting an eyebrow, Emily said, "Really? No problem?"

"Yeah. No problem. I've done this part before, Emily. It's not an issue."

"What do you mean? You've never had a girlfriend."

"No, but I've had a couple of long-term sex partners."

Emily turned and settled more comfortably in Blake's lap. "Want to tell me about them?"

"If you're interested." At Emily's nod, she said, "I saw an emergency medicine resident for most of the time I worked for Jean-Michel. But once she finished her training, she wanted more."

"More? What kind of more?"

"She wanted a girlfriend. You know. The whole thing."

"The difference between the whole thing and what you had was…?"

A frown settled on her face and she sat quietly for more than a minute. "I'm not exactly sure. I was only twenty-four, and the thought of being with anyone for good freaked me out. When she said she wanted more, I bailed."

"Was she hurt?"

"If she was, she hid it well. I think she realized it'd be tough to make it work, even if we lived together. I only had Mondays off and her days off moved around a lot. We were lucky to see each other twice a month."

"And you didn't mind being monogamous? Even seeing her that little?"

"I minded, but not much. If I know the reward is going to be worth the sacrifice, I can easily make the sacrifice."

"Did you ever hang out? Or was it just sex?"

"Sex." Slowly, a very sober look settled onto her face. "I don't want to sound like a jerk, but I don't need a lot of companionship. It's the drive to connect with someone that makes me want to give up my very limited free time."

"Hmm. That's not true for me. I like being around people, particularly someone I enjoy having sex with." She lifted her hand and caressed Blake's cheek, smiling when her eyes fluttered closed. "Even if we weren't intimate, I'd like to hang out with you."

"I like you too, Emily," she said, her expression very serious. "But I'm trying to be honest. When I have a day off, I'm not usually up for a walk or a movie. I want intimacy and connection, and the easiest way for me to get that is through sex."

"I don't think that's an insurmountable obstacle. I've got Chase and other friends from places I've worked. I can find someone to see a movie with."

"I'll see a movie with you," Blake promised. "I will. If you need to do something social, I'll adjust."

"It's a deal. You've told me about one woman, but you said you've had a couple, right?"

"Right. I saw a woman, a bartender at a place I used to go, for about six months. That was probably two years ago."

"Did you break up for the same reason?"

Shaking her head, Blake said, "Nope. It turned out she didn't have the monogamy instinct."

"Ooo." She lifted her hand and gently stroked Blake's face. "Did she hurt your feelings?"

"A little bit. She was pretty cool." Again, her head shook decisively. "I would have preferred an open relationship, but she insisted on being exclusive. I called her late one night, hoping I could stop by for a quickie, and another woman answered." She made a slicing motion at her throat. "Once you break a promise to me—I'm done."

"I'm the same way. I can't stand to be lied to."

Blake's hand moved to Emily's lips, and a finger trailed along them, making her giggle. "Is that your whole list? See each other, go outside once in a while, and be exclusive?"

"Pretty much."

Blake leaned over as far as she could to place a light kiss on the top of Emily's head. "How do I know you can be monogamous?"

She laughed. "I don't have a sofa in my office, and it's tough to lure people out to Queens." Roughly, she grabbed Blake's leg and shook it. "I've got one day a week when I have the time and energy to be with a woman. You're the woman I choose to spend that precious resource on."

"So I'm your choice when you're in New York. What happens when you go to Detroit?"

Emily gave her a wry smile. "We'll renegotiate every time one of us leaves town."

Blake took a minute to consider the terms, than nodded decisively. "You've got yourself a deal. Consider your New York Sundays spoken for until further notice."

Emily turned further onto her side, to be able to look Blake right in the eyes. "We'll go slow to make sure we're both into this. And I'll do my best not to be too demanding."

Blake leaned over, so their faces were close. "This can only work if you talk to me. When you want something, especially something important, you need to let me know. I suck at guessing."

"I'll do my best." She blew out a breath and told the truth. "I'm going to need practice. I'll probably screw up, so you'll have to bear with me."

"You're bearable." She lifted Emily from her lap, then stood and looked into her eyes for a minute, before speaking soberly. "Having you gone all summer was hard for me. I missed you a lot, and I'm sorry I didn't tell you that."

"You're telling me now. Now's really good." She put her hand on Blake's shoulder and pulled her close, snuggling for a minute. "Do you have an extra toothbrush?"

"Uh-huh. I use an electric, but I have some spare heads. But why don't we go have dinner instead of jumping into bed. We don't talk much once we get going."

"Dinner?" She let her eyes shift to the bed. "Don't you want to…?"

Blake wrapped her in a hug, dipping her head to murmur in her ear. "If we had three days it wouldn't be enough to satisfy the hunger I have for you." Her head lifted and those soulful eyes gazed at Emily for a few precious moments. "But I missed you so much. I want to hear about everything that happened this summer."

Charmed beyond words, Emily got up and started to put her clothes back on. "Even though I don't get the same pleasure from food that I used to, I still love the experience of going to a restaurant. Let's walk around the neighborhood and see what looks good."

"I'd like that. I'm awfully interested in how you got the bistro open, given Laurent insists you did it singlehandedly."

Emily looked at her for a second. "You know, he's a pretty perceptive guy. His hiring skills are weak, though. Felix is a bust."

They parted after Blake walked Emily to her preferred subway line. It wasn't late, only ten, but Emily was so tired she ached. Going back to Blake's was tempting, but she knew they'd be up half the night and she simply didn't have the energy. She leaned against the green metal railing that marked the entrance, with Blake standing between her legs, holding her tenderly.

"I thought we'd have sex on our first day as…whatever we are," Blake teased, clearly amused by the term.

"You said I could have a week or two off from servicing you if I needed it." She pulled Blake down and gave her the hottest kiss she had in her arsenal. "I'll make it up to you next week."

Blake started to smile, then every bit of pleasure left her face. "I've got to work. My last command performance of the year, I hope."

"What is it?"

A dark scowl settled onto her face. "Did you meet Jessica? Alan's wife?"

"She's the one who auctioned you off earlier this year."

"That's her. She's appointed herself my agent, and she's having a big end-of-season blowout disguised as a charity event."

"And you're cooking?"

"Yeah. Up on a friggin' stage they're having set up." Her good mood seemed to have vanished in an instant. "I never feel more like a trained chimp."

Emily lifted her hand and urged some of Blake's waves to lie the way she liked them. "You know what chimps like?"

"Mmm." She closed her eyes as she thought. "Bananas?"

"They like other chimps. Let me be your sous chef."

The good mood returned just as quickly as it had gone. "Really? You'd do that?"

"To spend the day with you? No question."

"Not bad," Blake said, nodding her head in satisfaction. "If this is what being in a 'whatever we are' is like, I'm gonna dig it." Her smile perked up even brighter. "Why don't you come up with the menu?"

"Me?"

"Yeah. You like to create dishes. Think of six canapés, a few salads, some vegetables and two mains. We'll need to grill the main courses, but everything else should be cold or room temp."

"What's the setup? Who's in charge?"

"Jessica's in charge, but she told me I could do anything I wanted. I'm supposed to send her my requirements by Tuesday. She's got two hundred and fifty confirmed, and money is no object. This is supposed to be for charity, but they don't mind spending a hundred bucks per person on food. Jerks," she muttered.

"Okay. I'll start thinking." She pulled Blake down and gave her a soft kiss. "Thanks for trusting me."

"You earned my trust a year ago, Emily, and it's only gotten stronger."

Chase was home, sitting on the sofa in the living room, watching TV while eating out of a Chinese carry-out container. "Hey, buddy," he said when Emily entered the room. "Want some sesame noodles?"

"No, thanks." She dropped her bag and leaned over the sofa to kiss him on the cheek, then moved around to sit on the side chair. "A gorgeous woman bought me some spicy Indian food for dinner. No Natasha tonight?"

"Nope. She's heading for a conference in Atlanta." He maneuvered his chopsticks to his mouth and slurped some noodles in. "So you met a hottie at the Angry Rooster, huh?"

"I did not." A self-satisfied smile fought its way to her lips. "I met this one about a year ago at her restaurant in TriBeCa."

"Oh-oh. Someone put her lust in control of her dialing finger."

"I did not..." She began, then trailed off. "Okay, I did. But she twisted my arm and got me to tell her what I was unhappy about. I'm still kinda stunned, but we're going to try to have a..." She trailed off again. "We're not sure what to call it, but it walks and talks like a relationship."

"Fantastic!" Chase held his hand out and they slapped their palms together. "I knew she was into you."

"She kind of is. *Much* more than I thought."

"Where'd you leave it? And why can't you call it a relationship?"

"Mmm." She bit at her lip, anxiety building when she thought of how ill-defined they'd left things. "If we're both in the mood, she'd like for us to get together every Sunday for sex."

He stared at her for a second, then barked out a laugh. "If you did a poll of every man in America, ninety percent of them would say that was the perfect relationship." He stopped, then looked at her carefully. "Most women wouldn't agree."

"I'm not most women, but I would like a little more than that." Rolling her eyes, she laughed at the absurdity of the whole thing. "I asked her to call me once in a while when we haven't seen each other. And to be monogamous. That's all I need." She blinked, thinking of the discussion. "I think monogamy's only in play when we're both in New

York, though. She said something about renegotiating when we're away from home."

"That's not much, Em. Will that really make you happy?"

"I'm not sure," she said, already worried that she'd asked for too little. "I clearly need more contact than she does, but I don't want to spook her."

He reached out and grasped her hand, holding it tightly for a few seconds before releasing it. "You also don't want to sell yourself short. Ask for what you need. That's the only way to get it."

"I do," she said, letting her defenses build up a little.

His level gaze knocked them right back down. "What do you tell me when I'm negotiating for something?"

"Ask for more than you want," she said, dropping her head. "But that's so hard for me to do!"

"I know it is," he soothed. "But you've got to push a little, Em. You can't expect her to read your mind."

"I don't..."

"Yes, you do. You always have. But you can change."

"I think I'm good with what I asked for. And if not, I'll try to renegotiate."

Chase put his hand on her cheek and patted it gently. "It's been nine years since Nicole broke up with you, buddy, but I think you're still stuck in that 'I can't look at her cross-eyed or she'll dump me' thing."

"I don't think that's true." She allowed herself to think of how she really was, not how she wished she could be. "It's definitely not as true as it used to be."

"You take what you're given, Em, even though women would be fighting over you in the street if they knew you. You're the cream of the crop," he insisted.

She sloughed that off, got up and sat next to him, her preferred position when Natasha wasn't around. "What about you? What's on your 'must have' list?"

His grin made him look slightly embarrassed. "You know I'm more of a girl than you are. I'd like to move in together, but Natasha wants to take it slow." He put his carton on the table and leaned into Emily.

"There must be some law of physics that two bodies don't spin in the same orbit. It seems like one or the other is always off by a few degrees."

She nodded, reflectively. It was pretty clear she and Blake were at least a few degrees from wanting the exact same thing, but her orbit was far too powerful to resist.

Emily rolled into Le Lapin bright and early the next morning. Since Laurent had made it clear she wasn't the poissonnier any longer, it didn't make sense to go in at her normal afternoon time.

The kitchen was pretty quiet, with just Helmut and Klaus, the sous chefs, and Manuel, the saucier, busily beginning their day. After spending a few minutes gossiping about Laurent Bistro, Emily jumped in and helped prep for Manuel, while the sous worked on checking in the day's orders. It was fun to knock the rust off her knife and perform the repetitive motions, doing something she was able to do in her sleep.

"She returns!"

Emily turned her head to find Laurent and Michael, his assistant, both smiling at her. "She does," she agreed.

"Come into the office and we'll talk," Laurent said. She noted that Michael looked down at his omnipresent tablet computer and pouted. It must have been a constant challenge to keep Laurent on a tight schedule.

Emily washed the tomato juice from her hands and followed them back to the office. Michael started to sit next to her, but Laurent made a dismissive gesture. "You don't need to stay. I'll let you know what we decide."

He had a hand on the back of the chair, and he clearly didn't want to remove it. But he did, reluctantly, and paused in the doorway. "Make sure to keep me in the loop." He leveled his gaze at Emily.

As Michael left, Laurent let out a soft laugh. "He wishes I were like the robot."

"He's not going to get his wish," Emily teased. "I uhm…wasn't sure what time to come in, so I showed up at the same time I did in Las Vegas."

"That's good. I'm sorry if you waited long."

"Oh, no, it was fine. I got to use my knife for the first time in a while. I missed it."

"Ahh..." He relaxed in his chair and nodded. She could see a bit of longing in his eyes. "I miss it too. Sometimes I think I was happier when I was chef de parti."

"Blake says that too." She paused for effect. "But I don't see her chucking it all and taking over as garde manger."

"No, once you're in charge..." He looked at his ever-present phone when it vibrated against the desk. "So. Here is what I think. I need another Michael—a Michael who can cook."

"He's not...?"

"MBA," he said dismissively. "I don't think he can poach an egg. No, I need someone who knows food and can create dishes and still be aware of costs and margins and all of the business things." He looked her in the eyes, pulling her in with the fire of his gaze. "You've proven yourself, Emily. In a few months you pulled Laurent Bistro out of the..." He put his hands together and pointed them to the ground. "Nose dive?"

Chuckling, she nodded. "I think nose dive is the right term."

He picked up his phone and rapidly typed. In seconds, Michael was there, looking at him expectantly.

"Do you have the gift for Emily?"

"Of course." He removed an envelope from his pocket and handed it to Laurent, then exited again.

Laurent opened the envelope and withdrew a check. Emily's eyes widened as she tried not to reach out and grab it. She'd never considered she'd get a bonus but now she really, really wanted it! "*You* opened the restaurant, Emily. I was going to give Felix a bonus for meeting the deadline, but he didn't earn it. You did." He slid the paper across the desk.

Hands prickling with anticipation, she picked it up and yelped, "Twenty-five thousand dollars?" She'd never seen such a big number on a check with her name on it. "Chef, this is so generous!"

"It's not," he said dismissively. "You've saved me much more. If I had missed the date…" He shook his head. "We will struggle to make a profit this year, so I can't give you what you deserve, but I hope this shows how grateful I am for what you did." His gaze settled on her as his mouth slid into a smile. "When does Blake have a day off?"

"Usually Sunday, but she's working this week. Why?"

"My wife and I would like you to be our guests for dinner. Next Sunday is good? I'll have Michael put you in the book."

"I'm almost certain Blake's free, but I'll double check." She sat back in her chair, buzzing with excitement. "I've always wanted to eat here."

"It's funny, no? We cook the food and never eat it. That surprises people."

"People don't understand how small our margins are. If the staff ate the product, we'd all go broke."

"Exactly. And that's why I want you to work with me. You understand the budget. You're not blind to cost, like so many are."

"Thank you, Chef. I didn't know I had the knack, but I surprised myself in Vegas."

His head cocked. "If you're going to work with me, I'd like you to call me Laurent. Is that fine?"

"Of course. It might take me a while, though."

"I am patient. So… You will take the job?"

"The job is what—exactly?"

He picked up his phone when it vibrated, but instead of letting it divert his attention he turned it off and flipped it over, now unable to see the screen even if the little thing managed to reanimate itself. He took a breath, as if clearing his head of the constant interruptions. "I need many things. The investors Blake and I spoke with in Las Vegas are partnering with me on another Laurent Bistro, this one in the Caribbean."

"I had no idea…"

"The public does not know, but the construction has begun. My goal is to be open by June. I'd like you to work full time on getting the kitchen going, but you can't do that until we have a kitchen. Until then, I'd like for you to be flexible."

"I'm very flexible. But..."

"Let's be honest," he said, his voice getting softer. "There is no job for you yet. But there is always work to be done. You can sub for a sous or a line cook who is out sick or on vacation. You can work with Daniel on the daily specials." His brow knit briefly. "You may have to go to Las Vegas to solve problems." He must have banished that thought from his head, as his hand waggled in front of him, shooing unpleasant details away. "I want only to know you will take a job that will define itself."

"I'll do it," she said, her heart beating rapidly.

He batted his eyes at her, looking surprisingly coquettish. "If I was going to take a job, I would ask how much I would be paid."

She swallowed, her nerves making her twitch. "How much will you pay me?"

The laugh he barked out surprised her. One thing you had to say for Laurent, he kept you guessing. "I have no idea how much we will pay. Michael will talk to you."

"You've been more than fair so far. I'm sure that will continue."

Soberly, he said, "That is the most important thing, Emily. I want to always be fair." He extended his hand, and she shook it. She was jumping in without knowing how deep the pool was, but Laurent would not screw her over. She was completely sure of his character. The rest of the details were just that.

At midnight, she dialed Blake's phone.

"I thought I was supposed to call you," Blake said, her soft laugh making Emily smile. "Did I get that wrong?"

"No, you're in charge of making phone calls, but I had to break the rule just this once." She took a breath. "Guess who got a cool new job, a massive raise, and a huge bonus?"

"I hope it's you because I don't want to waste time talking about people I don't know."

"It's me," she said, giggling like a teenager.

Blake's voice grew serious and certain. "You deserve that bonus, Emily. You pulled Laurent's ass out of the fire."

"He said I stopped him from doing the nose dive," she said, laughing when she thought of how he'd mimicked the plane crashing.

"You did. Now how are you going to make your mark at Le Lapin?"

"I'm going to be a jack of all trades. But the cool part, the really cool part is that I'll not only make more money, I can make my own hours. Five…days…a…week," she intoned dramatically. "Have you ever heard of anything crazier?"

"I want to be a jack of all trades," Blake pouted. "You'll be great at that. I can see you down in the Caribbean, working on your tan while you whip another Laurent Bistro into shape."

"Did I mention the Caribbean? Did I mention Laurent Bistro? My short-term memory must be on the fritz."

"Oops!"

"Did you talk him into giving me this job?" She spoke like she was chiding her, then laughed. "It's fine with me if you did. I hope you talked him into the raise too."

"Not at all. We just talked about your skills and I made a few suggestions. Honestly, Emily, he only wanted to figure out how to use you. I certainly didn't have to convince him you were a find."

"Thanks," she said, touched once again by Blake's faith in her abilities. "Hey, how about dinner at Le Lapin Sunday after next?"

"You did get a raise! I think Laurent's tasting menu's over three hundred bucks with wine pairings."

"We're being comped. By Laurent and his wife."

"I'm in. Way, way in." She waited a second, then said, "Could we maybe get together earlier in the afternoon and…"

"Yes, Chef," she said, putting on a weary tone. "You've made it clear part of the deal in being whatever we are is getting horizontal. If I want those phone calls, I've got to satisfy your voracious sexual appetite." She laughed, hearing her voice take on a sexy growl. "I'd come over right now if I hadn't volunteered to go in at nine tomorrow. Holding up that end of the bargain is going to be my pleasure…and yours."

CHAPTER EIGHTEEN

AT NINE A.M. ON Sunday morning, Emily perked up when a black Town Car moved slowly up her street. She was used to banged-up limos cruising around looking for fares, the outer-boroughs' version of Yellow Cabs, but this one stood out. Sparkling clean, tinted windows, shiny black tires. Lifting her hand to shield her eyes from the early morning sun, she blinked when the rear window slid down and a very pretty woman graced her with a smile. "Want a ride, little girl?"

Getting up and dusting off the seat of her jeans, Emily sauntered over and bent to poke her nose inside. "I have to keep adjusting my expectations with you. I assumed you'd rent a Zip Car for the day."

"Are you going to get in?" Blake tapped her big, heavy watch. "We've got rich people to feed, and they don't like to wait."

Emily'd been so focused she hadn't noticed a tall man in black approach. Instinctively, she yanked her bag close to her chest and turned her back so he couldn't grab it. Then Blake's amused laugh made her take a look at the guy.

Chauffeur.

Mortified, she stepped back and let him open the door for her. "Thanks," she said, hoping he hadn't noticed she'd thought he was going to mug her. "I'm such a rube," she muttered as she slid across the supple leather.

"You're a cute rube." Blake kissed her cheek, with Emily quickly dismissing the longing that often hit her when she breathed in and noticed…nothing. It was going to take a hell of a long time to convince her unconscious it was futile to hunt for the little notes that used to inform and enrich every bit of her world.

"I like that shirt." Blake's finger slid down the placket. "Ditch your whites and keep that on. I'd love to look at your bare arms all day."

Lifting an eyebrow, she said, "I'm going to get my one nice linen blouse dirty? Don't think so." She settled into the plush seat. "This is pretty high-class stuff, Chef. Was Hertz out of cars?"

"Don't know." She leaned over and rested her chin on Emily's shoulder. "Don't know how to drive."

"What?" She pulled away, with Blake's head falling a few inches before she righted herself and sat up.

"I left home before I learned."

"I thought you were sixteen when you left. Everyone I know got their license on their birthday."

"I had a lot of stuff going on during my sophomore year, and when I didn't take the driving portion of the class, I was out of luck. I would have gotten around to it, but…"

"A few years have passed since then," Emily said, trying to let this revelation sink in.

"Why bother? I can't afford to have a car in the city, and even if I could, I wouldn't want one. There are guys all over the place just itching to drive me around." Her smile was so damned cute it was a lethal weapon. "You see a yellow car and jump in. You should try it."

Ignoring the teasing, Emily said, "You didn't drive in France?"

"What would I have driven? I couldn't have afforded gas, much less a car." She chuckled softly. "One day, I'll take you on a tour. We'll go to each of the restaurants I worked in, and you'll see how silly these questions seem." Under her breath, she muttered, "Drive in France."

Emily took her hand and cuddled up against her body. It was a long, long way to the Hamptons and she was glad for every mile, very content to dream of the two of them leisurely traveling around France. Like they'd ever have the time, or the money, for a real vacation.

The house, an ultra-modern, cedar and limestone palace in Sagaponack, was the kind of place people dreamed of owning—if they had no social conscience. Emily didn't have a problem with people living in nice houses. If you could afford it, go for it. But there was a tipping point. A point at which you were saying, "I've got more money than God, and I need *two* outdoor kitchens so I don't have to walk to the north side of the house if I'm on the south side and want a hamburger." As they followed Jessica around the place, listening to her go on and on about her design choices, Emily had to remind herself that this ninety pound woman probably didn't eat many burgers. And she wouldn't have cooked her own, even if she had a hankering.

Even though the place was huge, and bore every possible convenience and luxury, it was too clean, making it more like a set than a house. The couple had kids, but there wasn't a discarded toy, or a drawing on one of the two restaurant style glass-fronted refrigerators, or a peanut butter and jelly sandwich abandoned on a table. Still, it was gorgeous. Clean and open and dramatic, with sweeping views of the ocean from the second floor deck that surrounded the place.

Blake was listening attentively as they stood in the master bath, a space big enough to wash one of the Range Rovers that took up a tiny portion of the mammoth circular drive out front. Emily caught her furtively checking her watch, then Blake said, "We're going to need a few hours to prep, Jessica. I'd love to see the rest of the house, but maybe we should hold off until after the party."

She stopped, then glanced at her own watch, held on by a big, gold-linked bracelet that probably cost more than Emily's childhood home. "Oh, shit. Good idea." She put her perfectly manicured hand on Blake's arm and propelled her toward the door, with Emily following behind. She wasn't normally a possessive person, but a big part of her wanted to knock that hand off. Touching Blake was one thing. Handling her like something you owned was another.

The outdoor kitchen was makeshift, but everything they'd asked for was in place and working properly. It seemed crazy to create a bare-bones kitchen on a stage when there were two fully-equipped outdoor ones on either end of the property, but she was hired help, not a decision maker.

The guests would be able to gather under two huge tents, with the ocean beckoning from behind sand banks dotted with saltwater-resistant plants. Their stage/kitchen was under a third, smaller tent, with a couple of industrial-sized fans to blow the smoke away from them, and, more importantly, the guests.

"Not a bad set-up for one day's use, huh?" Blake said, as she buttoned up her coat.

"Not bad at all. Want me to start on the lobsters?"

"You tell me." She checked herself out in the dull stainless steel door of a refrigerator they must have had to use a fork-lift to get onto the elevated platform.

"You tell me," Emily said. "You're the boss."

Blake turned and graced her with a dazzling smile. "Changed my mind. You're the chef. I'm the sous."

"What?" Her mouth dropped open, and she purposefully closed it. "Why?"

"Because it's your menu. You should decide how we attack it." She stood close and fussed with the stand-up collar of Emily's jacket. "I like that you decided to make almost normal food."

She smiled at her use of the term. "Lobster rolls, burgers with stunningly expensive blue cheese inside, and three kinds of ceviche isn't quite like a backyard barbecue."

"It is for these people. They'll be glad you're keeping it real. They have to get sick of foie gras."

"Truffle butter on the roasted corn might keep them from going into shock at the thought of eating something so ordinary."

"I hope so. I'm not in the mood to perform first aid." Blake clapped her hands together. "Give me my marching orders, Chef. We've got work to do."

By one o'clock it had gotten stiflingly hot under the tent. Blake disappeared for a few minutes, then returned wearing a pair of shorts that matched the color of her name on her jacket.

"Where'd you get those?" Emily asked, pointing with the tip of her knife.

"Brought 'em. Sorry I forgot to tell you to bring a pair. I learned my lesson earlier this summer when I almost fainted from the heat."

"Deck shoes?" She'd never seen her work in anything but her steel-toed chef's clogs.

"Yeah. I know you won't drop anything on me and I'm certainly not going to drop anything on myself. Besides," she said, looking down appraisingly, "these look better with the shorts."

Smirking, Emily got back to making corn chowder. Blake fit in better with the Hamptonites than she would ever admit.

Having purposefully made the menu easy to execute, Emily let herself relax and enjoy chatting while they cooked. She'd never been in a professional kitchen where people had normal conversations while cooking, but today was very different. More like an ultra high-end home barbecue than a restaurant kitchen. When the guests started to arrive, most of them stopped by, checking out the set-up as Blake plated food for the servers to rush over to the bigger tents.

Jessica and Alan brought a parade of people to introduce to Blake, with Emily marveling at her ability to perfectly arrange food on platters while charming the hosts and their guests. Many people were excellent, creative cooks, but only a few had the personality that made investors want to hang with you. Blake had it in spades.

After his guests wilted from the heat of the grill and moved out into the sun, Alan leaned against the refrigerator for a minute, watching. "Every once in a while I hear an East Coast accent out of you," he said, gazing at Blake thoughtfully.

"I grew up in Connecticut," she said, briskly snipping chives onto the lobster rolls.

"Really? I did too. Whereabouts?"

"Cos Cob."

Emily had never been to Connecticut, but Cos Cob gave her a mental image of clingy print sundresses, open-collared oxford-cloth shirts, and poplin shorts with sailboats embroidered on them. Just like every third couple wore today.

"Cos Cob, huh? Darien for me. We were neighbors." He narrowed his eyes, probably trying to figure out why a girl from his neck of the woods was cooking rather than being served. "What business was your father in?"

He didn't ask the question like a friend would. More like he wanted to check to make sure she really belonged in Cos Cob, wherever the hell that was.

"Insurance." She stood with her hands on her hips, assessing the platter before a server took it away.

"Really? What kind of insurance?"

"I honestly don't know," Blake said, now showing an easy, relaxed smile. "He left for the train at seven a.m. and came home for dinner at seven p.m. I made him a Rob Roy, while my mother put their dinner on the table." Her smile was more of a smirk. "Nice life. His office is on Madison, by the park. What is that? Like Twenty-Fourth Street?"

"He's still working?"

"Sure. He's only..." She seemed to be making a mental calculation. "Fifty-two or fifty-three. He'd like to retire at fifty-five, but only if the stock price stays high."

Alan was clearly perplexed, and Emily could see he craved more info. To figure out precisely where Blake fit in his world. But it was hard to ask that kind of thing directly. "You don't know the name of his firm?"

"It's..." She tilted her head and thought for a minute. "It's one of the big ones. He's gone from one to the next, and I forget where he's landed most recently. Actually, he might not be on Madison any more. I was in high school the last time I corralled my brothers and took them to visit him at the office."

"Shit!" Emily grabbed the pepper grinder and thrust it at Blake. "Ow, ow, ow," she whined, pointing at the blood pouring out of the knuckle of her middle finger. The one where a dark scar already rested. Blake immediately ground some pepper onto the cut, stopping the bleeding quickly.

"Did you bring a first aid kit?" Blake demanded.

Emily looked at her like she was nuts, not bothering to reply.

Blake had her by the wrist, keeping her hand elevated to prevent the slice from bleeding again. "Alan?" she said, her voice not showing a hint of concern. "Can you find some bandages?"

"He's not going to have blue knuckle guards," Emily groused as he left on his errand. "I've never used a flesh-colored bandage in a kitchen."

"Don't lose it in the soup and no one needs to know we forgot something important." She pulled Emily's hand close and took a long look at it. "Not too bad." When their eyes met, she said, "I don't think I've ever seen you cut yourself."

Emily didn't reply. Telling her she almost lost a digit upon learning Blake had siblings was way, way too embarrassing.

A group of shiny-faced, casually-coiffed blonde women, their dress sizes ranging from zero to two, were crowded around, watching Blake grill burgers, flipping them with effortless efficiency and visual panache. She was simultaneously drinking white wine with seltzer while answering questions and laughing at fairly lame jokes. If Emily had been told she'd one day see Blake cooking while drinking… It was too far-fetched to believe. But she seemed to know her role very well. They weren't true chefs today. They were acting like chefs while having fun with the guests. Flirting with the women was obviously part of the job, a part Blake seemed to know instinctively. Maybe because, deep down, she knew she could have been one of them.

The last burger was whisked off the grill at nine. As soon as Blake dropped her metal spatula, a group of guys from the equipment rental company descended upon them and began to clean and dismantle everything like they'd done it a thousand times before. They probably had. Blake unbuttoned her jacket, revealing a close-fitting white tank top that made Emily start to crave some closer contact. Then Blake took her hand and they went over to the bar, which was crowded with people. After refreshing their drinks, they worked the crowd for a while, posing for selfies with dozens of people.

One of the other owners pulled Blake away, and Emily moved to grab a chair at an empty table. Enjoying the relief that came from sitting for the first time since they'd been in the car that morning, she went to a popular social media site and searched for hashtags for the event. It didn't take long to find them. As expected, a bunch of photos of Blake popped up, with a few showing Emily's arm or a portion of her face. Of course, if she'd been the one who had a decent amount of notoriety, people would have been elbowing Blake out of the way to catch a photo of her. Fame ruled.

They finally stumbled to the town car that idled in the drive, each clutching an expensive bottle of Champagne and a small crystal globe engraved with the name of the charity and the date. "Do you want two? For bookends?" Blake asked, offering her globe up.

"One's plenty." She ran her hand over the etched glass. "I'm going to keep it, though. I want to remember the first and only time I got to boss you around."

"You didn't boss me around," Blake said, a warm grin lighting up her sleepy-looking face. "You're more of a leader than a boss. I could learn from you. I *should* learn from you."

Touched, Emily leaned against her, settling down for the very long ride home. "And I could learn how to flirt with straight women from you."

"Part of the job," she said, sighing. "Once men know I'm gay they might want to spar, but they rarely flirt. I don't understand why, but women do it constantly. What's the point?"

"You're great looking, and charming and…you look like you'd be fun in bed. Which you are."

"They're *straight* women. Why do they care what I'm like in bed?"

"It's a fantasy, Chef. People like to think about things they don't necessarily want to do. Plus, you've got some fame, which people are attracted to."

She let out a grouchy growl. It was so nice her little bit of fame hadn't gone to her head.

"I hate that part. I want to cook, not act like I'm cooking." Her head cocked and a thoughtful expression covered her face. "If I had my way, I'd only cook for normal people who really appreciated food."

"By normal you mean not obscenely rich?"

"No, I mean people who care about the taste more than the status. But I love to make complex food, and only wealthy people can afford it." She let out a wry laugh. "I need to find a heavily subsidized diner, where I cook whatever I want and only let in the people I know will truly enjoy it."

"Wouldn't every chef in the world like that?"

"I don't think so," she said, thoughtfully, as her dark eyes twitched. Remarkably opulent mansions, mostly hidden behind tall hedges, were impossible to ignore as they flew by them. "Every cook has different goals. Mine's always been to work. Leave me the hell alone and let me cook."

"Maybe someday," Emily murmured, snuggling against Blake's cushiony breast. "It's a nice dream."

/

On the following Sunday, Emily spent much of the morning getting ready for their dinner at Le Lapin. And for her afternoon in Blake's bed. She wasn't sure which event she was more excited about, but she was very much looking forward to both. After shaving her legs and carefully touching up the wrinkles in her dress, she decided to do something special with her hair. Whatever she did would be ruined after a roll in the hay, so she packed up some hair care products and put on her jeans and a sweater. It had started to rain, and a real storm was threatening, with black clouds looming over Queens like a vision of the Apocalypse. Right as she hit the front door, her phone chirped. It took a second to find it in her bulging carry-all, but she fished it out to find a text from Blake.

"Problem at restaurant. Call when done."

Damn. She almost took off anyway. Whatever problem had cropped up could probably use another pair of hands. But it was really coming down, and walking to the subway in a downpour sucked. Maybe Blake would finish by the time the skies cleared.

At four, Emily, Chase and Natasha were all in the kitchen, with Natasha and Chase making samosas under Emily's expert direction. "Make sure the oil's hot enough," she warned. "Then put one in at a time so you don't cool it down too much." She looked at her phone when it chirped. "Great. She's still not able to leave. We're going to meet at the restaurant."

"The storm will have passed by then," Natasha said. She looked out of the kitchen window, which, to Emily, showed nothing but trouble. "I bet the sun will be out by five."

She was a remarkably optimistic woman. Emily briefly wondered if she was a recent arrival. The city usually beat all of that cheery worldview out of you if you lived in New York long enough.

Pacing in front of the restaurant, Emily looked up at the patches of blue peeking out from dove gray, fluffy clouds. Natasha hadn't been exactly right, but she hadn't been very wrong, either. Maybe it wasn't a bad idea to assume good things would happen.

A cab pulled up and Blake hopped out, then strode across the wide sidewalk like she owned the place.

Emily purred when Blake's arms wrapped around her and hugged her tightly.

"Sorry I ruined our day," she said.

"You haven't. It's just starting later than we'd planned. What happened, anyway?"

"Drunk kids fighting on the street. One of them threw something and broke the glass in the entry door."

"What time was this?"

"Four a.m. Prime time for rowdy drunks. The security company woke me from such a nice dream." She sighed. "I had to race over there and wait for a guy to show up and cover it with plywood, then wait for another guy to cut the glass and install it. I got to sleep on the floor for an hour or two." She shifted her shoulders like the Tin Man between shots of oil.

"Why not sleep on your sofa?"

"I wouldn't have heard anyone if they'd come in. And believe me, someone would have come in if I hadn't been in plain sight."

They parted and Emily stepped back to check her out. "Nice suit," she said, letting her fingers trail down the lapel of the lightweight, navy blue wool. "It fits you as well as the gray one you wore to the Barstow Awards."

"It should. I had both of them made at the same time."

"Custom made suits," Emily said, smirking. "I should have known."

"My first ones. When I went to Japan last year I had a stopover in Hong Kong. I figured I wouldn't get back there very often, so I dove in." She slid her thumbs under the lapels and fingered the fabric. "They cost about the same as an off-the-rack model here."

"They look much better." She dipped her head toward the door. "Let's ditch dinner and go rock that bed of yours. A sexy woman in a great-fitting suit is a super turn on for me."

"Tempting," Blake said, with her eyes closing slightly, like she was really considering the offer. "But my bed, and my appetite for you will be there after I've gobbled down Laurent's perfect fish." She took Emily's elbow and guided her in as she held the door open. "It's time for you to sit on the other side of the kitchen for a change."

The room looked so darned nice, with subtle mood-lighting, candles and single gerbera daisies in tiny, elegant vases atop each linen-bedecked table. The place was packed, but noise was at a minimum, thanks to the sound-absorbing carpets and richly upholstered banquettes that surrounded the room. The statuesque model who served as hostess immediately led them to a banquette near the back, where Laurent was reviewing a sheaf of papers. As they approached, he looked up and jumped to his feet. "I am so happy you are here," he said, kissing them on both cheeks. "Now I can put this aside and have fun."

"Elodie?" Blake asked as she slid into the booth.

"Manon has a fever," he said, frowning. "I think she has the trick to be ill whenever we try to go out together, but Elodie says babies get sick even if their parents do not want to leave the apartment." He shrugged. "This I cannot prove."

"I'm sorry to hear that," Blake said. "I haven't seen Elodie since Manon's baptism."

"That is our fault. All our fault." He turned to Emily, giving her that sly smile. "I did not know a baby changes everything. Elodie told me, but I did not believe her." He reached for the wine bottle that rested in a chiller next to the table. As soon as his hand got close, a man in a suit sprinted to beat him to the punch. Laurent waved him off, acting like he was entertaining at home. That must have driven the servers crazy! "We used to entertain. I miss the days when we had friends over for brunch on Sunday. Now we eat whatever we can find. Like we're on a camping trip."

"Laurent comes from a long line of fabulous hosts," Blake said, as she tucked her arm around Emily's shoulders. "I've met his parents and his maternal grandparents, and they all love to feed a crowd."

"One day," he said, as he poured Champagne into their glasses, "one day Manon will allow us to have guests. You will come spend the day with us."

"I would love that," Emily said, damned glad simply to be allowed to have dinner at his restaurant.

"I know Blake will come," he said, chuckling. "From that first Christmas, when I took her to my grandmother's house, I learned you could take that sad face and brighten it with a good meal."

"Sad face?" Emily turned to Blake. "Why were you sad?"

Laurent answered when Blake didn't jump on it fast enough. "Because she was without a home," he said, his expression growing dark. "For Christmas, she was going to remain in her barn, fighting the chickens for feed. For one whole week!" he added, outraged. "A child, all alone. Abandoned."

Rolling her eyes, Blake said, "It wasn't like that. And I could have gone home if I'd wanted to. It was just…" She took a sip of her wine. "Excellent," she said, nodding to Laurent. "It was bad timing."

Emily could have kept her mouth shut and acted like she knew what they were talking about, but this seemed important, so she ignored her reticence and tossed a question out there. "Will you fill me in a little? I know almost nothing about that time in your life."

"When she was thrown from her home?" Laurent said, his voice getting louder.

"I wasn't *thrown*. I wanted to leave."

"I believed that in Nice. Now that I've been in America for ten years, I know people don't let their children leave home when they're so young. I don't care what Manon wants to do, she will remain with us until she's an adult."

Emily searched Blake's face for clues. While she didn't look upset, she certainly wasn't offering up any details. This wasn't the right setting for probing questions, but Emily was about to ask one anyway when Blake said, "Everything worked out for the best. If I'd stayed in Connecticut, I might be working at a big insurance company now. And no one would want that, most of all me."

Instead of ordering from the menu, Laurent asked for what he wanted, and their server ran to the kitchen to get it. After sharing some fantastically briny oysters that Emily could actually taste to a surprising extent, they nibbled on a seafood terrine that she couldn't. Then Laurent looked at his watch and rose. After leaning over to kiss them each again, he said, "I promised I would be no more than an hour. My time is up." Their server dashed back over. "My guests will order now," he said. "Treat them well and make sure their glasses are never empty."

"Yes, Chef," the young man said, so earnest it was comical.

"Thank you so much for inviting us," Emily said. "We've had a lovely time."

"It has been my pleasure." He caught Blake's eye. "It also gives me pleasure to see my friend so happy. It is time she found someone to love." He lifted Emily's hand and kissed it, then strolled toward the kitchen.

Emily was frozen in place. They were a long way from making that kind of commitment. Getting Blake to agree to call once in a while had been a big enough hurdle.

"He's funny, isn't he?" Blake asked as she leaned over and placed a gentle kiss on Emily's cheek. "He always makes it sound like I was an abandoned baby."

Their server appeared and asked for their choices. Emily hadn't even looked at the menu, but Blake obviously had. She rattled off their selections, choosing for both of them. As the server left, she said, "You don't mind, do you? I made sure to pick things with crunch and texture and as much spice as I could find."

"I don't mind a bit. But you should make sure you get what you like. You've got a working nose."

"I like everything on the menu. If Laurent serves it, it's good."

Their wine glasses were replenished, leaving them a few minutes of privacy. "Do you want to talk about leaving home?" Emily asked, reaching under the table to grasp Blake's hand. "I feel like I'm missing a pretty big piece of the puzzle."

"It's not a puzzle. I told you this already. I had some trouble at school and my grandmother found a way to help me get my training sooner than I'd planned."

"Uh-huh." Blake didn't look uncomfortable or even unwilling to talk about it. It was more like she didn't think it was a big deal. "Do you want to drop this?"

Blake sipped at her wine for a second, then placed her glass down at the proper spot, right atop the knife. "It wasn't a good time for me, Emily, but that's not a secret." Her lips pursed briefly, then she said, "I was involved with a teacher at my high school."

"Oh, shit," Emily whispered, truly shocked.

"Yeah," she said, tersely. "She was only seven years older than I was, but…"

"You were caught?"

"Kind of." She blew out a breath. "It was bad."

"It should have been bad for her, not you." She stopped. "It was a woman, right?"

"Uh-huh. The first person I ever kissed. When I look back on it, I think she was struggling to figure herself out, just like I was."

"You don't experiment with kids," Emily said, her anger growing by the second.

"I know. But she seemed like a peer. It wasn't abusive," she said, her eyes dark and intent. "Not in the least."

"Yes, it was," Emily said, not a doubt in her mind even though she didn't know the details.

Shrugging, Blake said, "My parents got involved, obviously, and the police. It was a huge mess."

"Did she go to jail?"

She shook her head quickly, then took another sip of her wine. "No. She gave up her teaching license, and pled guilty to a lesser charge."

"She should have gone to jail," Emily said, seething.

"Well, she didn't. But I felt like *I* was in jail. The whole school, the whole town knew about it." She let out a heavy sigh. "My parents were going to move me to a private school, but I wouldn't hear of it. Then my grandmother came to my rescue, found me a place in France, and I took off."

"Why not go home for Christmas?"

"Mmm." Now looking uncomfortable, she drank a little more wine, taking longer to answer. "I'd lost my parents' trust. We…agreed we needed a break."

Squeezing her hand, Emily said fiercely, "You didn't do anything wrong. You were still a child."

Blake's eyes had a certain fire to them when she leveled her gaze at Emily. "I knew better. Even a fifteen-year-old knows you shouldn't fool around with a teacher. But I was curious and she was… I'm not sure what she was, but I think she was frightened by her interest. We both knew we were taking a risk, but it's hard to control yourself when your hormones are in charge."

Emily tucked an arm around her and tried to pull her over for a hug, but Blake wasn't very pliant. It seemed to annoy her to receive sympathy for something she obviously didn't consider a violation. "I'm so sorry you got caught up in all of that, Chef. If you ask me, your teacher should have cooled her heels in jail for a good long time."

"She didn't have to pressure me. At all. I was *very* willing."

"You weren't old enough to give consent. Period." She brought Blake's hand to her lips and kissed it gently. "But I'm glad you don't feel like she used you."

"I don't. It messed me up a little, but once I figured out my sexuality, I let it go."

Emily gazed into her dark eyes, seeing tiny storm clouds in their depths. Blake might have gotten over her ill-advised fling. But the wound her parents inflicted was still open. Emily would have bet the farm on that.

They stood outside the restaurant, bellies full of great food and wine. Blake's hands were on Emily's shoulders, a teasing smile on her lovely lips. "What do I have to do to convince you to come to my apartment?"

"Mmm…" Emily thought for a minute. "You have to find a store that's open at nine in the morning, where I can buy something to wear to work. I can't go in this, and I don't want to have to go to Queens and then get back to the city. I work normal hours now, you know."

"I'll come to your place." Blake stopped for a second, then said, "If you want me to."

"You don't mind?"

"I don't mind the trip," she said, lips pursed. "My only issue is having sex when other people can hear." A lopsided grin showed. "I had enough of that when I was a kid. I was forced to be an exhibitionist, and that's not my thing."

Emily spent a moment looking into her eyes. There was definite desire there, but also some unspoken longing. "I'll come to your place. Then I'll take a car home later."

"Tonight?" Her head cocked, clearly confused.

"Yeah. No good?"

She shrugged, obviously unhappy. "That's okay if you need to get home. But…" Letting out a heavy breath, she spoke quickly, like she was in a hurry to get the words out. "I'd like to sleep with you, Emily. Sex is great, but it's not enough any more."

"Really? We've never slept together for a whole night. I didn't think you liked to..."

Blake took both of her hands and pulled them to her chest, with her eyes locked onto Emily's. "We're not just having sex, right? We're trying to have more than that." She bent and gave her a brief kiss, but there was a spark of feeling in it that belied its brevity. "I want to be in a whatever we're in, and to me that's more than sex. We need time to be close, even if we're only sleeping."

A burst of emotion filled Emily's chest. Being close wasn't something Blake had much experience with, but like everything she did, she jumped in and tried to do it right. "Damn, it's nice to be with someone who says what she needs. Let's grab a cab, Chef." Emily took her hand and led her to the corner. "I'll find something in your closet to tide me over until I put my whites on in the morning. We've got a full agenda tonight. Sex, snuggling and sleep."

Blake used the bathroom first, her electric toothbrush humming softly through the door. Given how earthy she was about almost everything, Emily found it a little surprising she seemed to need privacy for something as simple as dental care. When she came out, she wore only a smile, one that grew as she got closer. "How much time did I spend telling you how fantastic you look?" she asked as she stood next to Emily and slipped her arms around her waist.

"Not a lot, to be honest. You were distracted." She stretched to reach Blake's pink, minty lips. "But I can see how you feel by the way you look at me."

"No," she said, briskly. "That won't cut it. I want to make sure you know I appreciate how much time you spent looking extra good tonight." She put her lips to Emily's neck and kissed from the tip of her ear to the curve of her shoulder. "You were made to wear dresses. Strapless ones. When you took off your jacket, I wanted to throw it away so you couldn't put it back on." She took in a deep breath, clearly filled with longing. "Your shoulders are so beautiful."

"Yours are," Emily said as she ran her hands over them. "They're just about my favorite part of you."

"We both have them," she teased. "We can like the same part."

Emily grasped her by those pretty shoulders and delivered a long, soft kiss. "Why don't you get your bed set up? I'll go brush my teeth."

Blake didn't move. "Let me undress you," she said, her voice taking on that smoky, sexy timbre that always made Emily shiver with anticipation.

Slowly, Blake lowered the zipper, with her fingers tickling down Emily's back as it descended. As the dress pooled on the floor, Blake's interest settled on Emily's strapless bra. As her neck was delicately kissed, questing fingers teased across skin barely covered by fabric. When the fastener was released, Emily briefly wished for the days when women wore several layers of undergarments. It would have been so hot to have Blake unwrap her like a gift. But when Blake's fingers slid into her bikinis and eased them off, she decided it was nice to get right to the good stuff. Blake's tongue circled the dip between her collarbones as warm hands cupped and squeezed her ass.

"My teeth are not going to get brushed if you keep that up," she murmured, eyes closed, swaying when Blake pressed into her.

"Good. I can taste the passionfruit on your lips. It's like I'm still eating dessert." With one foot, she pushed the coffee table out of the way, while a hand pressed against the wall, releasing the catch for the bed. Blake had to let Emily go to lower the bed quietly, but as soon as it touched the floor they were lying on it.

"This is exactly where I wanted to be this afternoon," Blake murmured, hovering over Emily to voraciously kiss her ears, her neck, her throat, her shoulders. "We need this."

Emily pulled her onto her body, holding her tightly as they kissed, again and again. Blake was absolutely right. Now that they were building something together, they needed connection, touch, and time. She shivered at the depth of care she felt when she lay in Blake's arms. It filled the place in her heart that had been empty for far too long.

After a long, luxurious investigation of every hidden and not so hidden part of each other, Blake lay on her side, a fiendish grin on her face. “I think I’ve worn you out.” She ran a fingertip all around Emily’s lips, now swollen and hot.

“Possibly.” She turned and lay face down on the bed, stretching out her neck.

“Does this hurt?” Blake asked as her hand went to the stiff muscles.

“A little. I must have been in a funny position while I was making you squeal.”

Chuckling, she moved to sit astride Emily’s hips, then leaned over to firmly massage the tension away. “I did squeal, didn’t I? Good thing I don’t know my neighbors. I won’t blush when I see them in the elevator.”

“You seem like you’re still raring to go,” Emily murmured into the pillow. “Need a little more?”

Blake leaned over and took a nip out of Emily’s ear. “Need a lot more. But if you’re too tired…” She rolled off and took Emily’s hand, bringing it to her mouth for some kisses. “I can wait a week.”

With a grunt, Emily rolled onto her side, then held her head up with a hand. “Do you? Wait a week, I mean. I picture you with a devastatingly sexy look on your face, making love to yourself—porn style—every night.”

“I’m not sure what porn style is,” she said, laughing, “but your fantasy’s not accurate. I’m certainly not antagonistic to touching myself, but I don’t do it very often. Actually,” she said, looking thoughtful, “it’s pretty rare. It’s been weeks…” A sly smile lit her face. “I think you were in Las Vegas the last time I had the urge. I couldn’t pounce on you, so I had to pounce on myself.”

“Fascinating,” Emily said, gazing at her in the dim light. “You seem to need a lot of sex.”

“I guess I do, but I prefer sex with a partner. I’m more visual and tactile than I am…what? Imaginational?”

“That works.” Emily scooted closer and started to touch Blake’s back and side. “If I looked like you, I’d just tilt my chin to get hot. Looking down at my fantastic breasts would get me off.”

"You're so silly." Blake tucked an arm around her and pulled her close. "That's how I feel when I look at you. In just a second, I'm ready to go."

"I think you're always ready to go." Her hand slipped down and started to squeeze Blake's ass. "Let me watch you touch yourself," she whispered.

Clearly not needing much convincing, Blake raised her knee and planted her foot onto the bed. "Happy to." She let out a growl when Emily began to kiss her, while still squeezing her ass with both hands. Emily was too busy to actually watch, but it thrilled her to the core to feel Blake's breathing increase as her body got warmer and warmer. It took just a few minutes until Blake broke their kiss and let her head drop back. Her mouth opened as she sucked in a deep breath, then let it out as her whole body shivered, then stilled. "I'm good at that," she said, a soft laugh bubbling up. "Very efficient."

"You're fantastic. But now *I* need another turn." Emily slipped her hand between her legs to mimic Blake. "Touch me anywhere. Anywhere at all."

Eyes bright, Blake shrugged off her lethargy to slide her fingers inside, then, when they were slick, they slid lower to circle and tease. "Is this included in 'anywhere'?" she asked, watching Emily intently.

"Maybe…" She breathed in, concentrating on the sensation, testing it out. Blake was so intent it was a little disconcerting, but after a minute Emily relaxed into it and said, "Leave it to you to turn something I usually don't like into something I could probably really get into."

"If you're not into it, I'll stop." Those big brown eyes blinked slowly and Emily could see her swallow. "I have this need…" Looking strangely embarrassed, she continued, "I need to know every inch of you. If there's a way to give you pleasure, I want to do it."

Emily gazed into that beautiful, earnest face for a second. "Do you think you could keep that up while you kiss me? Nothing makes me happier than kissing you."

Her smile was so sweet Emily almost cried. Sometimes Blake looked a little cocky in bed, but tonight she was deadly serious. She probably didn't know that by revealing a little bit of her soul, she was giving Emily far more pleasure than any physical sensation ever could.

It was after midnight when Emily finally got to brush her teeth. She emerged from the bathroom and stood by the drawers where Blake kept her clothes. "Can I get something to wear in the morning? I'd never live it down if I walked into work in a strapless dress. That's the major league walk of shame."

"Sure. T-shirts and fleece in the middle drawer, tights, sweats, and shorts in the bottom."

"Shit!" Emily slapped herself in the forehead. "I only have heels! I can't wear a T-shirt, sweats and heels to work!"

"What size shoe do you wear?"

"Eight."

"I'm a nine," Blake said, frowning. "Wear a pair of my running shoes and lace them up real tight."

"I'm going to look like a friggin' clown," she complained, picking through Blake's clothes to find something that might fit. Taking a thin fleece top and a pair of sweats out, she also grabbed two pair of socks. "I don't know why I care. Many of the guys look like they've slept in their clothes." She laid everything out so she could sleep a little later, then climbed back into bed.

"I'm sorry I talked you into this," Blake said, a pout turning down the corners of her mouth.

"I'm not." Emily wrapped her in a tender hug and nuzzled all around her neck and shoulders. "I'm charged about sleeping with you." She moved away a bit and smoothed the curls from Blake's face. "Why have we never done this before?"

"Truth?"

"Uhm…sure. As long as it's not because you didn't like me enough to be with me all night."

"Yeah, that's it," Blake said, then she laughed. "No, Emily. Besides never having the opportunity, I've been told I'm horrible to sleep with. I take up the whole bed, and I sleep really deeply. A simple nudge won't get me to move."

Emily grasped her pillow and whacked Blake with it. "Now you tell me! I could be home now, looking forward to wearing shoes that fit."

Blake grabbed the pillow and tucked it under her arm. "I hope we're close enough that my subconscious realizes you're here. I need to train it."

"That'll be our fall project. Learn how to sleep well with others."

"Not others. Just you." Blake delivered a tender kiss. "You're all I need." She returned the pillow to its proper place, then scooted closer, so they were face to face. "Since we've never intentionally slept together, we need to figure out the ground rules. How do you like to start out?"

"We took a nap that day we met on the street." Emily let out a chuckle. "You took up the whole bed. And we've napped other times. You took up the whole bed," she repeated, smiling at Blake's troubled expression.

"I don't want to," she said earnestly. "I start out on my side, like a normal person, but I wake up right in the center, usually face down, with my arms and legs all spread out. I've been told I look like I've been shot in the back while fleeing the scene of a crime."

"Then let's start on your side of the bed. You'll have to work to push me aside."

Blake rolled over, hugging the edge. Then Emily scooted up behind her and tucked a protective arm around her waist. "How's this?"

"Really nice." She sighed as she took Emily's hand and pressed it to her breast. "I like being cuddled."

"Then we'll figure out a way to make this work. I'm determined to give you exactly what you need in this whatever it is we have."

"Thanks for coming over," Blake said, a yawn making her hard to understand. "I'm going to make a note on my calendar so I remember this. Tonight I slept with Emily Desjardins."

"I'll make one too." Emily tilted her chin to reach Blake's neck and place a kiss there. "I hope my note doesn't end with, 'Never again.'"

Emily's phone buzzed at eight, and she reached under her pillow to turn it off. Her brain slowly caught up with the sensations that surrounded her, most of those sensations consisting of Blake's body. Emily was lying on her side, with a warm face pressed between her shoulder blades, a heavy, limp arm draped across her body, and a thigh wedged between her own. Unconsciously, Blake had been trying to do her norm and take over the whole space. But Emily remained centered on her half of the bed, and was quiet sure she hadn't woken during the night. Not bad for one night's practice. Not bad at all.

CHAPTER NINETEEN

FOR FOUR BLISSFUL WEEKS in a row they spent Sundays together. Now that Emily had an earlier schedule, she was up by nine. But Blake had to rally to pry herself out of bed by noon. As the weeks ticked by, it started to seem like they weren't squeezing all of the juice from the orange. One Saturday afternoon in late October, Emily considered her options, then took the offensive and texted. "Want to have a sleep-over tonite?" If Blake was into it, they could work out the details.

The phone buzzed an hour later with a reply text. "Great idea! I'll call doorman. He'll give you keys."

Typical Blake. It was great being with someone who usually said what she wanted, but Blake didn't have a problem in the world with proposing her ideal solution to every issue. And those ideal solutions usually involved Emily traipsing over to TriBeCa. Not that she blamed her. Blake's apartment was nicer, quieter and had far fewer roommates.

It was strange going to Blake's apartment alone. Emily shifted a bag of groceries onto her hip and got the lock open. Entering, she switched on the light to find the place messy—for Blake. Her bed was unmade and still lying open, the toaster out on the counter instead of nestled in its cabinet. After dropping the bag onto the counter, Emily spent ten minutes neatening up. Having a small place meant anything out of order stuck out, but it also meant it only took a few minutes to put it all back where it belonged.

Even though she'd snooped in Blake's medicine cabinet the first time she'd visited, she wasn't tempted to poke around now. They'd become too close for that, which seemed strange, but also logical. Now that she was getting to know her, she could ask Blake almost anything. There wasn't any need to try to figure things out for herself.

Still, she'd never been in the apartment alone, and she found herself looking at things on the bookcases that bracketed the Murphy bed. For someone who hadn't graduated from high school, Blake had some difficult books on her shelves, including quite a few in French. That didn't necessarily mean she'd read them, but she wasn't the kind of person to put things out to impress other people. On the floor by the bed were several travel books, but not the kind for people planning a trip. These were memoirs by people who'd traveled extensively and written about their impressions of both people and place. The one on top was open, and Emily picked it up to find a sticky note near a passage recounting a fall afternoon spent eating a lamb, fig and olive stew after a long hike. A fond smile curled her lips at the thought of Blake reading before she fell asleep, unable to resist making a note about a recipe that probably reminded her of her years in France. If she had to bet, that stew would be on the menu soon, with something special to make it Blake's own.

Scanning across the shelves, an object made tears come to her eyes. There was a framed photo of a very young Blake, probably at her first job in Nice. She was wearing a short-sleeved, ill-fitting chef's jacket, and a bistro-style white apron around her hips. Her arm was around an older woman's waist, and they both smiled broadly for the camera. In the background, Emily could make out a tall, rough-hewn stone building, probably the barn where Blake slept. This must have been her grandmother, delivering her to her dream—or maybe just getting her away from home. Either way, Blake looked thrilled, and that's what mattered. She was a true survivor, someone who could take a bad circumstance and make it work. One of the many traits Emily respected about her.

A half hour later, Blake's key slid into the lock, and Emily called out, "Welcome home!"

When Blake turned the corner, her smile almost made Emily's knees give out.

"I'm always happy to leave work on Saturday, but tonight…" She closed her eyes, lifted her chin and sniffed. "Knowing you were here made me grab a cab, just to be home five minutes sooner." Her smile grew even wider. "If I'd known you were going to cook for me…" She moved around the counter and took Emily into her arms. "I might have skipped out while the dining room was still full. You're hurting my concentration." She bent to kiss her, slowly and tenderly. As her head lifted, Emily saw the sparkle grow in her eyes, and was almost able to see the fatigue leave her body. "And I don't mind a bit."

Emily put her hands on Blake's shoulders and let them slowly trail down her arms. "I know how beat you are on Saturday night, and I thought it would cheer you up to have some decent food waiting for you. You're hungry, right?"

"Very." She finally put her carry-all down, then slipped out of her jacket. "I got involved in something and didn't get a bite of the family meal."

"This isn't anything special. Just a croque madame. I know how you love a good egg, so when I saw fresh ones at the farmer's market in Astoria, I knew what I'd make for you."

"My mouth's watering. I can't imagine who wouldn't want the world's best grilled ham and cheese." She poked at the yolk with her finger. "Almost ready."

Emily took her by the arm and turned her. "You're off duty. Go wash your hands. It'll be ready in one minute. Exactly."

"Ahh… Why have I wasted my time with doctors and bartenders? A woman who can cook is the key to happiness."

When Blake returned, she took a long look at the beautifully plated dish and put her hands on Emily's hips. "I made a change when you were gone, but you haven't noticed."

Emily looked at her carefully, detecting nothing different. "Can I see it?"

"No. Well, yes." Her face scrunched up in thought. "You might notice its absence."

"I don't have any idea…"

"Here's a clue. If I ask for a kiss, give it to me."

Smiling, Emily asked, "Why would I ever refuse?"

"I don't know, but don't start." She sat at the counter and dug in, moaning with delight at her first bite. "As soon as I finish this, I'm going to need a kiss."

Emily grasped her ear and tugged on it. "What are you talking about?"

"I gave up my gum. I'm doing okay, but I crave a cigarette after I eat something I really like." She put another bite to her mouth. "And I really, really like this. Thank you for making it, Emily."

After throwing her arms around her, Emily gave her a big hug. "I'm proud of you. I've never smoked, but I can see how people struggle with quitting."

"I smoked for five years, and I've been chewing the damn gum for eight. I've *got* to stop."

Emily pulled her over and gave her a big kiss. "Anytime you need another, just ask."

Emily spent Sunday morning working on ideas for special first courses. Daniel, Laurent's chef de cuisine, certainly didn't need her to come up with so many of them, but when she had the time it was fun letting her imagination soar. And given how Blake was splayed out across the bed, completely inert, it was going to be a while before they got going.

Light filled the apartment, and she got up and closed the shades, trying to make the room perfect for sleeping. As much as she wanted Blake to get up and play with her, she needed her rest, and this was the only day she wasn't a slave to the alarm. Emily's phone vibrated on the table, and she picked it up to see a text from Charlotte. "Time to talk?"

Emily took the phone and tiptoed across the room to hide in the bathroom. A half hour later, Blake stumbled in, stopped in the doorway and blinked in confusion. Emily was sitting on the closed toilet, fully clothed. "Talking to my sister," she said, placing a kiss on Blake's cheek as she exited to give her some privacy.

Going back into the living room, she and Charlotte continued to chat until Blake emerged from the shower, clad in just a towel. Emily took a look at her still sleepy grin and said, "I've got to take off Charlotte. I think someone needs breakfast."

After they said their goodbyes, Emily got up and wrapped her arms around Blake's warm body, enjoying the damp heat that flowed off her. "What can I cook for you?"

She snuggled close for a few minutes, not speaking. It took her a while to fully wake up, even after her shower, but she finally pulled away. "Have you eaten?"

"Uh-huh. But I'm happy to make you something. I bought a few things."

A slow, sexy smile settled on Blake's lips. "I think we should go back to bed for a while. We can eat later."

"Not today. Get dressed while I make your breakfast." Emily turned her and gave her a swat on the seat. "We're going to go outside and get some sun. It's a lovely day and we might not get many more."

Grumbling to herself, Blake went to pull some clean clothes out of her drawers. "It'll be nice later, too. Give me an hour, and I promise to make your day."

Emily's hand stilled on the door to the refrigerator. Then she moved over to stand behind Blake and murmur into her ear. "If you'd rather have sex now, you won't have to work too hard to convince me."

Blake turned, showing a playful smile. "I'm just messing with you. Being outside's a good idea." She took Emily in her arms and gazed at her for a few moments. "But don't think you're getting on the E train before we spend some quality time in that bed."

"Wouldn't dream of it, Chef. That's my favorite time of the week."

They took the C train up to Central Park, their first subway ride, as well as their first trip to anything other than restaurants. Crossing the street at Seventy-Second, they dodged the young men vying for passengers on their bicycle/rickshaws, then walked across a small bridge with a canopy covered with now bare wisteria vines.

Emily took Blake's hand, but soon an arm was draped across her shoulders, holding her close. "I love living here," Emily said, looking over at Blake's contented smile.

"Is this where you want to live? I assume most people are here for the opportunity, not because they like it."

"Oh, no. I like it." She hooked a thumb into Blake's back pocket. "There aren't many places in the country where we can walk like this and not get a second glance."

She stopped and looked at Emily for a second, her head cocked quizzically. "I guess I never think of that."

"You don't?" They started to walk again, having no place in particular in mind. "That's because you've never lived in a less tolerant place."

"Maybe. But it's also because I've never had a whatever it is we have."

Emily bumped her with her hip. "You're a funny one. You've never done this, yet you touch me and kiss me and show anyone who might notice that you're perfectly comfortable being gay."

"I am," she said, a charming grin showing. "Perfectly. If people don't like it, they can kiss my butt."

"That's reserved for me," Emily reminded her. "We're exclusive, remember? At least when we're in New York."

When Blake looked at her, her gaze quickly filled with amused affection. "I do remember. And I'm really glad we are."

They were near the lake, with dozens of row boats skimming across the surface. The trees surrounding the water had just started to turn colors, some of their leaves tinged with orange and yellow, with a rare red one providing an unexpected treat.

"I've always wanted to rent a boat, but it seems like a lot of work," Emily reflected.

"It's a snap." Blake's confident demeanor came to the fore. "And if you haven't done it before, today's the day."

Emily pulled her down and placed a long, sweet kiss on her lips. "Only if you drive."

"My pleasure," she said, dark eyes twinkling.

Spending the whole day with someone you were starting to care about deeply was just plain awesome. Emily sat in the boat, facing Blake, who looked about as good as a woman could look. A red

Henley-style shirt, with the sleeves pushed up to expose her forearms highlighted her broad shoulders. Each long, smooth stroke of the oars had her leaning in toward Emily, pursing her lips for a kiss when she exaggerated the pull. "Don't take this the wrong way, but I'm awfully glad you didn't want to have sex this morning."

"How could I take that the wrong way?" Emily reached out and tugged the bill of a dark blue ball cap down, covering Blake's eyes.

She whipped it off and resettled it, after carefully making sure her hair was swept away from her forehead. "You know what I mean. It's good for me to be outside. It helps my mood."

"Mine too. I feel like I've missed a day off if I just lie around and nap on Sunday."

"That's it," she nodded. "When I was a kid, I was outside all the time. I get nature deprived when I only go to work and come home."

Emily's phone rang and she pulled it from her pocket. "It's my mom. Do you mind?"

"No, of course not."

After pushing the button, Emily held the phone to her ear. "Hey, Mom. What's going on?"

"Not a lot, honey. I just wanted to see how you're doing. Are you busy?"

"Uh-huh." She smiled at Blake, who'd really picked up the pace, blowing past boats full of kids who'd obviously never been in a row boat before. Even when she was doing something simple, she liked to do it all-out. "Blake and I are in a rowboat in Central Park. I have an absolutely gorgeous view." She took in the big plaza, filled with people, the magnificent statue representing the water that flowed into New York from upstate, the terraced stone steps and graceful arches that formed the plaza. "Not to mention my captain, the prettiest woman around. I'm having a great day."

"Then get back to it. Call me when you have a free minute."

"I'm working until about six tomorrow. Will you be home?"

"Uh-huh. I'm free all night. Say hi to Blake for me, okay?"

"I will, Mom. Give Dad my love."

"Bye, honey. Talk to you soon."

Emily took a photo of a grinning Blake, then shakily moved to her side to sit next to her and take a selfie. "For my mom," she said as she tottered back to her own seat and sent the photo. "The best way to show her how I'm doing is to send photos. I must be unable to fake a smile, since every one I sent after my accident had her calling to check on me." She looked at the photo fondly. "She's gonna like this one."

"They should come visit before it gets too cold," Blake said. "It'd be fun to hang out with them."

She thought about that for a second, then said, "It's a stretch for them. Hotel rooms are so expensive, not to mention how much it costs to eat. My mom wouldn't think of visiting without going to some nice restaurants, so it all adds up."

"When's the last time they visited?"

"Together? Last year. Not long before you and I started to work together."

A thoughtful expression settled onto Blake's face then she said, "Your parents can stay at my apartment and I'll stay with you. That'll help, right?"

"Really?" She was stunned. Absolutely stunned. "That's so generous of you."

"I like them." She turned her head to pass a particularly slow guy who was trying to impress his date with his technique, which was abysmal. "I wish I had more of a relationship with my family." Shrugging, she said, "I'm envious." The sun was starting its descent, with the golden light streaming through the waves that peeked out from the sides of Blake's cap. Emily was taken by it, and the wistful expression on her sweet face.

"Is your relationship tense?"

"Not much. Not now, at least. But when you leave home early and never live with your family again, it's easy to move apart and stay there."

"They're proud of you, right? You've accomplished so much."

"Doubtful." Her shoulder rose and fell as she used one oar to sweep around in a half-circle. "They wanted more for me. I was a good student, and could have easily gotten to swim for a top university. That's the path they thought I was on, and jumping off of it really disappointed them."

"That was never your path?" Emily asked gently.

"Once I learned about cooking school, I was just marking time until I could apply. Not finishing high school was a blow, but we would have had the same argument two years later."

"But you're not someone who dropped out and sat on the curb hustling for change. You're a big deal!"

"Not really. In my parents' world, there isn't any difference between a chef and a mechanic. Not that there should be." Her smile bore traces of sadness. "We're all tradespeople, not very high on the status scale."

"You're an artist," Emily said firmly. "And I'm *very* proud of you."

"I…uhm…don't want to screw things up by mentioning this, but…" A playful twinkle shone in her eyes. "Have we become girlfriends? I think we might be."

"I think that's a definite possibility," Emily agreed, her heart swelling in her chest at the look Blake was giving her. She looked not only happy, but excited about the change. "Who's going to screw it up first?"

Blake let out a hearty laugh. "Not me. I'm determined to prove that two cooks can actually have a relationship."

"I'd like to prove that too." She reached out and put her hand on Blake's knee. "So this is good? We're not moving too fast?"

"It's been ten months since we first had sex, Emily. Taking ten months to admit we're into each other isn't exactly warp speed."

Giving her a long, careful look, Emily said, "It is if it feels too fast for you. That's all that matters."

"I'm right where I want to be. With you. Only you."

Emily scooted across the boat on her knees, making it pitch more than was wise. But Blake just sat there and watched, a happy grin on her face. When their heads were almost touching, Emily put her hands on Blake's face and held it tenderly, placing soft, sweet kisses on her lips. She felt Blake inhale sharply, and when she pulled away she touched her lips with a finger, committing them to memory. "You were smelling me, weren't you."

"Uh-huh. It makes the kisses better." Her smile faded in an instant. "If I could give you back your sense of smell, I'd…I'd do anything. I'd even give you up, just to make you whole again. If you hadn't been going to my restaurant that day, you'd be fine. If we'd never met…" For the first time since she'd known her, tears formed in those beautiful eyes. Emily's heart skipped a beat, touched by the empathy she could feel pouring from Blake.

"Don't feel that way, Chef. That's not how fate works."

"I know but…" She bit at her lip, obviously trying to control her emotions. "Some people would hardly notice if they lost the ability to smell and taste. But it meant so much to you. Like a painter losing his sight," she said, her voice growing even softer. "I know what you've lost."

"You truly understand," Emily whispered, burying her head into Blake's chest as she wrapped her arms around her. "More than anyone, you understand. That means so much."

"You mean so much to me," Blake murmured, tilting her chin to place soft kisses on Emily's head. "I swear I'd do anything to give you back what you've lost."

Sighing, Emily scooted back to perch on her seat. The tenderness between them bubbled up inside her, almost making her cry. They were in a little boat on a crowded lake, but everyone else had faded away. Only Blake filled her vision. "I can ride in a nearly empty subway car now. That's a plus."

"I suppose I should know what you mean by that. But you know I don't," she said. "I'm not much of a New Yorker."

"The other day, a guy had all of his belongings in a cart, and he was wearing all of his clothes, layer upon layer. The stench must have been horrible, since people stepped on, then jumped back off, looking like they were going to hurl. I just sat there and smiled. I actually spread out and enjoyed the luxury of having the whole section to myself. I called it the Anosmia Express."

Blake touched her cheek while gazing into her eyes. "I know you don't like to dwell on it, but whenever you want to bitch, I'm here for you."

"I know," she said, grinning. "You *have* to listen to me now because you're my girlfriend."

On a surprisingly warm, blissfully sunny Sunday in November, Emily sat in her idling sub-compact rental car, waiting for Blake to emerge from her building. Right on time, she slipped out the door when the doorman held it for her. Clad in her perfectly fitted silvery suit, her head swiveled from left to right, then settled on Emily. Blake wasn't the type to be very histrionic, so instead of a hearty wave she simply smiled when Emily flashed her brights.

"I was hoping for a limo, but I guess this will get us up to Connecticut," she said as she slid into the tiny car.

"You look delicious, as usual," Emily said, giving her a once-over. "How many suits do you have?"

"Just two." She plucked at the knit of a very thin sweater she wore under her jacket. It was mostly silver, with an abstract white design incorporated into it. It made the suit a little dressier, but she retained the androgyny Emily loved. "Now you've seen my whole wardrobe." Blake's hand rose to grasp the fringe on the silk shawl Emily had draped around her shoulders. "I like this new addition."

"If I'm going to wear a summer dress in November I've either got to have a dressy coat or a shawl. Luckily, Natasha came to bat for me."

"Nice. I'm glad you didn't buy a new dress. I'll never tire of this one."

"I thought about it," she said, "but you would have figured out I'd done it just to impress you and…" She turned and stuck her tongue out. "You're already full of yourself."

"You're not the first to mention that." She fidgeted while trying to get her seat belt buckled. "I feel a little like we're in a clown car."

"It's tiny, but still stupid expensive. And it was the last one they had. If I hadn't reserved this the day after you invited me, we'd be taking the train."

The hand on her leg pressed into her flesh. When Emily turned her head, Blake was gazing at her intently. "I'm awfully glad you're coming with me. I don't think I could have gotten out of this, but I probably would have tried if I'd had to go alone."

Even though she was trying to get down a street clogged with double-parked cars and delivery guys on bikes, Emily spared as much of her attention as she could, trying to see what was going on behind those dark eyes. Blake looked a little nervous, or maybe agitated. Her temper wasn't flaring like it had the time her parents had come to the restaurant, but she put out the same kind of nervous energy she had that night.

"I don't know how your family works, but there wouldn't be an excuse big enough for me to skip my grandparents' sixtieth wedding anniversary." She reached down and patted Blake's leg. "Not that I'd want to. We don't throw a lot of parties, but they're always fun."

Blake was looking straight ahead, a sober expression on her handsome face. "We have more than I'd like, and they rarely are." When she turned, Emily could see a glimmer of a hopeful look. "Maybe you'll bring us luck."

Emily had to concentrate to weave her way over to the West Side Highway. Blake started to play with the radio, settling on a classical station. "This sucks," Emily heard her mutter under her breath.

"You don't like symphonies?"

"Not much, but I can't stand pop, so I don't have much to choose from. Commercial radio in New York sucks hard."

"You could sing to me," Emily said, sparing a quick look.

"I'll start after a drink or two. You'll beg me to stop," she added, chuckling.

Emily listened to the string section for a few minutes, finding she wouldn't have minded something a little more current herself. "I guess I don't have to ask if you're close to your grandparents, huh?"

"You can ask…"

"Okay. Are you close?"

"Not too. They spend more time with my mom's brother and sister." She shrugged. "They all live in New York, near the river, like Ossining or Croton-on-Hudson."

"Why have the party in Connecticut?"

Blake shrugged, something she did an awful lot when she talked about her family. "My mom likes to host parties." Another shrug. "I guess my dad doesn't mind paying for them."

"I'm a little nervous," Emily said. "It's been a long time since I've had to meet a woman's family—all at once."

"Yeah." She hooked her hands around a knee and stretched. "I can't promise much, to be honest. I guarantee it will be decorated nicely, and that the food will be as good as a big caterer can manage..." She let out a long breath. "As for fun? That's anyone's guess." After another second, she added, "I wouldn't count on it."

Blake hadn't specifically said where they were heading, so Emily was a little surprised when she guided her to a long, manicured drive that led to a series of stately yellow brick buildings. "If this is your parents' house..."

Having grown less talkative as they got closer, Blake let out a very brief laugh. "Their club. I almost had to look it up to remember how to get here. It's been years," she said, her voice almost a whisper.

Emily pulled up to a covered portico, where a gaggle of young men dashed from car to car to valet park them. Her rental cost about thirty thousand less than any other car in sight, but the clubhouse was so damned impressive she hardly noticed how their rental stuck out from all of the luxury cars.

Before she could speak, a guy had his hand on the door handle, then another guy flew to Blake's side to open both doors simultaneously. "Good afternoon, ladies," the guy at her door said. "How can I direct you today?"

Blake spoke up, simply saying, "Chadwick."

"Great. The Chadwick event is in the clubhouse. You'll see signs as soon as you enter." He handed Emily a slip of paper. "Just hand that to the attendant when you're ready to leave." He reached down and took her hand to help her exit. "Have a great time, ma'am."

"Thanks. We will." Then Blake's hand was on her elbow, guiding her not to the big building next to them, but around the side.

"Excuse me. Ma'am?" the kid called as he sprinted for them. "The clubhouse is behind you."

"I know," she said, turning to give him a polite smile. "I wanted to take a look at the pool. I haven't seen it in years."

"All right," he said, clearly not used to people taking off on their own. "Are you sure you know your way around?"

"With my eyes closed," she said, then started to walk again. As they moved away, she grumbled, "He'll probably report us to security. They don't like people going off-script."

They walked a short distance, coming up to a huge pool. "Holy crap," Emily gasped. "This is as nice as the one we had at Michigan, and that was for forty thousand students."

"It's pretty sweet. They tossed me in when I was about three, and I was pretty much in the water—here or at school—until I left for France." Her hands went to the fence and she held onto it like she was caressing it. Her gaze traveled all over; taking in the pool itself, the small grandstand near the far end, the stacks upon stacks of deck chairs.

"Do you swim now?"

"Nah." She pushed herself off the fence and settled her jacket. "I don't have time."

Emily looked at her, sensing she wasn't revealing the whole truth. Blake had a way of saying very little about the things that affected her the most. A very wan smile was the most she offered today. "I guess we'd better get in there. Don't want them to send the guard dogs after us."

Emily took her hand, letting Blake lead her back to the clubhouse. As they got close, cars continually pulled up, disgorging their passengers. "I'm glad lots of people are coming. We'll be able to sneak out whenever we want," Blake said, sounding a little happier. Emily almost suggested they get back into the rental and take off, but Blake was walking fast, like she was trying to catch a train.

The place had been decorated by someone who'd been told to make the clubhouse look like the classiest golf club ever. Acres of wood paneling, miles of plaid fabric on every vertical and many horizontal surfaces, flattering light fixtures, and big, bright event rooms. They breezed into the biggest of them, and headed right for Blake's parents. Emily's heart was racing, partly from nerves and partly from sprinting through the building. "Mom, Dad," Blake said, leaning in to offer each of them a kiss on the cheek.

"Blake," her mother said, grasping her by the shoulders and holding her still. A pleased smile that seemed very genuine made the skin around her eyes crinkle, but the rest of her face didn't move much. She had to be fifty or a little more, but her skin was easily as smooth as Blake's.

Her hair had probably been dark at one time, but now it was a few different shades of warm blonde, slightly wavy and very well styled. Emily didn't know the woman at all, but in a glance you could tell she spent an awful lot of her day trying to look as good as she possibly could. It was working—no question—but how much time and effort did you want to spend just to look younger than you were? Where was the payoff?

Blake grasped Emily's elbow a little harder than she probably intended and pulled her close so they were shoulder to shoulder. "You might not remember, but the last time you were at the restaurant you met Emily. I think she made a watermelon salad you liked."

Mrs. Chadwick blinked in surprise, but she quickly put on a warm smile. "Of course! It's lovely to see you again, Emily."

"You too, Mrs. Chadwick. It's good to see you both."

"Call me Dana," she insisted.

"Barry," Blake's dad said as he extended his hand to shake. "It's good to see you again." His shake was as firm and enthusiastic as a politician's. When Emily had seen him at the restaurant, he'd looked like just another middle-aged rich guy. But when he stood next to his wife, they seemed like a well-matched pair. Barry was tall and broad-shouldered, with an expensive dark suit covering his lean, athletic frame. His hair was starting to thin, but he kept it short enough that you didn't notice much. He'd either just gotten back from a week on a beach, or his summer tan lasted an awfully long time.

"You too," Emily said, trying to think of something else to say.

"How'd you two get here?" Barry asked.

"I rented a car," Emily said. "I think I got the last rental in Queens."

"Queens?" Barry said, cocking his head.

"That's where I live."

"Oh, right!" He laughed like he'd just heard a great joke. "Of course. I wasn't thinking. We don't get around much in the city. I probably couldn't find my way to work if I was driving."

"Don't feel bad. I think this is my first time in Connecticut."

"Have you seen your grandparents yet?" Barry asked, giving Blake a pointed look. He put his hand on her shoulder and turned her. "They're talking to your cousin, Hayley. I bet you don't even remember her."

"Good bet," she said, grim-faced. "See you soon." Again grasping Emily like she was afraid she'd bolt if she didn't hang on tight, they slipped through the large gathering, with Blake moving like she was guided by a laser. Emily couldn't tell if she was trying to avoid having people stop her, or if this was her normal way of cutting through a crowd.

As they approached, Hayley, the forgotten cousin, met Blake's gaze and gave her a quick wave, then took off. They approached from the side, with Blake once again bending to place light kisses on each grandparent's cheek. "Happy anniversary," she said when she stood.

Blake's grandmother, dressed in a cream-colored Channel suit, eyed her critically. "If I didn't see you on TV once in a while, I'd forget what you looked like." She put her hand on Blake's chin and moved her head a few degrees. "You're so much prettier in person. The TV doesn't show how tall you are."

"Thanks, Grandma. I brought a friend. This is Emily Desjardins."

The older woman's pale blue eyes narrowed, then her gaze moved from Blake to Emily and back again. "You brought someone? You never bring anyone."

"I did today. Emily, this is my grandmother, Frances, and my grandfather, Henry Blackett."

"It's good to meet you," Emily said, smiling as she shook each hand. Blake's grandmother had the ultra-soft skin and bony knuckles of a woman in her eighties, but her grandfather's hand, especially the palm, was tough-skinned and callused. He didn't seem like he'd done much manual labor, so he must have been a golfer or a tennis player.

His dark eyes scanned Emily critically. "You didn't get married, did you, Blake?" His gaze shifted to his granddaughter. "You'd at least tell us that, wouldn't you?"

Her laugh sounded as tight as a drum. "Emily's not crazy enough to marry me, but if I trick her into it, I'll definitely invite you."

"You can get married anywhere now," he said, almost glaring at her. "Did you pull your head out of an oven long enough to read about that?"

That brittle laugh came out again. "I think I heard something along those lines." She cleared her throat, looking so uncomfortable Emily longed to step in and save her. "But I'm usually too busy to keep up with current events," she added, her eyes not meeting the probing gaze her grandfather continued to fix her with.

"Don't let him get your goat," Frances said, scowling at her husband. "You know Blake only cares about cooking."

"There's a big world outside of that kitchen," he said. "You ought to get out and see it." He gripped the shoulder of her suit and pulled her closer. "Your mother tells me you could have your own TV show if you wanted it. What in the hell's wrong with you?"

Blake lifted her hands and turned her palms up. "I'm stupid."

"You're no such thing," he scoffed. "You're just hard-headed. You have to do everything the hard way." Almost to himself, he muttered, "A good-looking girl like you could easily make enough money to get out of that damned kitchen permanently."

She shrugged, looking more adolescent than adult. "I'm happy in the kitchen, Grandpa."

"That's a load of crap. You think you're going to be young forever, but you're not."

"Oh, I don't think I'm going to be young forever." Her smile was just for show. There wasn't a hint of sincerity in it. "My aching bones remind me of that every morning."

"Talk to me when you hit eighty." He turned and snapped his fingers at a server cruising by with glasses of champagne. "Slow down there," he demanded.

Blake waved at a couple a few tables away. "I have to go say hello to Lori and Jeff," she said, grasping Emily's elbow again. "We'll come back when we can sit down and chat."

"It'll be an hour before you make the rounds," Frances said. "You've got an awful lot of relatives here."

"I know," Blake said, starting to lead Emily away. They paused on the way to the next group, and Blake murmured, "If you want to wait in the car, I wouldn't blame you."

"I'm good to go," Emily said, amping up her smile. Events like this were the only bad part of being in a relationship. If your partner was stuck, so were you.

It actually took more than an hour to have a short, civilized conversation with each grouping of relatives. Blake's mom had an older sister and a brother, and each of them had three or four kids along with sons and daughters-in-law and a few grandkids. They spent a little more time talking to Blake's brothers, Bradley and Brett. As Emily watched Blake gently tease the boys, it became clear she liked them well enough—and equally clear they didn't have much of a current relationship, all behaving as if they were kids in older bodies.

When they moved to another table of beckoning relatives, Emily said, "Your brothers look a lot alike, but neither resembles you."

Blake gripped her arm as they turned toward a table, bent over a little and spoke quietly. "I've never been sure we have the same father."

Stunned, Emily stopped and stared at her, open-mouthed.

"Come on now," Blake urged, gently tugging on her. "You're gonna need some training on how to maintain family secrets if you want to keep up with the Chadwicks."

The cocktail hour turned into two, and voices grew appreciably louder. There was nothing like lots of alcohol in the afternoon to loosen a crowd up. They were near a group that included Dana and Barry when Blake said, "I've got to hit the restroom. Want to come with me?"

"Uhm…" Emily peered at her carefully. "Do you need help?"

That got a real laugh out of her. "I know how to do everything myself. I just thought you might not want to be alone."

"I'm okay. I'm not super social, but I can hold my own at a party."

Blake leaned in and placed a soft, sweet kiss on her lips, surprising the heck out of Emily. "I can't tell you how much I'd rather be in bed with you right now." Her eyes scanned up and down her body as a hungry-looking grin settled on her face. "Especially if you'd leave the dress on."

"Such a one-track mind," she said, turning her and giving her a push toward the hallway. "Call if you need help."

"You'll be the first."

Blake hadn't taken two steps before Dana was right at Emily's arm. Together, they watched Blake glide through the crowd, posture erect, head held high. Dana let out a sigh. "Does she talk to you, Emily? I mean, does she confide in you?"

"Uhm…" How much were you supposed to reveal to your girlfriend's mom? In her limited experience, not much. "Sure. Blake isn't the most talkative woman I've ever met, but yes, we're close."

"You *are* dating, aren't you? I guess I shouldn't assume…"

"Yes, we're dating." She laughed, thinking that was a strange word for it. "We don't have much time to spend together, but we see each other regularly."

"Good." She was still staring at the wide door Blake had exited through. "She needs someone. I'm not sure she knows that, but she does."

Boy, this was hard! Blake wouldn't appreciate Emily talking about her, but what was she supposed to do?

"I think she knows that. But you know how she is. It takes her a while to open up."

Dana turned and met her with a narrowed gaze. "She hasn't opened up to me yet, and I don't think it's going to happen at this late date."

Oh, shit!

It would have been a better idea to hide in the bathroom with Blake. "I don't know what to say about that. You know how busy she is…"

Dana's smile was just as forced as the one Blake had been pulling out all afternoon. "I don't think I've ever known what's going on in her head." Her gaze hardened. "Maybe if we hadn't let her go to France…" She shook her head decisively. "It's silly to let myself think about that. You couldn't tell her a thing, even when she was a baby."

"She knows her own mind," Emily had to agree. "No doubt about that."

"If Barry's mother hadn't gotten involved, we might have had more influence. If only we could have gotten her settled at a new school…" She stopped abruptly, the color draining from her cheeks. "You *do* know what happened to her in high school, don't you?"

"Yes," she said, deciding the less said, the better. But she was desperate to know more. To know Dana's perspective on the fling, as Blake called it.

"If it had been up to me, that woman would have been sent to jail. Actually, she'd still be there." She stopped, bit at her bottom lip for a second, then said quietly, "I know Blake's happy with…at least I think she's happy with how things turned out, but do you think that woman might have made her gay?"

Emily's eyes widened even more, and she found herself speechless.

Dana gripped her arm. "I don't think there's anything wrong with being gay. Really. But Blake had never given any indication she was attracted to girls before…"

"I don't think you can make someone gay," Emily finally said. "Lots of boys tried to make me straight, and they didn't have any success at all."

Covering her face with a hand, Dana said, "I'm making a fool of myself. It's just that I know her so little. I'd like to pull you aside and grill you for an hour or two."

Chuckling, Emily told the truth. "I wouldn't mind that, to be honest. Blake doesn't share her secrets easily, and I'd love to know more about her childhood."

Shaking her head, Dana said, "If you want to have children, have boys. They're a hundred times easier."

"I hadn't planned on it, but if I do…"

Dana laughed, her tone wry. "I'm sure the last thing you need is another old woman telling you what to do."

Emily could feel her eyes widen again. "That's a term that doesn't fit, Dana. When I saw you at the restaurant, I thought you were Barry's much-younger trophy wife."

"Bless you," she said dramatically. "It's bad enough having a kid graduating from college this year. But having a thirty-year-old? I hope it doesn't bother Blake, but I lie about her age. I've convinced an awful lot of people she's only twenty-three." She laughed to herself, patted Emily on the back and slipped away in the time it took Blake to cross the room.

"What was my mother bending your ear about?" Blake's piercing gaze followed her mother as she moved over to chat with a friend.

"Nothing much. We were both agreeing you're a handful."

Blake slipped an arm around Emily's waist and led her over to the bar. "Like you needed a second opinion on that."

By eight o'clock, the crowd was loud, the music blaring, and people were starting to dance. Blake tapped her watch and said, "Let's go get our pumpkin and have the white mice lead us home."

"Are you sure you have your glass slippers?"

"No, but I plan on being asleep by midnight, and I'd love to carve out time for dessert. You." She'd had a couple of drinks, but this wasn't the liquor talking.

"We'll see. Having a car makes the whole thing more complicated."

"Let's scoot." After quick goodbyes to Blake's grandparents, they hustled over to her parents. "We've got to run," Blake said. "Emily goes in early on Monday."

Dana took Emily's hand and held it in both of her own while looking into her eyes. "I'm very glad you were able to come. Let's all have dinner together one night."

"I'd love that," Emily said, meaning it. She knew it wouldn't happen, but she would have liked to get to know the Chadwicks better.

"Blake," Dana said, turning to put a hand on her shoulder, "I've got two boxes of your things in the hall closet. Since you have a car, will you take them with you?"

"Tonight?"

"When else have you had a car? Come on now, I'm going to have to throw them out, but I hate to do that without your having looked at them."

"We can go by your house," Emily said. "It won't take long."

"All right," she said, sighing. "Do you still have a spare key under the mat?"

"They tell me that's the last place a burglar looks."

That made Blake give her a genuine smile. When she let her guard down, that smile could make a statue smile back. "I'm glad we were able to come tonight. Grandma and Grandpa appreciate how much work you put into this."

Dana patted her on the cheek. "I appreciate the lie, honey. Now go get your boxes and get home safely. I hate to think of you having to go across the Bronx at this time of night."

"We'll be fine, Mom. We'll see you." She leaned over and gave her mom another brief buss, then they made a break for it. As soon as the heavy, damp autumn air hit her skin, Emily realized how on guard she'd been the whole night. It was like stepping out of prison after a short visit. Even though you hadn't been there long, it felt like years.

"How do I get roped into these things?" Blake asked, a half-smile on her face.

"You're a dutiful daughter. Or you've got some stuff in those boxes you really want."

"Could be both," she said, her smile growing. "You never know."

The Chadwick home was only ten minutes from the club. Ten minutes of beautifully rolling countryside. "Does anyone live around here? Is this some sort of nature preserve?" Emily asked, squinting to see signs of life.

"There are houses everywhere. They're just…I guess they're not obvious, are they." She laughed softly. "I never paid much attention. Take a left on the next street. Yeah. Hilton Heath."

Emily turned and slowed, creeping along the pitch-dark, private street. "No streetlights?"

"Absolutely not. No sidewalks either. I suppose that's one of the benefits of living here. You never feel hemmed in."

"I feel like Freddy Krueger's gonna jump out and slit my throat," Emily said, the dark streets and hidden houses making her ill at ease.

"I'm sure the Greenwich police would never allow that. They stop people for walking an unfamiliar dog." She pointed to the left. "Right at the end of the cul-de-sac."

Emily went even slower, then started down a long, curving drive. The house was big, compared to the houses she'd grown up around, but it looked like a mere mortal could own it. Nothing like those ridiculous mansions in the Hamptons. Hidden lights marked large flat stones, set in place in lieu of a traditional sidewalk, curving along a path that led from the parking area to the front entrance. More lights cast the home in a warm glow. They must have been hidden in trees, because you couldn't see a fixture anywhere.

The home was a buff-colored, two story Colonial, with a single story addition. On second glance, the addition might have been original, given how seamlessly it fit in with the main house. "Nice place," Emily said.

"Yeah, it's a good house," Blake said reflectively. "My parents bought it right before I was born. If my mom had her way, they'd move to the fancier part of town, but my dad's got a little New England thriftiness in him."

They got out of the car and climbed the slight incline. "It's really quiet back here," Emily said.

"Almost always. Every time someone has a loud party, someone calls the cops." Blake bent and whisked the key from under the mat. "Million dollar houses that a five year old could break into." She slid the key in the lock and opened the door, waiting for Emily to go in first.

Emily craned her neck, trying to peek around while she waited for Blake to grab her stuff. But Blake clearly had other ideas. After kicking the door closed with her foot, a sexy, sultry smile slid onto her face. "You know what I've never done?"

"Probably not much," Emily teased as Blake's arms encircled her.

Ignoring the jab, Blake said, "I've never had sex in my old room." She moved Emily back and forth playfully. "Come on. It'll be fun. Don't you want to fulfill my teenage dreams?"

"Hmm…" Emily linked her hands around Blake's neck and gazed at her. "What's in it for me?"

"The usual," she said, bending to place a soft kiss on her lips. "A mind-bending orgasm or two."

Emily tapped her nose with a finger. "You've got to work on your self-confidence. You'll never get anywhere with such a low opinion of yourself."

"Come on. You know you want to."

Emily let herself be led up the staircase, deciding this could work out for the best. If they got sex out of the way, she could drop Blake off at home and head back to Queens to return the car.

When they got to the landing, Blake stopped and touched the wall, absolutely dumbstruck. "My room…" After dropping Emily's hand, she dashed for the next door, entered and hung a right. Emily followed her, finding her standing in a very nice bathroom. "My room's gone!"

"This was your…"

"My mother's taken my room and my bath and turned it into a new bath and a huge closet!" She stormed into the massive space, filled with drawers and cabinets and double racks laden with more nice clothing than most boutiques held. "God damn it! That's why she's put my stuff into boxes. There's nowhere else to keep it!"

Emily was worried Blake was going to throw herself to the floor and have a tantrum. Being around her family brought out a side Emily had never seen, and wasn't looking forward to seeing often.

"It's their house," she said, trying to be reasonable.

Blake's face had turned a furious pink, eyes wide. "It's my room!"

Emily took a more thorough look around, noting a few nicks in the paint and some darkening of the grout in the bath. "They didn't do this in the last week. How long has it been since you've been home?"

She rolled her eyes, and moved around the new bathroom, checking everything out. "Two years, I guess," she finally said.

"Two years! And you still want to claim it?"

"I don't want to claim it," she said, sharply. "It's already mine. This is where they plunked me down when they brought me home from the hospital."

Emily was afraid she was going to cry. But Blake sat on the edge of the tub and sulked for a minute. When she spoke, she sounded more like her usual self. "It's their house. Of course it is. But…" She looked up and met Emily's gaze. "It would have been nice of them to at least mention it."

Her expression was so bereft, Emily sat next to her and took her in her arms, soothing her gently. "I'm sorry your parents didn't talk to you before they took your room. That was insensitive of them."

"It was, wasn't it?"

Emily had never seen her so vulnerable. So needing reassurance.

"It was. When my parents moved from our family home, both Charlotte and I were upset. And they gave us plenty of opportunity to take anything we wanted. If they'd done it without telling me…" She shook her head. "I wouldn't have been happy."

Blake dropped her head and took in a few long breaths. "I know it's none of my business what they do with the house, but it still hurts. It was…" She frowned, clearly struggling for words. "I felt like I was part of the family when I had a room here. Now…" She stood and extended her hand to Emily. "I'll go see if I want any of the stuff in those boxes."

"Why don't we just load them in the car? You can sort through them later."

"No. I'd rather take a look here. If I lug it all home, I'll wind up keeping it, even if it's junk I don't want. My mom's much more cold-blooded about throwing stuff away." They started to walk back down the stairs, with Blake mumbling, "Obviously," as they reached the hallway.

She opened a closet door and pulled out two moving boxes, both with her name written across them. Taking the first to the spacious living room, she sat on a large, upholstered sofa and started to unpack. Emily scanned the room as Blake worked. It was surprisingly cozy and warm, like the happiest people in the world lived here. Sunny yellows with splashes of cool blue reminded her of a crystal clear pool on a hot summer's day. Funny how you could never guess how someone's home would look. Emily would have bet money on a much more modern, streamlined home. Wrong on all counts.

Once the first box was empty, Blake started picking through the contents. Trophies, ribbons, and photos of Blake in or near a swimming pool predominated. The earliest pictures showed an adorable little girl, clearly pre-school age, and they spanned the time until she was about fourteen. Emily guessed at that number, since Blake didn't yet have awesome breasts.

"You weren't kidding when you said you were always in the pool," Emily said. "I've never seen so many trophies."

"I assume the next box is more of the same." She brought it over and went through it quickly, now that the trophies were larger. But there were also some beautiful little dresses and a couple of dolls that looked like they hadn't been played with. Standing over the piles, Blake put her hands on her hips and shook her head. "I don't need any of this." Without pause, she started to toss it all back inside.

Emily got up and put a hand on her arm, stopping her. "Take a second and think about this, okay?"

"What's there to think about? Am I going to put old swimming trophies in my living room?"

"No, I can't see you doing that, but..." She picked up a couple of the framed photos. "You look so proud of yourself here. How old were you?"

She looked like she wasn't going to play the game, but Blake reluctantly took the photo and gave it a moment's regard. "Four, I guess." A slow smile settled on her lips. "I beat some five and six-year-olds to take that ribbon. I thought I was hot stuff to beat kids in grade school."

"If you don't take this, I want it," Emily said, surprising herself as she slipped the frame from Blake's hands and clutched it to her chest.

A sly smile curled the corner of Blake's mouth. "Is that what girlfriends do? Hoard photos?"

"It is." Emily poked through the things lying on the sofa cushion. Her hand brushed past an unframed photo and she pulled it out. A ragged edge curled around Blake's image, her body now tall and square shouldered. Her breasts weren't quite as impressive as they were now, but they were close. "This one must have gotten caught on something."

Blake took it and regarded it for a full minute. "I can't tell if my mom tore this at the time, or recently." She dropped it into the box. "That's definitely her handiwork."

"Why would she tear a photo of you?"

"It wasn't me," she said, hoisting the box and carrying it back to the closet. "She was making an editorial comment about my coach."

"Because…?" Emily led.

Stopping to gaze at her for a few seconds, Blake said, "Shauna was my coach…and my lover."

Emily clapped a hand over her eyes. "Oh, shit. I had no idea. I thought she was a teacher."

"She was." Blake flopped down on the sofa, once again looking much younger than her chronological age. "But she wasn't *my* teacher. I only knew her from swim team."

"I take it your mom doesn't think you had a fling." Emily watched her carefully, seeing a swath of annoyance flash in her eyes.

"My mom thought I was an innocent *straight* child who this conniving pedophile molested." She slapped a hand on the cushion, making a muted "thwack" on the fabric. "She was wrong then, and she's wrong now."

"I don't know how it went down, but people who have sex with minors are guilty until proven innocent in my book." She shook her head. "And I'm not sure what could convince me someone was innocent, unless they were truly ignorant of the facts."

Blake sat up straight and leaned toward Emily, who was sharing the sofa with her. "I made the first move. Shauna never—not once—touched me until I made it clear I wanted to have sex with her."

"You were fifteen," Emily stressed. "She was in a position of authority over you. It's wrong, Blake. Pure and simple."

"Wrong enough to take away her teaching credential? To prevent a twenty-three year old from ever earning a living in her field? To put her on the sex offenders registry? She's probably working in a strip club now, all because of a mistake she made when she was one year out of college." She got to her feet and walked over to the mantle. When she leaned against it, Emily could almost picture her at fifteen, fighting for the woman who'd taken advantage of her.

"Yes," Emily said, trying to be as empathetic as she could while sticking to her beliefs. "You've got to send a message to teachers that it's never okay to have sex with students—even if the student wants it."

"We were barely eight years apart," she said, her cheeks coloring. "I was mature for my age and she was a little immature for hers."

"It's wrong on its face," Emily insisted. "But I can see why you think her punishment was too harsh. God knows people do worse things and get off scot-free." She started to put the remaining items back into the first box, but something stopped her. "If you didn't co-operate, how'd they get enough evidence to move forward?"

Blake walked over to the sofa and helped get the other things into the box. As she carried it over to the closet, she said, "Kevin Willard let his parents convince him to rat her out. Spineless jerk." She closed the door firmly, then went to the wall to start shutting off lights. "Ready?"

Emily wasn't going to leave until they'd finished. And they were nowhere near finished. "Who's Kevin Willard?" she asked, still seated on the sofa.

Rolling her eyes, Blake came into the living room and perched on the arm of the sofa. "Here's the funny thing," she said, her voice calm and reflective. "My mom thinks having sex with Shauna screwed me up. But it really didn't. In fact, it let me see how immature I was."

"I don't get…"

"I deluded myself into thinking she was as crazy about me as I was about her." Their eyes met and Emily's heart skipped a beat at the sorrow she saw in those lovely orbs. "She never told me I was the only person she was dating. I just assumed…" She shivered, like someone had opened the door on an icy night. "That showed me you can't assume stuff about people. I'm much more careful than I would have been if I hadn't met her, and I thank her for that."

Sick to her stomach, Emily quietly said, "Kevin was a student, too?"

"Not hers," Blake said, irritated. "Shauna coached the girls team, but both teams did laps together after school. I guess that's how they met. He got a year's worth of sex, which he happily took, then he told the police exactly what they wanted to hear." A short laugh bubbled up, surprising the heck out of Emily. "When I threatened him at school, my mom saw the light and let me go to Paris." She stood, then clapped her hands together like she'd finished a project. "At least that part worked out. There was no way I was going to transfer to some stupid boarding school in New Hampshire."

Emily got up and went to her, putting her hands on Blake's hips. Gently, she said, "Were you in love with Shauna?"

Her lips pursed tightly, then Blake nodded. "I thought I was. But I don't know..." She shook her head. "I guess it's not love if the other person doesn't love you back, right?"

"True. But that doesn't mean it doesn't hurt as much." She ran her fingers all over Blake's face, caressing her like the treasure she was. "I'm sorry she broke your heart."

"I am too. I was sad for a long time." She swallowed, and Emily could see her throat constrict. "Really sad."

"You told me you fooled around with guys when you were first in France. Did Shauna make you doubt your sexuality?"

She shifted around in Emily's hold, clearly not wanting to talk about this. But the information was important. Emily was certain of that. "I don't know." Letting out a heavy sigh, she said, "If I was so wrong about her, maybe I was wrong about everything, you know?" Those big brown eyes bore into Emily, begging for understanding.

"I do," she said, glad she really did understand her reasoning. Having your first love break your heart could easily shake your confidence in every area. "You didn't let guys talk you into things you weren't ready for, did you?"

"A few hand jobs," Blake said, chuckling softly. "The first time a guy successfully got his hand into my pants the experiment ended. No way that was going to happen."

"I'm glad you got it all worked out." Tilting her head, she met Blake's eyes, seeing them still looking a little spooked. "I think you're right where you belong. You're awfully gay."

Blake slung an arm around her shoulders and hugged her close. "Let's hit the road. I feel like I've been up for three days."

"I'd come back, but let's do it when we have the next day off, okay? This was draining."

"It's a deal. Given we never have two days off, we're home free."

They picked their way back down the professionally lit path, and Emily settled into the driver's seat after stowing the photo and a trophy in the back seat. Blake might not have wanted to display any of her childhood memorabilia in her apartment, but Emily couldn't stand to see her throw away the award she'd won at the state tournament. That was a big deal, despite Blake's glossing over it.

"You're going to have to guide me out of here," Emily said as she snapped her seat belt.

"I will." She pointed in the dark. "When you get to the first cross street, turn left."

"Left?" She peered down the street, confused. "I was sure we came in the other way."

"We did."

Taking a quick look at her, Emily could see Blake's surprisingly grim face. If they were going to drive around looking for Shauna...

"Keep going for about a mile," she said.

"Are we going anywhere special?" She asked the question with studied casualness, drawing a quick laugh from Blake.

"Yes, Emily, we are."

Over the months she'd learned Blake gave up her musings when she was damned good and ready, so Emily followed her directions without probing.

"Two more quick right turns," she said, then added in a quiet voice, "it seemed a lot farther when I was on my bike."

"What did?"

"Next corner," she said. "Will you stop for a minute?"

Emily pulled up in front of a large, rambling home, kind of a Tudor, with suburban Connecticut influences. The homes in this part of town were all larger, all set back further from the street, with more space between them. They still weren't ostentatiously in your face like the ones in the Hamptons, but there wasn't any doubt that the people who lived here were soaking in money.

When Emily turned to ask Blake why they'd stopped, she clapped her mouth shut before saying a word. Blake was staring at the house like a scientist peering into a microscope. Even in the dimly lit car, Emily could see her eyes checking out every window, then carefully looking around the yard.

"It looks…bigger," she said quietly. "Everyone says places from your childhood look smaller, but that's not true."

Emily put a hand on her knee and patted it gently. "Where are we?"

Not turning to meet her gaze, Blake said, "My grandmother's house."

"Ahh." Clearly not the grandmother she'd met earlier. "How long has she been gone?"

"Five years on the twenty-second of this month." Her voice took on a tender softness. "Too long."

Emily's hand slid off the knee to grasp Blake's hand, which was chilled. "You've never talked about her."

Now her head snapped to the left, eyes wide. "I haven't?"

"I know that she took you to France, but you've never told me what she meant to you."

Her head turned again to stare at the mostly dark home, with a single light illuminating an upstairs bedroom. "I don't know how to put that in words, Emily." Blake swallowed, clearly trying to keep her emotions in check. "She was always on my side. Always," she said, strongly emphasizing the word.

"That's so important for a kid to feel."

"It is."

"Did she get you into cooking?"

"Kinda." She gave an adolescent-looking shrug. "She loved good food, and took me with her a lot when she went out to eat." Now a genuinely warm smile settled onto her face. "We'd sit there until the chef had time to come out and talk with us. Grandma didn't care if it was midnight and I had school the next day. She loved to talk about food with people who knew what they were talking about."

"Aww, that's sweet," Emily said, gripping her hand tightly. "I'm so glad you got that from your grandparents."

"Not plural. My grandfather died when my dad was a little boy."

"Ooo, that's awful." Emily took another look at the grand house. "He must have had a good insurance policy."

"No, he didn't," Blake said, grim-faced once again. "The one message my grandma repeated again and again was never to marry for money. That's what she did when she got remarried to some insurance bigwig. She never admitted this, but I think the guy's bank account was his only plus."

"Hard to imagine how unpleasant that would be," Emily said.

"Yeah. Grandma wanted to make sure I had a way to support myself, even if I found myself alone with young kids."

"Was her husband a jerk?"

"No idea. He died before I was born. But she said there was no lonelier feeling than being in a bed with a man you didn't love."

"Damn, did she tell you that when you were young? That's a lot for a kid to take in."

"No, no, I was old enough to understand. We talked all the time, about anything. But when she took me to France she told me all sorts of stuff. I guess she wanted to make sure I didn't get into any more…" She shrugged. "Situations."

"She was cool with you being gay?"

Blake shook her head dismissively. "She didn't care who I loved, she just wanted to make sure I didn't get hurt again." Letting out another laugh, she added, "Her advice was to never put your own neck in the noose."

Emily's eyes widened. "She didn't want you to fall in love?"

"No, she believed in love," she said thoughtfully. "She just wanted me to be super careful. That was good advice."

Emily looked at her face, with the blue light from the dashboard making her skin a ghostly color. Blake's grandmother might not have been so doctrinaire if she'd known how doggedly her advice would be followed. Super careful didn't begin to cover how warily Blake traveled the road to love.

Blake's head was wedged between the window and her seat, where it had fallen not long after they'd left Cos Cob. That left Emily with little to do but creep down the congested interstate and stew about the evening. She felt nothing but empathy for Blake, certain she'd deluded herself about Shauna. It was probably too painful for her to admit she'd been victimized by someone she thought she loved. But she *had* been victimized. Her inability to form a significant relationship since then merely underscored how the whole thing had screwed her up. But she was trying now, thank god. Emily was going to continue to do her best to make this relationship the one that would convince her to ignore her grandmother's advice and let herself go—to trust—once again.

Chapter Twenty

LE LAPIN CLOSED ON Thanksgiving Day, a decision Emily found eminently reasonable. No one came to the best fish restaurant in the country for turkey, and if you didn't serve some form of it on Thanksgiving you were asking for trouble. Blake, however, ran exactly the kind of restaurant local people without family obligations and those not very tradition-bound chose for a festive holiday. She didn't seem to mind working on Thanksgiving, and Emily guessed one reason might have been a ready excuse to avoid spending the day with her family.

When Emily sat at her grandparents' table that Thursday, surrounded by her dearest relatives, she couldn't shake the pangs of sympathy she felt for Blake. Yes, she was an independent woman. Yes, she seemed perfectly happy to have to work today. But that was only because she didn't know the peaceful, contented feeling that filled Emily to overflowing as she held her sister's and her grandfather's hand when he led them in a short, emotional prayer of thanks. These people —every one of them—would come to her aid if she ever needed anything. She was one hundred percent certain they knew she'd do the same for each of them. That kind of connection, of love, wasn't something Blake got to experience. Emily was sure of that. And that knowledge made a few extra tears glide down her cheeks when her grandfather finished his prayer. Maybe one day Blake would be sitting beside her at this meal. Of course, they'd have to move the celebration to Sunday, and make it early enough in the day so they could fly back to New York for service on Monday. There was no way even the best Thanksgiving in the world would make Blake miss a day's work.

They'd established a new routine. Every Saturday night, Emily went over to Blake's apartment. That let them have all of Sunday together, still the only day of the week they saw each other.

She knew it was a little silly, but her arrival crept up earlier and earlier in the evening, leaving enough time to make something special for Blake's dinner. She was always hungry when she got home, and her tendency was to grab something from a late-night spot as she walked. But Emily wanted her to have a real meal, not just whatever was available.

That night, a cold, windy one in late December, Emily had made a simple risotto, having learned Blake craved carbs after a long day. As soon as Blake entered, she called out, "I hope I've made it clear this is the highlight of my week."

Emily wiped her hands and left the kitchen, catching Blake as she put her coat and gloves away. She wrapped her arms around her from behind, giving her a long hug. "Having a home-cooked meal one night a week shouldn't even make your highlight reel, Chef."

Blake squirmed from the embrace, turned and enfolded Emily in her arms. "I'm not talking about food." They kissed, the energy Blake had stored up from work bleeding over into her enthusiastic greeting. "I'm talking about how I feel when I open the door and hear you bustling around in the kitchen." Another longer, gentler kiss followed. "I love that you cook for me, but I hope you know you don't have to. I can easily grab some noodles or a curry on the way home."

Emily stood back and touched the crisply ironed placket on Blake's shirt. "I'll never understand how you manage to look so fresh after a long day in the kitchen."

"I send my shirts out," she whispered, bending to nibble on Emily's ear. "Extra starch, hangers."

"Put on your pajamas and I'll dish up our dinner."

Blake went to change, while Emily headed back into the kitchen. "I picked up some good mushrooms at the greenmarket," she said as she ladled the rice into bowls, "and I thought a risotto would show them off."

"I like that you wait to eat with me." Blake was back, standing so close Emily bumped into her when she moved to the sink.

"I like to. It's more special this way."

"It's very special. Like I said… It's the highlight of my week." She took a plate filled with slices of crunchy Italian bread over to the small table between the two chairs, then poured some olive oil onto a plate and nestled it into the scant amount of available space.

Emily carried the bowls, and they sat down after Blake moved her chair so close their knees touched. Emily had opened the wine hours earlier, and now she poured each of them a glass.

Blake took a sip, and closed her eyes as a smile made her look not only happy, but relaxed. "Spicy, with velvety tannins."

"We have a great sommelier, and we eat lunch together whenever he can get away." She laughed. "He probably feels like he's still at work, since I pepper him with questions, but I'm always trying to learn more about wine. The last time we had porcini mushrooms on the menu, he suggested a red from Mt. Etna. It took me a while, but I found this one."

Blake swirled the wine in her glass, then held it up to the light before taking another sip. "I like his recommendation." She took a big bite of her risotto. "Mmm," she purred. "Magnifico."

"I thought I might have been heavy-handed with the pepper. No?"

"It's perfect, Emily. Truly perfect."

"If I ever make a mistake, feel free to correct it. You won't offend me."

"No mistakes." Another forkful made its way to her mouth. "Perfection in a bowl."

They chatted about their weeks, then watched TV on Blake's computer until she started to fade. Emily cleaned the kitchen, and when she returned to the living room, Blake was sitting up in bed, with her head pressed up against the bookcase. Mouth slightly open, her breathing was already heavy and slow.

Emily slid in next to her, tucking her arms around Blake when she half-woke and started to protest. "I'm up. I'm up."

This was another Saturday night ritual. Blake seemed to think it was her duty to stay up long enough to have sex. But she was truly exhausted, and could never manage more than a few kisses before she conked out. Emily tugged her down until they were facing each other.

Then she wrapped her leg around Blake's hip and tenderly rubbed her back for a few seconds. Like a switch had been turned off, Blake fell into a sound sleep in a matter of moments. Her deep, regular breathing was normally a sleep-aid for Emily. Tonight, though, it didn't work its magic. In a few days Blake was taking off for Christmas. Her maternal grandparents had a house in Bermuda, and the entire family spent the holidays together. Given that Emily had to work, it made sense that Blake hadn't asked her to join them—but it still hurt. Knowing Blake, and her penchant for practicality, it wouldn't have occurred to her to ask. The invitation would have been a waste given Emily's commitments. Logically, that was completely true. Emotionally, it would have been awfully nice to be asked.

New Year's Day was on a Friday, giving Emily a three day weekend. She should have gone home to make up for missing Christmas, but the allure of two days out of three with Blake was too tantalizing to pass up.

When the elevator door slid open on the first day of the new year, Blake was right there, a massive grin on her gorgeous face.

"It's gonna be a very good year," she said, happiness beaming from her. "I'm looking forward to a whole lot of Saturday nights and Sunday mornings with you."

Emily slipped into her embrace, the warm safety of Blake's arms making her purr like a kitten. "Missed you," she whispered.

"Aww. Did you? We only missed one day."

When Blake stood up tall and took Emily's hand she looked pleased. Like she was glad Emily had gotten so hooked. Maybe even found it cute. As they walked the short distance to the apartment, Emily argued with herself over whether to say something. To reveal it hurt her feelings to admit to missing someone, only to have them find that funny or sentimental or whatever Blake thought. But Emily didn't want to spoil the day by complaining. She *had* missed her, and she wanted her to know that.

Blake led her into the room, took Emily's coat and hung it up, then went to pick up her computer. "Got a bunch of photos to show you," she said, going to sit down on one of her chairs, a playful grin curling her mouth.

"You do?" Emily took the other chair, waiting patiently while Blake brought up the proper program.

"Uh-huh," she said, now focusing intently. "While I was in Bermuda, I kept looking at my family with a different perspective." She met Emily's eyes and grinned impishly. "Yours."

"My perspective?" Emily asked, patting her own chest.

"Yeah. I wondered what you'd think of my grandparents' house, and the beach we go to. We played golf just about every day, and when I was taking pictures of the course it dawned on me I don't even know if you play."

Emily let out a laugh. "I've never had my hands on a club, much less swung one. My dad likes to arrange nature hikes, but that's the only outdoorsy thing we do as a family."

"Oh." Her smile dimmed a little. "Then you won't understand why I felt so good about getting a birdie on this really tricky seventeenth hole."

Emily reached over and grasped her knee, giving it a firm squeeze. "I know what a birdie is, Chef. All you have to do is explain why getting one on this hole was a big deal." She scooted her chair closer, draped her arm around Blake's shoulders, and got ready to have a Blake-eyed view of Bermuda.

After she'd brushed her teeth and gotten ready for bed, Emily rearranged the furniture and pulled the bed down. She slid in under the comforter as Blake dashed across the room, her nipples as hard as rocks. Jumping into bed and burrowing into Emily's body, she murmured, "Bermuda's nicer. I hate being cold."

Emily maneuvered her around until Blake's head was resting on her shoulder. Leaning close, she whispered, "I know this is a crazy thought, but you could put on clothes. They'd keep you warm."

A silly-sounding laugh tickled the side of Emily's face. "That's what you're for." In a flash, Blake was on top, hovering over Emily with a predatory smile on her face. "Among other things."

"I'm ready to perform my duties." Emily closed her eyes and draped a forearm across her face. "Just get it over with." She was joking. One hundred percent. But Blake moved her arm and peered at her with concern.

"You don't ever think that, do you?"

"Think what?"

Rolling off to lie on her side, Blake stared at Emily for a long minute. "You don't ever think I like you just…or even mostly…because of sex, do you?"

"Mmm." She closed her eyes to avoid having to look into that penetrating gaze. Blake was asking a serious question, and she deserved a thoughtful answer. "No, I don't think that," she said, almost reflexively. Then she took a breath and added the truth. "Well, that might not be totally accurate."

"How so?" Blake's eyes were wide open, watching like a hawk.

"I don't think we'd see each other every weekend if we weren't sex partners. I think you'd sleep all day and—"

Blake wrapped an arm around her and gave her such a forceful squeeze Emily had to gasp for breath.

"That's not true," she said, with a real urgency to her voice. "I thought about you dozens of times last week, Emily, and not one of those thoughts was about sex." Her lips pressed together firmly for a few seconds. "If we were only friends, we probably wouldn't see each other *every* week. But we'd see each other a lot. I'd miss the hell out of you if we didn't at least talk every week."

"You would?"

"Yeah. I would. I really would."

Now Blake's hold grew more gentle, and she pressed her lips just above Emily's ear. "I like talking to you, and hearing about what's going on with you. You get me," she said, "and I wouldn't want to give that up."

"I do get you," Emily said, feeling like she might cry. "And I feel the same. You're fun to be with, no matter what we're doing."

A low, sexy laugh tickled her skin. "But we do this one thing really well together, don't we?"

"We do, Chef," she admitted, nodding at her playful grin. "We do this one thing together very well. Let's double-check to make sure we haven't forgotten how."

"Awesome idea," Blake said, before dipping her head and giving Emily a kiss that would have warmed them even if they'd been outside —stark naked.

They hadn't forgotten how to do what they did together so very well. Emily lay on her side, playing with a sleeping Blake's curls. It was very dark in the room, with barely enough ambient light to see vague outlines of her pretty face. They'd been remarkably tender with each other, much more gentle than their usual frenzied expression of desire. Like something significant had changed. Deepened. At one point, with Blake lying atop her body, looking down into Emily's eyes, all of the lust drained from her. With nothing but tenderness remaining, Emily had almost confessed her love. She'd caught herself, but just barely. If things stayed on this trajectory, they'd get there, so she was especially leery about screwing things up if her timing was off.

Emily let her fingers trail down Blake's cheek, loving to feel its contours in the dark night. Certain she could content herself with this tiny intimacy for hours, she jerked when Blake's phone rang. Her usual ring was a nice, tinkling bell, but this was a klaxon. Both of them sat up like shots, with Blake fumbling blindly for the phone. "Hello," she said, sounding fully awake. Only two seconds passed, then she demanded, "Are you sure?"

Emily's heart was racing from being woken so rudely, but it was the tone in Blake's voice that was scaring the hell out of her.

"Have you called the fire department? Right." She was on her feet, diving for the cabinets where she kept her clothes. "Fire," she said, sounding preternaturally calm.

Emily jumped up and searched in the dark for her clothing, but Blake said, "Can't wait. I've got to run." Then she was across the room, grabbing her coat and blowing out the door before Emily could form a complaint.

After turning on the lights, Emily yanked her jeans on, pulled a sweater over her head, then found her phone and her keys, sticking them into her pockets as she shoved her feet into her boots. The elevator came quickly, and she spent the few seconds it took to reach the lobby tying her laces. As soon as she hit the street, she started to run. The restaurant was only a few blocks away, and she put her head down and kept going at full speed, even when her lungs started to burn.

When she turned down the short, angled street that housed the restaurant, a cry flew from her lips. The trendy Italian place next door was an inferno. Flames shot out from the roof of the single story restaurant, and as she watched, the front window blew out, glass projectiles arcing into the street.

Blake was nowhere to be found. Emily battled terror as she ran around to the alley. Sirens wailed in the distance, getting closer by the second. As she got near, she saw Blake kick in the back door while holding her coat over her face. Emily would never know what force propelled her, but she found her arms wrapped around Blake from behind, tumbling them both to the ground. "Are you insane?" she cried.

"Armando might be in there!" Blake fought to free herself, pushing off roughly, kicking Emily in the leg as she scrambled to her feet.

Instinctively, Emily grabbed Blake's ankle with both hands, holding on for dear life. Firemen stormed down the alley, huge tanks strapped to their backs. "Is anyone inside?" a guy in a white hat demanded.

"My night steward's usually here at this time," Blake said.

Knowing that the firemen wouldn't let Blake do anything stupid, Emily released her rabid hold, got up and ran back to the street, searching for Armando. She'd only seen him once or twice, but when she spied a guy standing in front of the building, looking like he'd just emerged from hades, she ran up to him. "Armando?"

He turned and looked at her blankly. The blank look of someone in shock. She grabbed his arm and tugged him along with her, heading back to the alley. In the few seconds she'd been gone, the police had arrived, and they closed the alley by running yellow caution tape across it. An imposing cop stood dead in the center, glaring at a few people who'd run to the alley to get a peek at the action. "My girlfriend!" Emily yelled when she was still ten feet away. "She has to know her employee's not inside!"

"Nobody goes through," he said, shaking his head slowly. "Nobody."

Emily yelled at the top of her lungs, fighting to be heard over the crackling fire, blaring walkie-talkies, and sirens still approaching. "BLAKE!"

In seconds, Blake was standing on the other side of the tape. "Thank god," she groaned when she saw Armando. She reached out and pulled him into a rough hug, slapping him repeatedly on the back. "Are you all right?"

"So fast," he muttered. "One minute smoke, one minute ceiling falls."

"You're all right," Blake said, soothingly. "Were you alone?"

"Sí." He looked at the restaurant next to theirs, now a burned-out shell. "I heard screaming."

"The captain over there said everyone was out. It was a close call, but he's sure no one was injured."

"You're gonna have to clear the area," the cop said. "This whole block might come down. Let's go."

Blake turned to take one last look, then she ducked under the police tape and took Emily's hand. When they got to the street, she pushed through dozens of onlookers to reach Spring, then hailed a cab and tried to load Armando inside. "Fuck. I don't have any money," she said.

"I've got my wallet." Emily took out all of her money—sixty dollars —and handed it to Armando. "Hurry home to your family," she said.

He nodded, still looking like he wasn't quite sure what to do next. The cab pulled away, leaving the two of them alone. "Do you want to go back?" Emily asked. She could smell smoke, but only in fits and starts. The whole neighborhood must have reeked of it, since ash floated overhead, lightly dropping onto their heads and shoulders.

Blake blinked slowly, then rubbed her eyes. Black smudges now marred her cheeks. "I don't know what to do. I guess…I guess I should call the owners, but…"

"There's nothing they can do tonight. Is there a rush in contacting your insurance company?"

"I don't know." She sighed, then coughed for a few seconds. "My lungs hurt."

"Let's get out of here." She started tugging her away from the fire, but Blake wasn't moving very quickly.

"I feel like I should stay…" She looked toward the street as another firetruck pulled in and shut off his siren. "Doesn't a captain have to go down with her ship?"

"It's not a ship." Emily took her more firmly by the arm and pulled forcefully. "You don't need to watch. Come on now."

Her dark eyes were trained on the street, but she made no effort to return. "It's gone, isn't it." Her voice was steady, but there was a child-like quality to it. Like she was asking a trusted adult if her bad dream had been real.

"Yes," Emily said, throwing her arms around her in a fierce hug. "I'm so sorry, but it's gone."

Abruptly, she started for the street again. "There were apartments over the shop next to us."

"The firefighters will check. People have had plenty of time to get out by now. It's okay," Emily soothed.

Blake started to cough again, and Emily took a moment to realize her own throat hurt. Then she began to cough as well, loud, harsh hacks that made her body shake.

Taking her hand, Blake headed for home, not stopping until Emily had another coughing fit. Blake held her shoulders as she looked at her critically. "Emergency room?"

"No, no, I'm okay." Her throat was raw and her eyes burned, but that seemed like a perfectly normal reaction to standing next to a raging fire for a few minutes. "Are you okay? Does your chest hurt?"

She seemed a little confused, but losing your life's work in seconds could account for that. "I have a headache, but it's not too bad." She took a deep breath and coughed a few times, then spit onto the street. "Let's go get this stink off ourselves."

When they reached the apartment, Emily let Blake go into the bathroom first. Normally, they showered together, but she thought this might be a night she needed some time alone. While she was gone, Emily double-bagged all of their clothes and shoes, then stuck the bag in the hallway. If the neighbors were annoyed, they'd have to get over it.

Blake was gone for a very long time. To avoid having her smoke-filled hair stink up the room, Emily washed it with dish soap in the sink, scrubbing her face as well. When Blake emerged, she didn't mention the fact that Emily had a dish towel wrapped around her head. She walked over to the bed and dropped to it. "All yours," she said, gesturing toward the bath.

She didn't seem like she wanted to talk, or even interact, so Emily went into the bathroom, heated up the shower stall and breathed in the warm, humid water until she could take a deep breath and not cough. She couldn't smell smoke, but she lathered her hair one more time, just to make sure. Then, wrapped in a bath towel, she went out to check on Blake.

Pacing across the room in a pair of sweats and a T-shirt, she spoke into her phone, calmly and slowly. "No, I didn't stay. The smoke was so bad I was getting light-headed. I'll ask again. Do you want me to call the insurance company, or do you want to?"

Emily met her eyes and walked over to the open drawer when Blake pointed at it. Inside were neatly organized T-shirts, and she took one out and slipped it over her head. Then she took Blake by the hand and led her back to the bed. They both sat and she put an arm around her shoulders, pulling her close. Blake fought for a second, but relented and nuzzled against her.

"I'm well aware I'm not the policy holder. I was merely trying to be helpful." She let out a long sigh, then coughed for a few seconds. "Yeah, I'm sure it would have been more helpful to have stopped the fire when it started, but I don't live at the restaurant." Emily could feel her body grow tense again. "I'm not a fire investigator either, but when I got there

Baci was burning out of control. We looked fine—from the street. It was a different story in the alley."

She jumped to her feet. "No, I will not go back. There's nothing I can do, Jeffrey. The building's gone." She started to pace again, her bare feet slapping against the wood floor as she walked. "Great," she said, her volume rising. "Check my contract and point out where it says I have to risk my fucking life to give you status updates on a building that's gone!" She pushed the "end" button so hard Emily feared she'd break a finger. Then the phone bounced onto the bed and both of them stared at it for a few seconds. Emily reached over and turned it off, preventing Jeffrey from calling back.

Gazing into Blake's troubled eyes, Emily said, "Tell me what you need. I can hold you, listen to you, talk to you…anything."

A tiny smile curled just one side of her mouth. "Thanks. If you don't mind…" She went to her drawers and pulled out a pair of socks. "I need to go for a walk. Is that cool?"

"You want to go alone?"

"Yeah," she said, bending to get the socks on quickly. "If that's okay."

"It's fine." Emily went to her and gave her a long hug. "Whatever you need." She put her hands on the sides of her face and gazed into her eyes for a few moments. "I'll be here for you."

"That helps." She went to the closet and stood in front of it for a second. "Where's…?"

"I put all of our clothes into a bag and left it in the hall."

"Got it. Thanks." She grabbed another coat, one that wasn't heavy enough for the weather, and went to the door. "I won't be gone too long."

"Take your phone," Emily said, rushing over to the door to hand it to her. "Call me if you're going to be gone more than an hour, okay?"

"I will." She looked at her as another sad smile settled on her face. "It's going to take me a while to let this sink in. But I'll be all right."

"I know you will. Just…be careful."

As she walked out Emily fought the urge to ignore what Blake needed and do what *she* needed to do—follow her. Sometimes, respecting a person's wishes sucked bad.

Both Saturday and Sunday were nothing but phone call after phone call, many of them ending in arguments. The owners, particularly that loathsome Jeffery, the guy who'd insulted Blake so badly that night in the kitchen, were putting pressure on her to fire the whole staff, and Emily had to sit on the sidelines, too interested to ignore the calls, but unable to participate in any way. The staff would never know how hard Blake had fought, but she was only allowed to keep her two long-time prep cooks, Carlos and Norma.

It was awful watching Blake wage a losing fight. She kept reminding each owner that their business continuation insurance would cover staff salaries, at least for a while, but they wouldn't hear of it. Blake did all of the work, and was the public face of the restaurant, but she had as little power as Grant—who was now out of a job.

Watching the arguments was draining, but listening to Blake dutifully call each of her employees and fire them broke Emily's heart. She was secretly relieved, albeit awash with guilt, when she got ready to leave for home on Sunday night.

They stood near the front door, holding each other for a long time. Emily's face was buried in Blake's shoulder when she murmured, "If you need me, I can take the day off. Even the week." She pulled away and looked into her stormy eyes.

"There's nothing you can do. I'll have to go meet the owners and the insurance adjuster, but..." She shrugged. "I should do that alone."

Emily put her hands on her shoulders and held her at arm's length as she stared into her eyes, hyper-vigilant for any sign Blake wanted her to stay. "Call me if you need me. Promise?"

"Sure. I promise." She leaned close and they kissed, gently. "I'll be okay."

"I still worry." She slid her arms around Blake's waist and hugged her tightly. "That's what girlfriends do."

"I'm glad I have you," Blake whispered into her ear.

"You can have me right next to you any time you need me. Just call."

Blake spent the week with fire investigators, insurance adjusters, and the owners. That all made sense. What had Emily worried was that she seemed to do nothing but sleep when she wasn't meeting with someone. After waking her at two in the afternoon on Friday, Emily said, "Go back to sleep. I didn't mean to wake you."

"S'okay. I should...do something."

"I'm going to come over after I get off work and make you dinner. Actually, I think I'll stay all weekend, if that's okay."

"Sure," she said, still sounding out-of-it. "Super. Keys. Doorman."

"Go back to sleep. I'll see you around six."

When Emily entered the apartment, Blake was lying on top of the bed, fully clothed. Her boots were still on, draped over the edge of the mattress as she lay sprawled across it, face-down. Normally, she was a heavy sleeper, but this was ridiculous. She didn't even flinch when Emily dropped a heavy can onto the floor. After putting the things she'd bought away, Emily went over and sat on the edge of the bed, then gently slid her fingers through Blake's hair, her concern growing when she shrugged off the caress and curled into a fetal position.

"Come on," Emily urged. "You've got to get up and get your blood moving."

"Don't wanna," she grumbled. "Tired."

Emily put her hand on her shoulder and forcefully turned her onto her side. "I don't think you're tired, Chef. I think you're depressed. Come on." She tickled under her chin, smiling to herself when Blake's eyes closed even tighter and she squirmed to get away. "I'm not going to give up, no matter how cute you look." Now she grasped a hand and pulled her into a sitting position. "You're already dressed, so all you need is your coat."

Blake's eyes opened halfway. "Coat?"

"Uh-huh. I stopped on the way over and bought you a membership at a public pool just north of Houston. Adult swim's until 7:30. After you swim, we'll go have dinner."

"Swim?" Now her beautiful brown eyes opened fully. "Swim? I haven't been swimming in a pool in…years." She blinked slowly, as if she couldn't get her head around the fact it had been so long.

"It's time to start." Emily pulled Blake to her feet and steadied her when she started to lean to one side. "It's too cold and slushy out to go for a long walk. Swimming will be good for you."

"I don't think I have the right kind of suit." She looked adorably confused, and blessedly malleable. "I have bikinis, but—"

"We'll stop and get you one on the way. Let's go." Putting her hands on Blake's back, Emily pushed her toward the hall, where they got her coat from the closet.

"Why are you being so forceful?" she managed to ask as Emily guided her out the door.

"Because you'll feel better if you use your body."

"Are you going to swim with me?"

"Not today. I like to play in the water, but I'm not much for laps. There's a place for parents to watch. That's where I'll be."

Finally, a weak smile appeared. "It's been a long time since anyone watched me swim."

"It's been a long time since I've watched anyone swim. Like forever." She took her hand and led her to the elevator. "It'll be fun."

Swimming must have been like riding a bike. Blake's first couple of laps were slow, almost plodding, with her hands slapping at the water as she clearly struggled to get into a groove. But once her muscle memory kicked in, she started to glide through the water like a seal, propelling herself, splash-free, with a beautiful economy of motion. Emily beamed with pride as a fit-looking guy got out and stood on the pool deck, watching her with what looked like envy—or desire. Either way, he wasn't going to sample Blake's talents. Those were for Emily to enjoy, maybe as soon as dinner was over.

When Blake appeared in the waiting area, she bore a sated smile. Very close to the one she wore after a roll in the hay. "You're gonna have to cut my meat," she said, shaking her arms like she had no control over them.

Emily put her arms around her and gave her a squeeze. "You're such a stud. I wanted to pull you out of the water and have you right on the pool deck."

Blake's eyes shimmered with interest. "I would have paid you to pull me out after about fifteen laps. I'm *old*."

"You're a total stud, and I won't hear a word of dissent." They exited into the icy night, with Emily snuggling up close. "What would my studly girlfriend like for dinner? You choose."

Blake pursed her lips in quiet contemplation. "Do you mind traveling?"

"Not a bit."

"Then let's head over to midtown."

Emily scoffed at her terminology. "Going to midtown is traveling? I thought you wanted to go to Ozone Park or something."

"I have no idea where that is. Midtown is as far as I like to go. Luckily, that's where some of my favorite restaurants are. Tonight, I want to feel the burn."

"Sichuan?"

"Yep," she said, her eyes narrowing in pleasure. "I want my tongue to burn as much as my shoulders do."

"You're on, Chef. I assume you know a good place."

With a dazzling smile, Blake nodded. "You assume correctly." She stood in the street, searching for a cab. "You don't mind, do you?"

"I know you're phobic about public transportation. I'll give in."

"I am not!" She laughed, then gave Emily another smile. "Maybe a little. But I'll pay."

"I'll contribute $2.50. That's all it's worth to me."

A cab screeched to a halt in the middle of the street, then backed up, nearly running Blake over. She jumped out of the way, then opened the rear door, letting Emily in first. "Thirtieth and Lex," she said, then settled into her seat. "Thanks for making me swim. I never would have thought of doing that."

Emily poked her in the side. "You might never have gotten out of bed."

She nodded, then turned to stare out the window. Blake didn't speak again until their driver stopped at Thirtieth Street. She paid him, then took Emily's hand as they walked down Lexington. "I guess I've been depressed." Shrugging, she added, "I've never had this much free time, and I have no idea what to do to keep myself busy."

Emily tucked Blake's arm close, and they both lowered their heads against the driving wind. When Blake pulled a large red door open, a very crowded entryway greet them. Blake threaded through the milling people and spoke quietly to the young woman at the door. Then they were being led to a table in the corner. "Who do you know?" Emily asked quietly as their menus were delivered.

"No one," she said, grinning. "But I know how to say I'm jonesing for some of their camphor-smoked duck. Either she liked the fact that I went out of my way to learn how to ask for what I like, or my pronunciation was so bad she wanted to get rid of me quickly."

"Maybe both," Emily said, sticking out her tongue. "Mmm... I love Sichuan food." She looked up and caught Blake gazing at her fondly. "Did you pick this hoping I might be able to taste something?"

"Who me?" She pointed at herself. "Never occurred to me." She ran her finger down the menu, saying, "I've had the braised whole fish, the conch, the chong qing chicken, the dandan noodles, and the fiery tofu. And the duck, of course." She smiled, showing her teeth. "Hungry?"

"If we order all of that, we'll have to pull another table over just to hold it. Why don't we stick with two mains, noodles and tofu? Will that satisfy you?"

Blake leaned over and spoke quietly. "Only until I get you home. I guess my libido only needed a week to mourn. It's ready for action."

"Then let's get eating, Chef. Mine's been primed since I saw you cranking out laps."

Blake sat back in her chair, looking very pleased with herself. "You've got yourself a date."

They arrived home at ten, both so full they were moaning. "We were pigs," Emily decided. "I was sweating and my mouth was on fire, but I couldn't stop. Even though I could barely taste it, that duck was like crack!"

"Agreed. But my stomach's going to hate me in the morning." She looked at her bed, unmade and open. "We can't lie down for hours or we'll have killer heartburn."

"Good." Emily took Blake by the hand and led her over to one of the two chairs. "I have news."

Blake sat and stared up at her. "Bad news?"

"It's not bad, but it's not..." Emily sat down and gazed into her eyes. "My work permit came through, so Laurent would like me to get going on the new restaurant." She squeezed Blake's hand when her eyes grew wide. "But he knows things are up in the air for you, so I can put it off for a while if I need to."

"He's a good guy," Blake said. "He's called me every couple of days."

"He *is* a good guy. He'd like it if I'd go now, but he's not pushing me. What do you think?"

Blake took in a breath and let it out slowly as her eyes narrowed. "If you need to go, you need to go. You made a commitment, Emily."

"I know," she said, searching her eyes for more information. "But I've made a commitment to you too." She grasped Blake's hand and kissed the back of it, holding it to her heart. "The girlfriend commitment is a pretty important one." Leaning close, she put her hand on Blake's cheek, holding her gaze. "There's no reason you can't go with me. Michael's arranged for a hotel room close to the restaurant. You couldn't work, but you could hang out at the beach all day. That would let you relax, Chef. Away from all of this stress."

Emily could see the desire in her stormy eyes. Nearly every part of her wanted to pack a bag and take off. She continued to think for a few seconds, finally saying, "Even though we're nowhere near getting paid off, we're supposed to start planning the new space. I should be here, Emily. I'm still getting paid, and that means I have to be available."

"But will you have enough to do to keep you busy?"

"If Jessica follows through like she said she was going to, I'm going to be busier than ever. She made it very clear I don't have any reason to refuse any and all promotional events."

"Your favorite things."

"Yeah. She's already got me booked for a trip to South Carolina next month. I'm sure that's just the tip of the iceberg."

"Well, I know you'd rather be busy than not. Maybe you'll get into it."

"I'm more interested in the rebuild. It's going to be much more work than last time, given we have to start from scratch. I want to get more involved with the planning. I'm going to fight for a bigger prep kitchen, and a better loading dock."

"You said you let Jessica make most of the design decisions last time. Will you do that again?"

She waved her hand in the air. "I don't care much about the color and the fabric or the kinds of tables or chairs she wants. But I'm not going to let her make one single decision about the kitchen or how much space I need. That's mine," she said firmly. Emily saw the determination in her eyes, impressed with how matter-of-fact she was about rebuilding. That was a very, very good sign. She was close to normal.

Chapter Twenty-One

A WEEK LATER, EMILY lay in Blake's bed, idly playing with her. She'd never been so hungry for a woman, filled with such a need to touch her, even while she was sound asleep. Tonight, sound asleep didn't cover it. Blake was out cold, splayed across Emily's body, with her head resting on a hip, arms bracketing her torso. If she could have reached her phone, Emily would have taken a picture. She couldn't imagine where Blake's legs were, given the bed wasn't nine feet long. But Blake never seemed to mind dozing in what looked like very uncomfortable positions. When she was tired, she slept, never concerned with the details.

Emily had a car coming for her in a half hour, but she was so unwilling to leave the warmth and comfort of Blake's bed and her tender embrace she knew she'd stay until she had to rush like a madwoman.

She'd had to fill in for Daniel the night before, not getting off work until midnight. Blake met her at the restaurant, and they'd gone out for drinks with Laurent, arriving back at the apartment at two. Then they'd played in bed for hours, unable to get enough of each other. Now the mean little clock was reminding her she just had a few minutes to relish Blake's body before she had to leave her for months. *Months!*

Blake stirred, then smacked her lips together. Nuzzling against Emily's belly, she placed a few kisses on her skin, then sighed and started to fall asleep again.

"I've got to get up," Emily whispered, patting her back.

"No," she groused, moving her hands to pin Emily to the bed. "Too early."

"I know it's early." She pried herself away from Blake's very welcome embrace, then got to her feet. Leaning over, she kissed her cheek. "Go back to sleep."

"Wake me before you leave," she mumbled, then started to breathe heavily.

Emily looked down on her, desperate to stay. They were in *such* a good place. Even though they only saw each other on the weekends, they got along so well that each weekend felt like a vacation. And she knew Blake felt the same. She didn't express her feelings with words very often, but she showed them by her actions. She was hooked. Emily was sure of it. But she hadn't once—not once—expressed any qualms about Emily leaving. Looking down at her, so peaceful when she slept, Emily's heart ached with longing for her. It was going to kill her to be apart for so long. But Blake acted like it was a regular week, and they'd see each other on the weekend. It was not, and they would not. Not by a long shot.

Emily had been on a few decent vacations; going to Europe with Chase after they'd graduated from Michigan, a long weekend in Montreal with her girlfriend when she was in cooking school, and a trip to South By Southwest with a group of people from Defarge. But she'd never been anywhere tropical.

As the plane dipped and skittered through the clouds, it burst through a big one to reveal a stunningly gorgeous, blue-green sea with a verdant island bobbing atop it. She almost elbowed her seat-mate to exclaim, but that was pretty amateurish. Clearly, she was the rookie on board, with everyone in sight acting like they were on the M1 bus, going down 5th Avenue. Just another uninteresting ride. People were so jaded! With a view so lush, so breathtaking lying right in front of them, most didn't look up from their phones or tablets. Right then, Emily pledged she'd never regard something so beautiful as commonplace.

Laurent's assistant Michael had made her travel arrangements, and he'd assured her someone would pick her up and take her to her hotel. That was a first, and she wasn't going to argue. She hadn't even taken the time to check whether people on Grand Cayman spoke English or Spanish!

The plane bounced a few times, and she was pushed back hard against her seat when they touched down. Then they slowed and eventually pulled up in front of a single terminal. Emily craned her neck to see a couple of guys wheel a set of stairs up to the plane, then they started to disembark.

By the time she'd moved past business class to approach the door, warm air was caressing her. Stifling the groan of pleasure that almost escaped, she shielded her eyes from the glaring sun and hoisted her bag onto her shoulder for the descent.

The tarmac was scalding hot, but New York had been cold and gray for what seemed like forever, so she was tempted to merely stand in the heat and breathe in the soothing air. But someone was waiting for her, and she moved along, assuming she could grab her bag and take off. There was a cover over a walkway that seemed to lead to the terminal, and she relished having the slanting sun out of her eyes. Then she and her fellow passengers entered an ice-cold room where the air-conditioning must have been set as high as it would go. Long lines of people sorted themselves into residents and non-residents, and she started to dig through her bag for all of the stuff Michael had given her, embarrassed to admit she hadn't even looked at the Manilla envelope upon which he'd written "Important documents." By the time she'd reached the front of the line, she'd figured out that English was the local language, a fact that filled her with relief. Her Spanish was worse than her French, which wasn't good at all.

The guy at the immigration booth seemed to think she was planning on overthrowing the government. Or at least that's how it felt when he questioned everything from her salary, her living situation, whether or not she had an employment contract, and every other detail she could imagine anyone caring about. Finally, he seemed vaguely satisfied that she wasn't going to just lie on the beach and harass the locals, and he stamped her passport, flashed a quick smile, and said, "Welcome to Cayman."

She actually did feel kind of welcome after all of that, and she strode into the terminal. It was small, the smallest she'd ever been in. A single baggage carousel moved lazily, bags still placed close together, waiting for their owners to work their way through immigration. Three of them were hers, and she wrestled them off, nearly wrenching her back as she chided herself for being just under the weight limit for each of them. After getting the ok from the customs officers to leave the secure area, she exited the building, trying to figure out how to spot her ride.

There was a handy place for taxi drivers to wait, and cabs filled the available spots. But a group of drivers were standing in the shade, chatting while they waited for people to exit. In the crowd, Emily spotted a really cute woman, very androgynous, clad in a sleeveless yellow cotton shirt and sky blue shorts. What caught Emily's attention were the tan work-boots she wore. Nearly every other person wore sandals or flip flops, and Emily smirked at the substantial footwear. Just as she was about to look away, she noticed the woman held a square of heavy white paper with "Desjardins" printed on it.

Emily dragged her bags over and said, "Are you waiting for me?"

A smile made the woman's face light up. "If you're Emily Desjardins, I am."

"Then you're waiting for me." Emily extended her hand, and shook one easily as callused as her own. But Emily didn't have a deep tan, sun bleached sandy-colored hair or a grip that could have bent steel.

"Joely Harris," the woman said, continuing to pump Emily's hand. "Great to meet you."

"Same here."

"Let me get your stuff." She tossed the smallest of the bags atop the largest, then held the third in her other hand. "Let's hit it," she said, rolling the big bag along the sidewalk as she carried the third bag like it was empty.

Emily followed along, trying to keep up with Joely's long strides. It was embarrassing to have trouble keeping pace when Joely was pushing a hundred pounds worth of suitcases, but she didn't have the nerve to ask her to slow down. They crossed a narrow plaza to reach a parking lot, and by the time Emily got to the truck, her bags were loaded in the bed. "Ready?" Joely asked.

"Sure. Just let me…"

Joely plucked the bag from her shoulder and tossed it into a tiny space behind the seats, acting like it weighed an ounce. Emily got in, and as she clicked her seatbelt, Joely said, "Are you ready to call it a day? Or would you like to see the restaurant?"

"Uhm..." Emily tried to figure out why her cabdriver knew about the restaurant. Maybe it was such a small island everyone knew everyone else's business. "You know about Laurent Bistro?"

Joely cocked her head, then blinked. "I'd better. I'm building it."

"Shit!" Emily clapped her hand over her mouth. "I'm so sorry. They only said someone would pick me up. I had no idea..."

Maintaining her puzzled gaze, Joely said, "Do you have any idea who I am?"

"No!" Emily started to laugh. "We talk about the restaurant all of the time, but we focus on the food and the staff and all of the practical aspects of getting the kitchen organized. I know nothing about the actual building."

"Well, I know nothing about running a restaurant. We'll have to work to narrow that gap a little bit."

Joely started to drive, and in a few minutes they were cruising along a road that snaked through stands of trees that Emily couldn't even attempt to name. "I'm not sure what these trees are," she said, "but I know we don't have them in New York. Ahhhh!" she yelped when a prehistoric...thing scampered across the road. "What in the holy hell was that?"

Joely was laughing hard as she slowed down. "That was an iguana. You're going to see a lot of them. This is mangrove, by the way, and if someone in New York planted one, it wouldn't last long."

Chuckling, Emily said, "I can say, without fear of contradiction, that this looks nothing like New York. It's so...tropical."

"Compared to New York, it definitely is." She gave Emily a quick look. "Have you traveled much?"

"I went to Europe right after college, but that's about it. I've never been to the Caribbean."

"Ahh. Then you're going to experience a whole different climate, as well as culture. If you're like most people, you'll start trying to figure out a way to stay."

"I wouldn't mind being warm in winter, but other than that, I'm happy in New York. It sure would be nice to come down here to knock the icicles off once in a while, though."

"It is. The furthest north I've ever lived is Florida. I don't think I'd do well in cold weather."

"You're not from Florida, are you? I can hear little bits of an accent, but I can't quite make it out."

"I've been here most of my life, but local people tell me I sound like a foreigner. And my relatives in England assure me that I don't sound English at all. I suppose I've picked up bits and bobs without really noticing."

"Got it," Emily said. "Another one!" she called out. "Damn, you could easily hit one of those things."

"You look like you're about to climb up onto the roof." Joely laughed. "They won't hurt you. Promise."

"That sounds like I might encounter one—up close. Tell me I'm wrong!" she said, knowing she was talking much louder than she needed to.

Unable to hide a smirk, Joely said, "You might see one up close, but it'll be lying in the sun, enjoying itself. It's not going to chase you. Promise."

While trying to get her heart to slow down and beat at a normal rhythm, Emily realized she hadn't said whether or not she wanted to go by the restaurant. But Joely clearly wasn't the type to let a little indecision stop her. Soon they hit a road that led them to the beach Emily had been certain she'd see the minute she landed. "Ahh, now we're talking," she said, grinning at the sight. "I love being near water."

"You're going to be very near it." A minute later, she pulled into the parking lot of a pretty standard-issue motel. "Let's get you checked in, then we'll swing by the restaurant."

By the time Emily got out, Joely had the tailgate down. Effortlessly, she stepped onto the bumper and jumped up into the bed of the truck, then placed the suitcases near the tailgate, jumped back down and got them organized again. "Ready?" she asked, allowing Emily to carry only the small bag she'd stored her travel stuff in. In her heart, she was pretty butch. But she clearly didn't give off that vibe, given that just about every powerful woman she'd ever met treated her like a damsel in distress.

In just a few minutes they were back in the truck, with Joely saying, "The building's in Georgetown, which I think was a good choice."

"That's a…town?"

"Yeah. That's where the office buildings are."

"Office buildings? I think we'll have to rely on American tourists to build a reputation. Do you really think—"

"It'll be great," she said, clearly confident. "It's close to where the cruise ships tender their passengers, so you might be able to lure traveling Americans in for lunch or drinks. And you'll do a great business for breakfast and lunch from the office workers. They're always looking for something new."

Chuckling, Emily said, "I haven't heard anything about dinner. I don't think Laurent's looking to run a luncheonette."

"Trust me," Joely said. "Being in Georgetown is the right choice. If you were out by the beach, you'd never get the office workers. If the place is as good as Laurent says it's going to be, the locals will flock to it."

"You know Laurent?"

"We've met, but I get most of my direction from—"

"Michael," Emily supplied. "He's in charge of everything except cooking."

"That's the guy. Laurent wanted to be by the beach, but Michael and I and the real estate guy all ganged up on him to convince him to be in town."

"Laurent's not easy to convince of things," Emily said. "Not that I've tried."

"No, but he's reasonable. He listened to me, even though I'm just the builder. I appreciated that."

"He's a good guy," Emily agreed. "He gave me a job when I was pretty down about my cooking abilities, so I'll always be a fan."

"You cook?" Joely asked, a grin appearing.

"I cook," she said, realizing she was sure of her identity as a cook, even though she wasn't going to touch a knife for months. Cooking wasn't what she did, it was who she was, and losing her sense of smell didn't change that fact.

It took a while to reach the job site, but Joely eventually tucked the truck into a muddy spot in front of a shell of a building, now only a foundation and a steel frame. Midsize to large office buildings surrounded them, most of them modern and relatively new. "Here's your new home," Joely said as they both got out.

"Looks a little rough. I don't think I'm ready to put the appliances in yet." They climbed up a hand-made set of three steps, and Emily walked around the perimeter. "It looks strangely small."

"It's not. The restaurants in the luxury hotels are bigger, but this will be one of the biggest free-standing places on the island. Depending on how you lay it out, you could seat two hundred customers in here."

"That's a lot of covers to spit out every night."

"Covers?"

"Meals. Laurent's flagship restaurant, where I work, seats a hundred and fifty, and it takes a huge staff to crank it out."

Joely slapped her hand onto one of the metal supports. "You won't be serving two hundred all year. You'll be lucky to have fifty in the summer."

"Really? Why?"

"The heat, mostly. People like to come to the Caribbean when it's thirty at home and seventy here." She moved over to the rear of the building. "If I had to design the place, I'd section it off so you could close the big room when things are slow. Then it won't look like it's empty."

"Have you talked to Michael about that?"

"Oh, sure. I think he agrees, but he's not much for committing himself." She let out a soft laugh. "I think he likes to act like Laurent makes the decisions." She bent to pick up some wicked looking screws discarded on the floor.

"He actually does," Emily said. "But he's much more into food and service than buildings. He gave me a lot of independence when I helped open up his place in Las Vegas."

"So this isn't your first rodeo?"

"It's my second. I didn't get to Las Vegas until the build was nearly finished, though. This will be a very different experience."

"A better one, I hope." Joely's grin gave Emily her first hint that she might be amenable to a little flirting along with their business needs. *Damn.* The last thing she'd expected was to wind up in a tropical paradise with a friendly, flirty, attractive lesbian, but she'd been around long enough to know when a woman liked what she saw. *Great.* Emily had been single for a heck of a long time, never coming across a woman she even wanted to see twice. Now, when she was happy with Blake, a great opportunity she had no interest in pursuing dropped into her lap. Timing was everything.

Blake knew the Caribbean, but she'd never been to Cayman, so Emily took her tablet with her wherever she went, sending texts and short videos.

Since Blake had no fixed schedule to keep, they could spend hours talking at night. It was weird, with both of them being much more verbal than they were in New York. Maybe that was only because they couldn't get their hands on each other.

One night, a week after Emily arrived, she sat on her balcony, listening to the faint sounds of waves lapping at the shore. It was an almost perfect night. All she needed was a certain chef next to her and she would have been in heaven. Blake had her tablet computer resting on a pillow, angled so Emily could see her from the waist up. Blake gazed into the camera, a happy smile curling her mouth. "Are you enjoying this as much as I am?"

"Totally. I feel super close to you, even though we're hundreds of miles apart."

"Wish I was there," Blake said, sounding a little melancholy. "I've got just enough to do to keep me here, but not enough to keep me busy. That leaves me a lot of time to mope."

"No progress with the insurance company?"

"No," she said, a frown covering her face. "We had another conference call today. They insist on having a certified report from the fire investigator. I think they're just stalling, but our attorney says that's not an unusual request."

"Are you working on the plans for the new place?"

"Not enough. Until we know exactly much money we're going to get, the owners don't want to make any firm decisions. But I'm going to be on a panel at some lecture series at the public library, and a writer for a food magazine is going to interview me next week."

"See if there's a link so I can watch your panel. And I want that magazine, too. I'm going to keep a scrapbook for you, since I know you aren't the type to keep one for yourself."

She chuckled. "I don't mind stuff like that, but I'd rather be cooking. I'd *much* rather be cooking."

"Then cook. Call some of your friends and ask if you can guest chef for them. I bet a lot of people would love a few days off."

The camera was focused on Blake's face and Emily could see the idea lodge in her brain and process for a minute. "You're a freaking genius, Emily! I'm gonna make some calls." She narrowed her eyes, probably looking at the clock on her bookshelf. "It's only eleven thirty. This is a good time to catch people as they're finishing up." She blinked. "Do you mind?"

"No," she said, chuckling. "Go find a way to keep busy. I know you need to."

"I really do," she said, so earnest she took Emily's breath away. "Call me tomorrow. With any luck, I'll be cooking soon!"

Emily was sitting on the edge of the concrete foundation of the restaurant, scanning a supply catalog. She hadn't rented a car, given that Joely always insisted on picking her up and dropping her off at the end of the day. She would have refused, but it really was silly to have a car sitting around idly all day. Besides, keeping her expenses low looked good to Michael, who pinched every penny possible.

Her phone vibrated, then Blake's ring made her smile. She'd recorded her chopping a bunch of carrots, loving the way her knife zipped decisively through the flesh, and the audio was now her personalized ringtone. "How's my favorite chef?"

"Good. Better. Starting Monday, I'm going to sub for Gunther Brandt for a week at Sommer. Know it?"

"Is that on Park?"

"Yeah. In Midtown. I'm going to be at the end of my leash up there, but I'm really happy. I've never cooked German-inspired food."

"I'm *so* glad to hear that. You'll be much happier with something to do, and cooking a different cuisine will be good for you." Emily looked up to see Joely jump down to the ground, then perch on the edge of the foundation, waiting.

"Are you still at work?" Blake asked.

"Uh-huh. I'm waiting for my ride."

"Your contractor?"

"Yeah." She let out a laugh. "I've never had a chauffeur, but I'm getting used to it. I'll be so out of shape from not walking anywhere that I might not be able to make it to the subway when I get home."

"I have my doubts about that. I bet you're still on your feet all day."

"This is true. Speaking of being in shape, have you been swimming today?"

After a lengthy pause, Blake said, "I guess I have to, huh?"

"You should, Chef. You know you feel better when you get some exercise."

"Fine," she grumbled. Emily could just see her pouting. "It's twenty degrees, but I'll go swimming."

"Don't whine. You know you could come here if you wanted to be warm." She was about to add how she'd like to warm her up, but didn't want Joely to hear anything too private.

"Wish I could, but the second we get the okay from the insurance company, I'm gonna be more than full-time busy."

"Just offering alternatives."

"I appreciate that, Emily. One thing I know I can rely on is you caring about me."

"You've got that right. Call me before you go to sleep, okay?"

"It's a deal. Later."

Emily clicked off, stood and put her phone back into her pocket. "Ready to go?"

"Uh-huh." Joely pulled her keys from a small gear bag she carried. "Have you got anything scheduled?"

Emily walked alongside as they picked their way across the construction detritus, heading for the truck. "For tonight?"

"Yeah. Tonight."

"You're the only person I know on the island, so…no." She chuckled. "I'm going to do my usual. Order room service, then walk over to the beach and watch the ocean for a while."

"What?" Joely said, her eyes wide. "You're wasting your evenings ordering room service?"

"I could go out, but I'm not crazy about eating alone."

"Then eat with me." Emily turned and took a good, long look at Joely. Now that they'd been working together for a bit, she didn't seem flirty anymore. Friendly and outgoing, but that was about it. "All right. I just need to be home by ten."

They got into the truck, and Joely turned the engine over, letting it growl for a second before she put it into drive. "Late date?" she asked, her casual tone seeming like it was studied.

"Uh-huh. My girlfriend and I do a video chat before bed. My exciting life," she added, laughing at how lame it sounded.

"That could be really exciting, depending on the girlfriend. How long have you been together?"

"Not very. I could be wrong, but I don't think she's the sexting type."

"Prudish?" Joely asked, her eyebrow rising.

"Yeah. She's prudish," Emily agreed, not interested in telling a stranger just how sizzling hot her girlfriend was.

Emily organized herself in bed, getting her tablet set up so they could see each other, as well as look as good as she could. It took a while to make sure she didn't look like she had a triple chin, but she eventually perched the tablet on the dresser. With the lens angled down, she looked pretty darned good.

Her phone rang at ten, and she hit the video button. "Hi there," she said, getting a zing each time Blake's face popped up on the screen.

"Hi." Her smile grew as she gazed at Emily. "You look awfully good. There's just one change I'd make."

"What's that?"

She patted the empty space beside her. "You'd be a little closer. I like being able to talk, but you know what I'd rather be doing." She had such a lecherous tone when she was trying to be seductive. If they needed voiceover artists for sex scenes, Blake would have been employed full time.

"I know what you'd always rather be doing," Emily teased. "But if you were working full time you'd be sound asleep by now, waking up just long enough to insist you were ready to go."

Blake laughed, the sound warming Emily from the inside. "My stamina never matches my desire. I'm all talk."

"I wouldn't go that far. When you're actually awake, you're as good as they get, Chef."

Soberly, Blake said, "I wanted this to be a surprise, so I didn't tell you about it, but I bought a ticket to visit you next week."

"That's great!" Emily saw the pouty look, then said, "Oh, crap. You're subbing at that food festival in San Francisco."

"Exactly. I was going to stay a whole damn week." She scooted around in bed, finally winding up flat on her back, her T-shirt riding up to expose her belly. "I tried to change my flight to come in late February or March, but I can't be sure I'll have a week to spare then. So I tried for any Friday or Saturday morning, thinking a weekend was better than nothing, but was shut out. Why'd you have to go someplace everyone wants to be?"

"That sucks so bad," Emily said, unable to hide her disappointment. "But I'm really pleased you tried. Did you get stuck with the ticket?"

"No, I'll get a credit. And have to pay a change fee. There's no chance of you coming home, right?"

"Mmm, I'm not super busy now, but I could get away for a weekend."

"No, you can't. I'm not kidding when I say there aren't any tickets available for weekend travel. You've got to fly on a weekday to get a seat."

She tried to get a read on how Blake was feeling, but it was hard to see her clearly, given the low light and poor picture quality. "Let me make one thing clear, Chef. I'll come tomorrow if you need me."

"You don't want to know how much a last-minute ticket would be." She sighed, then tilted her head so Emily got a clear picture of her face. Thankfully, she didn't look sad, just disappointed. "I guess we'll see how our schedules sync up. You open in June, right?"

"Uh-huh. Laurent wants to open in the summer so we work any bugs out before tourist season starts."

"That's my boy. He's always been cautious." She picked up her tablet and extended her arms so more of her body was revealed. "How about you? Feeling cautious…or…what's the opposite of cautious?"

"Daring?"

"Yeah," she said, "that's good. Feeling daring?"

Given the look on her face, Emily didn't have to guess what was making Blake feel adventurous. Amazing how a woman's expression could make your whole body tingle, but as Emily settled deeper into the mattress, ready for whatever Blake had in mind, every part of her was ready to go. "I'm all in."

Chapter Twenty-Two

THE NEXT WEEK, EMILY was fairly sure her cell phone was going to be permanently welded to her ear. For four or five hours each day she took calls from Michael, Daniel, and Laurent about the layout, with Joely in the background, trying to guess how the conversations were going to impact her. Emily wasn't sure how they'd found Joely, but they'd lucked out. Every time Emily needed her, she was right there, supervising carefully while handling the constant decisions that came with building any sized structure. Given this was going to be a large place, every decision bore repercussions. If you placed a piece of equipment improperly, it threw off the placement of a dozen more.

Joely was a dynamo, filled with nervous energy and a work ethic that rivaled Blake's. She was so hyper, not one member of her crew could seem to match her pace. Emily often watched her urging the guys on, trying to get them to fly around like she did. But that wasn't how her crew attacked a project. They were good-natured guys, never outright refusing a request. But they moved at their own speed, doing precise, neat work that you couldn't complain about. It must have driven Joely crazy, having to wait for every single task. But she never showed her frustration. Instead, she acted like a cheerleader, complimenting her crew effusively when they sped it up just a hair.

Emily was sure Joely's job would have driven her nuts. With only four full time guys, she was forced to rely on a large number of subcontractors, over whom she had very little control. A lot of the guys listened to her, but all of them seemed to think she was a little crazy. Women general contractors were clearly something these guys didn't have to deal with very often, especially women who followed you around, nipping at your heels like a terrier.

While Emily was confident the work was being done carefully, she stuck to Joely most of the time, trying to oversee things, even when she had no real idea of what she was looking at. Doing that was Blake's suggestion, and now that Emily was on the site, it seemed to be working. People were more careful when they knew someone would see them taking a shortcut.

Blake had been at Sommer all week, not getting home until well after Emily was in bed. As much as she loved talking to her, Emily couldn't afford to be up until two or three, even for phone sex, which she'd found they both had an affinity for. They were in the same time zone, but that didn't help much. By the end of the week, Emily's longing for contact was making her a little cranky, and she was damned glad it was the end of the day.

Joely wandered over and put her hand on the wall they'd finished earlier in the day. "Nice to see it's still standing," she said. "It's so embarrassing when they fall over before you can even slap a coat of paint on them."

"Ugh. Don't remind me. We've got to test paint samples to make sure they look good in different lights."

"We've got a lot more walls to put up. No rush."

"I guess that's true, but each day that passes is a day closer to our opening. I've got to bring this baby in on time."

"We'll get there," Joely said, cheering Emily when she made it clear the deadline was just as important to her. "How about dinner?"

"We've eaten together every night this week. Are you sure you're not sick of me yet?"

"Not even a little." She stuck a hand out and Emily grasped it, allowing Joely to pull her to her feet. "Since I've been single, I've spent a lot of nights alone. It's been nice having someone to talk to."

"I feel the same." They started for the truck, with Emily pausing in the street, gazing at the sunset. It would have been so nice to have Blake beside her, enjoying the warm temperature and the spectacular display the clouds were making. Maybe she'd be able to come for the opening —four months away.

Emily could have spent the weekend learning to scuba dive. But she didn't think it was a good idea to have dinner with Joely every night *and*

spend the weekend with her. Even though the flirty vibes had stopped, spending all of your time with someone sent a message she didn't want to transmit. But she was lonely. As lonely as she'd been since she'd gotten to Cayman. Blake was in San Francisco until Monday, then she was going over to Napa for a week to participate in a food and wine festival.

Emily's hotel had a small pool, and she spent the morning sitting by it while she read. Her phone woke her and she cleared her throat before answering. "I thought I was reading, but obviously not. I almost jumped out of my skin when the phone rang."

"Sleeping?"

"Yeah." She yawned. "Where are you?"

"In a cab, going to the event space. I'm going to astound a few hundred people with my cassoulet."

"Jealous," Emily sighed. "I'd love to be in San Francisco, eating your cassoulet."

"What's on your agenda? Besides sleeping."

"Nothing. Joely wanted me to go scuba diving with her, but I thought she should have some free time."

Blake didn't respond for a few seconds, and when she did her voice was playful. "Going for hard to get?"

"Ha! You know better than most how easy I am to get. No, I'm not playing mind games. I'm a little afraid of being underwater with all of that equipment on."

"Really? If that's all that's stopping you, give it a little thought. How many chances will you have to learn to dive in such a pretty place?"

"Not many. But how often will I do it in the future? Not much scuba diving in New York."

"Emily," she said, her words slow and filled with fondness. "Go outside your comfort zone. It doesn't matter if you never go near another ocean. You're by one now."

"You make a good point, Chef. I think I'll reconsider."

"Do that. But be safe. Make sure Joely really knows what she's doing. Promise?"

"Oh, I'm sure she's an expert. You know, she reminds me of you in a lot of ways. When she says she can do something, she owns it."

"I'm like that?"

"You know you are, but I appreciate that you at least try to be modest. Speaking of owning it, I think my new career might be phone sex given how you responded last time. When can we do that again?"

"You're an ace, you sexy devil. But I think we're going to have trouble finding time to talk for long. The festival in Napa's in the evening, and I probably won't get out of there before midnight. That's three in the morning in the Caribbean."

"We'll get back to it when you're in New York again. You're just in Napa for a week, right?"

"Right." She spoke to her cab driver, then said, "Got to go. Have fun with the fish."

"Thanks," Emily said, but Blake was already gone.

By late March, the restaurant was starting to look like a place you could have dinner. But that was just a facade. They had a heck of a lot of work to do to finish the plumbing and electrical, put up the interior walls, then get flooring down. But once they had all of that, the appliances could go in and Emily could start hiring people.

She'd met all of Joely's friends, mostly bartenders, servers, and cooks who'd welcomed her into the service-class of the island. It was different from New York in some big ways. Weather was, of course, a huge change. But she had to admit people were nicer, friendlier, and less competitive than her fellow New Yorkers. People in the service industry still didn't earn much, they still couldn't afford nice apartments, and very few of them had cars. But they also didn't have to slog through snow to get to the subway for an hour long ride to work.

Blake's predictions about the insurance settlement hadn't panned out. The owners were engaged in a ferocious battle with their insurer, with the whole thing probably headed for court. But she wasn't letting that get her down. She was actually making out very well financially, given she was still being paid her regular salary. The money she made from occasionally subbing for friends was icing on the cake, and given how happy she seemed to be as a vagabond, Emily bet she wasn't in a rush to get back to her own place.

One of the nicest conversations they'd had was just a week earlier when Blake reported that she'd finally placed every single one of her former employees with another restaurant. It was so cool to listen to her talk about everyone's strengths and how she'd worked hard to find places her people would thrive in. She was a darned good boss, even if she did throw a pan or two when things weren't going her way.

One Saturday night, Emily was at Erin and Gretchen's place, cooking dinner. None of Joely's friends could cook, even though half of them were in the restaurant business. So Emily had agreed to show this new couple how to make a few basic dishes to save them from blowing all of their money on dinner out.

"Okay," she said, as both Erin and Gretchen sat at the kitchen counter, alert expressions on their faces. "The first thing you should learn is to prep your mise."

Erin cocked her head. "Should we know what that is?"

"No," Emily said, chuckling. "It's a French term. Mise en place. Your mise is all of the ingredients you need to make your dish. If you've got everything lined up, you won't ever have an unpleasant surprise."

"Got it," Gretchen said, nodding as she made a note.

"Do you and your girlfriend do this when you cook at home?" Erin asked.

"We've only cooked together once," Emily said, thinking of the early morning when Blake tried to create a burrito that would shock her taste buds back into action. "But we would, if we ever got the chance. She's a workaholic." She let out a laugh. "I guess I am too."

"She works too hard to visit? Even once?" Erin asked, getting a not-too-subtle elbow in the ribs from Gretchen.

"It's okay," Emily said. "I know it looks funny she hasn't visited, but she's so busy we barely have time to talk on the phone."

Erin shrugged, looking like she was going to comment further, but feared Gretchen would elbow her again.

"Our relationship is solid," Emily said. "We're just off schedule. I'm at work by seven, and she's working from noon to midnight this week. Then she's going to some big event in Montreal. When she does one of those, she doesn't have a moment to spare."

"Do you talk on the weekend?"

"Oh, yeah. Usually for a few hours." She bit her tongue, realizing that was kind of a lie. "Well, we do when she has a day off. For the past couple of weeks she's been off on Monday, which is always my busiest day. But she's been staying up late, just so we have a little time together." She put an onion on the cutting board and had it chopped in seconds.

"How in the hell did you do that?" Gretchen demanded. "I could barely see your knife!"

Emily started to laugh at her stunned expression, distracted when her phone rang. "Gotta take this," she said, dashing into the living room for privacy. "What's wrong?"

"Does something have to be wrong?" Blake let out a soft laugh. "You've turned into a real worrier."

"Well, you're never, ever free at this time of night…"

"True. And I'm not really free now, but service doesn't start for fifteen minutes, and I wanted to hear your voice."

Relief flooded her. "Aww, that's so romantic."

"I wouldn't go that far, but if you think it is, I'll claim it. What's going on?"

"Hold on a sec, will you?"

Joely had stuck her head into the living room, holding Emily's beer. She entered and dangled it right in front of her nose.

"Thank you. I needed that," Emily said.

"Needed what?" Blake asked.

"Oh. Nothing. Joely was just taunting me with a beer."

"You're with Joely again?" Her tone was casual, but there was an odd edge to her voice.

"Yeah. Is that… You know we hang out."

"Sure. I knew that. I guess I thought you usually just had dinner together after work. No big deal."

"She's my only real friend," Emily reminded her.

"Are you at dinner or…"

"No. I'm cooking for a change. All I've done so far is chop an onion, but even that felt great. I've really missed it."

"You don't have a kitchen, do you?"

Emily laughed. "No, I'm not living large like I was in Las Vegas. You've seen my room. Were you too stunned by my naked body to notice I didn't have a stove?"

"Yeah, I guess I was. Uhm…you sent me a bunch of pictures when you first got there, but you stopped. I have no idea what Joely looks like."

"Really? Well, I can remedy that." She put her phone to her chest and called out, "Hey, Joely!" In a few seconds, she came back into the living room.

"What's up?"

"Come here and pose for me."

"Pose?"

"Yeah. I want to show Blake a picture of the cutest lesbian on Grand Cayman."

Grinning, she walked over and stood next to Emily, who lifted her phone and took a couple of selfies. "Thanks."

"No problem. I aim to please."

"Okay," Emily said, addressing Blake. "I took one of us together. It's pretty cute."

"Of course it is," Blake said, suddenly serious. "If you're in it, it has to be cute."

Three heads appeared in the doorway, one atop the other. "We're starving," her hosts moaned.

Laughing, Emily said, "Don't rush me. Eat some chips or something."

"You'd better go," Blake said. "I didn't mean to interrupt."

"It's not possible for you to interrupt me, Chef. You're my priority."

"I never doubt that in New York," she said softly. Then her tone shifted, sounding brighter, but also a little forced. "I've got more competition when you're away."

"It's not competition, Chef. I'm just trying to stay busy."

"I want that for you," Blake said. "I want you to be happy, Emily. I really do."

"I know." She looked up as someone waved a white kitchen towel in the doorway. "I've gotta go. I'm not going to have a minute's peace until I get dinner moving."

"Call me tomorrow," Blake said. "If you can spare the time."

"Of course I can. Are you working?"

"I go in at noon tomorrow. Does that work?"

"Perfectly. I'll call by ten. You'll be up by then, right?"

"You can wake me. I'd rather have you here in person, but I'll take what I can get. G'night."

Emily hung up, even though she didn't feel they'd really connected. They'd have to do better, 'cause this just wasn't cutting it.

The next morning, a big group of women spread out across Cayman Kai, a beach a lot of ex-pats preferred for snorkeling. They'd all brought something to share for lunch, but as Emily looked through the bags, she said, "Everybody brought chips! I swear, people here eat worse than they do in New York."

Joely laughed, her usual response when Emily compared Cayman to New York. "We can walk down the beach a mile and go to a great bar. They've got food."

Emily rolled her eyes and took out her sunblock, watching their friends run to the water and begin to toss a foam football around. "I don't know why I expect a bunch of lesbians in their twenties to bring a sensible, well-balanced meal, but everyone I've met acts like tomorrow's never going to come."

"Huh?" Joely rolled on her side and shaded her eyes with her hand. "What's that supposed to mean?"

"Nothing bad," Emily assured her. "But at home everyone I know is planning their next move, or worrying about anti-oxidants or only drinking vodka because it's got fewer impurities. Everybody worries."

"Not here," Joely said. "Of course, most of these girls won't last. People cycle out after a few years."

"They die of malnutrition!"

Chuckling, Joely said, "That's not what I mean. If you don't have resident status you have to leave after seven years. They all know they're just passing through, so why put down roots?"

"What about you? Are you permanent or just cycling through?"

"Permanent. Since my parents were born in England I could move there, but I have no urge to leave. It's paradise for me." She leveled her gaze and her volume went down a little so Emily had to lean close to hear. "If I could find someone to love, I'd be set for life."

"Hey," Emily said, giving her a gentle shake. "You've been single for less than a year. You'll find someone new."

"That's the problem. I don't have any trouble finding people to sleep with, but that's not what I'm after. I want a relationship with an adult. I'm tired of sleeping with recent college grads trying to piss off their parents by being a beach bum."

"I don't know," Emily teased as they looked out at the women playing in the water like a bunch of kids. "Some of those bums are pretty cute."

"No argument. But I want more than a nice ass." She lay down and tilted her cap so it shielded her eyes. "I don't mind sampling a few more while I wait, but..."

"Just as I suspected." Emily sat up and took out her phone. "I'm going to wake Blake up with a picture. Maybe I can lure her down here if I taunt her enough."

Joely got up and plucked the phone from her. "I'll take a few for you. Try to look pretty," she joked. Emily posed playfully, attempting to look like a swimwear model.

When she got the phone back, she shook her head. "Stick with construction. I'm in shadow in every one of these." She twitched her head. "Stand behind me. I want to show Blake what kind of tan she could have if she chucked everything and moved down here."

Joely whipped off her tank top, exposing her sun-darkened skin. "I'm going to look like a piece of driftwood in a few years, but I'm too damned lazy to put sunblock on all the time." She got on her knees behind Emily, steadied herself by putting her hands on her shoulders, then they smiled as the shutter clicked a few times.

Emily assessed the pictures. "This is how you do it," she teased, holding the phone in front of Joely's face. "Good composition. Good light."

"I'll take notes, but first I'm gonna go show those kids how to throw a football correctly. Wanna come?"

"No thanks. I've got a full battery so I'm going to drain it by talking to my girlfriend." Emily sent a text, with the best of the photos attached, asking if Blake was up yet. In just a few seconds, her phone rang. "Good morning, sunshine."

"No sun here," Blake said. "Let's do a video chat and you can see what you're missing."

Emily called her back and made tsking noises when Blake held her tablet up to the window to show a steady stream of cars descending into the Holland Tunnel, their windshield wipers working hard against the rain. "That's dreadful," she said. "Maybe you should hop on a plane." She turned her phone to capture the miles of white sand and azure water. "This isn't awful, Chef."

"I'd have to agree." As Blake moved over to her chair, Emily saw her guitar lying across the footstool.

"You'd rather be in dingy, gray, New York, plucking away at some depressing song, huh?"

"How'd you know?" She put the tablet on the table, then adjusted it so Emily could watch her pick up the guitar and start to strum it.

"When do you have to leave for work?"

She shrugged, not looking up. "I should leave in an hour, but the sous I'm working with can handle the place until I'm damn good and ready to show up."

Stunned, Emily finally got out, "You're intentionally going in late?"

"Not feeling it," she admitted, wearing an expression that showed she didn't want to explain further.

"Uhm..." Emily wasn't sure if she should try to get to the bottom of Blake's unbelievably laid-back attitude, or switch topics. "Wanna play me whatever you're working on?"

Even the shrug she gave didn't have much emotion.

"Not one of my girly songs?" Emily joked, knowing her favorite styles didn't appeal to Blake in the least.

"Nah. I heard this yesterday, and started thinking about how many times I sang it when I was a kid. I thought I'd learn it."

"You can just pick your guitar up and start playing?"

"You can find anything on the internet. Took me two seconds to get the chords."

She looked so cute. Hair tousled, wearing a dark fleece turtleneck over flannel pajama bottoms. Like she could be in a cabin in Vermont, with snow falling as a fire burned in the hearth. The difference in their weather highlighted the miles that separated them, filling Emily with melancholy. Given her glum mood, Blake must have been feeling the same. As she played, her eyes closed halfway as she got into the tune.

Then she peered at her laptop, where she must have had the music. Emily watched her go through the first part of the song, not singing along. That was normal for her. She needed to know a tune pretty well to be able to sing while she played.

Emily thought the song was familiar, but their listening tastes were so incompatible it wasn't rare for either of them to play something they were certain was very well known, only to have the other not recognize a note.

After Blake played a few more lines, she nodded slightly and started to sing. "You float like a feather, in a beautiful weather. You're so fucking special." Then her voice grew quiet, almost a whisper as her features contorted, making her look like she was about to cry. "I wish I was special."

Emily stared at her, amazed and troubled at the emotion Blake started to pour into her playing. Her head bounced with each chord, and she leaned forward, really throwing herself into it. Finally, she got to the end, then continued to strum, working on the last few chords as if she were totally alone. Emily didn't say a word, allowing her to finish. Then Blake dropped the instrument to the footstool and leaned back. "It'd sound better with my electric. It just tapers off with the acoustic."

"Did you listen to that song when you were…in high school?" she said, wincing at how clumsy the question sounded. But she didn't want to ask if this was a post-fling song, even though she would have bet money it was.

"Yeah," Blake said, adding nothing.

"I could listen to you all day, even when you're playing something sad." She hesitated, then spoke to the feeling that was going through her. "I get more of you when you play. You're most you when you cook and when you're singing."

"Yeah, I guess," she said, picking up the instrument again to fiddle with the tuning.

"You just started to work on that?"

"Uh-huh. I heard the electric version, then remembered they did an acoustic one. I thought you'd like that better."

Waiting a beat, trying to think of a way to offer her opinion without being too blunt, Emily said, "I love the way you sing it, but it's a little dark for me. I like my music to cheer me up."

"I guess that'd be smarter." Blake looked directly into the camera and Emily gasped at the sadness she saw in her expressive eyes. "Sometimes a song really gets under my skin." She focused on her guitar again, probably only to avoid looking into the camera. "This is one of those. It grabs my heart and squeezes it until…" She shook her head dismissively. "You know."

"Are you all right?" Emily asked, cupping her hand around the phone to make sure Blake could hear her.

"Yeah." She turned her head and looked at her fingers as she moved them along the frets. "Probably the weather. It's hard to be cheerful when it's so gloomy."

"Weather doesn't usually affect you. Are you *sure* you're all right? I'm worried about you."

She shrugged, looking as adolescent as she had during their one trip to Connecticut. "I'll play something happier." She started to strum an old song. As she often did, she bit at her bottom lip as she concentrated. "I'll take Manhattan. The Bronx and Staten Island too..." Then she dropped the guitar onto her lap. "That was one of my grandmother's favorite songs. Damn, she had a beautiful voice." She sighed and tossed the guitar away. It must have landed on the bed, since Emily didn't hear a crash. "Yesterday was her birthday. Five years without her, but it seems like forever."

"Oh, Chef," Emily said, closing her eyes at the pain she could see on Blake's face. "Wanna talk about her?"

"Don't think so."

"Do you want to stay on the line? I don't want to pressure you when you're feeling down."

"I'm *fine*." She smiled, but it didn't have much wattage. "Thanks for making me jealous with that beach picture. I'll send one back so you can show your friends how New Yorkers spend their Sundays." She tried to look soulful and tragic as she stuck her hand out to take the picture. "It's too dark in here for that to be clear, but it's the best I can do."

"Have you eaten yet?"

"I don't have anything in the house." She stood and picked up the tablet, letting it jostle and bounce as she walked to the window. She must have put the tablet right against the glass, because all Emily could see were cars coiling into the tunnel and rivulets of rain sliding down the window. "Looks like a good day to order in, doesn't it?"

"I wish I was there with you." Then she thought of how dumb an idea that was. "Actually, I wish you were here with me. I'd love to have you right beside me until I'm finished here."

"You're too busy."

"Says who? I'm doing my job and making the most of my free time, but I'd give you every spare minute if you'd come down."

Her head dropped for a few moments, and when it lifted again her face had taken on a terribly wistful look. "It's Sunday," she said quietly. "Remember how great Sundays used to be?"

"I do. We didn't get many of them, but those Sundays we had once we became girlfriends were the best."

"Yeah," she agreed, nodding. "Now Sunday's just another day."

"We can try to bring some of that back. Let's make an effort."

Blake shrugged. "We had something special, didn't we?"

"Very special, Chef. What we have is awesome. We just have to be in the same city to get the spark back."

"You seem to have plenty of spark. You're looking great, you're rested, and you're always in a good mood. I think you've found a good situation."

"I like it here," she admitted. "And I'm having fun hanging out. But I'd rush right back to the hotel if you were here."

"Being in the Caribbean for long would drive me nuts if I wasn't working." She picked up the tablet and held it at arm's length, staring into the camera. "How about you? Could you live there?"

"Probably," Emily said, not having given it any serious thought. "I can easily see how people get seduced. You start to think every day is a vacation and that your home just doesn't measure up." She started to laugh, thinking of how absurd that was. "Joely acts like she's still twenty, but it hasn't seemed to hurt her. Maybe living like there's no tomorrow keeps you young."

Blake's big, brown eyes blinked slowly, but she didn't speak for a few moments. "I've got to stop for breakfast, so I'd better get going."

Emily did *not* want to let her go. Something was bothering her, but with so little time to wear her down, she was powerless. "Call me when you get home."

"It'll be late. We go until eleven." Her mood changed the moment she'd decided to get going. A business-like efficiency colored her voice as she stood and started to make her bed.

"I don't mind. I want to talk to you."

"Sure you'll be around?" She was across the room, but Emily could see her eyes land on the lens for a second.

"Of course. Where else would I be at midnight?"

Blake didn't respond. Instead, she looked at the camera for a few long seconds. "Okay. I'll talk to you then." She strode across the room and leaned forward, then the screen went dark. For a long while, Emily went over the whole conversation. Something was definitely wrong. It was possible she had PMS, or the fights about the insurance settlement were finally beginning to wear her down. But Emily was afraid her depression was coming back. Urging her to get back to work had probably been a mistake, since working with people she hadn't hired and didn't truly control clearly wasn't her thing.

After annoying herself with idle speculation, she stowed her phone and went to join her friends. They weren't close friends, but she could rely on every one of them to pull her out of this melancholy mood. With a sick feeling in the pit of her stomach, she reminded herself that Blake didn't have access to that same kind of support network. She had good friends, long-standing ones. But she wouldn't reach out to a single one of them when she was down. Emily knew her far too well to think there was even a possibility of her doing that.

Emily forced herself to sit in the chair in her room, determined to stay awake. A day at the beach tired her out more than a full day of work, but she wanted to be alert when Blake called.

It was almost midnight when she had a shot of insight. There was no reason on earth she had to be at work at seven every morning. Just because Joely and her crew started then didn't mean she had to. She wasn't building the damn restaurant, she was supervising, and she could easily do that starting at nine or even ten. Her self-imposed start time was screwing up her connection to Blake, and it was going to stop. They were going to make time to talk when Blake got home, no matter how late it got.

That vow was still running through her mind when her head jerked, startling her awake. She got up to relieve herself, then took a look at her phone on the way back to her chair. One a.m.

Damn it!

Forcing herself into alertness, she dialed Blake's number.

After a few rings, Blake picked up. "What are you doing up this late?

Irritated, Emily said, "You promised to call after your shift. What happened?"

"It's one in the morning. I'm not going to call you now when you get up at six."

"I know when I get up. I also know I asked you to call, no matter how late."

"Sorry," she said, her voice unusually soft. "It's important for you to get your rest."

"I don't have to punch in, you know. I'm going to start going in later so we can talk." She let out a sigh. "Call me back so I can see you."

"Really? I look like hell."

"Blake," she said, her patience at an end. "I'm not interested in how you look. I'm interested in how you *are*."

"I'll call you right back." Then she cut the connection, giving Emily a second to turn on a light and set her tablet up.

When both devices buzzed, she answered quickly. Blake was still dressed, her nice grey turtleneck making her look very cuddly. "Why do you say you look bad? I love you in that sweater."

"I dunno," she said, dropping down onto one of her chairs. She had a plate in her hand, filled with chunks of cheese and crackers. After popping one into her mouth, she said, "I'm as gray as the weather."

"Tell me about that."

"Dunno. Just feeling bad. Depressed, I guess."

"Have you been swimming?"

Blake stared into the camera for a second. "Swimming isn't the key to happiness, Emily. And, no, I haven't had time."

"All right. I don't want to supervise you, Chef, but it seemed to help before, and I thought it might now."

"I know," she said, her shoulders rising and falling after she took a deep breath. "I'm really unhappy with this gig. The sous is a guy I worked with when I first came to New York. He never liked me, and now he's pissed I'm his boss. I know he's shifting a bunch of stuff onto me that should be his responsibility, but I hate to call Youssef to rat him out." She made a sour face. "I should be able to handle a jerk for a friggin' week."

"You're just there until the weekend?"

"Uh-huh. I guess I'll put up with his games. It won't kill me." She yawned, then took a bite of another cracker. "When's your sister coming?"

"Tuesday."

"You're gonna have a little family reunion?"

"Very little. Chuck was supposed to come, but he had to cancel. They were going to stay at a ritzy resort, but I talked Charlotte into cancelling that. Even though she's got a lot of money, it's silly to throw it away. We'll have an extended sleepover here in my little room."

A small furrow settled between her brows. "Is she just gonna hang out and wait for you to finish work?"

"No. I'm going to take a few days off. Joely will call if she hits any decision points. I've got her trained by now."

"Good. Good." She ate another cracker, then put the plate aside. "I hope you guys have fun."

"Oh, we will. When she's got time, Joely's gonna drive us around to some of her favorite spots. I don't know what I was smoking when I thought I could get by without a car, but I don't want to rent one now. Michael watches my expenses like I'm taking money out of his own pocket."

Blake leaned over, her eyes filling the screen. "Luckily, you don't need one. You've got a built-in taxi service."

"And it's much cheaper than a cab. So what's up next for you? Any prospects?"

Blake shrugged. "A bunch. I'm trying to decide which one to take next."

"Jessica doesn't have anything lined up for you?"

"Nope." She slowly shook her head. "Haven't heard from her in a while."

"Any news on the restaurant? You haven't mentioned it for weeks."

"No news," she said, her voice so dismissive Emily decided not to bring it up again.

She took a breath, trying to figure out a way inside. But she was stumped. Blake clearly wasn't her usual self, but that could have been for a dozen reasons. Thinking back, Emily was reminded of the day Blake's parents came to the restaurant. She was equally snappish then, and just as curt. "Are you sure you're okay?"

"I am fine," Blake said, her diction very precise.

"All right. I guess I'll let you go. Unless you want…" She was going to suggest they have phone sex. It had been weeks since they'd been on a schedule when they could seduce each other, but Blake was giving off fewer sexy vibes than a rock. "Anything."

"I want a lot of things, Emily. Whether I get them is another issue."

The next Saturday morning, Emily slapped at the bed, trying to silence her ringing phone. It took a few seconds for her brain to register Blake's knife-work, but when she did, she grasped the device. "Give me a second. Gotta wake up."

"Oh, shit. I'm sorry. I didn't pay any attention to what time it was."

Emily fought to focus, then blinked at the display. "It's only eight. What are you doing up?"

"Couldn't sleep. Got too many things racing around in my brain."

Joely walked into the living room, smirked at Emily's clearly disheveled self and said, "Want coffee?"

After putting her hand over the microphone, she said, "Yes. Lots of it. Lots of milk."

"What?"

"Sorry. I was just asking for some coffee. I got carried away last night and my head's throbbing." Emily grasped her pillows and propped herself up, wondering if Charlotte was also nursing a hangover. "What's going on in that brain?"

"You can make coffee?"

"Of course I can make coffee," she said, smiling at her little joke. "I'm a chef."

"Right," Blake said brusquely. "Got an offer." She was using her business-like shorthand. "South Beach. Start tomorrow. Indefinite."

"South Beach?" Emily bit her tongue, trying not to be a scold. If Blake could spend an indefinite amount of time in South Beach, why couldn't she go a little farther and visit Cayman? Before she could stuff a fist in her mouth, the words leaked out. "That's awfully close to the Caribbean, Chef."

"Yeah," she said, oblivious. "Do you know Jenny Thien?"

"I've heard of her. She does some kind of Latin fusion thing, right?"

"That's Jenny Tiant. Different Jenny. This one does Vietnamese/ French. Her mom's ill, and she needs to go to San Jose to be with her. She's leaving tonight, so I've got to hustle."

"And you'll stay…as long as she needs you?"

"Not sure. I might. I don't have anything going on here."

"Since when? Don't you have a restaurant you're trying to reopen?"

"Depends on the day." She cleared her throat. "I'm trying to get things in order, Emily."

"What kind of things?" Her blood pressure rose as Blake continued her oddly rambling comments. She wasn't herself, and hadn't been for weeks, but Emily couldn't find a way to get into her head.

"Everything. Before you left…" She took an audible breath, then spat the rest of the sentence out in a rush. "We didn't specifically talk about some things."

"Things?" Now her heart was thrumming hard in her chest. This wasn't good. She could feel a punch coming for her, aimed right at her head.

"We said we'd be exclusive when we were in New York, but we didn't renegotiate when you left."

Oh, fuck!

Emily began to shake, almost dropping the phone from her trembling hand.

Blake continued, haltingly. "We said we'd talk about that when we had to be apart, but we didn't."

"I didn't know we needed to have that conversation," Emily said, her voice shaking. "I thought it was obvious."

"I'm out of my element here," Blake said, sounding just that. "What's the norm when people are apart?" She took another breath, sounding like she'd been running. "How do they stay together if they…" Utter silence for a few seconds. "Aren't able to be exclusive."

Fuck, fuck, fuck!

Emily's guts were in such a knot she was sure she was going to be sick. "What are you asking?"

"Uhm… I guess I'm asking about the best way to structure an open relationship. You said Joely was in one. How did she do it?"

Joely? Why the fuck did she care about Joely? Emily closed her eyes while trying to make her thoughts coalesce. It took a minute, but she was finally able to answer. "Joely and her ex dated other people as long as they got clearance first. Is that what you're asking for? Is that what you want?"

"No, no," she said, her voice rising. "That wouldn't work for me. I'd rather have it left unsaid."

"Tell me what's on your mind, Chef. Don't beat around the bush."

"Uhm, okay." Emily could hear her suck in a breath. "If it's just sex… That's not a big deal. I love the closeness I feel with you, Emily. And it'd kill me to lose that. So if it's just sex—nothing serious or too emotional—that's okay. That's much, much better than breaking up. Right?"

She swallowed, trying to keep the tears at bay. "I don't want to break up. But…" Several long, slow breaths let her control her voice. "I guess we should have talked about this before I left. I didn't realize being away a few months would—"

"Everybody has needs," Blake interrupted, her voice now gentle and soothing. "There's a difference between sex and what we have. At least there is for me."

"There is for me too," Emily said. "I love…I love what we have."

"Good. That's good." She sounded so relieved! Like this was one item she could check off her list. Pack for South Beach, sharpen knives, have meaningless sex with strangers. "So, we'll go with that, right?"

"Not so fast. I need to think about this."

After a pregnant pause, Blake said, "Which part?"

"*All* of it, Blake. I need to decide what I really want. I'm not sure I can be casual about sex."

"Oh. I thought… Didn't you just agree there's a difference between having sex and being girlfriends?" She sounded so hurt. *She* was hurt? She's the one who started this bullshit!

"There is. For me, it's a big difference."

"You've got to let me know what you're thinking, Emily. I want things to be clear. I'm not very good at fumbling around, trying to guess what's going on. I want to agree on some rules we both agree to and then stick to them."

"You don't have to fumble," Emily said, her anger starting to rise to the surface. "Go to South Beach and enjoy yourself. We'll talk more when you finish there."

"It might be weeks," Blake warned. "Does that mean we'll just be discrete until we have time to talk about this again?"

"Yes," she said, absolutely exhausted. "Call me when you're in the mood."

"Hey," Blake said, her voice soothing and soft, "I'm always in the mood to talk to you."

Emily tried to let the warm tones comfort her, the way they had so many times before. But now Blake sounded like a bullshit artist. Someone who said what she needed to say to keep you on the hook.

"You might be in the mood, but we won't talk often. You know that's true."

"It probably is. This is a big restaurant, and it's open all the damn time. I haven't cooked Vietnamese food very often, so I'm going to have my hands full. Why don't you call me? My mornings are free, and I don't mind if you wake me up."

"That's my busiest time. I thought I could make my own schedule, but things started to get away from me. Now I'm back to going in at seven and checking every single thing the crew does. Every one of those subcontractors has me breathing down his neck."

"I'm proud of you," Blake said, her voice breaking. "You're doing a fantastic job. Laurent's so lucky to have you."

"We'll see. If I don't get the place open on time, he'll chop me up and put me in one of those huge stock pots I just ordered."

"You'll be fine. Now don't work too hard. I'll be thinking of you."

"Yeah. Me too." She was already thinking of her, wrapped around some sexy, tanned, South Beach beauty. "Good luck."

After pressing the "end" button, she dropped the phone to her lap and stared vacantly, her brain not registering a single image. To stop herself from doing what she wanted—ripping Joely's apartment apart with her bare hands—she went into the shower and stayed there until her skin started to prune. When she emerged, shaking and furious, she found her shoes, grabbed her bag and headed for the door. "Thanks for putting me up this week. I've…" She was *not* going to cry in front of Joely. While they were friends, they were also co-workers and you didn't show your guts to your co-workers. "I've got to get home. See you on Monday."

Joely's mouth hung open as she stared at Emily. "Let me drive you."

"No, I'd rather walk. Really nice day," she said, then slipped out the door to have the stunning brightness of the sun hit her full in the face.

Her backpack held four days worth of clothes, shoes, toiletries and electronics, and it was getting heavier by the second. The sun was scorching, even though it was barely nine a.m., but there was a decent breeze, and she could see the majestic ocean glimmering in front of her, like a gorgeous postcard. If she could have reached it, she would have spit in it. All of her dreams of playing on the beach with Blake had vanished by the time she'd hung up the phone.

She was panting when she slipped her card key into the lock of her motel room. "Fuck me," Emily gasped dropping the backpack to the floor. "What a stupid idea!" She collapsed into her chair, hitting it so hard she thought it might break. "I've had the shittiest day I can remember, and that includes the day I fractured my skull."

Charlotte was still in her pajamas, obviously having just gotten up.

"What's wrong?" she asked, coming over to put her hand on Emily's shoulder.

"Where's Mom?"

"She went to the little restaurant down the street to get coffee. What is *wrong*?" she demanded, her grip getting stronger.

"My girlfriend, and I use the term loosely, called at eight a.m. to tell me she wants a free pass to have sex with strangers."

Charlotte's eyes popped open wide. "What?"

"Just what I said." Emily got up and went into the bathroom, where she wet a washcloth and wiped her face and neck with it. "I don't know why I'm so damned surprised. We've never even said we love each other."

Charlotte entered the room and gently put her hands on Emily's arms, looking at her image in the mirror. "But you do."

"Yeah, I do," she said, her lower lip starting to quiver. Then she found herself wrapped in her sister's embrace, crying into her shoulder.

"Poor thing," Charlotte soothed. "She's an idiot if she can't keep her pants on for a few months. A big, fucking idiot."

"No, she's not. She needs a lot of sex and I guess she's able to separate sex from love. But I can't. I don't want to."

"Did you tell her that?"

"Not in so many words. I told her to do whatever she wanted, and we'd discuss it later."

Charlotte pushed her away and stared. "Why'd you say that?"

"I was so stunned. I never expected this from her. She gave me no warning at all!"

"Did something…happen?"

"Yeah. She got an offer to go to South Beach and fill in for some hotshot chef. I guess she wanted to let me know she was going to take a look around down there." She sighed. "At least she told me before she started cheating on me."

"You don't have to take that. You don't have to settle." She held her at arm's length and gazed into her eyes for a long time. "You're a very special woman, Emmy. You don't have to take this kind of shit."

"I'm so fucking special," she grumbled as she pulled away. "Give Blake a call and tell her that. She's clearly forgotten the words she sang to me just a week ago."

X

Late that afternoon, Emily sat at the airport with her sister and her mom, waiting to see if their plane would take off on time. It had been a shit-fest of a day, with her doing nothing but crying while her support team tried to convince her this was just a bump in the road.

But it wasn't. Even though Blake was sometimes as hard to figure out as a treasure map, in some ways she was very simple. When they'd first gotten together Emily had jokingly agreed they'd negotiate each time one of them went out of town. They hadn't done that when Emily had left for the Caribbean, but Blake was at the end of her leash and now wanted some wiggle room. She knew that Emily wouldn't like it, but she was an honorable woman, so she forced herself to wade through her nervousness and ask for what she wanted. You had to give her credit for that. She was a shit, but she was a shit with fortitude.

Her mom had either been holding her hand or stroking her hair since nine o'clock that morning. It was all too much like it had been after her skull fracture, and Emily could hardly wait to get them onto the plane so she could stew in private.

Charlotte was the most pragmatic one of the group, and she came over to sit next to Emily. "Look," she said, very businesslike. "Here's what makes sense. You've been away from each other for months now. That's longer than Blake can tolerate, right?"

"Obviously," Emily grumbled.

"So? Don't be away from each other that much. Jesus, Em, you can't trust most guys to be away from home for months at a time. What makes you think women are more loyal?"

Emily took a long look at her sister. They had such different views of the world, but she knew Charlotte's advice was heartfelt. "I don't think women are superior in that way, but I thought Blake was. I thought what we had was important enough to go through a little discomfort."

"How do you know it's not? Talk to her, Emmy. Don't just write her off."

"She made her position clear. She wants meaningless sex while we're apart. I might have agreed to that originally, but not now. Not after I..." She sucked in a breath, so sick of crying she was ready to slap herself for being unable to control her emotions.

"You let yourself be vulnerable," her mom said softly. "That's what hurts."

Emily fell onto her shoulder, crying like a baby. "That's exactly it," she sobbed. "I was happy to just have sex with her. But we've been making love. Or at least *I* have."

/

Even though she'd wanted to, Emily wasn't able to keep her personal life separate from her professional. Not long after they started work on Monday, she told Joely the whole story. They were too busy to get into much detail, but they agreed to go out after work and have a drink. But even with the promise of a sympathetic ear, she couldn't concentrate. That afternoon she snuck away, going to sit on the bed of Joely's truck and call Chase.

"Aren't you afraid to pick up?" she asked, chuckling wryly when he did.

"Never. I'm here for you, Em. How are you feeling?"

"I'm better. Not a lot, but a little."

"Have you heard from Blake?" he asked tentatively.

"Just texts. Today's was really playful. Like she was trying to be ingratiating, which isn't like her."

"Maybe she regrets asking for a free pass."

"No, she'd say so if she regretted it. She's very blunt." Sighing, she pulled up the text, after putting Chase on speaker so she could see it. "It's a picture of her in her new jacket, looking like the cat that ate the canary. The woman's never happier than when she's in charge."

"But she doesn't get to be in charge of you. You don't need to put up with her bullshit."

"I know." She got up and started to walk down the road, trying to get away from the grating sound of a circular saw. "Maybe I'll stay here for a while. Laurent would love it if I'd run the place, at least until we get all of the kinks worked out."

"Do you like it enough to stay?"

She thought about that for a minute. "You'd have to be crazy not to like it here. It's warm and sunny and clean and I'm hanging out with a bunch of super friendly people. I might get bored, but I think it would take a while."

"That wouldn't work for me. I like morose, tortured New Yorkers." He cleared his throat. "If you're gonna stay for a while, why don't we think about the apartment? I could move in with Natasha…"

"You want to, don't you," she said, having gotten a few vibes from him over the last months.

"I love our apartment, Em, but I'm not crazy about the flight attendants shuffling in and out at all hours of the day and night. I've been at Natasha's the entire time you've been gone."

"When's our lease up?"

"Two months. I talked to Ray and Olivia, and they'd like to stay. If you want to, we could have the landlord sign them to a new lease." His voice grew stronger. "But I'm not pushing you. I'm fine with re-upping. I promised I'd never abandon you in the big, bad city, and I'm going to keep my word."

Tears filled her eyes as she let herself think of how fantastic it was to have someone so solid and reliable as Chase in her life. "Same for me. Let me think about it, okay?"

"Take your time. I want you to be happy, Em, and if you'd be happier there, you should stay."

"I'd be happier with Blake," she said, the annoying tears starting to fall again. "But I can't be with a woman who has to be supervised."

"I don't blame you for being mad," he soothed.

"I'm not really mad. I'm sad. I'm damned sad, Chase. I wanted something Blake couldn't give, but I shouldn't be surprised. She'd never seriously dated anyone. Why did I think I'd be the one person in the world to convince her to settle down and be monogamous?"

"Because you're awesome," he said, his voice so full of certainty it made her cry all the harder. "And if she can't see that, she's not the right woman for you."

"But she was," Emily sobbed. "She was the *perfect* woman for me, but I'm going to cut her loose."

Chapter Twenty-Three

ON FRIDAY, THE CREW spent the day installing paneling on the lower halves of the walls, making the space much warmer and more like a place you'd want to dine. It had taken hours longer than Joely had predicted, but she'd ridden the guys like racehorses, forcing them, despite their grumbling, to finish before they packed it in for the weekend. As the last of the crew drove away, Emily sidled up to her.

"How about a nice dinner as a thank you?"

A cute smile settled on her face. "You don't have to thank me for doing my job. That should have been a day's work, pure and simple. The guys weren't feeling it, but that doesn't change the facts."

"Yes it does. You got in there and *made* them feel it. And I want you to know how much I appreciate it."

Joely stepped back and gave Emily a long, assessing look. "A nice dinner? Like 'no swimsuits' nice?"

"Nicer than that."

"Hmm," she said, her head cocking slightly as she considered the offer. "I don't think I've ever had dinner in a place where you couldn't wear a swimsuit."

"Then this will be a new experience."

With a pleased but puzzled smile, Joely said, "I guess that means I'd better go get cleaned up. Ready to go?"

"I am. I'll find us a place to eat when I get to my room. I'll try for seven thirty. Is that good?"

"Sounds great. I'll be starving by then."

As soon as Emily got home, she used her phone to search for a good place. It was near the end of high season, and a little easier to get into highly recommended places on a weeknight. Not that Emily had personally been to any nice places, given that Joely and her friends were a burger and beer crowd. But Emily had noticed Joely seemed to light up when they talked about the kinds of dishes Laurent Bistro would feature. While cooking was her favorite way to share food, Emily enjoyed introducing people to the delights of interesting dishes through other cooks' labors, too. After spending a long time reading reviews and checking out menus, she was able to snag a table in the dining room of the most exclusive hotel on the island at seven-thirty. That would be perfect. They could have a drink in the bar, then pull out the stops and have a good meal.

Emily hadn't brought a lot of clothes, mostly because she owned so little. So she stopped at a boutique on the walk home and bought a brick-red, slim-fitting, linen shift. Actually, it was some sort of man-made fiber, but it looked like linen, which was good enough for her. Although she didn't wear dresses very often, the restaurant she'd chosen was very upmarket, and she wanted to fit in with the idle rich. Besides, dresses were much cooler in the heat that had started to invade her tropical paradise. It was only a few degrees hotter than it had been in January, but those few degrees made the whole island feel substantially warmer.

Joely didn't get the message about dresses being cooler, but she was as well turned-out as Emily had ever seen her. She liked wearing bright colors, and tonight she sported a pair of slacks that were as blue as the tropical fish that surrounded Cayman. She didn't seem to own any shirts with sleeves, but the white cotton sleeveless one she wore made her tan glow.

"You look fantastic," Joely said, eyeing Emily with more interest than she was comfortable with. One more good reason not to mix your business and professional lives. The body wasn't even cold yet, but Joely was clearly tempted to kick Blake's carcass aside and take her place. But that wasn't going to happen. Definitely not now, and probably not ever.

Emily took another discrete look when Joely's attention was elsewhere. She was definitely cute, definitely fun, and would probably be a party in bed. But those were just things you ticked off a list of requirements. Once you'd truly given yourself to a woman the way she had with Blake, you reached a depth of connection that all of that surface stuff didn't come close to touching. No matter how long Emily mourned the loss, Joely would never measure up to Blake. Emily's stomach lurched when she considered the very real possibility that no one ever would.

She had to fight with herself to hang in there and focus on the moment. It was stupid to go to a nice place and spend the time thinking about Blake. Pulling her focus away from her emotions, she tried to look at the building and see it in a way that put her newfound construction knowledge to work.

Not surprisingly, the restaurant was very, very fancy. Understated, like most really expensive places tried to be, but also elegant. Joely laced her hands behind her back and assessed the details in the entryway while Emily checked in with the hostess.

"Damn, they spent a load on this place," Joely said as they walked to the bar. "They have five different types of molding all tacked together to make those impressive door-frames. Money was no object."

Emily accepted a hand to help her scoot onto a high bar stool. "The same's true for our dinner. I don't want you to worry about the prices. Order whatever interests you."

"I'm not sure what interests me. My mom's a simple cook, and I've never had the opportunity to branch out much. I'd rather you told me what I should order."

"I'm good at that," Emily said. "But for now, lets get some drinks."

Joely put her hand on Emily's when she started to lift it to signal the bartender. "Let me get the drinks."

"You don't need to…"

"I want to." The bartender approached, and she said, "I'd like a nice bottle of champagne. Can you hook me up?"

"Of course," the guy said. "Let me get the wine list."

"You're in deep," Emily quietly teased. "This isn't the place to buy champagne."

The server came back and Emily watched as Joely's eyes widened. "Holy fuck," she mumbled.

"There's a nice prosecco," Emily said, pointing. "That's just as good as champagne."

"Are you sure?"

"Positive." In fact, Emily loved Champagne much more, finding the bubbles too large and the taste too bold in most proseccos. But she wasn't going to let Joely spend two hundred bucks on a bottle of wine that Emily couldn't even taste well. That was nuts.

They'd finished most of their wine by the time their table was ready. After they sat down, Emily took the menu and made some suggestions, trying to suss out what kinds of flavors appealed to Joely. They finally had things sorted out, and she ordered for both of them, then allowed Joely to add another bottle of prosecco to her charge card.

"We really should have had the sommelier recommend some wines to go with our food, but I'm pretty happy with what we have. It should go well with the fish."

"I eat way too much meat," Joely said. "I should really start mixing things up with some fish."

"I've spent what feels like years butchering fish," she said, sighing. "I miss using my knife."

"Butchering? Isn't that what you do to a cow?"

"Yeah," she agreed, chuckling. "I say butchering for any animal I break down. Does filleting sound better?"

"It sounds less…bloody," Joely said, swallowing nervously.

"You'll have to come watch us in the kitchen once we get rocking. It's a mess. An organized mess, but it's still a mess."

Emily looked up as a runner delivered a hefty portion of burrata, surrounded by sautéed mushrooms, and drizzled with bright green olive oil. "Ooo, that looks good," she said. "If you like cheese as much as I do, you're gonna love this."

Joely picked up her fork and poked at the burrata tentatively. "It's supposed to look like a wet baseball?"

Laughing, Emily nodded. "It is. But a good burrata is smooth and creamy and slightly rich. It should have just a hint of salt, too." She waited patiently for Joely to cut off a piece and pop it into her mouth.

Watching someone experience something you loved was kinda cool. It was easy to take things like this for granted, to assume everyone put food up on the altar of things most holy. Hanging out with Joely had been good for her. It let Emily see how far from the norm she and her fellow cooks really were. As Joely chewed, she began to smile. "It's really good," she said. "Creamy, like you said, but not like cream cheese or anything like that."

"No, they're very far apart," Emily said. "This should be very light."

"It is. I like it," she said, digging in for another bite. Emily joined her, hoping it registered, then brushing off the disappointment when it didn't. Every once in a while she got an almost normal amount of flavor from a bite or two. She couldn't count the times she'd thought she might actually be back to normal, like she'd been cured in an instant. But that was how long it lasted—an instant. Somehow, her olfactory nerve connected for a moment, like a balky pair of headphones she owned. Clear, full sound—then crackling static when the connection faltered.

She hadn't told Joely about her head injury. So few people truly understood what she'd lost it seemed pointless to bother. Plus, it was depressing to talk about. A therapist might not agree, but sometimes Emily preferred to ignore the things that caused pain to focus on the positive. That's why she was going to enjoy this dinner. The other option was to sit in her hotel room and mope, and that wasn't a good idea. Life had to go on, even when your heart had taken a thorough beating.

Prices for good meals on Cayman were as bad as they were in New York. Emily gulped when presented with the bill, but she knew good food cost good money. Besides, she'd enjoyed taking Joely on a short culinary journey, and it was much cheaper than a trip to Italy.

When she reached into her purse to extract her credit card, her gaze flicked past the bar—where a pair of dark, stormy eyes bore into her. As their gazes met, Blake must have consciously tried to wipe the glower from her face, with a mildly pleasant smile taking its place.

"Blake," Emily choked out, staring.

Joely turned to look, then quickly scooted her chair back. "Do you want to see her?" she asked, getting to her feet.

"I..." The back waiter came by and picked up her card. Looking up at Joely, she blinked a few times, then said, "I don't know."

Before Emily could say another word, Joely strode across the room, heading for the bar. Emily wanted to tackle her, but she was locked in place, frozen between running to jump into Blake's arms and giving her a sharp kick to the shins.

Joely stood directly in front of Blake's chair, blocking her from rising. Given the angle, Emily couldn't see Blake's face, but Joely's body language reminded her of a rooster about to peck another bird's eyes out.

The back waiter was going to have to search for her. She had to get involved—pronto! On the short walk, she berated herself for pouring her heart out to Joely. But the *last* thing she'd expected was to have her appoint herself some kind of knight in shining armor, especially in this situation.

Blake didn't look particularly intimidated by the obviously angry woman. Emily would have characterized her expression as puzzled more than anything else. Then she heard Joely speak. "You're the first East Coaster I've heard of who wasn't interested in coming down here during the winter." She leaned over slightly, getting right in Blake's face. "It's not like you can claim your job kept you in New York, since you don't *have* one."

Oh, shit!

Blake's attention was split between Emily and this insolent stranger. She tried to stand, but Joely's shins were up against the lower rungs of the chair, effectively stopping her. Blake gave her a curious look, then said, "Shouldn't we wait to be introduced before you start posturing?"

"I know who you are," she snapped. "So? What's your deal? Why couldn't you get your ass down here at least once to visit your girlfriend?"

Blake's puzzled expression turned to annoyance in a flash. "If you'd back it up, I could say hello to her. Would that make you happy?"

"No," she said, not giving an inch. "You've got your work cut out for you on that score."

Blake gave her a withering look, then spoke calmly but forcefully. "I don't know you, and I don't care to. I'm here to see Emily, and I'm going to stay here until *she* asks me to leave."

Emily wedged herself between the women, then pushed Joely away with a hip thrust.

"How did you find me?" Emily said, her first words, curtly enunciated, to a woman she'd been dying to see for months.

Standing, Blake gave Joely another quick look, then composed her face into some semblance of her usual self. "You still have that 'find my phone' thing on."

"That doesn't give you the right to stalk her," Joely said, her voice far too loud for the muted conversations at the bar. Emily looked up as a few of the closer guests snapped their heads around to stare at the three of them. She had to calm this down *now*.

Blake's fuse was longer than Emily would have guessed, but it had reached its end. She leaned to the side, so she and Joely were facing each other again. "Buzz off!"

Joely stuck her chin out and spoke way too loudly. "Emily doesn't want to see you *now*. She wanted to see you in January…or February. You know. When she was lonely."

Blake's hands went up, palms out, obviously poised to give Joely a firm push. But Emily grabbed and held them, finding them surprisingly difficult to corral.

"I'm not stalking you," Blake said fiercely, her eyes narrowing again.

"I didn't accuse you of that, Chef. I'm just surprised."

"You don't work for her any more," Joely said. She's not your *boss*."

Turning, Emily stared at Joely's fierce glower. "She's not what?"

"You can call her by her name, Emily. You don't have to be under her thumb."

"Oh, God," she murmured. "I'm not under her thumb. That's kind of joke between us."

"There's nothing funny about a woman trying to dominate you," Joely said.

"What is *wrong* with you?" Blake demanded, also too loudly. Everyone at the bar was now staring at them, with all of the people in the first row of tables also taking a peek at the fracas.

Then a man in a dark suit was right at the edge of Emily's peripheral vision. "Pardon me," he said quietly, addressing Blake. "If you wouldn't mind stepping outside, I'll take care of your bar bill." Then he moved behind the stool and put his hand on her shoulder, trying to guide her out.

"You're tossing me?" she demanded, clearly incredulous as she whirled around to glare at him.

"Blake," Emily said sharply, using her given name for one of the very few times in their history. "Grab a cab and meet me in my room." She found her card key and thrust it at her. "Now," she added, her tone making it clear she wasn't playing around. "The address is on the card. Room 215."

Her mouth opened and closed, then she stared at the floor for a second. While giving no verbal indication she was going to comply, she took the card and walked straight for the door, with every damn person in the bar staring after her. What a great way for Emily to introduce herself to the fine diners of Cayman!

The back waiter approached, giving Emily a funny look while extending a metal tray with her credit card on it. "I'm sorry I—" He blinked in surprise when the manager took the tray, his sober gaze still on Emily.

"If you'll leave quietly, I'll take care of this."

"No," Emily said, standing her ground. "We had a lovely meal. It's not the restaurant's fault my personal life's gotten out of hand." She yanked the tray away from him, placed it on the bar and signed her name to the chit. She just hoped everyone forgot it before Laurent Bistro opened in two months. This was *not* the kind of publicity her boss was looking for.

Emily's hand was visibly shaking when she lifted it to knock on her hotel room door. Blake answered quickly, obviously nervous. "I'm so sorry," she said, her face contorted into a mask of embarrassment. "I had no damned idea how hard this would be."

Sliding into the room, Emily dropped her purse and gazed at Blake for a while. She looked haggard, like she hadn't slept. But her color was good, probably from sleeping on the beach while she waited to go to work. They kept their distance, which felt so damned odd. Blake seemed to know the ax was going to fall, but if that was true, why come down?

She'd been thinking so hard she'd ignored Blake's comment. But then it sharpened in her head. "What are you talking about? What's hard?"

Blake sank to the bed, her head drooping, normally erect posture absent. Tonight she looked sad, and tired, and utterly ill at ease. Her head slowly lifted, and Emily could vividly see pain in her eyes. "Seeing you with another woman," she said as her chin started to quiver. By the time Emily got in front of her, Blake was crying, tears rolling down her cheeks.

"That's insulting even to consider," Emily snapped. Her tone had been sharp, but her instinct, so strong it made her fingers twitch, was to comfort Blake, to wrap her in her arms and soothe her. But that wasn't what you did to a woman you were breaking up with. Especially one who was trying to turn her bullshit on you.

"I respect what we had, Chef, and because of that I'd never start one thing before I was finished with another." She took a deep breath and spit out the words she'd been practicing in her mind. "We should get this over with, and you can get back to your gig." She walked over to the sliding door and opened it, unable to look at the tear-streaked face that gazed up at her with such trust. "We should call it a day. We obviously don't view what we had in the same way." She was going to let it lie right there. She *should* have let it lie right there. But she was so deeply hurt she couldn't stop herself from getting in a jab. "I thought we were building a relationship, but you were happy to have an available, enthusiastic fuck buddy."

Blake jumped to her feet, her cheeks turning pink in seconds. "Me? Don't try to make this about me!"

"Who else is it about? Who called asking for permission to fool around?"

"What?" Blake grasped her arms and held her still. "What are you talking about?"

"Do you have memory loss? It wasn't even a week ago you asked for permission to fuck people while you were in South Beach."

"I never…" She stopped and put her hands on the sides of her face, like she was trying to keep her head from exploding. "I didn't do that, Emily. I was only giving you permission to keep…" She swallowed. "Doing what you were already doing." The tears started back in full force, and she wrapped her arms around her waist, comforting herself. "I was trying to hold onto you any way I could." Great, heaving sobs made her grab onto the dresser to stay upright. "I knew I was losing you, but I love you so much." The pain she obviously felt distorted her features so dramatically Emily's guts began to knot. "I was trying to find some way to hold onto you."

"What?" Emily ran to her, grabbed her by the shoulders and shook her. "Have you lost your mind?"

"I heard you on the fucking phone!" Blake spat out. "You were in her bed, Emily. Jesus Christ! It's one thing to need some freedom, but I never thought you'd lie right to my face!"

Her thoughts hadn't been so jumbled since she'd fractured her skull. None of this made a friggin' word of sense. Emily put her fists to her eyes and pressed them against the bones, trying to think clearly. "You heard me on the phone…"

"When your sister was here. I woke you up, then I heard Joely offer to make you coffee." Her eyes narrowed and she looked like she wanted to slap Emily right across the face. "You don't have a coffee maker, so you had to have been at her house. You obviously couldn't stop banging her even with your sister in town."

Now things got clear. Crystal clear. So clear they made her blood boil. She spat the words out slowly. "As a surprise, Charlotte paid the change fee for my mom to use Chuck's ticket. I was at Joely's—on her lumpy sofa—so the three of us didn't have to share that bed." She pointed at the full-sized mattress, with both of them staring at it for a few seconds.

Blake's voice was soft now, and filled with doubt. "So you weren't sleeping with Joely? At all?"

"Of course not!" She gripped Blake by the shoulders and shook her. "I'm committed to you. Are you saying you didn't want to sleep with other women?"

"Other women?" Blake's big, dark eyes blinked slowly. "You know how I am. If I can't have the best, I wait. I'm the same way with women and food."

"Oh, fuck." All of the anger drained from her and she started to see the Blake who was standing in front of her—wounded and nervous and desperate to hold on. "You still want to be my girlfriend?"

"No." She took in a breath and blinked a few times. "I want to be more than that. A lot more. I want all of you, Emily. Every bit of you."

Emily wrapped her arms around her shivering body, then buried her face against Blake's neck. "Do you mean that?" she whispered. "Do you really love me?"

Blake pulled away and stared at her. Then her eyes closed when she whispered, "God, yes."

Emily caressed her damp, flushed cheek, so puzzled her head was throbbing again. "You have never, ever said that, Chef. *Never.*"

Still shivering, Blake bit her lip, clearly reticent to speak. Finally, she forced her words out. "I've never been in love before." She swallowed, her mouth obviously dry. "I wasn't sure how or when to…" Sighing deeply, she admitted, "I didn't have the nerve."

"When did you…" She shook her head. "Did you just realize this when I left?"

"Of course not." As if her self-assurance was being poured back into her body, she stood tall and squared her shoulders. "Do you remember when we went out for dinner the first time? To Gustavo's?"

"Of course I remember." With Blake starting to act like herself, Emily found herself drawn to her like a knife to a magnet. Her hands rested on her waist, her palms reveling in the feel of Blake's sturdy body, so deeply missed.

"That was the first time I felt…something. It was more than lust, even though I had a lot of it that night." She put her hand on Emily's cheek, her touch like a salve. "Even though I could tell you would have liked to get together, I couldn't risk it."

"You can't possibly convince me you loved me back then!" This was making her head spin. They'd barely gotten to know each other at that point.

"I felt something," Blake said, her certainty rock-solid. "When we were eating, I had this dream of walking home with you after we finished work for the night. I could picture it, Emily. We were holding hands and talking about what a shit day we'd had, but we were going home—together." Her eyes closed tightly. "I couldn't let myself feel that way. Even the fantasy was too dangerous. So I let you get onto that damned subway when all I wanted was to wrap my body around yours and make love to you."

"You've *never* called it making love. Only sex."

Blake's touch was as gentle as a whisper when it caressed Emily's cheek. "I act like I love you, don't I? Don't I make you feel loved?"

"Yes," she said, closing her eyes. It was so hard to look at Blake's tear-streaked face, to see the pain lodged deep in her gaze. "You do. You have since the second time we were together. I was…amazed," she said, sucking in a breath. "I felt cherished."

"That's exactly it," she soothed, leaning in to let her lips touch the shell of Emily's ear. "I cherish you. Every time we're together I feel like I've been given a gift."

"God damn it," Emily murmured, letting herself really feel Blake's body in her arms. The heat that poured from her, the emotion she could feel pulsing through her flesh. Every sensation so heady she got a little weak in the knees.

Then they were sitting on the bed, touching at just the shoulders and hips. Just that little bit of contact was supremely reassuring. Like a force-field of love and affection was protecting them both.

"I'm so sorry I didn't come home when I knew you were struggling. I didn't know what was wrong, but I knew something was," Emily said, tears spilling from her eyes. "That was the stupidest mistake I've ever made."

"It was hard being apart. I lost track of you. I couldn't tell what was going on the way I could when we were together. It was like there was a…" She struggled for the right word. "Some kind of screen I couldn't see through."

"I know. I know," Emily soothed. "It was fine at first, but as we both got busier we started to lose our connection."

Blake pulled away and looked deeply into Emily's eyes as her fingers slid across her brow and down her cheeks. "I missed that connection more than I'll ever be able to tell you." Her eyes closed briefly. "I'm so dependent on you. That's never, ever happened to me before, and it scares me."

"There's nothing to be afraid of," Emily soothed. "Our love will make us stronger. I promise you that."

"I don't feel very strong now," she admitted. "I'm a nervous friggin' wreck."

"Then we need to fix that."

"Okay," Blake said, looking into her eyes, clearly seeking guidance.

"We need to reconnect." Her arms slid around Blake's body and tightened. "I've missed you so damn much. I missed your company, the way we talk so easily, your sense of humor, the way you look at the world…" She tilted her head and kissed her, with all of her senses coming alive at the first touch. "All of that stuff matters. But the magic we have when we touch…" Shivers covered her body when she looked up into Blake's glittering eyes. "That's the glue that's going to hold us together when we start to lose touch."

"No, no," Blake said, her eyes growing wide as she leapt to her feet, looking like she'd fight the person who tried to separate them. "We *can't* let this happen again."

"We won't," Emily pledged, standing to put her hands on Blake's hips and hold her still. "Now that we know how easy it is, we'll know what to look out for."

"Don't leave me again," Blake said, bending over to whisper into her ear. "Stay with me, Emily."

Emily wrapped her arms around her neck as she stared into those watchful, wary eyes. "I will. As soon as I'm done here, I'll be home."

"Would you like some help?" she asked, flinching a little. "I don't have a work permit, and I know you can't pay me, but I guarantee I'd be the best free help you ever got."

Emily pulled her down for a long, sweet kiss. Then they looked into each other's eyes for a long time, getting used to being this close again. "Will you stay? God, I'd love that."

"I will." She let out a soft laugh. "I brought one pair of shorts, one T-shirt, and a pair of sandals. Will that hold me until you open?"

"I'll hold you until we open. Every minute I'm not at work, I'm going to be holding you." She started to do just that, but stopped cold. "What about your restaurant? How can you stay?"

"I quit." She blinked slowly, then repeated herself. "I quit. I told them I'd only reopen if I could hire you as executive chef. They told me to go fuck myself, so I told them the same."

"What in the holy fuck?" Emily's entire body tingled. "You did what?" A shiver of fear ran down her spine. "Did you do that just to… hold onto me?"

"No. Not at all," she said, her bright, clear eyes radiating honesty. "I told them not long after you left. We argued for two months, but I couldn't convince them. My contract wasn't up yet, but I told them they didn't have to continue paying me if they cut me loose early. Jeffrey was happy to see me go," she said, her eyes narrowing. "The feeling was mutual."

"What are you going to do?"

"Right now? I'm going to make love to you."

The smile that bloomed on that beautiful face made Emily's knees weak. Then Blake swept her into her arms and carried her the few feet to the bed. As she had the last time she'd tried this, she dropped her from a height, panting from the effort. "This always looks so easy when you see people do it in the movies."

"It's always a guy doing the carrying," Emily said, grabbing her by the shirt and pulling her down onto her body. "You're pretty butch, but you're no guy." She started to kiss the bit of exposed skin at her throat, then worked to expand the territory. Her fingers popped the buttons open one by one, with her mouth following along, kissing every inch of skin revealed. "I missed you so much," she murmured between kisses.

Blake's hands moved to her face, holding her like a fragile, cherished treasure. "Do you love me?"

"I do. I love you so much."

Suddenly, Blake found another burst of strength. She grasped Emily around the shoulders and pulled her up so they were nose to nose. "Kiss me," she begged, the slightest bit of hesitation in her voice. "Convince me."

A burst of pain stabbed at her heart. She'd shaken Blake's confidence, her certainty about them as a couple. All because she'd let things slide. But no more. Blake was her priority. From this moment on, she was going to show her that she mattered more than anything. "I love you," she said, her voice clear and sure. "You're never going to doubt my love again, Chef. I promise that."

"This is new for me," Blake said, her vulnerability still showing in her gaze. "All of it. Being in love, putting someone first, making time to be together... You're going to have to be patient, and you might have to tell me how to do things. But I'll try hard, Emily. I promise."

"We can work through anything," Emily pledged. "We just have to both be committed to this."

"I'm all in," Blake said. "You're the woman I've been waiting for my whole life. The only woman I've ever truly loved."

Emily cradled her in her arms, then kissed her cheeks, her nose, her eyelids and finally her supple, warm lips. "I'm so glad you waited for me."

"I'd wait two lifetimes for you," Blake whispered. "But I'm so glad you're here now. That we're here. Together."

The sincerity of her words made Emily's entire body shiver. "See what you do to me?" she asked, holding out her arm, revealing the goosebumps that covered it.

Blake grasped her body and flipped her, then hovered over her for a moment, like a predator. "I want to see exactly what I do to you." Her cocky grin was back, with Emily able to see her dominant personality sliding back into place, right where it belonged. Quickly, Blake began to undress her, leaving her naked and trembling with desire in less than a minute. Then Blake stood and slipped out of her own clothes, with Emily watching her avidly as the pulse beat between her legs. No one was sexier than Blake when she undressed. She knew she looked good, her shoulders and waist having gained definition from months of swimming. But even if she'd been sitting on her butt for the past months, eating chips and drinking beer, she'd still be as sexy as hell. That came from her personality more than her body. Her personality would always be a ten. Emily was sure of that.

That warm, sturdy body cuddled up next to her, and Blake spent long minutes exploring Emily's mouth like it was a place she had to reacquaint herself with. A former home she desperately needed to inhabit once again.

Emily lay next to her, opening herself up in every possible way to her love, her desire, her affection, her need. There was nothing in the world Blake could ask that she would refuse. Her sole desire was to please her.

Blake trailed a finger down the center of Emily's chest, smiling as goosebumps broke out again. "I love you," she murmured, her gaze so avid Emily wasn't sure she knew she'd spoken. Another kiss held significantly more heat. "I love you when we're talking. I love you when we're just sitting around watching TV. But I love this one thing we do a whole lot." Her lecherous grin was so cute Emily had to pull her close and kiss her.

"I hate to be pushy," she said as she nudged Blake onto her back, "but I've got to try something." She slowly worked her way down Blake's body, kissing and nibbling while delighting in the wonder of her. Then she nestled herself between her legs and took in a deep breath. A delighted smile lit her face as she met Blake's curious gaze. "I can tell you're...you," she said, her eyes closing in satisfaction.

"You can?" Blake gripped her shoulders, possibly leaving imprints. "That's fantastic!"

"Not anything like it used to be," she warned, "but it's definitely improved." Her face hovered over Blake as she delicately sniffed every part of her. "I've been able to taste food a little better, but I longed for the most important scent." Their eyes met again. "Yours."

"Oh, Emily, that makes me so happy. Maybe it'll keep getting better and better."

It broke her heart to look into that hopeful face and see the innocent longing Blake held for her. Emily dipped her head to revel in the hints of scent Blake's body revealed. It would never be the same as it had been. But she wasn't going to complain. The desire she felt for Blake would easily make up for what she'd lost. Their love could heal the broken parts of her—creating a new, invulnerable bond. One unlike any she'd experienced before. Blake was all she'd ever wanted. The woman she'd always needed. Her soulmate. Her Chef.

One Year Later

THE WARM SUMMER SUN bathed her face when Emily walked out of their apartment building and started down the street. Their neighborhood was especially quiet in the morning, with just a few parent and kid pairs heading off to daycare. Living in a neighborhood that was so relentlessly American was taking Emily a while to get used to. She truly missed the Columbian, Ecuadorian, and Pakistani diners where she used to go for a bowl of something delicious. A smile came to her lips as she thought of the Korean meal she and Blake had shared late one night. If there was anyone making a top-notch kimbap in Detroit, she hadn't found it yet. But that was cool. She'd gladly sacrifice budae-jigae to have the restaurant of their dreams.

As she approached Agnes Street, a flutter of activity caught her attention. It wasn't much, just a delivery truck's loading door slamming shut before it rumbled away. That was the same level of noise she used to experience in her old neighborhood at around four a.m. on a national holiday. But even though the West Village now had very few commercial concerns open at this time of day, that was going to change. Emily was sure of it. Their little neighborhood was on the verge of becoming a hot spot, and Emily Blake was going to be a part of that revitalization.

She normally entered through the back door, but today she walked around the building to see the awning, newly installed. Her heart beat a little faster, and she pressed her lips together to avoid crying. Having her name up there, side by side with Blake's... She was still amazed that Blake had insisted hers go first. For her, Emily Blake simply sounded better than Blake Emily. That's just how she was. Always practical. Her ego didn't come into it.

Emily was a little shaky when she went back around to her normal entrance, then tears once again slowed her down when the faint scent of roasting bones reached her nose. For her, the scents of a professional kitchen first thing in the morning was as evocative and emotion-laden as smelling mom's apple pie perfuming your childhood home.

The tall, shy kid she'd hired to be their morning prep cook had his back to her, oblivious to being observed. He was raw. Very raw. But his lack of experience wasn't going to be a problem. Reggie was a sweet kid, not only eager to please, but just as hard a worker as she was. While the bones roasted for stock, he was chopping bundles of celery exactly like she'd taught him. Even though he'd been trained at a local high school, his knife work was a mess. Over time, his knife would be a blur. They simply had to be patient while he learned.

"Good morning, Reggie," she said, smiling to herself when he jumped in surprise.

"Hey, Chef." He turned and gave her a shy smile. He seemed like he was frozen, waiting for instructions.

"Finding everything?"

"Yes, Chef."

"Do you have the menu?"

"I do. I've never cooked for eighteen people at once, but I'm ready to try."

It was hard not to laugh at his naïveté, but she managed. "You'll do fine." She picked up a piece of celery, nodding at his dice. "Nice job. Did a pretty woman fly through here about fifteen minutes ago?"

He pointed with the tip of his knife to the door on his left. He swallowed, paused, then said, "I think she likes to be alone in the morning."

Emily laughed at his expression. It would take him and everyone else a while to get used to Blake. Actually, she was sure it would take a while for everyone to get used to working for women who were also lovers. But she'd made it clear what the setup was, and had quickly eliminated anyone who seemed uncomfortable with their relationship. Thankfully, that was only a couple of applicants. Everyone else was more concerned with the hours and the pay than the orientation of the chefs.

"She just gets focused and forgets to converse." She patted him on the back, then pushed through the door.

Blake was sitting on the counter, wearing jeans and the Tigers T-shirt she'd bought when Emily took her to her first baseball game. Her hair was still wet from the shower, but her clogs were on her feet, showing she wasn't just fooling around. The paperwork from their various suppliers was in two neat piles, and a bunch of hand towels rested at her hip. A roll of blue painter's tape was in her hand, and she stuck her tongue out as she carefully wrapped it around the end of a folded and rolled towel—a job she used to assign to the newest of her unpaid apprentices. It was a routine job, simply making neat clean-up towels. When service started, they'd put them in a pan with a little hot water, then use the moist towels to wipe away any morsels of food that dared stray from where Blake placed them on the plate. Still, she was doing it with such concentration she didn't hear a sound until Emily stood between her spread legs and slapped her thighs.

Those surprised eyes met Emily's gaze, then a guilty look settled onto her lovely face.

"I cannot believe you snuck out of the apartment while I was still asleep."

"Couldn't help myself. I ran," she admitted, an embarrassed smile making her look significantly younger.

"Nervous?"

That dark head nodded forcefully. "Very. You?"

"Yep." She moved away, then walked along the D-shaped counter, looking at the space from every angle. Ducking under it, she stood inside the D, where JoJo would reign. Luring him away from New York had been her idea, and she was still surprised he'd agreed. He'd been nervous about bringing his family to a new town, but when he'd discovered he could afford a house, as well as private school for his kids, he couldn't sign up fast enough. Since that time, he'd convinced both of his cousins to join him, and they were determined to turn a small section of Detroit into a Gambian outpost.

They'd had a fun reunion a few weeks ago when he'd come by to have the final tailoring done on his suits. He'd brought his youngest son, Koba, and Blake had gotten onto the floor and played with the kid until JoJo had to leave to pick up his older two from school. One thing Emily was sure of. JoJo was going to be the sharpest-looking commis de rang in town, not to mention the most eager. The energy he'd had that day had almost matched Koba's, and the kid was only two years old.

She was beyond happy with the way the space looked. They'd worked it over and over again in their heads and on graph paper, finally bringing in a commercial kitchen designer to firm up the plans. Their space was small, and they were only able to squeeze in eighteen seats, but that would be plenty. Better to have people trying to get in than have a bunch of empty seats.

The phone in the prep kitchen rang, and Emily scrambled to get out of the serving area and answer it. Reggie wouldn't answer a phone if it called his name, and once Blake's concentration was locked-in she wouldn't have heard it. "Emily Blake," she said.

"Reservations?" a guy said, sounding unsure of himself.

"Yes, this is the correct number." For the time being. Once the voice mail system was set up properly they wouldn't answer at all.

"Yeah, I wanna come on Friday. 8 o'clock. Four people."

Her eyes opened wide. This guy hadn't heard the buzz. "I'm afraid we're fully booked through July. If you'll call back on Monday, May eighteenth, you can book for August."

Dead silence for a few seconds. "Are you serious? You're not even open yet, are you?"

"That's correct. But we've been featured in several national magazines, as well as all of the local papers and blogs. The phone started ringing off the hook as soon as the number went live."

"What's the deal? I just heard it was supposed to be different."

"It's a *little* different," she admitted. "We have a fixed menu of ten courses, with optional wine pairings. When you make your reservation, you pay for your meal."

There was a long pause, then he said, "You know you're in Detroit, right?"

"I do," she said, smirking.

His annoyance started to grow. You didn't have to be in New York for people to feel entitled to demand a table whenever they wanted. "Is this another hipster chef from Brooklyn coming to town to show us how to eat?"

"I'm one of the chefs, and I was born and raised here. I can guarantee no one's ever called me a hipster."

That kept him quiet for a second, but he couldn't stop himself from getting in a dig. "I don't care where you're from, lady. You're gonna lose your shirts."

He slammed the phone down and Emily went back to the front of the house. "Some guy wants you to take your shirt off," she said, giving Blake a quick tap on the leg.

Blake glanced up, only a small part of her attention on Emily. "Huh?"

"Nothing. I was making a joke, but I need an audience to get a good reaction."

Slapping a properly formed towel onto the stainless counter, Blake slid off and held Emily in her arms. "You have my complete, undivided attention. What's this about shirts?"

"Someone called to make reservations, and when I told him the deal he said we were going to lose our shirts." She looked up into Blake's dark eyes, glad to find nothing but confidence reflected back at her.

"We're going to be busier than mustard trying to ketchup." She barked out a laugh. "Chef humor—grade school edition."

"I wouldn't have a worry in the world if we were in New York. But there are only four or five hundred thousand people in Detroit, and not many of them can afford us. We're not lousy with investment bankers and stock brokers around here."

"Hey, you're the local. Where's all of that civic pride that's been pouring out of you for the past year?"

"Hiding," she said, a little embarrassed to be so unsure.

"There are over four million people in the metro area, Emily. We only need eighteen of them to show up five nights a week to fill these seats."

"I know but…"

"We own the building," Blake said, her voice gentle, but persuasive. "Something we never would have been able to do in New York. If we have slow times, we'll be able to hang in there. And when we're a huge success, we won't have to pay jacked-up rent." She gave Emily a slap on the butt. "We're good."

"I guess we'll get a preview tonight, huh?"

"We will." Blake bent to kiss her, a tender kiss that touched her heart. "And I guarantee every part of tonight is going to be fantastic."

Blake's phone buzzed when she was checking the dairy delivery. Without checking the name, she flicked her finger across it and held it to her ear. "Yeah."

"Hey. It's Chase."

"Hey. What's up?"

"Do you have a plumber? I mean, I know you have a plumber, but do you have one you like?"

"Yeah, I like the guy who did our work. He's always swamped, so he's tough to nail down, but he's sharp. Why? What's going on?"

"I'm trying to get this garden set up and I must've broken something. There's a stream of water trying to reach the street."

Blake chuckled to herself. Since Chase and Natasha had moved to Detroit and purchased their first home, he invariably called her when he had any kind of homeowner problem. Why he thought she knew more than Emily was a puzzle, but she didn't mind. Emily was so damned happy to have him close, Blake would have let them move in and camp in the living room.

"Sounds like you need help fast. I know a guy who's not very good, but he knows how to do simple things. And he's usually available, since he's kinda awful. I'll text you the number."

"Since I've got no choice, I'll take him," Chase said. "Need anything for tonight?"

"Steady hands," she said, laughing a little. "But I don't think I'm going to get them. I've never been so damned nervous!"

At eight o'clock, each of their eighteen seats were filled. Emily had been both surprised and pleased when Blake's parents and grandparents had agreed to come, but she wasn't sure Blake was as glad. Over the last year she'd made a real effort, calling her family more frequently and trying to keep them informed about the build-out. While she was definitely making progress with her parents, Emily had a feeling her grandfather would always be tough to take. The old grouch was just an occasional annoyance they'd have to put up with. No big deal.

Rock music played from hidden speakers, the volume low. JoJo was gliding around his small space, placing tiny plates of amuse-bouches before their guests.

She and Blake stood next to one another, their backs to their guests, each working on a different dish. Without speaking, Emily touched a spoon to the mousseline she was finishing and stuck it into Blake's mouth.

Her brow furrowed slightly. "Lemon juice. Just a dash."

Emily made the addition and nodded, not bothering to recheck. Their two chefs de parti, local women who'd both worked in restaurants for years, were on either side of them, silently working away. Emily was sure Geneva and Jaclyn would loosen up quickly and display some of the personality each of them had shown when she'd interviewed them. They'd just have to get used to working with Blake, who radiated such focus they were probably afraid to say a word.

After Blake finished the third course, she wiped her face with a clean towel and slipped under the counter to chat. As soon as Emily could hand off to Jaclyn she joined her, insinuating herself between Blake and JoJo, who was clearing the second course.

"What do you mean, you're *renting* an apartment?" Blake's grandfather said, his dark eyes narrowed. "You can buy a place in Detroit for ten bucks, can't you?"

She ignored the insult, stuck her arm out, and tucked it around Emily, pulling her in close. "I used the proceeds from the sale of my apartment to cover the down payment and renovation of the building."

"Out here in the…" He cast a quick glance at Emily and chose what he probably thought was an inoffensive word, "Ghetto?"

Blake didn't flinch. "That's not a term you should use, Grandpa. And it's not accurate, either. This is a well established neighborhood, and even though it's mostly residential, more businesses are starting up all the time."

"We went past areas that looked like they'd been carpet bombed! It looked like Phnom Penh during the war." Emily rolled her eyes. He often made references to the war, but Blake assured her the only uniform he'd ever worn was the blue blazer and white slacks from his yacht club.

Blake shrugged, looking completely unconcerned. "Detroit has its problems. But there are a lot of hard-working people who live here, all hoping for prosperity. We've been treated very well by our new neighbors." She gave Emily a firm squeeze. "I'm really glad we were able to come back to Emily's home."

"They're urban pioneers," Blake's grandmother said, obviously trying to be supportive.

"Not really," Blake said. "That implies this was unsettled land before we got here, which it definitely was not. We're not trying to take over, Grandma. We just want to fit into our new home."

Blake's grandfather acted like he hadn't heard that portion of the conversation. Or, more likely, he simply didn't want to listen. "How much money do you have left?" His dark eyes scanned the neat, clean, modern space. "You didn't have to use everything, did you?"

"We've got enough left for a down payment on a house. As soon as we've built a following, and are sure we'll make it, we're going to start looking." One shoulder rose and fell in a casual shrug. "Of course, if we don't build a following, we're screwed."

Emily knew that was a joke. Hell would freeze over before Blake failed at this, the apogee of her life's work.

"Sure, sure. You're young and cocky. Everything's possible. But let me tell you something, missy, the only way to get rich is with other people's money. Your grandmother wouldn't have wanted you to blow your inheritance on a pig in a poke. Especially *here*."

It took just a half-second for her grin to vanish, and another equally short moment for her to lean over and say, very quietly, "If that's what you believe, you didn't know her at all."

"He's just worried about you," her grandmother said, clearly trying to keep things polite. "This neighborhood is so…" She put on a bright smile. "What's the word people use? Diverse?"

"It's not all that diverse," Blake said. "Especially compared with Emily's old neighborhood in Queens. I only hear English when we walk around. It's kinda weird."

Henry looked like he wanted to get in another dig, but he either caught himself or his wife kicked him. His fork was in his hand, and he trailed it around the tiny stripe of sauce left on the plate. "I certainly can't complain about the food. What did I just eat? Whatever it was, I loved it."

"Wagyu beef with a black truffle sauce," Blake said. "I made sure to include some beef for you."

"Why don't you run over there and make me about three more of those," he said, a hopeful smile making Emily see that Blake might have gotten a little of her charm from the old grouch.

She reached over and patted him on the shoulder. "The next course is sea bream. I'll swap that out for beef." Turning, she said, "Emily? I believe we've got some cooking to do."

As service progressed, Emily kept trying to keep an eye on her mom, sure she was enjoying the heck out of the food, but the pace had been too rushed for her to peel away to visit. She made an exception when she plated the poached lobster with veal ravioli. Slipping into the center just as JoJo placed the dish, she crossed her arms over her chest and watched her mom take a bite.

When her mom's eyes filled with tears, Emily's did too. "I'm so proud of you," Carol murmured, reaching out to grasp Emily's hand and squeeze it. "You've maximized every bit of talent you were born with, sweetheart, and that's something not many people can claim." Her chin started to quiver. "To be able to cook like this after your accident…"

Emily leaned over and kissed her on the cheek. "I made this with you in mind, Mom. I still remember the first time you urged me to order lobster. It freaked me out, but you helped me crack it open and showed me how to use the fork to get every bite out." She let out a laugh. "A lifelong love affair was born that night."

"Do you mind if I take a photo? I know that's not allowed…"

Emily let out a laugh, thinking of Blake's insistence on having a note at the bottom of the menu asking their guests to refrain from using cameras during service. "We're not going to confiscate people's phones. We just want everyone to taste the damn food while it's hot. It drives Blake nuts when people spend ten minutes composing a photo instead of eating."

Blake's arms were around her and she was enfolded in a hug. "What drives Blake nuts?"

Chuckling, Emily said, "I've got a long list. That's why I'm in charge of personnel."

"Hold on there, you two," Carol said, before they could part. "I need a couple of shots for the family album."

They posed until Carol was satisfied. "As soon as we finish, we'll have time to sit down and talk," Blake said. "But now…" She started to walk backwards, with Emily leaning into her until Blake had to set her back on her feet. "Come on, you slacker," she joked, with Emily turning to give her a sharp whack on the seat.

Once they were on the proper side of their cooking station, Blake leaned over and said, "You do realize you just swatted me on the ass, didn't you? In front of my aged grandparents, no less?"

"Yes!" Emily said, feeling her cheeks turn pink. "In front of *my* aged grandparents. Even when we're at work, I can't keep my hands off you."

"I hope that's always true," Blake said, leaning close to kiss her, briefly. "Let's finish up and start drinking some wine. I want to see what kind of trouble you can get into by the end of the night."

"I'm gonna be lucky not to slice a hand off with your cute self next to me."

"Yeah, that's you," Blake said, chuckling. "You're so easy to distract when you cook."

At ten o'clock, JoJo moved around his compact space, delivering the final dish, a deceptively simple, perfectly executed lemon tart, accompanied by housemade strawberry sorbet. Geneva had the makings of a good pastry chef, but was also very adept as a line cook. Emily wasn't going to brag that she was the one who'd found her. That would have been unseemly.

They slipped into the prep kitchen and took off their jackets. They had a fan in there, and they stood in front of it for a few minutes, cooling down. Emily removed her baker's cap, dunked a fresh towel in cold water and held it to her face for a minute. Then she chilled it again and ran it across Blake's face and neck, smiling when she leaned into her hand.

"Do we have any soap that won't peel the skin right off our faces?" Blake asked.

"Yeah. I brought my toiletries." She produced some gentle foaming soap and they both washed their faces and hands. Then Emily took the band from her hair and brushed it, while Blake dug into the bag and found their toothbrushes.

"You really came prepared," she said, loading hers up with paste. Then Emily did the same, with a more moderate amount. She dabbed at her mouth, then checked herself out in the mirror tucked behind the door.

"Ready?" Blake asked, putting her hands on Emily's shoulders as she gazed into her eyes.

"One hundred percent, Chef. Let's do it."

Emily took a fresh jacket from Blake's cubbyhole and held it up for her to slip into. Then she patted the restaurant name, embroidered over the breast. Blake returned the favor, then they buttoned up and snapped the fabric into place, both now fresh and clean.

This time, instead of going into the center of the workspace to reach their guests, they exited through the prep kitchen, then had to walk around the building to enter through the front door. When Blake pushed it open, all of their friends and family stood to applaud. Tears wet her eyes as Emily took in their guests' smiling faces. Blake squeezed her hand, then draped an arm across her shoulders. "I think we need a few bottles of Champagne. JoJo? Can you set us up?"

"Oui, Chef," he said, heading to the wine cooler.

Soon they all had glasses in their hands, with tiny bubbles escaping to tickle Emily's nose when she held the glass close.

"I think it's obvious this is a labor of love for Emily and me." Blake tapped her glass lightly against Emily's, sparing a love-filled smile. "We've put our hearts and souls into getting to this point, and I'm certain we're going to love working together once again."

"Hear, hear," Barry said, looking very proud of his daughter.

"I know it was a long trip for many of you, and we wanted to make sure you got a big bang for your buck."

Emily leaned against her, amazed at the amount of energy she had after their twelve hour day. "We're beginning our adventure as restauranteurs tonight," she said, waiting a second for the punchline, "and as spouses."

"What?" Henry yelped. "You told me you'd never get married without inviting us. You couldn't wait?"

"We did wait," Blake said. "You've helped us kick off the restaurant. Now you can help us kick off our married lives."

"You're getting married now? Right now?" Dana asked, paling a little. "Don't you want a *real* wedding?" Her gaze locked on Emily, clearly hoping she'd be more reasonable than Blake. "Ever since it's been clear how serious you are about each other, I've been planning something…"

Ooo, Emily had been afraid Dana would be upset. But Blake had refused to tell her family beforehand, not wanting her mom to have time to complain about their plans.

Blake let go of Emily and walked over to her family. Quietly, she said, "If you'd like to throw a party for us, we'd love that, Mom. A reception at the club or something like that would be fantastic. But this is what we want for our wedding. Just the people we love the most, in the place we'll call home." She put her arms around her mother, and Emily got a lump in her throat as Dana enfolded her in a long, emotion-filled hug, then let her go by putting a hand to her cheek and patting it gently.

Moving back to Emily, Blake took her hand again. "We know this isn't traditional, but it's what we want." She tugged at the hem of her coat. "Neither of us would be comfortable in wedding gowns, but we're bowing to tradition by wearing white. These are the clothes that mean the most to us." She looked up and waved at JoJo. "Ready?"

"Oui, Chef." He dashed out the back, then entered through the front a minute later. He was a very fastidious man, and his pewter-colored suit was a spotless as it had been three hours earlier. A snow white shirt gleamed against his ebony skin as he stood in the center of the restaurant for a moment, obviously gathering himself. Then he nodded at Chase and Charlotte, who moved over to stand on either side of him. Blake had insisted that Emily's closest friend and her sister be their attendants, and Emily was so happy she had.

JoJo's hand shook when he removed a card from his pocket, upon which he'd written everything they wanted him to say. Emily looked across the small bit of space to catch a glimpse of Chase, who moved closer and put his hand on Blake's shoulder. He would always have both of their backs.

Then Blake moved to stand directly in front of Emily, then grasped both of her hands. When those warm, callused hands enfolded her own, Emily felt a burst of certainty, of utter confidence in herself as well as their bond.

Up until this moment, she'd spent the last months dreaming of their restaurant, utterly focused on watching it come to life. Now she was locked into the moment, realizing *this* is what mattered. Giving herself, her future, and her life to Blake. There was no one she'd ever met whom she trusted more. No one she'd ever been more certain of. Blake was her North Star, the center of her universe, and she couldn't wait to have their futures legally and permanently joined.

Gripping Blake's hands tightly, Emily gazed up into her eyes, with JoJo's silky voice raining their carefully crafted words upon their heads. There wasn't a doubt in her heart or in her mind that she would love, honor, and cherish Blake Chadwick for as long as they both would live.

She took in a breath, gathered herself and spoke the two most important words she'd ever uttered. "I will."

The End

By Susan X Meagher

Novels

Arbor Vitae

All That Matters

Cherry Grove

Girl Meets Girl

The Lies That Bind

The Legacy

Doublecrossed

Smooth Sailing

How To Wrangle a Woman

Almost Heaven

The Crush

The Reunion

Inside Out

Out of Whack

Homecoming

The Right Time

Summer of Love

Chef's Special

Serial Novel

I Found My Heart In San Francisco

Awakenings: Book One
Beginnings: Book Two
Coalescence: Book Three
Disclosures: Book Four
Entwined: Book Five
Fidelity: Book Six
Getaway: Book Seven
Honesty: Book Eight
Intentions: Book Nine
Journeys: Book Ten
Karma: Book Eleven
Lifeline: Book Twelve
Monogamy: Book Thirteen
Nurture: Book Fourteen
Osmosis: Book Fifteen
Paradigm: Book Sixteen
Quandary: Book Seventeen
Renewal: Book Eighteen
Synchronicity: Book Nineteen
Trust: Book Twenty

Anthologies

Undercover Tales
Outsiders

Wait, there's more!
A chapter set in Cayman didn't fit in the way I'd hoped it would, so I didn't include it. If you'd like me to send it to you, I'd be happy to.
susan@briskpress.com

Information about all of Susan's books can be found at
www.susanxmeagher.com or www.briskpress.com

To receive notification of new titles, send an email to
newsletters@briskpress.com

facebook.com/susanxmeagher
twitter.com/susanx